BURIED SEEDS

DONNA MEREDITH

Wild Women Writers
An Independent Publishing Company

BURIED SEEDS

This book is a work of fiction. Names, characters, places and incidents are either the product of the author's imagination or are used fictitiously. Any resemblance to actual persons, living or dead, or to actual events or locales is entirely coincidental.

ISBN: 978-0-578-65237-5

Published by Wild Women Writers, Tallahassee, FL

Logo design by E'Layne Koenigsberg of 3 Hip Chics, Tallahassee, FL
www.3HipChics.com

Printed in the United States of America

BURIED
SEEDS

Also by Donna Meredith

The Glass Madonna (2010)

The Color of Lies (2011)

Magic in the Mountains: Kelsey Murphy, Robert Bomkamp, and the West Virginia Cameo Glass Revolution (2012)

Wet Work (2014)

Fraccidental Death (2016)

For Susan B. Anthony

and all the women
who march.

We shall someday be heeded, and we shall have our amendment to the Constitution of the United States, everybody will think it was always so, just exactly as many young women now think that all the privileges, all the freedom, all the enjoyments which woman now possesses always were hers. They have no idea of how every single inch of ground that she stands upon today has been gained by the hard work of some little handful of women of the past.

- Susan B. Anthony, 1894

what didn't you do to bury me
but you forgot that I was a seed

-Dinos Christianopoulos

Young people will have the seeds you bury in their minds, and when they grow up, they will change the world.

-Jack Ma

Prologue

YOU'VE PLAYED JENGA—YES? Held your breath while removing yet another block from a tower wobbling from so little support? In every game, there comes a moment when stasis tumbles toward chaos, and collapse is inevitable.

The underpinnings of our history, our individual lives, are not as easily observed as the removal of the final block that causes a Jenga crash. Did the American Revolution begin with Paul Revere's ride—or was it preceded by more subtle loosening of the King's grasp? Some scholars cite the King's edict forbidding settlers from moving west past the Appalachian Mountains. Others credit passage of the Sugar Act or the Stamp Tax.

But most likely, the upheaval began with one man—or one woman, who would never receive proper credit because of her sex, bless her heart—lying sleepless in bed, twisting the blanket in fists, deciding something had to be done—now, not later—and it couldn't be left up to someone else. That one human roused another and another until a chorus of protest filled the colonies. They swelled into an army. A revolution. Our teacher strike, I think, evolved much the same way.

Dewey says it's fruitless to dwell on the past. As he likes to remind me, a human is not a science experiment that can be planned, manipulated, controlled, replicated. Maybe so, but still my thoughts sift through the memories, relentless as a tongue poking a sore tooth, to explore the sharp edges of what I nearly lost and assess what I might have gained. To question the risks I took.

Did my frequent insomnia this past year result merely from wobbly middle-aged hormones, or did I sense more fundamental wobbles in the underpinnings of my life, my job, and even in the larger world outside my little realm?

Angie Fisher

SWEAT SOAKS MY PILLOWCASE, the air heavy with the humidity of late summer and the lingering odor of the salmon I sautéed for supper. I glance at the red LED readout on my clock. Quarter after eleven. Half an hour, I've been lying awake. I roll onto my back, close my eyes. Deliberately, I begin to count my blessings, picturing each family member and friend, a relaxation technique to forget my worries. To forget the heat. At last I feel myself adrift in the sweet forgetfulness of sleep.

The light on Dewey's side of the bed flares on, the visual equivalent of a screeching fire alarm. He thrusts his body upright with an obnoxious whump that rocks the mattress and scares the freaking daylights out of me.

"What's wrong?" I ask.

"Angie, I gotta tell you something. I didn't want to, but it's better if you hear it from me."

The blood drains from my head and shivers race along my body, now cold against the damp sheets. Is he about to confess he's cheating on me—or he wants a divorce? These prospects skirl through the fish odor and curdle my stomach.

"There's rumors going around . . ." He pauses.

The wife is always the last to know. "Just spit it out, Dewey."

"I heard Dynamo Deals is shutting down almost a hundred stores nationwide. Ours is one."

The tension melts away. He isn't leaving me. But by the time I wiggle my toes and have time to think about what he's done, my muscles tense up tight as a double fisherman's knot. He could have told me when he got home from work or over dinner. But no, he waits until I'm asleep. I make an effort to suppress anger, to be sympathetic. Obviously, he's been lying there on the other side of the bed stewing over this news, and no wonder.

"Geez, Dew, that sucks." I dig my fingers into the spot where his cervical spine ends and massage my way down the center of his back. What rotten luck—the third company he's worked for in the last decade that's folded.

Was he agitated throughout dinner? I can't remember looking at his face, not even once, since he came home from work, preoccupied first with fixing the rice, the fish, the salad; the washing of dishes; and finally wrapping up paperwork on a grant I'd received to take students on a summer field trip. I hadn't paid attention to him at all. I shrug off my guilt. When I first started painting red highlights in my hair, it took a week before he noticed—and then only because my mother asked him if he liked having a redhead as a wife. Chalk it up to decades of marriage—you take each other for granted the way you do your favorite chair or gravity.

He flops back onto his pillow. I study him now and like what I see as much as I did when we met my senior year of college. Thick brown hair, though not as thick as it used to be. Hazel eyes. Gently upturned nose. Oversized ears, an imperfection I find endearing.

His arms are crossed behind his head, lower lip sucked into his mouth. He blows out a puff of air. "If the rumor's true, I sure hope the layoffs don't happen until after the new year."

"We'll make do," I tell him. I'm not sure how, but we will.

As manager, he's always the one who has to axe people he's worked with for years. They are more than employees. They're our friends. Neighbors. Parents of my students. I feel bad for all those folks, but I can't help worrying about our own family. Dewey's employer hired him as an independent contractor—so, no unemployment benefits. How will we pay our bills on my measly teacher salary? Years ago, Mom needed an experimental treatment for cancer. Her insurance wouldn't cover it, so Dewey and I took out a second mortgage. Then came Trish's college, numerous dental crowns, and the recession—followed by Dewey's purchase of an expensive, gas-hog truck. I've never aimed to be rich, yet somehow I thought our finances would be more secure by the time I neared fifty.

Dewey turns off the light and rolls over, thoughtlessly pulling the entire sheet over to his side. I reach over and yank it back. I can't sleep without the comfort of a sheet, no matter how hot it is. How the devil can he sleep anyway? I punch my pillow and roll away from him. The longer I think about his waking me up, the more annoyed I get.

My hub is not what you'd call a go-getter. Not lazy—never that—but laid back. I worry he won't push hard enough, move fast enough, to find another job. There are so few out there. Last time, he was out of work for eleven months, despite having an MBA. We ate through what little savings we had, yet somehow there was always enough money for another case of beer.

Some folks are movers, and some are shakers. If you want to change the world, you have to hop off the couch, take a deep breath, and boldly charge into the den of power. In other words, become a mover and shaker, which is different than either one by itself. The only thing Dewey ever shook up was a beer can once as a joke when we were camping with friends. When bubbles erupted, he laughed— *Look, Ange, West Virginia champagne.* I can hardly criticize Dewey for not putting himself out there. I'd rather eat live toads than stand in the spotlight. I hunker down inside my comfort zone less than ten miles away from the thirty-acre farm where I grew up. Home is Clarksburg in West, by God, Virginia. I have a tap root like a carrot or a beet. I wouldn't transplant well.

Dewey happily plods along doing whatever needs to be done. He hammers new shingles on our leaky roof. Replaces splintered boards on the porch steps and malfunctioning flapper valves in the toilet. He's a good man to have around when anything goes wrong. He knows how to fix things. I appreciate this—I do. I count him among my blessings, but sometimes he drives me crazy.

His bedside light comes on again. "I was thinking, maybe you could ask your brother-in-law to refinance the mortgage. Should be easy for him to arrange, his being a hot-shot banker."

A shudder travels down my spine. "Nope. Not a good idea."

"Why not?"

Where to start? "You've heard the rumors about his pay-to-play schemes. You want a state government contract, you gotta pay State Senator Ted McNeil, a.k.a. Ted McSteal."

"That's nothing to do with us. A word from him, and his bank could cough up a loan. He could even co-sign."

"I would rather swallow week-old roadkill than take money from that creep."

"That's ridiculous. You just have a thing about rich guys. Think they're all crooks."

Dewey turns off the light again, correctly reading my silence as refusal. His head falls onto the pillow. "I'll ask Ted if you don't want to. I'm not afraid of a guy just because he wears an Armani suit."

"Don't." It's a command, but after a pause I throw in *please* to be polite.

I lie in the dark and stare at the ceiling. It isn't the suit I am afraid of, or even Ted's money and political connections. If you can believe the hints my sister drops, Ted may become the next State Treasurer—or even run for Governor. I suppose that's why she's stayed with him when he's cheated on her for years.

Dewey knows nothing about the long history between Ted and me. My sophomore year in college I had half a dozen dates with my future brother-in-law. One Sunday night, he showed up with an eye-popping engagement ring and proposed a summer marriage, spinning out his vision to transform me into a stay-at-home wife with country club memberships and Caribbean vacations. I proposed he seek help from the nearest psychiatrist. I was not dropping out of college to become his little lapdog.

Ted didn't even wait for the weekend to put the hustle on my freshman sister. Three months later he placed that same eye-popping ring on MacKenzie's finger and convinced her to drop out. Wasn't hard. Except for the social aspects, she never cared much for school anyway. Ted swept her up in a tornado of parties, culminating in an obscenely expensive wedding with a dozen fluffy bridesmaids. Including Yours Truly, even though flannel is more my forte than fluff. I have kept his proposal secret. MacKenzie and me—we are not always kind to each other as it is.

After I turned him down, the computer disk containing my psych term paper disappeared from my dorm room two days before it was due. Frantically, I cranked out another one from notes. Ted turned my paper in as his own.

Once a snake, always a snake. We will find another way to get by.

~~~

THE COFFEE THIS MORNING tastes bitter. I add more creamer to my cup, Fiestaware, like the plates hung in an arc along the kitchen wall in all the cheerful colors of a rainbow. I fix two bowls of cereal and place them on the table.

Dewey saunters out of our bedroom wearing baggy shorts and a faded Yuengling tee-shirt, his WVU baseball hat slapped on backwards. In the kitchen he plunks a six-pack and pretzels into an insulated nylon lunch sack.

I aim a stink eye at his shirt. "Maybe you shouldn't advertise your plan to drink beer during the tournament."

He harrumphs. "Angie, what they gonna do—arrest me?"

That's my Dewey. Never worries. Says I do enough fretting for both of us. Hard not to, when our income will soon be halved and a potential employer might attend the bocce tournament, the first event in the annual Italian Heritage Festival. The main festival is still weeks away over Labor Day weekend.

When we arrive at the bocce court in nearby Shinnston, I am relieved to see not many spectators have turned out to watch. I would prefer to join them instead of competing, but I agreed to be Poppy's partner because the festival means so much to him, a connection to his mother's family who had emigrated from Italy three generations ago to work in the coal mines. Poppy, though, has never been inside a mine, thank goodness. For three decades, he owned two restaurants specializing in Italian recipes he'd learned from his mother. Baked rigatoni and meatballs. Mostaccioli with broccoli alfredo. Limoncello cake with mascarpone filling. Yummy doesn't begin to describe Poppy's delectable kitchen creations. Sadly, age necessitated his hanging up his apron.

I step onto the court and roll a few practice balls. Dewey waves from his perch on a wooden rail. His other hand cradles a rubbery red koozie, partially obscuring his beer. A sweat ring is already darkening the neckline of his tee-shirt. Small wonder. The sun screams down, throwing a wicked tantrum, no breeze at all. Despite the shade offered under the pavilion, I feel sticky as flypaper.

Beside me, my sister shoots a couple of selfies, and then removes the fancy extension stick from her phone. "Angela, I switched this over to video. You want to film my next practice roll?"

I live for it trips to the edge of my tongue. In the interest of family peace, I stifle it and capture Mac's athletic toss for posterity. While filming, I can't help but notice, with a trace of unbecoming glee, her blonde hair is more straw than strawberry these days. Too many years of bleaching. Makes me feel better about those auburn highlights I've been painting into my hair. I pretend they're for kicks, not because of the unsightly gray wires that stick out like I've been playing Ben Franklin with a kite in a rainstorm.

Mac studies the playback. "Choppy. Let's try it again."

Dutifully, I record Take Two and Take Three. By then I've had enough. "Facebook will have to get along without Take Four." I smack the phone back onto her palm. "Here you go, Movie Star."

She laughs, choosing to ignore my sarcasm. Just as well.

In addition to the festival, my family is celebrating the rare return of our superhero, MacKenzie Adams McNeil. Unlike me, Mac is a mover. After she married Ted, she sashayed off to Charleston so fast the dust is still settling behind her decades later. I can count on both hands the number of times she has come home for a visit, even though she lives only two hours away. Mac's motto: so many cosmic causes, so little time. My sister is Chair of the Hospital Fundraising Committee. And let us not forget, Secretary of the Men's Rights Activists. In the World According to MacKenzie, her lawyer son faces unfair competition from pushy women scrambling to make partner. MacKenzie has journeyed alone to the north central part of the state because Senator Ted is busy shaking down people in the capital.

For the umpteenth time, my eyes roam the metal bleachers full of folks who have shown up to watch the tournament. Funny, how I can stand in front of students all day every day, no worries, but plunk me down in front of adults and I squirm like an earthworm suddenly exposed to blinding light. I wish I hadn't let Poppy talk me into this.

The match begins, so I gotta forget about MacKenzie, forget about the spectators stacked up on the bleachers. No one really cares if my fat jiggles or if I trip over my own shoelaces. The match moves right along, and Poppy and I are holding our own against MacKenzie and Mom. It comes down to the final roll. I take a deep breath and send the ball up the smooth court. A strong toss, it comes to rest two inches to the left of the pallino. Dewey whoops his approval. I wince but love it all the same.

As I turn my attention back to the court, MacKenzie releases her beetle-green ball, and darned if it doesn't thunk into mine. Her ball practically French-kisses the pallino, nailing the win for my sister and mother.

My stepfather's bushy white brows descend into a deep vee. I nudge him with my elbow in a friendly way. "S'okay, Poppy. No big deal, right? We had fun, didn't we?"

Although he nods, bunched brows say he isn't convinced. It doesn't help that my sister is making such a spectacle hollering and fist-pumping, blonde ponytail swinging, spotless white tennies tapping out a victory dance. Darn her, anyway. How does she always manage to look so perfect? I glance at my running shoes, whose soles went gray so long ago they plumb forgot what white is.

"Knocked you right out of contention, Angela." MacKenzie's voice is loud, bordering on unseemly.

You'd think my forty-nine-year-old little sis had snagged a Super Bowl ring. Our rivalry results, I guess, from our being only slightly less than one year apart in age. I suppose I'm too old to smack her.

"Congrats. You and Mom played a super match."

Poppy leans over until his mouth practically touches my ear. "Who's that girl?"

My breath catches. I sneak a sideways glance at my sister—nah, she's so absorbed by the grand victory she didn't hear. I tuck Poppy's arm through mine, herd him quickly to the bleachers, and whisper back, "That's MacKenzie, Poppy. You raised both of us—remember?"

Hamilton Squires, known as "Hambone" to his friends and "Poppy" to Mac and me, frowns. "But she doesn't live with us."

"No," I explain for the fourth time since MacKenzie arrived for the weekend, "she lives in Charleston with her husband. That's where she raised her children. Your grandchildren."

Poppy's mouth squinches up as if he were sucking one of those lemon drops he is partial to. On the outside, Poppy looks perfectly healthy; inside, deteriorating neural connections are a constant source of frustration. Like forgetting where the bathroom is in the home he's lived in for six decades. Or figuring out how to transfer soup from the bowl into his mouth. Dewey can plug holes in the drywall, but not even he or the best doctors know how to plug the holes in Poppy's mind.

My hub ambles over and kisses my cheek. "You'll beat them next year, Ange. Keep the faith. I'm taking off to the barbershop."

"Not too short in back." I wink at him. "Those little curls on your neck are kinda cute."

"Yes, Miss School Marm." He grins because he knows I hate it when he calls me that, and off he goes, just the right amount of bounce to suggest he's easy in his own skin. He jokes about having Dumbo ears and crooked teeth. He never lets these distinctions bother him the way my clunky bones and long nose bother me. But he hadn't grown up comparing himself to MacKenzie, she of the roses and cream complexion, the petite upturned nose, the fine bone structure.

I deposit Poppy on the bench beside MacKenzie and Mom, who have overtaken us. We watch the next match. Then those winners are pitted against MacKenzie and Mom, who win again and are declared this year's champs.

Afterwards, MacKenzie prances over to the bleachers and tugs me to my feet. Her eyes roam over the slightly rumpled big shirt I wear to disguise the fact that I no longer have Scarlet O'Hara's waistline. Not that I ever did.

"I've been playing a lot of tennis," she says.

"You do look fit. Very buff."

"It has done wonders for my muscle tone. Angela, you should give it a try." She jabs a forefinger toward my midsection in case I missed her hint.

"Sure, Mac, one of these days I hope to retire, and then I'll be more than happy to trade work for play."

Mom laughs—and when she does, she is so beautiful, those blue eyes shining, each wrinkle a testament to a life well-lived. "You have a lot more free time, MacKenzie."

"Understatement," I grumble.

Mac's pert little nose comes up. "You did have the whole summer off."

"Newsflash—I taught summer school and then Dewey and I took a bus load of students on a camping trip to Dolly Sods, Cranberry Glades, and Seneca Rocks to expose them to the botanical and geological wonders of our state. Trust me—it was no vacation supervising those little squirrels."

"You are a very devoted teacher, Angela, better than the ones around Charleston. That's why I home-schooled my kids. Ted and I were concerned about what kind of values they might pick up in public schools."

What I'm thinking: *Yeah, we public school teachers are a dangerous lot, encouraging wickedness and rewarding criminal behavior every chance we get.*

What I say: "You're a very devoted mother."

My niece and nephew seem to have turned out all right—not that I know them very well. Neither has married, though both are past thirty. I expected Mac to push them into youthful marriages if only to protect their virginity so it could be sacrificed at the altar. God only knows how she will react when she spots Trish's swollen abdomen, but my daughter is twenty-eight. Old enough to know what she wants. And what she doesn't want.

I swipe sweaty palms against my capris.

Poppy stares suspiciously at MacKenzie and tugs on Mom's flowered shirt sleeve. "Helen, who is that woman? Do we know her?"

Mom and I freeze, watch as MacKenzie's face cracks into a million pieces.

After what seems like an eon later, Mom's tinkling laugh shatters the silence. "Oh, honey, you remember MacKenzie. She and her husband sent us on that cruise to Alaska. Remember that?"

Poppy's face lights up. "We saw bears."

"That's right. And whales."

"Lots of whales. And moose. We saw Mickey Mouse, too, with the girls."

"Let's get out of this sun." Mom guides him toward the parking lot.

MacKenzie shifts her weight from one foot to the other. "Well, I'd better go."

"And I'd better unlock the car and get the AC on for the folks. You're coming out to the farm for dinner, right?"

MacKenzie nods. I still can't believe she would choose to stay in a hotel instead of at the farm or with me and Dewey—*don't want to inconvenience anyone*, she says. Ha—more like she doesn't want to inconvenience herself by slumming with poor relations.

We walk back to our cars in sunlight so bright it pains my eyes despite dark sunglasses. "Thanks for coming back for the tourney."

"Wouldn't have missed it." The usual brass is absent from her voice. "I think this will be the last time Poppy will be able to play."

The inevitability of that loss lodges in my throat. A loss my sister would share. I squeeze her shoulder and quickly stride away. Mac's finger-pointing at my midsection replays in my mind. I entertain excuses for my extra pounds: Poppy's cooking, no time to work out, menopause. I swat Mac's insult away. I refuse to judge myself by the shape of my body. I am more than that.

I am driving my folks back to our farm just outside of town so I can help Mom prepare a feast for MacKenzie. Grass-covered meadows hug both sides of the road, broad green expanses brightened by flashes of color: buttery giant swallowtails floating above purple ironweed, candy-corn blooms of butterfly weed, white swaths of Queen Anne's Lace and poison hemlock. Behind a barbed-wire fence, Herefords graze and lumber about, captives bored by the tedium of their day. Vultures scatter on my car's approach, temporarily abandoning the remains of a possum they are cleaning from the asphalt.

We pass by grassy mounds I'd climbed countless times as a girl so I could launch myself downward, arms spread wide, wind and seeds tangled in my hair, defying gravity for long seconds, airborne, a human kite with sky dreams. Behind those hills lie secret patches of thimble-sized wild strawberries, known only to me and my sister. On the other side of the road, we had tromped through sumac-laden meadows with our mother where raspberries and blackberries brambled promiscuously, begging to be plucked, simmered in sugar, and ladled into Mason jars. I had made sure my daughter grew up knowing the thrill of riding a silver saucer down the snow-covered hill behind the house, just as Mac and I had. Poppy almost always went down first so his extra weight would pack the fresh fallen snow. We zipped downhill ever faster as the morning wore on and the path grew slick with ice. If we didn't veer hard right at the bottom, we'd slam into the white aluminum siding that girded the crawlspace under the back porch. The siding still bears dimples and dents from our mishaps. Mac and I had such fun as kids.

I glance at Poppy in the seat beside me and briefly let my eyes flick to the rear mirror at Mom. I am grateful, overwhelmingly grateful, to have been adopted into such a loving home. I blink furiously to disperse the unshed tears that threaten to cloud my vision. Gotta cut out this foolishness. Keep my mind clear and focused on my driving—lives depend on it. Hasn't Mom emphasized that repeatedly since she first let me behind the wheel when I was fifteen? A car is a lethal weapon, she says.

As if I don't know. As if I could ever forget the day my Daddy died.

We were on the way to Myrtle Beach, Daddy, Mom, Grandmother Adams, MacKenzie and me. A family vacation, the first we'd ever taken. MacKenzie and I were both five years old. We shared the back seat of our ancient baby blue Ford sedan with our grandmother. The car's swooping side fins resembled wings—a big blue bird ready to fly down the highway.

SUMMER, 1972

I SLIDE DOWN to the floor behind my father to play with Barbie. Mine has long brunette hair bunched behind her head. Her bathing suit is hot pink with greenish stripes along the sides.

"Angie, you shouldn't sit down there," Grandmother says. "You'll get your shorts dirty."

"I like it down here."

"The rumble will make you carsick."

"I like the rumble." Besides, I don't like to see the scary drop-offs. Down here I can pretend they aren't right outside the window.

Daddy's calm voice floats over the seats. "It's okay, Mom. She sits down there all the time." Daddy is almost always calm. Laid-back, Mommy calls him. It makes me think of Daddy's brown chair. You could lay back in it, which is lots of fun—even though Mommy says his chair is ratty. Not even fit for a yard sale.

"Well, I don't want a carsick child sitting near me."

"She never gets carsick." Mommy's voice grows sharp edges when she speaks to Grandmother Adams.

"I don't see why she can't be good like her sister and sit on the seat by me."

"Both my girls are good children, thank you very much, very good, very precious."

Grandmother's nose wrinkles as if she smells something nasty. She pretends to study the view out her window. I can tell she's pretending because I feel her eyes stab me every few minutes.

I clamp my teeth together. Why had we brought her along? She always makes trouble. Like the time she scolded Mommy for over-cooking the steaks. Grandmother likes her meat red inside, juicy, she says. What she means is bloody. Gag a maggot. Besides, Daddy grilled the steaks, so why did Grandmother blame Mommy? They argue about even more stuff than me and MacKenzie: was it okay for us girls to wear slacks to church, had the vacuum cleaner bag been changed since Christmas, why did Mommy insist on keeping smelly food scraps in the kitchen for composting. The worst argument of all was over weeds on the back porch, which was just crazy. There aren't any weeds on the porch, just Mommy's pink begonias.

I make my Barbie hop toward the Grump Hump that divides the floor into two equal halves, one side for me and Barbie, the other for grumpy grandmother's feet. The hump could be a diving board.

"Look, my Barbie's diving into the ocean," I tell MacKenzie and swoop Barbie headfirst toward the floor. Can you dive into the real ocean? I'm not sure. I've only seen the ocean in pictures.

"My Barbie's diving into the ocean, too." MacKenzie drops her blonde Barbie onto the car floor. "Let's trade dolls," she says.

I shake my head. "I don't want to." I set blonde Barbie back on the seat beside my sister. Our Barbies' hair matches our own. Mine is almost as dark as Inky the Cat's fur; MacKenzie's, light as duck down.

Grandmother Adams strokes MacKenzie's hair with her wrinkly hand. "Your Barbie is prettier, anyway. The one with dark hair looks like a dirty wop."

"What's a wop?" my sister asks.

Mommy hisses, "See, Joe? See what your mother is teaching the girls? I won't stand for it, I just won't."

"Helen's right, Mom. Little pitchers have big ears. We don't use that kind of language."

I know me and MacKenzie are the pictures, but pictures of what? Doesn't make sense. Daddy and Mommy use that funny expression when grown-ups talk about bad stuff, stuff children aren't supposed to know about. What does that word—*wop*— mean? Whatever, I'm glad Daddy let Grandmother Adams know she isn't the boss, even if he is still using his easy-chair voice. Grandmother Adams isn't boss. He is. And Mommy.

MacKenzie snatches my Barbie right out of my hands and stands up on the back seat, shrieking, "I got her!"

"Give her back!" I reach for my doll.

Grandmother Adams swats my hand. "Let MacKenzie have it a while."

The car swerves hard to the left and Mommy screams. My head crunches against the car door. My Barbie's headless body flies by, bounces off the back of Daddy's seat, and dive bombs onto the ocean floor.

LATER MOMMY FILLS in the missing parts of that day. My father had swerved across the center line, skidded off the road, and smashed into a pine tree. MacKenzie broke her arm; Mommy cracked her collarbone; Grandmother ruptured her spleen. I hurt my head, a mild concussion, Mommy explains.

Daddy's funeral is held a week later. At the funeral home I can hardly breathe. I feel sick—the fragrance from three walls stacked from floor to ceiling with rainbows of lilies and tall flowers Mommy calls glads; the crowd of grown-ups, pressing in on all sides, towering above me, brushing fingers against my cheeks or latching onto my hands; the big box in front of the room. Mommy says Daddy is lying under the lid. Not asleep. Dead. I understand, sort of. I saw Laddie, the neighbor's dog, hit by a passing truck, lying stiff and still beside the road. And Inky, the cat, sometimes deposits trophies on our doorstep: a dead robin once, another time a field mouse. But I hadn't known dead could happen to people. To Daddy. I wonder if he is stiff and still like Laddie. Can he breathe under that lid—or is the odor of the flowers smothering him the way it is me? Will dead happen to Mommy? To me and MacKenzie?

When MacKenzie whispers that she needs to "go," I am happy to leave the room, so heavy with smells, long faces, the box. MacKenzie needs help with her clothes, what with her arm wrapped up in that cast. I help her pull her underpants down, and a few minutes later, help her tug them back up.

Holding hands—MacKenzie's good hand—we return to the

viewing room, quiet as little mice. I hope no one else will pat our heads and pinch our cheeks. We linger in the back. Everything about this place feels strange. Why do they call it a home? Who lives here?

In the sea of strangers I find Mommy's face and relax a little—until I see who she is talking to. I tug on MacKenzie's hand. I don't have to tell her why. She sees Grandmother too, in a wheelchair, black hat, scratchy-looking veil covering most of her gray hair and her eyes, a woman in baggy white hospital clothes resting big knuckles on the chair handles.

"Honey, you shouldn't be here." Mommy uses her worried voice, the one for bike spills, skinned knees, coughing, croup, and finding money to pay the bills. "The hospital wanted to keep you another week."

Grandmother's voice, loud and mean, washes over the room, drowning out every other sound except the buzz inside my head. "You should be ashamed."

The sea of visitors slowly drifts away, a few steps at a time, edging toward the door.

"A decent wife would have left off having the funeral until his mother could attend."

"But it's been a week already. The doctors said they didn't know when they could release you, when it would be safe. At least another week, they said. Did the doctor release you?" Mommy looks at the hospital worker, who shakes her head. Mommy bends over grandmother, taking both her hands. "We'd better get you back to—"

Grandmother jerks away. "My son would still be alive if you hadn't adopted that child. With that complexion and hair she surely has Tally blood. Maybe even a touch of Colored. Most likely her mother was a drug addict, a whore. That child'll never amount to a hill of beans."

I know she means me, but I'm not dirty. I take baths and Mommy is my mother.

Mommy steps backward as if Grandmother had smacked her. "What a despicable thing to say!"

"Everybody knows it, the Tallies are just as bad as Colored. Why, in my day, their sort weren't allowed to buy homes in the good neighborhoods. Said so right in the covenants. Couldn't swim in our pools, either."

The buzzing in my ears grows louder, like a swarm of crickets rubbing their wings together. I can't breathe—is it because of the lilies? I feel myself swaying and in the distance I hear MacKenzie calling my name. An arm encircles my shoulders and another slips beneath my knees. One of my mother's friends carries me to a folding chair and props me upright. MacKenzie climbs onto the empty chair on my other side.

"Is Angie going to die too?" my sister asks.

"Of course not, sweetie." Mommy's friend calls out, "Helen, Angie needs you."

Mommy rushes over and kneels down on the carpeted floor. "Oh no, my sweet girls, you didn't hear that, did you?"

Guests eye each other nervously. Cocooning us in her arms, sobbing, Mommy sweeps us away into the private room the funeral home keeps for family members who are crying.

Grandmother is left alone in front of the big box.

AUGUST 2017

IT WAS NOT THE BEST WAY in the world to learn I was adopted. Oh, Mom explained she and Daddy had been overwhelmed with joy when they brought me home from the adoption agency, that they had longed for a child and after a decade of marriage despaired of ever having one. She explained how MacKenzie probably would never have happened if it weren't for me, a strange and wonderful blessing occurring sometimes after adoption. Sudden fertility.

Mom insisted I should forget every unkind word. "Older people sometimes hold onto bad notions they were raised with, ugly prejudices we want nothing to do with now."

Still, I couldn't erase the feeling that I was inferior to MacKenzie. Even worse, I was the reason Daddy died. If only I hadn't been fighting with my sister.

Grandmother Adams's words planted seeds of shame in my soul. Yet from that dirt grew a blessing, the gift of recognition. If one of my students had no one to lunch with, I invited him to hang out in my room and shared apples and crackers. Or if a girl carried the shame of being dateless to Homecoming or Prom, I complimented her new haircut or her smile. If they were teased for wearing the same jeans for weeks on end, I offered wage-paying jobs: babysitters for Trish when she was young or farm hands to help Poppy with haying and harvesting.

My grandmother was right about one thing: in Clarksburg's not too distant past, those of Italian heritage were forbidden to live in middle class neighborhoods, forbidden to swim in community pools. We were not welcome. At one time or another, most ethnic groups found themselves labeled and dumped onto the wrong side of the social spectrum: kikes, micks, dagos, dumb Polacks, jigaboos, slant-eyes, bohunks, redskins, and wetbacks. So ugly, those labels. Even though courts had struck down the restrictive covenants my grandmother revered, and my rational mind understood how wrong ethnic divisions were, I couldn't quite erase the feeling I was not good enough.

And the odor of hothouse lilies or bloody steak? Gag me with a spoon.

THE LAST CLUMP of ricotta and spinach slides into a giant pasta shell. The shells look like cute turtles flipped onto their backs. I smother them in Poppy's marinara—he is still allowed in the kitchen with supervision—and slide the pan into the oven.

We think, but don't know for sure, that MacKenzie might be vegetarian now, so the shells are for her, in case she won't eat the meatloaf Mom made. If she turns out to be vegan, there's always salad with Mom's beefsteak tomatoes and Poppy's signature vinaigrette, and the Italian bread Trish picked up at Tomaro's Bakery. A kettle of water is on the stove to steam ears of corn fresh from Mom's garden. I could live off that corn, heavenly sunshine harnessed in every kernel.

Trish slices the bread, her long, thick braid swinging across her back, her skin radiant, glowing from all those good hormones.

Vases of crayon-colored zinnias adorn the center of the dining room table. Mom has laid out her best white damask tablecloth, Grandma's Forget-Me-Not china, and the good silver. And naturally, MacKenzie's place at the table is set with the red plate—the special plate for the guest of honor. My place has never been set with the red plate.

With my sister due any minute, I take off my apron, a necessity when you put me anywhere in the vicinity of tomato sauce. Before the day is out, despite my best efforts to be careful, my blouse will be smeared with colorful splashes worthy of a Jackson Pollock painting.

The purr of an engine alerts us to MacKenzie's arrival. "Here's my girl!" Mom rushes outside and approaches the car before the tires stop spinning, repeating her greeting—"Here's my special girl!"—all open arms, the bear hug mandatory, even though it's only been a few hours since the bocce matches.

MacKenzie hugs Mom back, though it seems to me her arms are braced to keep a little space between them, probably doesn't want her blouse mussed.

"I'm not your special girl." MacKenzie's voice sounds scratchy like she's swallowed shards of glass. "That would be Angela, the daughter you chose. I'm the accident that came after her."

I have never given credence to demonic possession, but I might have to change my opinion. Who is this person speaking? Can't be my sister.

My mother looks crestfallen. "How can you say that? You know how much I longed for a baby. And I love you both the same, always have."

MacKenzie makes a sound I've never heard from her before. Not quite a snort. Not quite a snuffle. A snorfle.

I try to make light of the moment. "Give me a break, Mac. You've always been the perfect daughter. I was the troublemaker. Remember my plan to raise chicks for Easter—and those soft white eggs I found by the creek and hatched in my bedroom turned out to be snakes and it took weeks to find them all? I was the tomboy who deliberately steered my bike through mud, while you skirted the puddles and kept your clothes clean. It's a wonder they didn't send me back."

Mom throws her hands up in the air. She looks so frail it's a wonder she doesn't pitch right over with the motion, but I know she's stronger than she looks. "Stop it now, girls. I love you both the same."

"We know." I hold out my arms for the requisite sibling hug, but MacKenzie needn't worry about my crushing her clothes. I know better. A hug with space. A space filled with the dread of moving aside because behind me is Trish, my beautiful, athletic daughter, lushly ripe, ready to bear the fruit of her womb.

MacKenzie pushes past me. "Trish!" Her arms open wide and then waterfall, flowing down the front of dazzling white capris. She whirls around to me. "My only niece is having a baby and you didn't tell me?"

"You should return phone calls once in a while."

"We were together all morning at the bocce court. You might have mentioned it."

"Didn't seem like the place for a family chat."

My sister back-steps, a thought visibly climbing her throat, choking her red-faced. Her voice crackles like tires on gravel. "You didn't invite me to the wedding!"

"Girls, all this fussing is going to spoil your appetites," my mother says.

I am ready to scream, but Trish only laughs. "Take it easy, Auntie Mac—there hasn't been a wedding, but if there ever is, yours will be the first invitation I send out."

Oh, lordee, call the firemen! Mac's face is really burning now—and she wonders why I didn't announce the news at the tournament.

"Not married!"

"I'm not at all sure I want to get married."

My sister glares at me as if this was all my idea. "What does Reverend Carr have to say about this?"

"He hasn't commented," I say.

"What about the school board? Won't she lose her job?"

"And be sued? This is 2017, Mac. Wake up."

Trish plants her hands on her hips. "Hey, you two, cut it out. You're talking about me as if I'm not here. It's my life and I intend to live it my way. I want a baby now, but I refuse to get married until I find the perfect husband."

To my surprise, Mac says aloud what I am thinking: "Good luck with that."

Trish laughs. "At least he has to be perfect for me. Anyway, I know you are going to be a great Great Aunt, Auntie Mac—the best ever. Because you sure have been good to me."

I almost blurt out a *huh?* but bite my tongue. In some ways, Mac has been a good aunt. She comes through with the perfect gifts for birthdays and Christmas from the smartest fashions to the smartest phones—stuff I can't afford to buy. But it's not as if she ever took Trish shopping or went for walks in the woods or even shared family stories.

Trish pulls my sister into a real hug. Mac is smiling again, her bestness reaffirmed.

I remember reading somewhere that flattery works best on insecure people. It dawns on me that my sister may not be the arrogant Queen of the Capital after all. She seems more messed up than usual. Why? The answer washes over me in a nasty wave. Something's gone wrong in her marriage.

Something beyond the fact that her husband is Ted. That part has always been wrong.

PREPLANNING DAYS MEAN MAJOR HUSTLE to prep my classroom to receive students. With a box cutter, I slice into cartons of supplies I ordered at the end of last term. I unpack beakers, slides, Petri dishes, pipettes, and multi-packs of probes for measuring pH, temperature, and soil nutrients. Then I carefully unwrap three new basic model digital microscopes, which at three hundred dollars each, ate a big hole in my budget. No choice. To meet the new state science standards, lessons have to be lab-centered—and that means more equipment. I would give my eye-teeth for a couple of research-quality microscopes, but I can only stretch the dollars so far.

Next I unload another big ticket item: preserved specimens. Sure, these days students could do virtual dissections on the computer, but virtual experience just isn't the same as the real thing. So specimens: one worm for each student to serve as an introduction to dissecting, and one fetal pig to be shared by eight students in my human anatomy classes. I sigh. It should have been a pig for every four kids, but at thirty dollars each, this was as far as the budget would stretch. The legislature screwed us over once again. I can use my personal credit card to buy sterile soil at the local garden center. They know I'm a teacher and always throw in little black plastic pots for free. I've saved thousands of Black-Seeded Simpson lettuce seeds, enough for all my students. Just once it would be nice if I didn't have to use my own money for school supplies. Yeah. Might as well wish for world peace.

Despite harboring evil thoughts of slashing cheapskate legislators' tires, tingles slide up and down my spine as I look around the classroom that has been mine for the last twenty-five years. The desks and whiteboards are neat and clean. One wall is brightened by my "Mrs. Fisher's Seeds for Success" bulletin board. It uses a winding garden path as a metaphor for getting along in my room, and, I hope, in life as well. I turn off the lights and lock my door.

The first day of school is only a few days away. If ever I don't feel this rush, this hope, this I'm-ready-to-change-the-world-one-child-at-a-time at the beginning of the school year, I will know it's time to retire. I feel optimistic, even though experience has taught me my shining enthusiasm will dim by the time I issue the first report cards and will darken right along with winter skies in the weeks leading up to the Christmas holiday. Luckily, I rebound over the break.

I jog down the hall to Rebecca's room and call through the open doorway, "Going out to lunch?"

Rebecca is standing on a chair, wobbling as she pivots toward me. A short brunette, she carries thirty excess pounds—"ten for each child I birthed," she claims. I don't have that excuse since I only birthed one child. Instead I blame Poppy's pasta and tiramisu.

"Come help me pin up the last pieces of this bulletin board and we'll head out." Rebecca, in a gesture I've witnessed a hundred times, tugs a tuft of her short hair straight out from her scalp. She wears it in a spiky, gelled style, a bit wild and youthful, a deliberate contrast to the premature silvering. In her early forties, Rebecca still has school-age kids. Our principal asked me to serve as her mentor when she arrived here straight out of college. Since all my friends from high school and college had long since moved out of state and Rebecca was new to town, our work relationship soon expanded into caring and sharing; in short, a friendship.

On her desk I find a thin cardboard red and blue circle graph and hand it to her. I pass Rebecca little cardboard cars that reinforce the concept of three-fourths. Repetition. Eventually most kids will conquer fractions, though they prove perennially difficult for Rebecca's special needs kids to grasp. Rebecca is a saint. It takes incredible patience, perseverance, and determination, when student progress arrives in baby steps rather than leaps and bounds.

"Nice board," I say.

She hops down to admire her work. "Thanks. I made all the pieces myself."

"Paid for the cardboard yourself, too, no doubt."

"Do I detect a touch of sarcasm, missy?" Rebecca chuckles and slings a suitcase-of-a-purse over her shoulder. "Yeah, I bought it. How else is a body gonna get supplies around here?"

"Some things will never change."

Rebecca holds the outside door open and lets me pass through ahead of her. "Not true. We can change education policy through AFT and WVEA. Things are different this year."

She has to say that, as president of the local chapter of the American Federation of Teachers. The other union is the West Virginia Education Association. I'm a member of AFT, the inactive type.

"People say that every year and nothing changes."

"No, really. This time our unions are working together instead of competing. You'd know that if you ever came to a meeting."

"I'd rather eat chalk than sit through long, boring meetings. Besides, you might as well believe in the Education Fairy. She's going to wave her magic wand and every room will be lined with SMART Boards and state-of-the-art computers, all raggedy lab equipment will be replaced, and we'll get free A-plus health insurance."

We stride to Hilltop High's teacher parking lot. "My car," I suggest. My electric vehicle, a Bolt, is one small way I try to lead students by example. It makes talking about clean air easier in a state where people can get mighty defensive over any suggestion that burning coal and petroleum products might not be as clean as coal and oil company commercials claim.

Rebecca climbs in the passenger seat. She tugs on another spike of hair, and then for good measure, tugs on two more. "You need to get more involved. You're coming with me this afternoon to our first meeting of the new school year, and I won't take no for an answer."

Great. I had hoped to use that first hour after this teacher-prep day to tweak directions for my all-time favorite biology assignment, one that lasts all year: making each kid responsible for determining the exact ecology of his or her own small plot of undeveloped land, cataloguing every living and non-living thing, no matter how small or large, and determining how it sustains its life. During the year they will create models for food chains and nutrient cycles for their little piece of Planet Earth. They will record their observations regularly in their science journals. I want GPS coordinates of individual plots ready for the start of the school year.

Someday I'm going to learn to keep my snarky comments to myself. I've heard the grumbling. I've grumbled too. No pay raises for years. Health insurance premiums increasing astronomically. But I can't afford to be branded a troublemaker, can't afford to lose my job. Especially now that Dewey is likely to lose his.

We head into a downtown that's pretty enough, with attractive streetlamps, smooth sidewalks, and tidy facades, but it sure isn't the same downtown I knew growing up. One by one, locally owned businesses— Broida's Bridal Shop, Parsons Souders Department Store, Mellet's Clothing for Men, and Palace Furniture—and even Sears and JCPenney's closed their doors. Of the old stores, only the James and Law Company, a stationer and bookstore, remains, though new businesses inhabit a few of the old buildings now. First the money fled to the Fairmont and Bridgeport malls, and then moved on to East Pointe, New Pointe and White Oak, those sprawling outdoor strip malls. Rebecca and I try to patronize locally owned establishments, so we head out Bridgeport Hill to Twin Oaks, which has been part of the Clarksburg-Bridgeport scene forever. Or at least for all of my life. The restaurant is housed in a tan-sided building with a giant sign near the highway. A red arrow beckons guests to enter. The décor is unpretentious: wooden tables with paper placemats and slat-backed, padded-seat chairs.

Over meatball hoagies oozing mozzarella and marinara, Rebecca outlines her goals for AFT. "I think you would make a great vice president. Peggy can only serve until October, and then she'll be out on pregnancy leave, so I need someone to finish out the year."

"No way."

Rebecca holds her palm up like a traffic cop. "Hear me out. You have tons of classroom experience. No one knows what these kids and teachers need any better than you do. You've been a member of AFT forever, so how about it? Give something back."

"As if I need one more thing to do."

"Who does? But change only happens if we all work together for it. Think about it, okay?"

Finally I agree, if only to get Rebecca to turn off the lecture mode. There are better people than me to take the lead. Later I'll find some excuse to renege. Meetings suck. Which reminds me, I'd called a science department meeting for 1:30—one with a tight agenda that will take no more than fifteen minutes. With a napkin, I mop smears of marina and cheese from my mouth and push my chair from the table.

"Back to the grind," I say.

"You know you love it."

Truth. I can't imagine any more rewarding—or aggravating—way to spend my life.

LATE AUGUST 2017

TWO WEEKS PASS and it's still hotter than blue blazes. I can hardly touch the steering wheel when I first get in the car. As I pull into our driveway, I spot several ripe tomatoes in the pots along the side of the house. I stop to pick them before going in. When we first moved in twenty-five years ago, our middle-class neighborhood was already fraying around the edges, a loose awning here, broken window there. Now half a dozen houses have deteriorated to the point they deserve demolition rather than renovation and folks with money have moved to Bridgeport. Dewey, though, has repainted our modest two-story with a fresh coat of white. New windows and thirty-year shingles on the roof, too.

He meets me at the front door. "Angie, your mom called. She wants us to come over for supper tonight."

"Not tonight. I had a crazy, crazy day at work."

He takes my purse and satchel of papers, sets them on the end table by the sofa. I collapse into the cushions. They are lumpy and on the verge of collapse themselves.

Dewey trudges to the fridge, brings back a glass of iced tea for me. He settles in beside me. "What happened? Tell Dr. Dewey all about it. Big smooches gonna make it all better."

The smucky sounds he makes are so silly I can't help but smile. Two long sips later, I sigh. Where to start?

"Kev dropped one of my microscopes in first period and broke it. Another one quit working because the gear mechanism locking the stage down is stripped and it won't focus. I had to send both off for repairs. A forest ranger I'd scheduled as a speaker tomorrow called and said she couldn't make it. And the assistant principal tried to twist my arm into becoming an assistant girls' soccer team coach. I refused." I stop to take another long drink.

"Yeah, Ange, but none of that would have driven you over the edge."

He knows me too well. "Marla Harding's mom dropped by on my planning period and it took her half an hour to insist that her child must sit in the front row because she has poor eyesight and refuses to wear glasses because some boy made some crack about how ugly they were. Right before my next class came in, Mrs. Harding sneaked out the real reason for her visit. She wants to be sure I don't teach her daughter about that—" I finger air quotes—" 'sacrilegious evolution garbage' or she is going to homeschool her."

"So let her—fewer papers to grade."

Dewey can't understand how that suggestion distresses me. I truly like Marla, a no-nonsense, big-boned awkward girl who reminds me of myself at that age. I truly believe a strong public school education will enable her to develop her full potential.

"I want to keep her in my class, Dew. I suggested the best place to study creationism was Sunday School."

"I take it the mom didn't like that."

"Nope. After school I got called into Mr. Esposito's office to see if I couldn't make accommodations for Marla and her mother. Like what? Nail myself and the biology text to a cross on the front wall?"

"Ange, I know you didn't tell him that."

A visit to the principal's office causes brain freeze worse than sucking down a whole slushy in one gulp. It's not that Mr. E. isn't nice to me—he is kind, helpful, paternal, an older gent with thick salt and pepper hair and a waistline that tells me he loves pasta and warm bread as much as I do—but there's something about being called to the principal's office, whether you are eight or over forty-eight. Shame hangs around your neck like a big scarlet *P*. Once I stood before the man, every glimmer of a smart-alec comeback faded away.

"I politely agreed to everything Mr. E. suggested. I will send Marla to the library if we are specifically using the word *evolution* and let her study something else. It's kind of hard, what with the new state standards. Heredity and Evolution is one of the five core ideas that I'm supposed to teach in biology. In the text, evolution doesn't come up until Chapter Five, but the new standards mean biology instruction centers more on lab work than text reading. I don't see how I can send Marla out of the room every time one of our five core principles comes up."

"You want me to call Mrs. Harding and tell her off?"

I burst out laughing. Dewey has never told anyone off in his life.

"I just want to curl up in front of the TV tonight and zone out."

He jangles car keys at arm's length. "I know how much you want to, but you can't. Your mom's making a special dinner for your birthday."

"The only gift I want is to fall asleep over mindless TV shows and a bowl of popcorn."

All day long I have been purposefully forgetting the special significance of this day. The half century mark. The big Five-O. It's all downhill from here. Before long, my boobs will sag to my waist, I'll be trading bikini underwear for Depends, I'll be eating prunes and won't dare to eat a peach. This is cause for celebration?

"She told me to remind you *some* woman went through twenty hours of labor fifty years ago today, so no arguments."

I laugh at Mom's little joke. I know when I'm beaten. "Okay, okay. But I'm getting out of these slacks and putting on something comfy. No bra."

"Angie, you gotta wear one."

"Seriously?" My bra's elastic band has tightened like a noose, cutting off circulation all the way to my toes.

"Yeah, trust me. Bind those babies up."

I make a face; I hope it's as ugly as I feel. "All right, but I'm wearing my stretchy jeans." Ones that accommodate a fifty-year-old waistline comfortably. And a roomy shirt to hide the love handles.

As soon as I spot all the cars pulled in at odd angles onto the lawn, I know I am in trouble.

"Dewey, I can't believe you didn't tell me." I tug my sloppy shirt down over my belly. "How could you let me leave the house looking like this?"

He has the nerve to grin. "I wouldn't want you to be uncomfortable on your birthday."

At least he had convinced me to wear a bra. Doggone it! I begged Mom not to make a big fuss. Why hadn't she listened?

Might as well get this over with. I throw open the front door. A glittery "Big Five-O" sign is strung from one end of the living room to the other over everyone's heads. And I do mean everyone in the whole town. Pretty near everyone I know, anyway, and they all are shouting "Surprise!" and "Happy Birthday!" I wander around the room delivering greetings. First, my hugely pregnant daughter accompanied by live-in boyfriend Dakota. Then aunts, uncles, cousins, neighbors, minister, church organist, and people from school: the whole science department, my buddy Rebecca, and even the principal, Mr. Esposito, for heaven's sake. Lucky me—I get to see him twice in one day—yay.

I make my way to the kitchen where Mom is setting out paper plates and plastic silverware. "Mom, how on earth can we afford a party like this?"

The microwave beeps and she pivots to remove a casserole she's warmed. "Covered dish. Hardly any expense at all. Don't you worry none. Just enjoy your day."

The dining room table looks ready to buckle under the weight of fried chicken, baked ziti and meatballs, ham, scalloped potatoes, mac and cheese, five beans bake, broccoli rice casserole, loaves of Italian bread, raspberry gelatin salad with pecans and cream cheese, and more sweets than you can shake a stick at. Not to mention the birthday cake I spot on the kitchen counter. It must have taken all the chocolate in Willy Wonka's factory to bake that monster.

Mr. Esposito is telling me not to worry about Marla and Mrs. Harding. "It will all work out. I really like that girl. Smart as a whip."

"I like her too."

Dewey comes up and squeezes my shoulder with one hand. The other reaches surreptitiously for my butt and delivers a pinch. With epic effort, I maintain a neutral expression, as though I am still enthralled by the words tumbling from Mr. E's mouth. I will get Dew back for this before the night is over, that old devil. The sneaky pinches are an old game between us, one we haven't played since the first year of our marriage. I suspect he's had a few beers too many, or he wouldn't have tried this while I was talking to my boss. I also suspect he's trying to assure me I'm still the sexy girl he fell in love with, even if I am officially an old lady now.

People load their plates and laugh and tell family stories I've already heard three gazillion times before. In the background, Dean Martin croons, and Poppy waltzes the church organist through the kitchen. He may not remember the organist's name, but he sure remembers how to dance.

As the night wears on, I notice Trish, alone on the sofa, legs extended out nearly straight, baby bump facing the ceiling. If she leans back any further, she'll be lying down. Everything I hate about myself is translated into perfection in my daughter. My big bones became athletic and sturdy on Trish, my long nose shortened just enough to look patrician.

Dakota seems oblivious to my daughter's discomfort, an indication, perhaps, that Trish is correct in her assessment that he may not be husband material. She seems quite sure she is capable of caring for a baby on her own. At twenty-eight, she doesn't want to delay motherhood any longer. Handsome, sturdily built and intelligent enough to earn a business degree from WVU in four years, Dakota is a suitable sperm donor. As for marriage, Trish is reserving judgment until she sees how Dakota handles fatherhood. When I was young, so-called shotgun weddings were the expected conclusion of premarital pregnancies. I admire the self assurance of young women who would rather go it alone than hitch up to a man resembling a horse's behind. They maintain control over their own lives and avoid the pain of divorce. It's not a choice I could have made, but times have changed, and Trish is her own person.

I join the little group Dakota is entertaining with a tale of the seven-point buck he'd bagged last winter. "Hey, you'd best carry Trish on home. Her ankles look swollen. She needs to get those feet up."

"Yeah, sure, in a minute." Dakota jumps back into his story.

Call me a cynic, but I harbor doubts about the length of the delay. In the kitchen I fix several containers of leftovers for Trish. I carry them to the living room and shove them into Dakota's hands. A blatant ploy to move the Official Sperm Donor toward the door.

Dewey, bless his heart, pulls Trish to her feet and booms out in a friendly way, "Time for our mommy-to-be to scoot on home."

That sparks Dakota's dash for the exit, Trish waddling out behind him. A bevy of other guests follow. In their wake, every conceivable surface is littered with wadded up napkins, empty soft drink and beer cans, and half-empty glasses of tea sweating condensation rings onto Mom's furniture. I scoop these up first before they cause damage.

Near the front door, Dewey is thanking our minister for coming. On pretense of reaching for a paper plate beneath a folding chair, I stoop behind Dewey and land a strong pinch on his backside. He shifts his weight to the opposite foot, and I stifle a giggle. *Gotcha, mister!*

As the crowd thins, Rebecca helps me clean the kitchen and load a few last take-home plates. She massages one hand over the small of her back. A troubled expression flashes across her face.

"What's wrong?" I ask.

She shakes her head, and then fingers a couple of hair spikes to assure herself they still spring out, porcupine-style. "Nothing. Just a little back pain again. Probably hurt it hefting desks around." Sniffing out an ally, she launches phase two of her campaign. "Helen, wouldn't Angie make the best AFT vice-president ever?"

I shoot Rebecca a *Not Fair* look and continue to scoop potato salad into a plastic container. I snap on the lid. All my life I have shunned leadership roles, the guts and glory garbage the exclusive domain of MacKenzie, Miss President of Everything. "I prefer to stay behind the scenes."

"You should do it, honey," Mom says, as if I couldn't see that response coming. "I know you have good ideas about what our schools need. You've shared them with us for years."

Different. Private. Just venting. If my complaining became public, I'd be out of a job.

Rebecca rinses out an empty casserole dish in the sink. "See? Everyone thinks you'd do a great job."

Everyone—defined as my best friend and my mom. Other teachers have more charisma, are more extroverted. "A younger teacher would be better. I plan to retire in a few years."

My mother huffs. "Experience counts. Give Rebecca some of that ham. We'll never eat all this stuff."

Dutifully, I lay half a dozen slabs on a paper plate and Mom covers it with plastic wrap.

Rebecca cradles the leftovers in her arms. "No more—goodness, I won't have to cook for a week as it is." At the door she lingers, pressing the issue. "Your mom's right. Experience matters. Say you'll do it."

"Don't think so, but thanks for asking." I've been hearing the "s" word bandied about. Not that one, the really bad one. *Strike.* Trouble is brewing all across the state.

Mom walks with us to the front door. "Don't you worry, Rebecca, I'll work on her. Like I always tell her, she can do anything she sets her mind to."

"I am selective when it comes to my mind's agenda."

Rebecca and Mom exchange a look that reeks of conspiracy, so I close the front door between them, cutting off any further attack, but they have planted a whisper in my mind: Maybe it's time to venture outside my comfort zone, get out from behind my desk; maybe it's not enough to let other people do the work for AFT. I am thinking of something Martin Luther King said: "There comes a point when silence is betrayal." I suspect we teachers are at that point.

I kiss Mom's cheek and suggest it's time for me and Dewey to head out too. "Where is that husband of mine?"

"He offered to get Hambone ready for bed. The crowd tired him out."

Poor Poppy. I can only imagine how confused he must have been trying to figure out who all these people were.

I turn toward the hallway to retrieve Dewey, but Mom stops me. "I have a present for you."

"Oh, no, Mom. You've done more than enough already. No presents. I don't need a thing." Except new tennis shoes, and they aren't something anyone else can buy. Though I'd worn the same size of shoes since my freshman year of high school, my feet started growing again two years ago. If it kept up much longer, I'd resemble Big Foot. So bizarre, the changes happening to my body.

Mom disappears into my childhood bedroom, which she has been using as a craft and hobby workshop. She emerges with a scrapbook so bulky I marvel that she can hold it with those arthritic hands. I follow her to the sofa. On the cover, gold embossed letters—the kind with sticky backs—spell out "Angela Marie Adams Fisher" in a slightly crooked line.

"This is your story, Angie, and the story of your family."

"Oh, Mom, what a special gift."

I leaf through the first pages of baby photos, me and MacKenzie in matching outfits Mom had sewn. Next is a receipt from one of those genetic testing companies—she has ordered a testing kit for me. The science behind these tests isn't strong, but I don't have the heart to tell her. I turn another page and notice bold tabs divide the contents into "Forever Family" and "Birth Family."

Lips pressed together, I close the book and when I can finally speak, my voice cracks. "You didn't."

"You say you don't care about your birth family, but like it or not, they are part of who you are. There are some very strong women, important women, in your family tree."

"Sorry, but strong women don't give their children away. My family is the people who raised me."

"Always and forever. But it's time you learn the rest of your story."

She means well, I know she does. I fan through the pages—typed pages full of words, news clippings, photos. I can only imagine how many hours it took to assemble.

"Thanks, Mom. This is really special." I lean over and kiss her cheek.

"I have another little something for you. It's over there on the bookshelf—see that brown ceramic thing-a-ma-jiggy? Bring it here."

She is motioning toward a vase about as tall as a wine bottle, a bit wider, curvier, burnished walnut with amber shading around the raised artwork. Once seated again, I trace my fingers over the design. A swath of maple leaves. And on the other side, a pair of seed pods—samaras. "MacKenzie and I called these helicopters when we were kids."

Mom grabs her reading glasses and leans closer to inspect the vase. "I thought those were angel wings."

"Nope, seed pods. Mac and I would toss them up and watch them spin through the air."

She removes her glasses, studying me with the same intensity she had directed toward the vase. "You two had plenty of good times growing up. You were like two peas in a pod."

I know Mom is wondering what happened. Hard to pin down to any one thing, but Mac's and my paths diverged in junior high. Mom wanted me to join this teen group at the country club. Junior Debs. Ladies offered instruction on proper manners and organized dances for the kids. I knew I'd be one of those girls the boys groaned over if they got stuck with me as their date, so I refused to join. Instead, I stayed in 4-H and Girl Scouts. When Mac entered seventh grade, she relished the opportunity to wear frilly dresses on these pre-arranged dance dates. Mom was delighted that at least one of her girls was popular. The boys, unnaturally stiff in Sunday suits and ties, were motored to our door by their mothers. Their fumbling attempts to pin pastel corsages on my sister's shoulder were painful to watch. They were as uneasy as I would have been in their shoes. Later, though, in the school hallways, I'd overhear their bragging if they got to escort my sister to a dance. She was easily the prettiest girl in our school. And she read every issue of popular teen magazines cover to cover. She knew what to say to awkward boys to put them at ease. My inept attempts to joke with them between classes only made them feel more gauche. By the time Mac and I entered high school, open sarcasm characterized our relationship. I made snide remarks about her obsession with teen magazines. She poked fun at my perfect report card. *Who wants to be valedictorian?* she said. *I'd rather be Prom Queen.*

We both attained our goals, but we lost each other.

Uneasy with Mom's scrutiny, I turn my attention back to the vase. "This is really beautiful. I like the subdued coloring and raised design."

"One of your ancestors was a rather famous potter back in the early 1900s. The design is hers."

"Seriously?" I am curious now. "How did you ever find this?"

"Miss College-Educated, you aren't the only one in the family who knows how to do research." Mom smiles, cat-like, so smug I can almost see the canary feathers protruding from her mouth.

I run my finger around the rim, not chipped—amazing, considering its age. "I'll treasure it—always."

"When I die—"

A chill slides down my spine. "You're not going to die, at least not any time soon." I examine her more closely, so thin, flesh hanging loose from fragile bones, muscle and fat nonexistent. Does she have cancer again—or is this what eighty-two looks like? "Have you been drinking those nutrition boosters I bought you?"

She ignores the interruption. "When I die, you must be the glue that holds our family together."

"What about MacKenzie?"

"Can you imagine her on her own?" She answers her own question. "No, she married a rich man to take care of her. She's not as strong as you are, and someday she's gonna need you to lean on."

I remember my intuition that Mac's marriage was in trouble. Had Mom sensed something wrong as well?

Mom's eyes rise to the wall beside the mantel where photos of me and my sister at different ages have hung as long as I can remember. All those matching outfits—until junior high school when I insisted on store-bought jeans and casual tops.

"Why do you think your sister is so competitive?"

"It's MacKenzie's nature, has to be the best."

"She has always tried to measure up to you, Angie."

As if! "Don't be silly. MacKenzie is Miss Perfect. Miss President-of-Everything."

"She could never best you at school, so she tried to win in other ways. You were the smart one. You got a college degree, a career. You will be this family's backbone when I'm gone. You come from strong women. You're going to need to draw on that strength sooner than you think."

I touch the cover of the book, the first one I've ever been half afraid of. After all my years of purposeful forgetting, Mom insists on dragging out my birth mother's sins. Behind the cover of this book lies the whole truth of who I am. *I am the child whose mother gave her away. I am the child who caused the accident.*

My mother shakes her head. "You didn't cause the accident."

Did I say it out loud? Must have. "Yes, I did. I should have given Mac my doll."

"Sweetheart, you didn't cause the accident. Your father was driving under the influence. I loved him dearly, but he couldn't leave the drugs alone after he came back from Vietnam. He stayed stoned most of the time."

My mind reels as if I am the one under the influence of mind-altering drugs. "How could I have known? You never talked about it."

"I had no idea how to explain your father's demons to five year olds. He was a good father in many ways, always willing to read to you, to tuck you in at night. I always thought you married Dewey because he reminded you of him."

Maybe I did: the laid-back approach to life, the chirpily happy voice, but no drugs, thank goodness, other than the occasional beer.

Memories surface, vague images of my daddy singing me and MacKenzie to sleep, "Puff the Magic Dragon," "Bridge Over Troubled Water," or "Me and You and a Dog Named Boo."

I remember my father reading my favorite Dr. Seuss book aloud, *Hop on Pop*. Soon MacKenzie and I knew all the words and read it aloud to him instead. We giggled like maniacs when we got to the page where two little critters hop on Pop's tummy. We tackled Daddy on the bed, rolled around on him, his arms strong and sure, sometimes hauling us in tight for a tickle, sometimes pushing us off if we bounced too vigorously, and then he would drop his voice an octave and call out, *Enough, you little banshees, enough!* at which we giggled and bounced more insistently.

Other words from the story flash back to me, words shadowed with new meaning, my father's demons lurking beneath them: *Dad is sad. Very, very sad. He had a bad day. What a day Dad had!*

Now those arguments over weeds on the porch make sense. Grandmother Adams was upset because she realized someone was smoking pot on the porch. Suddenly I feel sorry for my grandmother—not too sorry, but a little. It must have been hard to admit her only son had addiction problems, impossible to admit he had caused the accident, caused his own death.

How had I not known this years ago? The needless guilt.

I am stunned when my mother starts crying. I don't know what else to do, so I hand her a tissue.

"You and MacKenzie had another sister, Jo Beth."

"What?"

"In the seventh month of my pregnancy, the doctor told me my little girl had died. He induced labor and we buried her next to my grandmother. Your father's addictions became much worse after Jo Beth died. I wanted to curl up in a ball and die myself, but I couldn't. I had to be there for you and your sister. That trip to the beach was supposed to help us both get past our grief, to bring your father and me back together. His mother was supposed to watch you two while we had some alone time."

Instead the accident gave us all new grief.

"Your father's death—maybe it was for the best. I don't think he could have ever healed everything broken inside, couldn't have gotten sober."

Finally I hear what she's telling me: they wouldn't have stayed together. I squeeze her hand and we sit in silent reflection for a few moments.

Her revelation is shocking.

It's good. Sort of.

I am innocent. Mostly.

I call out for Dewey. It's past time to go home.

Mom nudges me with her elbow. "I'm glad to see you and Dewey still have a little fun together."

"What do you mean?"

"You know perfectly well what I mean."

I assume my best mystified look and shrug.

"Oh, come on. The pinches."

My insides are blushing purple. "What—?" I can't bring myself to say *pinches*.

"Harmless fun. Every marriage needs a little of that."

I wonder who else has seen us.

"Don't worry. No one else knows, but I'm your mother. I see everything."

Oh dear. That is not comforting.

I drive home since Dewey has downed a few too many beers. I hate driving his truck, the big beast he just had to have. His dream machine, he calls it. A raised 4x4 with huge tires, dual exhausts, and custom paint job of a man fishing in a mountain creek on the tailgate. His dream, my nightmare. It's so big I feel as if I'm always crossing the center line or alternatively, riding off the road's shoulder. Besides that, it's a gas hog and we are still making payments on the darn thing.

As if the day hasn't been strange enough, Dewey detonates another bomb. "Did you notice the way Dakota was making goo-goo eyes at that Belinda Talkington? Something's going on there."

I am so surprised I can't speak. Sure, Dakota and Trish aren't married, but I thought they loved each other. They have lived together for over a year and are going to be the parents of my grandchild. I swear I'll beat the living tar out of Dakota if he does anything to hurt Trish—or the baby bump I already adore beyond all reason.

When I get home and Dewey is brushing his teeth, I open the scrapbook to the Birth Family Tree. I slide my finger down to the bottom branches to the name of the woman who gave me away. Deborah Wellington Springer. I say her name aloud twice. A lump in my throat prevents me from continuing. There's no father on the space beside her name. I guess Mom's research didn't turn one up. Anyway, my birth mother's name is all I can handle right now.

I don't think I will sleep a wink all night, but I climb into bed beside Dewey anyway, my mind jumbled with scenes from the party, Rebecca and Mom teaming up to make me say yes—no, no, no—the swollen curve of Trish's ankles, the baby bump, the pinches, my mother knowing about the pinches. The present fades into the night, swallowed by the past. A guitar strums "Bridge Over Troubled Water," a voice whispers *Deborah Wellington Springer, Deborah Wellington Springer,* and my mother is saying, *How could I explain, you were just a child, just a child, just a child,* just before I lose consciousness.

LATE SEPTEMBER 2017

DAKOTA CALLS US TO MEET HIM at United Hospital Center for the birth of Bella Fisher-Jones. Like every other family, we believe little Bella is the most beautiful baby ever born, perfect in every way. Like every other baby, her skin is wrinkly and red, her face a tad mashed from its journey into life, a full head of walnut-hued fuzz that springs out comically no matter how much gel Trish smoothes onto it. She is beyond adorable, beyond precious, scarily tiny and vulnerable. Each of us knows we will do anything, no matter how difficult, however impossible, to protect this child from all harm.

At the moment of Bella's birth, the ground shifts under me. My role is upended. My daughter is a mother; I am a grandmother. One of those people who seemed so old when I was young.

The world has changed in other ways when I wasn't looking, seismic shifts that haven't touched me personally. Until now. Dewey and I are allowed in the hospital room with Trish and the baby. When I had Trish, babies were sequestered in a nursery, brought out only at feeding time. Only mothers and nurses were allowed contact for fear of exposing newborns to germs carried by fathers, grandparents, aunts, uncles. Now the baby interacts with family from its first moments. I see the change and it is good.

While Trish rests in the adjustable bed, I cradle Bella gently against my chest, close my eyes, stifle an urge to crush her against me. Instead I stroke the unutterably soft skin of her tiny arm and almost weep when she grasps my finger, her nails no more than tiny sharp flakes, her lashes long and black against her cheeks. Oh, the exquisite button nose! The smells of baby lotion and milk are almost painful, too intense to bear. I understand Lennie in *Of Mice and Men,* how he crushed the puppy against him, not because he wanted to harm it but because he so dearly loved the soft new life. That's me. I am Lennie.

We float on a cloud of happiness.

Until an audiologist visits Trish's hospital room. A slender woman with short blonde hair, she is possibly in her mid-forties, neatly dressed in black slacks and a loose floral blouse. She introduces herself but the name doesn't stick. I sense immediately she bears bad news.

"We conduct screenings of all infants. Unfortunately, we discovered Bella has congenital hearing loss, and we want to run more definitive tests." she says. My heart drops to the floor. "She is not alone," the audiologist continues. "One in five hundred develops some form of hearing loss in childhood."

Small consolation, fellow sufferers. It is this child we cherish, this child it is our duty to protect.

Tears slide down Trish's cheeks. How can I possibly comfort her?

After another set of tests, the specialist informs us Bella is not completely deaf. "With hearing aids and speech therapy in the early years, Bella will grow into a happy, healthy girl. She may benefit from cochlear implants eventually, but it's too early to tell if that will be necessary."

Despite the assurance Bella will be able to learn, I can't quiet my doubt until my pal Rebecca arrives at the hospital with balloons. "A perfect name for a beautiful baby. She'll be fine, Trish. They've made so many advances in hearing aid technology today. We start speech therapy right away, and it makes all the difference."

We are relieved she will be able to learn language skills, but oh, the anguish that we can't just kiss her and make it better. I am more thankful than ever for Rebecca's friendship—and thankful for all the special needs teachers out there helping all children reach their potential. The shortage of these teachers scares me. If we don't increase their pay, we will never be able to attract more young people to the field.

Trish pales when she learns hearing aids will cost around six thousand dollars, not covered by health insurance. They will need replacement every three years. The thought of that ongoing expense makes me dizzy.

Dewey clasps her shoulder. "Don't give it another thought," he tells Trish. "We'll take care of it."

I'm grateful he stepped forward so quickly, but I avoid making eye contact. He has to be as worried as I am about another unexpected expense.

On the last morning of Bella's hospital stay, the obstetrician stops by. A trim woman of Asian heritage, Dr. Chen leans over the crib for a last look at the baby. "Very alert for a newborn," the doctor says. "She already seems to follow movements with her eyes. Such a beautiful baby, too."

Poppy, grinning foolishly, moves so close he brushes against the fabric of her white doctor's coat. "You're quite the looker yourself."

Mom takes his arm and pulls him away. "Sorry."

Since Mom is too embarrassed to explain, I walk with the doctor to the hallway. "His social filters don't always work anymore."

"Dementia?" the doctor asks.

"Yes, Alzheimer's."

Dr. Chen tells me about an experimental program getting underway at West Virginia University's Neuroscience Institute. They plan to use focused ultrasound treatment to disrupt the blood-brain barrier in regions of the brain affected by Alzheimer's. "They hope the ultrasound will reduce cognitive decline. You might want to find out if your father is a good candidate for the trials."

I promise to look into it and thank her for her kindness. Ultrasound is so completely different from the other avenues of research into brain disease, I allow my hopes to rise. This could reverse Poppy's decline, could restore the personality we know and love. A phone call later, my hopes are dashed. Poppy's case is not likely to be accepted because of other complicating health issues. That's so often the way with these trials. Every factor needs to be controlled. So far, every avenue we've explored has been discouraging. He was in one trial that was halted when doctors discovered the drug had serious side effects. We continue to hope, but it's difficult to be optimistic.

The evening news covers one disaster after another—and these, on top of the polarized politics dividing our country, make me dread tuning in to stay informed. Three hurricanes cause tremendous devastation: Harvey, Irma, Maria. Fires burn all over the American West destroying acres of forest and threatening wildlife and towns. In class we talk about the impact of climate change. The news isn't good at home either. For all Dakota's good looks, muscular definition, and educational attainment, he proves Trish's reservations well conceived. He is not up to the demands of a child facing extra challenges. He moves out of Trish's apartment and into Belinda Talkington's a month after the baby's birth. Maybe he was planning to all along.

Screw him. He isn't good enough for my girls anyway.

OCTOBER 2017

I SPEND MY SUNDAY MORNING deadheading the pots of chrysanthemums on our porch and picking the last tiny green tomatoes for bread and butter pickles. Dewey pulls up the spent plants and wheelbarrows them to the compost bin in the back yard. Sunlight glints and dances across the orange, red, and golden leaves of our maple, creating the illusion of a lively campfire.

After our customary Sunday brunch at the farm, Trish nurses little Bella in the family room, burps her, diaper draped on her shoulder to catch dribbles and sour spit-up, the inevitable reality of life with a baby. Not every smell is sweet as baby lotion.

"I've decided to find a smaller apartment," Trish says. Her nose twitches, a giveaway that she isn't being entirely truthful. "I don't need as much space with Dakota gone."

"The baby will take up just as much space if not more." My mother motions from a sofa that's nearly as old as I am. "Give Great Nana the baby."

That sofa has been recovered at least three times, always in plaid. I sink down onto the opposite end, moving a throw pillow Mom has placed over a thin piece of metal sticking through the couch fabric. My finger can't resist touching the defect. "These springs are shot, Mom. You really need a new sofa."

"You, Missy, should appreciate my environmental responsibility. I'm reducing and reusing. Besides, this old thing will last as long as me and then you can haul it off to Goodwill."

I chuckle. "Don't think they'll want it."

Mom continues waving her hands. "Come on, gimme the baby. Let me hold her a while."

Trish takes Bella over, swaddled in the yellow blanket Mom has knitted, and gently lays her in her great grandmother's arms. Mom dandles the little bundle until I'm sure the baby will spit up all the breast milk so recently swallowed.

"You always been so rough handling younguns?" I ask.

Mom finally lays the baby down in her lap, and Poppy blows a raspberry on Bella's belly. She opens her eyes and smiles. "You sure is a pretty baby, Trishie Wishie," Poppy says.

"She sure is," Mom agrees. It's easier than explaining. Lost in a time warp, Poppy is never going to understand who the baby is, and what difference does it make? Fooling around with the baby's tiny feet and hands makes him happy.

After all the time Trish spent transforming the spare bedroom into a nursery, I can't believe she would give her place up on a whim. "What's really going on, Trish?"

Trish's shoulders wag from side to side, an admission of sorts. "I'm reducing my hours to have more time with Bella."

Her job is secretarial and administrative work for the county school board. "The board is okay with that?"

"Family hardship leave. It's only for a few months until I see how everything works out with Bella. I'll have to take her to speech therapy and practice with her at home too. Another worker has agreed to cover for me. I already found a cheaper place to live. It will be fine."

"Nonsense. You can move in with us." I glance at Dewey to make sure this is okay with him.

"Damn right," he says.

"We can take her to therapy sometimes. Practice speech with

her, too. It would be our privilege."

"Absolutely." Dewey whips off his ball cap and slaps it back on. "Besides, if you move back home, your mom will have a reason to finally clean out all the junk she's shoved into your old bedroom."

Always a joker, my husband.

"Are you sure?" Trish asks.

"Of course." I am pleased my very independent daughter has agreed so quickly. Ahhh—sometimes I am slow on the uptake. Trish was hoping for the invitation. With Bella's extra needs, Trish will need our help but is too proud to ask.

Both thrilled and a little unnerved, I am just beginning to consider how much our lives are about to change. Waking up to cries in the middle of the night. Dirty diapers. Toys scattered everywhere—it's inevitable. Oh, it'll be fun, a delight, another unexpected blessing.

"We'll redecorate," I say. "When do you have to give up your apartment? A baby shouldn't be exposed to paint fumes."

"I'll help, Mom," Trish says. "Relax, we don't have to be out until the end of the year."

In a playful turnabout, I suggest Dewey could clean out all the junk in the garage so Trish could park her car inside.

Trish giggles. "Good one, Mom."

Dewey shrugs good-naturedly. "It's not junk. I need that stuff."

"Sure, hon, everyone needs cans of paint that dried up twenty years ago. Very valuable, very useful."

"Or boxes of *Rolling Stone* magazines from the '80s," Trish adds.

"Hey, those are collectible," Dewey protests.

We are all laughing, so Dewey feels compelled to defend himself. "Well, they might be some day."

"I'll be sure to save them for Bella, so she can sell them and get rich," Trish says.

Mom's laugh tinkles out. "You can have all those Avon bottles I collected. They were so prized back in the day, but aren't worth the shelf space in antique shops anymore. Come to think of it, I haven't seen any *Rolling Stones* on the shelves either."

The baby lets out an obscenely loud belch. Mom lifts the baby from her lap and rubs her back.

"Not you too, Bella," Dewey protests. "No fair—all you women ganging up on me."

Mom also offers to take Bella to speech therapy. "You might carry a recessive gene for hearing loss, Angie," she says. "I wonder if that DNA testing company looks at defects in that particular gene. Have you gotten the results back?"

Caught—I am forced to confess I haven't spit in the test tube the company mailed to me yet.

Mom shakes her head. "I bet you haven't read about your ancestor, Rosella Krause, how she not only was a talented potter, but also an activist for women's rights. I recollect she had some health issues with her children, too."

She knows me too well. "I read all the 'Forever Family' stuff, the family I care about. The family that cares about me." I haven't read past the name, Deborah Wellington Springer, the woman who gave me away. But if knowing about my birth family will help Bella in any way, I will spit in a test tube and read every word in the scrapbook.

"I promise to start reading the rest tonight—even though I have papers I need to grade."

"You always have papers to grade. They'll wait. Read your story, Angie. Leadership is in your genes. Have you told Rebecca you'd serve as AFT vice president?" Mom asks.

"Someone else would do a better job. Besides, I don't have time."

"Mom, you have to do it," Trish says. "Be the change you want to see."

"That's a cliché."

"Because it's true. Come on. I've found time, so should you."

The guilt trip starts working on me. Even though Trish had already been pregnant as the "Me Too" movement took off over the summer, she spoke out about harassment she'd experienced in college and organized a meeting of local women to share their experiences.

I'm not ready to give into to the "do it" whispers in my head yet. "I'm just a one tiny cog in a humongous system. Who's going to listen to me?"

"You have power, even if you don't realize it," Mom says. "You can be an organizer like Rosella Krause." Mom stares over the baby's head at empty space near the ceiling as if she sees something the rest of us are missing. "Just think about Evelyn Maddox."

Evelyn? Hadn't she died a few years back? Mom's train of thought is impossible to follow. "That woman with the reedy voice who used to sing in the church choir?"

"Right, Evelyn Maddox. When Evelyn was singing one of her pitiful solos, you could hardly hear her. But when the whole choir was singing together, why, the joyful noise rocked the rafters of the sanctuary. Their voices drowned out the preacher, the man in charge. You want Governor Justice and them legislators to give you a raise, the whole chorus has to start singing. Drown the tightwads out."

I swallow a giggle. So often Mom brings dead people into conversations as if they are still among us, but I see her point.

Trish crosses the room and retrieves the baby from my mother. "Do it for Bella, Mom. She's gonna need good public schools."

The whisper morphs into a roar. Why doesn't insurance cover children's hearing aids? What if we can't afford to give little Bella all the best care she deserves, that every human deserves?

"Okay, okay, I'll do it for all of us."

Back home that night, I curl up in my favorite chair with a cup of tea, the scrapbook in my lap. I'm not ready for Deborah Springer's story. Not yet. Instead I turn to the fattest section of the book, the one labeled "Rosella Krause."

I sink deeper into the chair cushion, amazed by how much work went into this project. The first page is a sepia-toned photograph of Rosella, taken when she was possibly in her late teens, dwarfed beside a strapping fellow who resembles Clark Gable, clearly older than she. Despite her diminutive size, the lively spirit and self-assurance she exudes dominates the photograph. Or maybe I am predisposed to focus on her because my mother has gushed over her so. I wouldn't call Rosella beautiful, but she is striking, dark-eyed, full-lipped, with long, thin fingers, close-clipped nails, that look as capable of milking a cow as shaping a vase from clay. A small embroidered cape fastened with a brooch partially hides the bodice of her gown, three-quarter sleeved with a thickly braided hemline, a frock designed to give any woman confidence. My mother's handwritten caption indicates it might be a wedding photograph. Although I study the woman's face closely, I cannot discern any resemblance to me. She is dainty; I am big-boned. Her hair, caramel; mine black as coal. At least, it used to be. The one feature we might share is dark eyes, though who can really say from a faded photograph.

I flip through several pages of news clippings about Rosella's pottery. I am impressed. She was important enough to merit her own show in an art gallery in San Francisco. I doubt if many women achieved that kind of recognition way back in 1920. I flip to the next page and unfold a photocopy of the entire front page from the *Examiner.* How important this woman must have been to make the front page of a city paper!

Absently I reach for my teacup with my right hand, letting the index finger of my left hand trail down the photocopy until it rests on a bold headline containing my ancestor's name. As the headline's meaning sinks in, the teacup slips from my fingers and clatters back onto its saucer.

Rosella

THE TEACUP SLIPPED from my fingers and clattered onto its saucer. It seemed some ghosts from my past refused to stay buried. I scanned the headline again and let my breath hiss past my teeth. How in tarnation could the *Examiner* print such scurrilous lies! Now that the Great War was over, it seemed all the newspapers wanted to print was scandal and gossip and lies. Tardily, I inspected the teacup, caressing the curve of the handle. The piece was hand painted, a gift from Nellie Priester, and I would be loath to allow the slightest harm to come to it. I started every morning with that cup in hand—even when I traveled—to remind me of my dearest friend. I found the china intact though tea had sloshed onto the hotel's tablecloth.

I scanned the first paragraph again, hoping the words were merely the product of a mind still cobwebbed by dreams or nightmares. But the massive headline, so oppressively dark in typeface and thought, assaulted me anew. As if my hands possessed no more substance than empty gloves, bereft of starch and bone, they released the *Examiner,* its pages spilling atop buttered toast, a pot of fragrant plum jam, and what remained of my chamomile tea. I would have appreciated this room service more had it not included the newspaper. My hands flew to the hollow at the base of my throat, as if to shield that most vulnerable stretch of skin. Were authorities about to arrest me? Imprison me? Hang me by the neck until dead?

Considering the power of the Puritanical crusade waged by Compton and his ilk, it is no wonder that I was first overcome with fear, but let me assure you, after a few deep breaths, outrage replaced fear. Oh all right, I was afraid too, but the ridiculousness of that headline. *Lock her up!!!* Yes, the paper deemed me—all ninety-two pounds, fully dressed out in petticoats, corset, and leather shoes—me, worthy of three exclamation marks. Three! Why, the very morality of the nation must be at stake. Gasp! What woman's husband could possibly be safe as long as such a harlot remained free. *Lock her up!!!*

Oh, I had spent a night in jail when I was arrested for picketing the White House, but other women shared the same fate then. Awful as it was, I had company in my misery, other women who ate beans and cornmeal crawling with weevils, who were kicked and beaten, manacled to the bars of prison cells, and denied even the simple luxury of a toothbrush. That last bothered me more than anything else. I do like clean teeth.

This new threat singled me out in a personal attack. Who among my acquaintances had fed the reporter this mishmash of fact and fiction? Hardly anyone knew the few details that were accurate. Who? Who? Who would betray me this way?

I had barely noticed when Solina rose from the breakfast table and tiptoed behind me to see what had caused such alarm. By the time she spoke, I suppose she had already read most of the story over my shoulder.

"Mama, I know you are different from other mothers, but how can they say these things about you?"

Different? I wasn't that different. Although I grant you, most mothers didn't have clay under their fingernails. And not many had arrest records—but it wasn't as if I had committed any criminal acts. None I deemed criminal anyway. I caressed the petal smooth hand she placed on my shoulder without turning to look at her.

When I didn't respond, the hand on my shoulder tightened, her tone more insistent, the pitch higher, trembling. "Mama?"

She was so young, only fourteen, an innocent, but I could procrastinate no longer. Even though I'd often rehearsed my story mentally over the years, now that the moment had arrived, I felt unprepared.

"Only a fool could believe I set out to become a bigamist—and I know you are no fool, Solina, because I raised you."

She resumed her seat at the breakfast table, unable, poor girl, to eat a bite, her eyes never leaving my face until I delivered the newspaper into her hands.

"Most certainly I am not now nor have I ever been a baby killer or a whore," I told her when she finished reading the scandal sheet—for what else could you call it? "You cannot believe those things about me. Such despicable fabrication is beneath even Hearst and the *Examiner*."

But oh, I shuddered as I considered the damage this would do. Picture my fine circle of patrons and friends as their eyes alight on this sordid gossip. See their finely embroidered handkerchiefs clasped to the delicate pink of their lips. Hear them call to their maids for smelling salts. But quicker than my friends can order up a carriage, they will be overcome by a Christian impulse to share such dreadful news. Feel the air shift as front doors whiz open and click shut along Russian Hill as these ladies rush to each other's homes. Beware: A ninety-two pound Satan has darkened your doorways. An exorcism is in order. Or at least a glass of sherry.

For a moment, I speculated about the fate of my pottery. Would they destroy my precious art, now view it as tarnished by the wicked hands that created it? No, no, 'tis more likely notoriety would increase its value. Every piece, an opportunity to waft a pale, smooth hand in a ewer's direction, and declare *I knew the artist*, and then in the lowest of whispers—lean in closer, ladies—here comes "A Tale of Two Men in Two Cities." A tale far racier than anything Dickens ever wrote, though hardly as profound.

"My story—the real story, Solina—begins on our family farm in West Virginia," I said.

One side of her mouth lifted in an expression I'd noticed all too often lately. A scowl. Quite unattractive.

"Mama, I have a right to know. Is Papa really—"

I posed the rude question before she could finish. "Really your father? He raised you, didn't he? He deserves that title. But if you consider simple biology, the answer is rather more complicated."

My daughter's eyes grew wide with horror. "Mama, right now I feel as if I have no idea who you are."

"Don't be ridiculous. Let me assure you, the story I am about to share will vindicate my actions."

I would have told her long ago, should have, but the moment never seemed quite right. She deserved to hear the truth, a virtue entirely—well, almost entirely—absent from the *Examiner* story. "Seriously, darling, what woman would willingly assume the responsibility of caring for two husbands simultaneously? The Good Lord knows one man can be trouble enough."

Especially if one of them was Jack Joyner.

"Give me a chance to explain."

She slouched in the chair and crossed her arms, pulling the fabric of her nightgown tight against her budding breasts. "I'm listening."

The tone of her voice had hardened slightly. But even though her lower lip eclipsed the upper in a slight pout, I was amazed anew by how lovely her face had become—an exquisite oval with features arrayed in perfect symmetry. Her dark eyes, which reminded me so much of Jack's, and every bit as much of Val's, rested on me expectantly, but I hardly knew where to start. Truth—did anyone ever really grasp the whole truth, the bitter truth? More important, did Solina really want to hear it? I wasn't sure how much to divulge.

My eyes fell back onto the newsprint and my teeth clamped together. Instead of the photograph of the most beautifully textured design I'd ever created, one employing both slip trail and sgraffito, the *Examiner* had wasted space on Jack's and Val's mug shots. The scandal completely overshadowed the opening of my show at Kenneson's gallery, mentioned almost as an afterthought. Men! Must they always dominate everything? Poof! All the years I had spent honing skills, perfecting technique, building toward the kind of recognition every artist longs for—my own show in an important gallery—eclipsed by outrageous tittle-tattle.

Who had ruined what was supposed to be my moment of triumph? I was going to find the source behind the *Examiner's* story and then I would—well, I didn't know what I would do, but I would be forceful. Merciless. Vengeful. If it was that conniving Alexandra Underwood, I would slap the arrogance right off her face.

I smacked my hand down on the table. Solina jumped and Nellie's teacup rattled in its saucer.

HARRISON COUNTY, WEST VIRGINIA, 1899-1903

A THIEF AND MAGICIAN, that's what Jack Joyner was. Though I sketched him many times, I never could quite capture his ever-changing eyes. Through sleight of hand, one day his eyes would steal the burnished brown of chestnuts, but the next day, he'd sidle up beside the very same tree, and before those poor leaves knew what was happening, he'd stripped them of their green. Some days his eyes gleamed golden, and I knew he'd fooled the sunlight yet again, perhaps with another card trick. No girl could resist his twinkle or his wink. Jack Joyner was indeed a thief. That trickster stole the heart of many a girl, including mine. I should have known he'd prove just as fickle as the color of his eyes. Jack was a jackass, but I couldn't see it then. No, I was certain he would rescue me, that he would keep me from turning into my mother. Don't get me wrong— I adored the dear woman—but she allowed my father to swallow her identity. I swore by all that was holy that would not happen to Rosella Krause. And it didn't, so it's only fair to credit Jack for his role in shaping the independent woman I became.

The Krause farm amounted to sixty-five acres of rolling hills suitable only for grazing. We raised cows to keep us in milk and meat. No matter how cash-poor we might be, there was always plenty to eat. My father had plowed up our only two acres of bottomland where we planted corn, pole beans, tomatoes, peppers, and squash. His skin was sun-darkened and pebbled like an orange; his fingers, so rough they snagged on cloth, sandpapered your skin if he happened to touch you. His face, narrow, trapezoid-shaped, broader at the forehead, tapered to a squared chin darkened by a trim beard.

Besides tending to the needs of a husband and seven children, my mother managed that vegetable garden, stocking our root cellar with Mason jars to see us through winter. They were beautiful, those jars, shiny rows of raspberry jam, red and green peppers simmered in tomato sauce, golden corn relish, the dull green of pole beans, and pickled cucumber spears. The jars I cherished above all were the green tomato pickles we canned in late fall.

My mother also kept a small flock of buckeye chickens she'd obtained from a woman in Lumberport, ten miles north of our farm on the outskirts of Clarksburg. My mother claimed they were the best chickens ever bred. Killed mice better than our cats. Summer evenings when she was too exhausted to take another step, my mother would sit in her rocker on the porch, and several of those hens took turns nestling in her lap while she stroked their feathers. Baby substitutes, you see, after my youngest brother Timmy grew too big for lap sitting. Following Timmy's birth, my mother took to sleeping in the bedroom that had been Mark's and Paul's before they left home for jobs in the coal mines and Josiah's before he married and worked construction jobs in town. The room was once shared by two older brothers, so I'm told. They left home soon after I was born to log the magnificent red spruce, yellow poplar, white oak, and hemlock that once carpeted the Alleghenies. Many trees ranged from ten to twenty feet in diameter, if you can believe the letters my brothers sent home. Those giants are all gone now and my brothers disappeared into the wilds of the western states. We last heard from them almost a decade ago.

In any case, my mother passed off the new sleeping arrangements as a joke, that it was the only way to get any rest because my father snored.

By the time I was ten, I had wrung the necks of chickens under the direction of my mother and had sent a bullet spiraling into the sweet spot of a deer after hours hovering in a stand with Josiah. I had tried but failed to snag a wild turkey, those creatures being far too wily for the likes of me.

My first attempts at art were rather crude pots, functional pieces my mother taught me to make. We hauled wet clay up from the creek and shaped vessels to hold water and large bowls to hold apples from our orchard. My mother showed me how to use a sharpened stick to incise simple designs in the wet clay, the shape of an oak leaf or the outline of a tree. But my favorite way to capture any aspect of the natural world was with a pencil. I fancied myself an artist. The school mistress had shown us sketches of bobwhite, crows, and a golden eagle done by John James Audubon who lived in nearby Kentucky. He had become famous for his drawings, she said. Since she had complimented my drawings, I was certain I could become famous too.

Besides farming, my father, the right Reverend Herman Krause, supported us as an itinerant preacher. Weekends, he set out for Bristol, Pennsboro, Center Point, Clarksburg, Quiet Dell, Shinnston, Saltwell—any nearby community that would welcome a sermon and allow him to pass a collection plate. No matter how exhausted my mother was, if his destination was close enough, she put on her one good dress and got all of us cleaned up to accompany him. She would leave a small roast with vegetables in a cast iron pot inside the woodstove so we could eat upon return. When I was a little tot, my older brothers would sometimes tell jokes at the table. That seemed acceptable to my father, but if my mother dared to laugh at the boys' remarks, he blessed her out with a fiery sermon. Women must not laugh at off-color stories. Women, in Herman Krause's book of rules, must hold themselves to higher standards than men. Women must serve as pillars of light, leading their men folk down the paths of righteousness. He even used to sing "This Little Light of Mine," just for me, his little light. I didn't aspire to be anyone's light or pillar—the heck with that—but I learned to follow my mother's example and only laughed at my brothers' antics when my father wasn't around. Through small deceptions like this, I remained in my father's good graces. Grudgingly. Already I resented the way my mother allowed him to control her actions, the way her light dimmed in his presence.

The summer everything changed, I was but eleven. Early in the morning, I had helped my mother with the wash and hung the bedding and clothes on the line to dry. Afterward, I peeled potatoes for our dinner. The trouble began when I carried the peelings out to the garden compost pile. Nimrod, my father's prized Hereford bull, snorted behind the fence as if he were calling to me. We stared at each other for a full minute. Then I ran back to the house for my sketchbook. Before I knew it, an hour had passed and I had filled several pages with drawings of the bull, a patch of Queen Anne's Lace, the gay blooms of a Rose of Sharon, and a wooly worm inching its way across a hickory twig. I trotted toward the barn, sketchbook swinging freely from one hand, pencil box from the other, eager to share my latest drawing with my father. I pulled up short when I saw him forking fresh hay into the stalls. My chore, which I had shirked. Again. I tended to lose track of time when I was drawing.

But maybe, just maybe, when he saw my sketch of Nimrod, he'd forget to chastise me. I had labored to capture every detail. The precise pattern of red and white. The bony kneecaps. The broad horns and pointed ears. The symmetrical testes. The large furred sheath pointed straight at the ground, except for the last bit of the tip. My father often bragged to neighboring farmers about the conformation of the bull's male parts. Their efficiency caused our neighbors to part with hard-earned cash to breed their cows with Nimrod.

I held out my drawing. "Look, Daddy, you can show my picture to other farmers and drum up more business."

My father's spine stiffened like the bull's penis when it spotted a cow in estrus. He marched the sketch back to our two-story farmhouse and cornered my mother in the kitchen. "Ann, you take this girl in hand, or I will." He ripped my drawing into miniscule pieces that fell onto the wooden kitchen table where we took all our meals.

"I'm sure Ro meant no harm," my mother said.

"She is out of control, totally out of control."

Eyes burning with unshed tears, I retrieved a few pieces from the table, though I'm not sure what I was thinking. There was no way to rescue the drawing. How many times had I heard my father stand before a congregation and preach about the perfect beauty of God's creations? "You're not being fair, daddy. I drew Nimrod exactly the way God made him."

"You jest hesh-up, young miss, before you get the blistering you deserve." My father's lips quivered, the rage in his belly boiling up a mess of spittle. Then his work-roughened hands snatched the pencil box and sketchbook away from me. He shredded sketches of goldenrod, morning glories, squirrels, sunflowers, joe pye weed, and the shimmery silk dangling from a fresh ear of corn.

Finally I could hold back no longer. The tears fell, and my throat was strangled by sobs.

He destroyed portraits of my brothers—Mark, Paul, Josiah, and Timmy—and now my mother joined in the weeping. As if to punish her for showing sympathy, he ripped up the drawing of my mother in her rocker, her hair arranged in a disheveled topknot, two hens with their little pea combs and feathered bodies nestled in her lap, the scene framed by the Reine de Violette and Gloire de Dijon roses that twined up the porch posts and braided their way across the ceiling, secured by loops of twine fastened to nails.

If he could have spared that one sketch—just that one—I might have forgiven him. If I close my eyes even now, I can smell the heady scent of those roses. A few shattered blossoms have spilled their petals onto the wooden steps. My mother basks in the last amber rays of the evening sun. If I close my eyes even now, I can smell her, the light sweat evaporating from her gingham housedress after a day of chores. I smell the dusting of flour brushed down her apron while she makes dumplings for dinner. And if I push really hard, I can detect the fragrance of lavender and rosemary sachets she sewed and scattered throughout the painted chest of drawers in her bedroom.

She smells exactly like love.

After my father stomped back to his fields, she helped me pick up the pieces.

For six months, my father banned drawing from our house. Twice I heard my mother plead with him to lift the punishment. "I love her drawings," she told him. "They give me such pleasure." Her efforts on my behalf only succeeded in renewing my father's wrath. Their heated voices seeped through the walls, my mother accusing him of being self-righteous, father retorting that she was spineless.

"Leave it be, Ann," he said, "afore your indulgences ruin the girl. She must learn to be a proper wife according to the word of God: 'To be discreet, chaste, keepers at home, good, obedient to their own husbands, that the word of God be not blasphemed.'"

"Surely, forgiveness is a virtue. God gave his only son so that 'we have redemption through His blood, even the forgiveness of sins.' As a man of God, can't you find it in your heart to forgive such a small sin, one that surely was unintentional?"

"You forget yourself, wife. The Bible commands women to be silent, to be obedient to their husbands."

Man of the cloth he might be, but my father could never surpass my mother in quoting Bible verses. She answered him from Philippians. "I am obedient. Yet I think you might strive to be reasonable: 'Let your reasonableness be known to everyone, the Lord is at hand.'"

He erupted with such fury he likely curdled the cows' milk and they were far from the house in the barn. "Damnation, woman, don't you quote the Bible to me."

My mother suggested they should lower their voices lest we children could hear. After that, I could only make out a few words of their back and forth: *hard-hearted, rigid, forgiveness, joy.* I had little trouble guessing the context of each.

The door slammed soon after, my father's temper on full display.

Finally at Christmas, he relented. My present was a new sketchbook, presented to me Christmas morning by my father. Stubborn creature that I was, I refused to take up drawing again.

My mother had moved back into my father's bedroom. Within

months, she was expecting again. This time, neither she nor the baby survived a long and complicated labor in mid-January when the ground was frozen solid. Their interments were delayed until the cloud of white blossoms on the serviceberry signaled sufficient thawing. For two months, I was tormented by the thought of my mother lying inside that cold receiving vault. Not that the thought of her being underground would offer much comfort, but at least our family and community could perform proper tribute and ac-knowledge our grief.

Many years later, though long before I heard of Margaret Sanger and learned to despise Anthony Comstock, I understood what my mother had traded for that sketchbook. My mother taught me much about sacrifice. Much about love.

AFTER MY MOTHER'S DEATH, the family fell on hard times. My mother had trained me well and I did my best to take over her du-ties in the household. My education had ended after completing the sixth grade, though I continued to borrow books from the school mistress, who had befriended me.

The farm was heavily mortgaged and to pay off debts, my father accepted a permanent position at a church in nearby Clarksburg. The loose dirt hardly settled atop my mother's grave when he mar-ried Martha Saunders, a woman barely out of her teens. Martha was a pious soul, long of face, with a disposition as severe and tightly wound as the mousy hair she pulled into a bun. She always occupied the front pew, hanging on every word as if it came straight from the Holy Ghost to Herman Krause's mouth.

Soon after they married, she beat my brother Timmy with a stick right there in the churchyard so everyone could bear witness to her piety. During the sermon, Timmy had crept under a pew and tied Lester Palmer's shoe laces together. At the end of the service, there was much hooting and hollering and general commotion when Lester tripped and tumbled into Miss Moore, knocking her flow-ered hat askew. When we returned home, my stepmother slapped my face. "You shouldn't have laughed," she said. "You are wrong to encourage the boy, you wicked girl."

I couldn't help myself from indulging him. Timmy was an ador-able scamp with brown eyes like a puppy's. A motherless child in need of cuddles and hugs, not scoldings. One summer afternoon after I'd finished my chores, Martha happened upon me in my favorite spot in the whole world. I was sprawled beneath the largest of our weeping willows, the music of the creek trilling in my ears. I was reading Dickens' *Little Dorrit,* a loan from the school mistress. Martha couldn't wait to tattle to my father.

"You shouldn't allow her to read novels," she announced at the end of our supper of beef she'd over-roasted until it was utterly dried out, bloodless—the Martha approach to life. She read aloud a passage from Dr. Mary Wood-Allen's book, *What A Young Woman Ought to Know*: "Romance-reading by young girls will, by this excitement of the bodily organs, tend to create their premature development, and the child becomes physically a woman months, or even years, before she should."

My father glared at me, remembering my sketch of Nimrod, I suppose, and he forbade novels from entering his house ever again. "What husband wants an uppity book-read wife anyway?" His question was rhetorical, and I knew better than to mouth the smarty-pants response that was running through my mind. "You want to read, read the Bible," he added.

The ban only intensified my desire to read and plunged me headlong down the path of breaking the fifth commandment. I sneaked novels borrowed from the schoolmistress into the house at every opportunity, though it was difficult to squeeze reading time into my schedule of chores. I no longer honored my father's wishes. Any of them.

SEVERAL YEARS PASSED with Timmy and me trying to stay out of trouble, mostly succeeding by evading my stepmother. I did my chores faithfully but avoided her. If she set to cleaning the kitchen, I scrubbed the bedroom floors; I wrung the chickens' necks and left the stew pot to her while I wandered off to weed the garden or dig potatoes. I churned butter when she hung clothes on the line. She never commented on it. Avoidance was mutually acceptable.

When I turned fifteen, my duty, according to my father, was to marry a good man. He had one in mind. Gunner Beck.

I cringed, imagining Mr. Beck's farm-roughened hands touching me. Besides being twice my age, he smelled as musty as the goats he raised. He had three children from his first wife, who had passed away delivering the last. Just like my mother, except Mama had lost the baby too.

During the next Sunday service, I studied the Becks in side-long glances. Mr. Beck's mother was jostling the newborn against her shoulder. It looked like every other baby and failed to stir even a smidgen of maternal feeling. The older boy, possibly about four, wiped his nose on the sleeve of his shirt, leaving behind a slimy trail of snot. The two year old was kicking his shoes against the pew, until Mr. Beck reached over and smacked his chubby knees. After that, the child alternated between pouting and hiding his face in his armpit. I didn't blame him. I wanted to hide from his father too. A memory surfaced of the only advice my mother had offered concerning marriage, once when she'd been angry with my father: *Don't marry a self-righteous man.* Mr. Beck, I felt certain, was just such a person. Anger surged through my chest and turned down my lips. Why hadn't my mother followed her own advice? How could she have left me alone at the mercy of my father and Martha?

When we got home from church, my stepmother mounted the next phase of attack. "Isn't Mr. Beck's baby adorable? What a blessing you would bestow on that family if you married him. And consider how well off you'd be."

The last statement was true. The Beck farm consisted of at least two hundred acres. "Money is the root of all evil," I said.

My father held out his palms as if supplicating the Lord, a gesture I'd seen him make a thousand times in church. "Not always. Think of the glory you would achieve in the eyes of God for accepting this burden."

Burden was right, and I was too young and too ambitious to chase after that particular glory. I wanted to choose my own husband. Someone handsome and dashing. Someone who would take me far away from these backwoods West Virginia hill towns and show me the world. That night I prayed fervently that the Lord would deliver me from Gunner Beck, from his goats, from his snot-nosed children. If that was a sin, I would fully accept culpability.

The following Sunday, Jack Joyner ascended the church steps, morning sun glowing behind him like a nimbus, his eyes shining as if they'd stolen beams from Apollo's chariot. An inexplicable magic infused him. The perfect symmetry of his cheekbones, dark with a hint of stubble, generated heat in my belly when he smiled at me. I smiled back and wondered, with a sense of awe, if my prayer could have been answered this quickly. He accompanied his aunt, Elizabeth Barnes, a well-off widow who lived in one of the large homes on Main Street in Clarksburg. His aunt had often spoken of him to me. Elizabeth had been a dear friend of my mother's, so dear that when Elizabeth had fallen ill with the croup the winter I was nine, my mother had sent me to stay with her for a week. I fixed her meals and did small housekeeping chores, as well as reading stories aloud to her from the *Saturday Evening Post*. She was so pleased with a sketch I made of her cat Herkimer that she thumb-tacked it immediately to her wall. I almost busted my buttons when she told my mother I was the daughter she wished she'd had. Sadly, she was childless. I often visited her after that—until my mother's death, when my own chores consumed all my time.

My father's sermon addressed accepting one's duty willingly. God commanded women to serve their families and communities, he said, by easing the burdens of others—and the task, my father assured us, was the greatest and most rewarding part of every woman's life. "Woe be to the woman who shuns her God-given role in life, for she will reap naught but sorrow and pain," he said, finger pointed directly at me.

Father's intention to shame me with that accusatory finger failed. Was he that anxious to get me out of his house? Hadn't I been a good daughter? If he loved me, he wouldn't force me to marry an Old Goat. Well, I would not be shamed into marrying Mr. Beck, though I was somewhat ashamed of myself for thinking of him in those terms. It was unkind.

Throughout the service, I imagined I could feel Elizabeth's nephew's eyes on my back. I wondered how old he was—perhaps eight or ten years older than I. Maybe even as old as Mr. Beck, but far less shopworn. His suit appeared newly sewn from fine cloth. A city fellow, then. I scoffed at myself for indulging an overactive imagination. A fellow like him wouldn't be interested in me. I was plain—and plainly flat-chested. But later as I stood in front of the congregation to lead the singing of "Amazing Grace" and "Doxology," I glanced his way—and yes, he was watching me—he certainly was.

So was the Old Goat, but I refused to make eye contact.

At the end of the service, I couldn't wait to escape the pressure of my family's expectations— and to avoid shaking Mr. Beck's hand. I raced down the church steps into the shade of the grand maple that shadowed the lawn and breathed in the fresh air like someone who'd been on the verge of drowning. I believe I had been holding my breath throughout the whole service for fear of inhaling the odor of Gunner Beck's goats.

Tingles shot up my spine as I caught the fragrance of tobacco— sweet, like overripe apples. Instantly I knew Elizabeth's nephew had followed me onto the lawn. His features thrilled me from the square lines of his jaw to the way his smile carved vertical creases in his cheeks to the ever-elusive, mesmerizing color of his eyes. Jack and Aunt Elizabeth walked partway down the lane with me where black-eyed susans, Queen Anne's Lace, and ironweed sprinkled their merry colors along the ditches. Jack plucked two umbrellas of Queen Anne's Lace and presented one to his aunt and one to me.

"Do you remember how you used to put these in colored water so they'd turn pink or blue?" he asked his aunt. "How'd you do that?"

Her laugh tinkled out. "You remember that, do you? I crushed berries to turn the water colors."

I recalled my mother doing the same for us as children. It was a sign, surely. He was meant for me.

Our courtship was no different than any other, so I'll spare you the details. I was flattered when he singled me out after Sunday services, when he paid attention to me though far prettier girls paraded through our town streets. No local boy had ever made me feel so desirable—or desiring.

Once, I invited him and his aunt home to share Sunday supper. As soon as he departed, my father chastised me. "You aren't near half as smart as you think you are, Rosella, or you wouldn't be taken in by a man jest 'cause he's got a purty face."

Was that such a sin? Didn't make a lick of sense to dislike a man just because he was handsome. I couldn't wait to find out what that mustache of his felt like on my lips.

My father raked callused fingers through his thin brown hair, making the pale streaks of scalp that peeped through even more noticeable. "You had half the sense God gave a snail, you'd marry someone solid, like Gunner Beck."

"I don't love Mr. Beck. I love Jack Joyner."

My stepmother huffed. "What you feel ain't love, my dear. It's lust. It's sinful. It takes time for love to grow."

How much time? Four months? That's how long it took after my mother died for this woman to latch onto my father. Besides, Martha was showing off her ignorance. Mama said only ignorant folks used *ain't*, and she wasn't raising her children up to have ignorant ways.

"Daddy, we met in church. That should earn points in his favor. And we've known his aunt practically my whole life."

My father shook his head. "Only a fool would marry a railroad man. You tie up with the likes of him and you'll be alone like a widder woman, only not so good. You won't be free to find yourself another husband."

"I won't want to marry someone else. I'll draw while we travel." I hadn't drawn since my father had torn up my sketches, but as soon as I made this declaration, it felt like destiny, as if the Hand of Providence had taken charge of my life. I would marry Jack Joyner and become an artist.

My father snorted. "Colored pencils will be cold comfort when he takes up with a different woman in every town."

Wrong, wrong, wrong. I started sketching again, the weeping willow by the creek, the black-eyed susans by the fence, a crow sitting on a post. He loved them all, Jack did. And so I drew his face, over and over in all its expressions. I drew him standing in the church door, I drew him striding down the aisle and standing under the maple in the church yard. I made excuses to go into town and saw him behind my father's back. Twice, he drove his aunt's carriage out as far as the bend in our road and walked the rest of the way. The moss under my favorite oak was our carpet; the stars, the only light required.

Jack Joyner was going places and taking me with him. It didn't hurt that Jack's clothes didn't smell like a musty goat. Besides, he had a rambunctious laugh that tickled me right down to my soles. There'd been little enough laughter in our home since my mother died. Oh, I'll admit it—I burned, burned, burned for him. What's more, I didn't care if I burned in hell for lusting after him.

My feelings did not go unnoticed.

"I won't allow you to see this man again outside of church services," my father said. "I forbid it. You *will* marry Gunner Beck."

My stepmother's lips parted in a thin smile. "That's settled then." She turned to my father. "Don't worry, my dear. I'll arrange everything."

I wasn't her *dear,* and I knew better than to argue any further, but settled? Over my dead body.

SAN FRANCISCO, LATE SEPTEMBER 1903

I HAVE ESCAPED! Oh, you can't imagine the thrill that swept over me every time that thought crossed my mind. I felt as if I had been born anew, with a new name, new store-bought clothes befitting a fashionable lady, and a new husband.

But the reflected image in the Pullman's window appeared so young and silly I unclasped my hands. I looked like nothing more than a little girl ready to jump for joy, not the way Mrs. Jack Joyner should look. But how could I contain myself? That was the Pacific outside, my first ever glimpse of an ocean. If only I could stop the train and dip my hands in water that had touched the shores of places I had only read about in school. Australia. Japan. Hawaii.

I leaned closer, my breath feathering the window, and I could just make out gray waves breaking white against slate-colored cliffs. A little further out, a fishing skiff pitched and rolled. I longed to hear the waves crash, but couldn't hear a thing over the metallic scrape of wheels against track, a sound I'd grown numb to over the past eight days as we journeyed west. My lungs felt clogged with smoke from the coal-fired engine. That annoyance fell away as I glimpsed white birds with long curvy necks pecking through the tidal marshes. They looked a bit like those cow birds that pecked grubs from cow patties, but more elegant, with greater wing spans and far longer legs.

"What are those gorgeous critters?" I asked.

"Great white egrets," Jack said. "So many ladies fancied their feathers for hats, they nearly died off a few years ago."

I had never considered that someone might actually kill birds to feather hats. I assumed someone gathered stray plumes that fell out naturally. I frequently found them about the farm. Never again would I buy a hat with a feather. It was sinful to kill such a stunning creature. *Far more sinful than eloping, Father,* I thought. I wished I could stop thinking about him. I wished I could stop worrying about Timmy, left alone with my father and the hateful Martha. I had left a letter under his pillow telling him not to worry about me and that I loved him dearly and always would.

As an egret took flight, I grabbed my sketchbook and outlined its form. For a moment I imagined I was in the air, listening to the flap of my own wings. On the next page I drew the s-curve of an egret half hidden in tall grass and in my mind I could feel the unwinding of that sinuous neck, could feel the cool water against the beak, the gentle lap of a shallow lake pulling against those impossibly long legs. I could taste the morsel it snapped up from the muck. If only I could stop the train to take in more details.

Jack snatched the pencil from my hands. "You'll have plenty of time to draw all the birds and flowers in California. You don't have to accomplish the entire collection in one day."

"That's my decision to make." I reached for the pencil, but he whipped it behind his back. How dare he! No man ever again would be allowed to restrict my artistic endeavors.

"You're devoting too much time to those little sketches."

Little sketches! His dismissal piqued me. He had praised my drawings while we were courting. Was the honeymoon already over? I had to make up for those lost years after the clash with my father. At every rail station I had drawn whatever I saw. Cactus. Prairie flowers. Gophers. Rattlesnakes. Elk. Mountains—especially the mountains. They were so different from our West Virginia hills. Grander, but more fearsome too. The world was absolutely glorious and I was going to draw it all. Becoming an artist was as much a part of my destiny as my escape with Jack Joyner.

"You had best get it through your head," I tapped his thick curls, only partly in play, "I am devoted to my art."

He drew me away from the Pullman's window, his head ducking beneath my hat to nibble on an ear, whereupon his mustache tickled my neck in the most delightful way. His hand slid up the front of my cotton blouse until it rested beneath my breast. I caught the fragrance of his tobacco and heat raced up the small of my back. All thought of art and rebellion evaporated.

He flashed that self-assured, lopsided smile I found so endearing. "I am hoping that you'll devote yourself to me, Mrs. Joyner."

For the next half an hour, I devoted myself to exploring every inch of Mr. Joyner's delicious skin.

NOISE ASSAULTED US FROM ALL DIRECTIONS as we rode through the business district of San Francisco in a carriage. Cable car bells clanging. Horse hooves clopping. Fog horns moaning in the harbor and automobiles honking their way through crowded streets. I wished I could squeeze my ears shut. And my nose. The smell of so much humanity and so many horses packed into a few square miles was overwhelming. So much chimney smoke, and everywhere, the stench of fish markets and offal tossed into alleys.

I was light-headed, my senses overwhelmed. The many-storied buildings along the city streets both delighted and frightened me. The horses carried us onto a residential street where houses lined up like rows of crops as far as the eye could see, each fighting for its own patch of dirt. The hilly terrain felt familiar. Hills, I knew. But these hills were different. Busier. Alien.

Jack was chatting about our destination, a boarding house he had frequently patronized. It was operated by a young widow, he said, but I paid more attention to my surroundings than to his prattle.

Two cable cars whirred by, barely missing a woman crossing the street. A man on a bicycle zipped between two automobiles—putting his life at needless risk—and everywhere people rushed past on foot or in carriages. The entire conglomeration of people and conveyances crisscrossed each other in a scene of utter chaos. Accidents waiting to happen. Whole streets splayed out with no sign of tree or shrub or flower. Despite the herds of people, the city proper felt dead, devoid of all things green or growing.

Jack called out for the carriage to stop and he helped me out. Much as I anticipated exploring this new city, my legs nearly buckled from the strangeness of it all. Never had I imagined any place in the world like San Francisco.

I waited one step below Jack on the boarding house stoop, my attention riveted on automobiles rumbling down the street. The pair of horses harnessed to the carriage whinnied and stamped nervously. Understandable. The contraptions made me nervous, too, though I longed to ride in one.

The Widow Hansen did not invite us in. Perhaps the age of my stepmother but much more attractive with a fine figure and full, pouty lips, she stood on the threshold of her three-story frame home, upturned nose tilted toward an overcast sky. "I'm very sorry, Mr. Joyner. My rooms are all let."

Jack pulled me forward and bestowed his lop-sided smile on the widow. "Come on, Mrs. Hansen, be a sport. My wife has had a long journey. The sign in the window says 'Rooms Available.' It's not as if I ran out on my bill the last time I stayed with you. You know me."

The chin raised a notch. "Yes, I do."

I prickled at her tone. If I wasn't mistaken, it implied censure.

The widow looked me full in the eyes without a hint of warmth or welcome. "I'm sorry for your pretty little wife—"

I stiffened. What had I done to offend her, to deserve this hostility?

"—but I rented the last room a week ago," the widow was saying. "Been so busy I haven't had time to take down the sign."

Jack pressed his lips together. "Fine. There are plenty of boarding houses around that want our money." He took my elbow and guided me back to the carriage. The driver clucked at the horses and the carriage lurched forward. I looked back at Mrs. Hansen's boarding house. A hand brushed aside the curtain and whisked away the sign advertising rooms. Perhaps I'd imagined her disapproval.

A few blocks away on Sacramento Street, my husband called out for the driver to stop. Jack bolted up the steps to a house nearly identical to the Widow Hansen's, except it was brick. This time the hostess welcomed us. Mrs. Priester was considerably older than Mrs. Hansen, perhaps in her late thirties, with a round face blessed by cheery dimples, her hair arranged in a pleasantly sloppy topknot. Where Mrs. Hansen's eyes had been cold, Mrs. Priester's eyes were as warm and brown as the cup of hot chocolate she offered to make if we decided to stay.

She showed us the rooms, apologizing. "I'm afraid the bedroom is rather cramped."

Behind Mrs. Priester's back, Jack waggled his eyebrows at me. "Plenty big enough for its purpose."

I made a face at him, feigning displeasure and swallowing a

bubble of laughter. We followed Mrs. Priester into a sitting room smelling faintly of lavender. I choked back a sob, thinking of my mother. "It's right homey, Mrs. Priester."

Actually, it was fancier than any home I'd ever seen, but I was trying to pretend I was used to such luxury. Pale lemon walls warmed with light from the windows. A seafoam green loveseat and matching brocade chair were grouped around a mahogany coffee table with what I later learned were called Queen Anne legs. A sampler in primary colors hung on the wall, embroidered, I suspected, by Mrs. Priester herself. One corner held a tea cart, and in another, a captain's chair was pushed under a mahogany secretary. I could imagine writing a long letter to my brother Timmy while ensconced in that chair, and we could use the narrow slots to manage household bills.

Jack threw open the window and hailed the driver to carry our trunks to the second floor.

After Mrs. Priester withdrew to make cocoa, I hung my gowns in the chiffarobe to the left of the bed. I touched up my hair in the oval mirror mounted above the dressing table. The only other furniture in the bedroom was a ladder back chair in front of the table, but Mrs. Priester had made the room welcoming with floral wallpaper, rose-colored curtains at the window, and a matching dust ruffle on the bed.

When I re-entered the adjoining sitting room, I found Jack sprawled across the loveseat. He dallied one hand up my calf, lifting my skirt as he progressed. When he reached the back of my knees, I smacked his hand lightly.

"That tickles."

"I predict we will put this loveseat to good use."

I sat next to him and rubbed my nose against his. "You are a wicked man, Jack Joyner."

"You love it."

Mrs. Priester rapped at the door to the apartment. "Cocoa's ready whenever you are."

Jack ran his tongue around the hollow of my neck and whispered, "Send her away."

I straightened my blouse. "Be right there."

"Our new landlady has quite a bay window, don't you think?"

Jack said, referring to her belly, on his way downstairs.

"I expect the birth of two younguns accounts for the loss of a girlish waist."

"How do you know she has children?"

"Portraits in the parlor."

Jack's eyebrows raised, questioning. "No sign of brats around."

"Don't mention them," I whispered. "She might have lost them. You wouldn't want to stir up a pot of sorrows."

"Hadn't thought of that."

Course he hadn't. Just like a man to think he knew everything.

Once we were seated near the center of the twelve-foot dining table, Mrs. Priester served the cocoa in china cups, each a different pattern. "Sorry the cups don't match, but you can pick up such bargains at auctions if you're willing to take broken sets."

My cup was silver-rimmed with pink and violet flowers. We Krauses had never owned anything half so lovely. "They're charming. Really, the whole house is."

Mrs. Priester settled into the chair across from us and beamed. "Your house now, too. And you must call me Nellie—short for Eleanor—since we are to share a home."

"Everyone calls me Ro," I said, smiling.

Jack said, "Time to leave childhood nicknames behind. You're married now." The smile fell from my face, and perhaps realizing how annoyed I was, he added, "Besides, Rosella is such a beautiful name. It would be a shame not to use it."

That somewhat mollified me. "I'm glad you fancy it, but Nellie must call me Ro. It will make me feel at home. Everything's so strange here. Living in such a big town'll take considerable getting used to." My voice didn't even sound right in this parlor. The words tumbled out all wrong. Bumpkinish. Not like Nellie's manner of speaking at all. Did I sound funny to Jack, too? Probably not, since he had West Virginia kin. I realized I didn't even know where he'd been raised. He brushed off all questions about his family.

A flash of irritation crossed Jack's face when I expressed my preference, but he deferred to me. "If that's what you want."

Nellie Priester rushed to dispel this uncomfortable clash of opinions, and at once I recognized in her similarities to my mother, both peacemakers, both so busy making their nests comfortable for others they were always a bit harried and disheveled themselves. "It'll be so nice to have another woman around. One left two months ago when she married, and her new husband whisked her off to Oregon. Said it was too crowded in the city for his taste. Seems as if no one can settle in one place for long. Whole country's got moving fever."

Jack finished the last of his cocoa and leaned away from the table. "That's good news for the railroad business. I'll be up in Oregon myself quite a bit late this fall and in El Paso as well. I'm happy to know my wife will have your company while I'm away."

As the reality of his impending absence sank in, my ribs squeezed together until I thought my heart had slid up and lodged in my throat. Surely he wouldn't stay away long. I rose and wandered over to a large hutch, unable to resist stroking the ears of a small brown stuffed animal. "Is this one of them Teddy's bears?" It seemed the President had started a fad.

"Yes, I think they're so cute. I made this little fellow myself."

The front door squeaked open and the homeliest man I had ever seen entered. He was tall and thin, a candlestick of a man, with fevered intelligence burning in his eyes. Wire-rimmed glasses perched on his nose. When he removed his hat, however, his thick hair was the rich color of freshly ground nutmeg.

Nellie Priester rose to fetch another cup. "Valentine, you're just in time for cocoa with our new family members, the Joyners."

"So pleased to meet you," he said.

"How do," I replied.

For the briefest of moments, the young man hesitated, an eyebrow lifted, and shame crept over me. I'd said something the wrong way. I realized then I hadn't heard anyone say *how do* since I'd left home. People would think me odd. A bumpkin. A backwards hillbilly. Then the widest of smiles lit his face, completely transforming his features, so much so that I revised my first impression. He was not homely at all.

"If you're going to be family, you must call me Val." He dropped a handful of Tootsie Rolls on the tablecloth. "Your favorite, Nellie, I didn't forget you. There's enough for everyone. Help yourselves. I've just seen the most amazing stereograph of natives in the South Pacific. By golly, I'd like to visit those islands someday. Ever been?"

No one had, so Val stumbled onto the next subject, the Chautauqua he attended the week before in Boulder. He took cello lessons from a master cellist, studied mathematics, brushed up on his French, and heard lectures on women's suffrage and self improvement.

I listened with amazement to the young man's enthusiasm on every subject.

Nellie Priester noted my wide-eyed expression and laughed. "Our Val is quite accomplished."

"What's your profession, Mr. Martin?" I asked in my best proper English, though I could hear in my vowels a twang missing from Mrs. Priester's voice. How would I ever fit in here if I sounded strange to everyone?

He grimaced. "I fear I neither play the cello nor speak French well enough to pay the bills. I am a medical student."

"He's overly modest." Nellie gathered the cups. I rose to help. "Val is quite wonderful at everything he does. He's even experimenting with medicinal compounds, isn't that right?"

His brown eyes sparkled again. "I have this idea to distill willow bark—everyone knows it kills pain but upsets the stomach, right? So I mix it with peppermint, chamomile, and ginger, which dispel the gastronomic side effects. I regret to say I have yet to perfect the formula."

He excused himself and I listened to the tapping of his steps as he fairly ran to the third floor.

"An interesting fellow," Jack said.

"Kind, too. They don't come any better than our Mr. Martin. I will share a secret, though. His family surname was Martino. They anglicized it when they came over. I can't blame them—the way some people carry on about the Italians, the Polish and the Chinese, but I don't hold with such nonsense. Our Val is a fine fellow. Always pays his rent on time. If it bothers you living with an Italian, you'll have to find somewhere else to stay." Jack and I looked at each other, shook our heads, and Jack assured her we harbored no objection.

"His secret is safe with us." I pinched my lips between my fingers to show my mouth was sealed.

Two other small rooms on the third floor were let periodically to a variety of gentlemen whenever they were in town. "I don't consider them family, though," Mrs. Priester said. "They don't often take meals with us or visit in the parlor."

Her gossip finished, she urged us to follow her through the downstairs rooms, pointing out things she'd made: needlepoint upholstery for the dining room chairs, candlewick pillows on the parlor settee, a cupboard drawer full of afghans, fanning through them to expose blue, emerald, and garnet yarns in various patterns.

I knelt down and lay my palm against the soft texture of one. "Must have taken years to make all these."

"Not really. Crocheting goes fast. One of my friends has a little store and sells my pieces on consignment. You must choose one, any one you like."

I could feel my face redden. It must have sounded as if I had been fishing for this invitation. "I couldn't."

"Nonsense, I insist. My wedding gift to you."

After multiple professions of gratitude, I settled on a soft green design.

Nellie drew water for our baths. I soaked a long while, then dressed, and relinquished the tub to my husband.

Following an early meal in the dining room, Nellie nodded, a motion that doubled the folds under her chin. "I expect you'll need a rest after such a long journey."

Jack grinned. "I expect we do."

Dec. 21, 1903

Dear "Favorite Sis,"

How I laffed when I saw how you signed your letter of November 23. Even if I had a dozen, you would still be my favorite sister. I bout busted my buttons when I read the part about you expecting a new addition. If ever a girl was born to mother, it's you, Ro. Josiah's wife expects a new arrival round the same time. They moved in with us soon after you lit out. The house is sumwat crowded, but after father cut his leg up in a haying accident, he needed Josie's help. Oak Hall construction was nearly done anyway, and Josie would have soon gone looking for another job.

Remember how we used to squirt each other during the milking? You should bring your little un home when he gets

growed some and I could teach him stuff. Milking. Turkey calling. Jumping into the nearest hidey-hole when Martha comes
hunting you for chores. I think it'll be a boy, don't you? We'd
have us some laffs.

You sure are having a grand time in San Francisco. I hope
to visit some day and see the things you describe for myself.
The train ride would be the best thing of all.
We shore missed you at Thanksgiving and know Christmas
won't be the same without you at all.

You asked about father. No, I am sorry to say he has not
forgiven you yet. Steam fairly boils outa his nose and ears
when anyone's fool enough to speak your name. Seems he
borrowed a pile of money from Gunner Beck. They had them
an understanding that once you two married, the land along
the willow pond next to Gunner's place would be deeded over.
Father's finances are a mess—again. Gunner is grousing about
the broken agreement, but I'm sure they'll come up with new
terms for the loan once tempers cool down.

Martha's tongue hasn't softened any since you left. She
is fussing mightily over father's idea to give Josie that land
along the willow pond to build a house. In return, Josie would
hire himself out to Gunner as a farm hand till the loan is re-
paid. Also, he would continue helping father on the farm. A
good deal for us, since otherwise Josie would keep his family in town and hire onto another construction crew. But you
know Martha—real angshuss to get Josie and Louisa and little
Hermie and Sally out of the house before their new baby arrives. She is no more fond of children than ever, especially
Hermie—poor child always feeling the sting of her switch.

I'm not sure Martha knows how bad father's injured.
Ever step is hurtful, though he does his best to hide it. I do the
chickens and the milking, but now that school has started up,
I have less time for other chores. Martha is nagging at father
to take me out of school. He says no, but for once I agree with
that womin. I am nearly eleven and how much schooling do I
need for farming? None, I say.

Sending much love from,

Your Favorite Brother (Me, I hope)
Timmy

JAN. 10, 1904

Dear Timmy,

Don't you dare stop going to school. At least stick it out through the rest of the year and finish sixth grade. You are the brightest of all my brothers and can make something of yourself. Why, you are so quick with numbers, someday you could work in a bank. Or a hardware store. Maybe once you are growed, you will come to San Francisco and Mr. Martin (our fellow boarder) will get you a job at the U.S. Mint where his father works—imagine that!

I am sorry to hear of father's injury. I am hoping he improves soon. I knew nothing about this agreement with Gunner, but if I had, I still wouldn't have married the old goat. I am sorry the rest of you must suffer because of father's broken promise. Learn from this, Timmy. Never make promises you can't keep.

Tell Josiah and Louisa I am happy about their news. Now, you must keep this to yourself, but you are and ever will be— pinky swear—my favorite. Our secret, right?

Much love,
Your Favorite Sister, Ro

SAN FRANCISCO, MAY 1920

"GROWED? MAMA, I'VE NEVER ONCE HEARD you use such poor grammar," Solina said, the thin paper of my letter crinkling between her delicate fingers. "This doesn't even sound like you."

Well, it wasn't. The Rosella who had written that letter was a girl lost long ago, a girl still cloaked in the greens of the hills and hollows, whose voice still echoed with the burble of creeks, a girl more familiar with the smell of damp hay, cow manure, and warm milk than the French perfumes sold in the city's department stores. She was Ro Krause. Rosella Joyner was a different creature altogether.

As soon as Jack and I had settled in at the boarding house, I approached Nellie. "I want you to learn me how to talk proper so as I fit in here."

Gently she corrected my grammar. "I'd be happy to *teach* you, honey. In no time at all, you'll catch on." Under Nellie's tutelage, I left that country girl behind. And I insisted that no child of mine would ever sound uneducated, so Solina had never heard me use bad grammar.

"People change over the course of their lives, dear. Remember when you used to detest potatoes—and now you love them?"

Solina shook her head, and I couldn't resist touching the lovely dark curls tumbling down her shoulders. "That's different. Mama, none of this makes sense. Why would you have this letter, the one you wrote to your brother?"

I sighed. "Timmy let it slip that we were writing to each other. My father intercepted my letters and returned them, unopened. Timmy wrote a few more times, wondering why I didn't write back. That's how I knew what was happening, so I mailed letters to Jack's Aunt Elizabeth and she would pass them to my brother secretly."

"Your father was such a meanie. I still don't understand how you—what you could have done to make the newspaper say these things about you. A bigamist. A baby killer. Why would they say these things?"

I wasn't quite sure how the paper had come up with all the details in that story, such a mixture of truth and falsehoods, but I was determined to learn their source. Who had spread this poison and what did they hope to gain?

"I've done nothing to be ashamed of," I said.

Solina tilted her head to one side. "Why would the reporter make up those horrible lies?"

"No more questions until I'm done telling the whole story— that's what we agreed. You'll understand everything, all in good time. Now, let's get dressed. Nellie will be here soon. We're going over to the Kennesons to oversee preparations for the reception." At least I hoped there would still be a reception. Hoped the gallery wouldn't cancel my show.

I smiled with more confidence than I felt. "I'm looking forward to seeing Mindy. It's been ages." I could picture Mindy's sweet heart-shaped face with its delicate features, nearly perfect except for a slight concavity, as if the Good Lord had pushed gently against the center with His thumb. A face that reminded me of Nellie's jam thumbprint cookies, though the comparison seemed unkind. Mindy favored pastel fluffy, ruffled gowns, her step so light she appeared to float, untethered by the same gravity affecting mere mortals. Her fairy-like appearance led many, including myself on more than one occasion, to underestimate her depth, her intelligence, her ingenuity.

"Does Aunt Nellie know the truth?"

Mostly, but this was no time to be wishy-washy. "Absolutely."

"Do the Kennesons?"

"Stop fretting. Nellie will defend me should anyone repeat these lies." But I could count on Nellie's old friend Alexandra Underwood to spread the gossip to all with ears. Would Alexandra attend the reception? She owned quite a few pieces of my pottery, some of which she'd loaned to the gallery for the show, according to Mindy.

"How well do you know the Kennesons?"

"They have been dear friends since well before you were born." I'd met the Underwoods and Kennesons soon after we'd moved in to Nellie's. "I'll tell you all about it when Aunt Nellie picks us up in her new car."

"Is Aunt Nellie rich?"

My goodness—questions questions, and more questions. "No, but she has done quite well for herself since we moved back east. Now scoot and get dressed so we don't keep her waiting."

Finally Solina stopped interrogating me, and I went down to the lobby to check for messages. When I returned, Solina was still not dressed. Instead, she was furiously scribbling in that diary of hers. Whatever did she find to write about in there every day? I feared she was complaining about me, her appalling mother, the bigamist and baby killer. I sighed. I suppose she found solace in writing as I did in my art and pottery.

I crossed the room and placed my hand over hers to still the flow of words. "We must go. Please get ready."

She made a face, but closed her little book and donned a rose gown with pink sash that looked stunning with all those dark curls tumbling down her shoulders. A truly beautiful young woman, though I could take little credit for that. As we descended to the hotel lobby, Solina wavered, as if she might bolt back to our room at any moment. "Mama, how can you hold your head up after all the things they said?"

I reached back and tugged her hand. "That's exactly why we're going out. You must always hold your head high, no matter what anyone says about you. You are just as good as anyone else, always remember that."

Even if you feel puny because of your country bumpkin ways.

Especially then.

JANUARY 1904

THE TELEGRAM DANGLED FROM MY FINGERS. I stared out the front window at the carriages hurtling down the hill in front of the boarding house. Jack—delayed again. Already he'd been gone three months and we were behind on our rent. Nellie said not to worry, but how could I not? I pulled his shirt from the chiffarobe and pressed it to my face. Traces of his apple-scented tobacco scent melted my bones. If only I could hold him for a few hours. Even a few minutes. I missed him so—and yet . . . quite unexpectedly, our excursions together to San Francisco's department stores had stirred in me an attitude of generalized resentment toward the world. Inevitably, shop girls looked to Jack for approval of purchases, rather than to me—even if it concerned a gown that, obviously, I would wear. But did the girls ask if I liked it? Not at all. I was dismissed with barely a glance. Their eyes were all for Jack—and not simply because he was young and handsome. His jurisdiction over all financial concerns gilded him with a stature that I, as a woman, lacked. The shop girls' betrayals wounded me.

When he'd forbidden me to explore the city on my own without him or Nellie to accompany me, my resentment had multiplied ten-fold. Why could men roam freely when women couldn't? Although I was somewhat mollified as my husband explained certain neighborhoods were dangerous, his attempts to restrict my movements still angered me. He was gone so often, and Nellie had a boarding house to run. I had a bad case of what we would have called cabin fever back in West Virginia.

Besides, no man, not even my husband, was going to dictate what I could and could not do. Never again. I refused to spend another minute cooped up in these rooms. A walk, fresh air—that's what I needed. I should be perfectly safe as long as I remained on the main streets.

It never got as bitter cold here as back home, but often there was a damp cold that settled in the bones. I pulled on my coat. I slipped out of the house and gave the streetcar conductor a nickel for a ride downtown. I nodded at a working girl who looked about my age. She had broad, plain features, Polish perhaps. I tried to imagine where she worked—in a hotel as a maid? Afternoon shift in a factory? I smiled and then theatrically offered a half-grimace, shaking my umbrella for emphasis. "I expect it will rain today."

The girl wrinkled her nose. "Rains every day," she said in heavily accented English.

She was right. Every day a downpour.

Even such a pitiful, tenuous connection to a fellow San Franciscan lifted my spirits, but I could think of no way to extend the conversation. Opening my sketchbook, I drew a rough outline of the girl's face. Her nose turned up, her best feature.

At Mission and Third, I got off and made my way toward the Claus Spreckels Building. Its crenellated rotunda towered above the other buildings and kept me oriented. I strode as if I had a purpose along this street where mostly men hurried along to conduct their business at the Winchester Hotel, Mutual Bank, New York Loan Office, or the *Chronicle* News Office—the buildings visible but still at some distance. I made sure to walk by the San Francisco Mint where Val Martin's father worked. "The Granite Lady" was mostly built from sandstone rather than granite, according to Val, but it was one of the city's most famous landmarks. Inside, prospectors' gold was turned into coins. By the time I reached the Spreckels Building, it had indeed begun to rain and I put off my plan to sketch the skyline. I caught a streetcar back to Mrs. Priester's. Growing up with five brothers, two parents, a cat, a flock of chickens, and small herd of cattle, I had never had opportunity to be idle. With little to do, I found myself bored. If only Jack were beside me!

When I opened Mrs. Priester's door, I detected the fragrance of tea brewing. In a small dish in the foyer lay a calling card from Mrs. Alexandra Underwood. Again. Mrs. Underwood, whom Nellie Priester claimed was one of her oldest friends, sent her card over with a servant every Wednesday yet never came herself. I had never heard of calling cards and didn't know what to make of this silly custom. Back home, if we wanted to see a friend, we just dropped by their house and we sat a spell together on the front porch if it was warm and in the kitchen if it wasn't. To Nellie, I had confessed how awkward I felt, as if I'd been dropped smack dab into an alien world where folks spoke a different language and had such different ways.

To my surprise, strange voices came from the parlor. I walked through the arched entrance.

Nellie sashayed straight over and placed a sisterly arm about my shoulders. "Here she is, our Rosella. I'm so glad you got back in time to meet Mrs. Myrtle Kenneson and her lovely daughter Miss Mindy."

"How do." The greeting slipped out automatically. I winced and faked a cough that I hoped sounded ladylike, pressing a handkerchief to my mouth, to cover my error. "Pleased to meet you," I amended.

The Mrs. sat on the left side of the rose settee with the daughter on the right. Mindy wore a pale blue gown with a low-cut, puffed bodice and narrow waist emphasized by a satin sash. I observed every detail of these obviously new clothes and the masses of honey-colored hair styled in the latest Gibson fashion—until I realized my examination bordered on rudeness.

I apologized, professing myself overcome with admiration for Miss Kenneson's hairstyle.

Nellie suggested I try one of the lemon tea cakes our guests were already enjoying.

I placed a teacake on a china dessert plate and sat down across from the visitors. I lifted the golden cake to my lips and indulged in a bite, pronouncing it delicious.

Nellie's eyes warned me I'd made a mistake—but what? She side-eyed the tea table where the dessert forks lay, then flicked her gaze to the Kennesons' forks resting on their plates.

I flushed. What a country mouse I must appear! Back home, the tea cake would be considered nothing more than a cookie, a finger food. Here I was—surrounded by thousands of people—and I had never felt more alone in my life. The Kennesons chatted about their favorite restaurants and about a recent trip to Paris. I tried to nod at appropriate times during their travelogue.

"Have you traveled much, Mrs. Joyner?" Mrs. Kenneson asked.

"I'm afraid not. Unless you count the train ride across the states to get here."

Mindy smoothed the lace on her bodice. "So you're from back East?"

"I grew up on a farm in West Virginia."

"How wonderfully healthy that must have been," Mrs. Kenneson said.

"I love Virginia." Mindy's voice shimmered, a pastel bouquet of rose, apricot, and lemon. "We often visit my cousins there. They raise quarter horses. Do you ride?"

"Uh . . . yes. Yes, I do." Only old work horses, not the thoroughbreds they referred to. I refrained from correcting their impression that Virginia and West Virginia were one and the same. They were clearly so well-traveled, West Virginia's statehood was probably the only thing I knew about the world that they didn't. Thinking of the farm made me homesick. I missed my brothers. I missed the hill behind our home, sprinkled with wild strawberries in June and with luscious raspberries and blackberries later in summer. I even missed my father when he was in a good mood. I didn't miss Martha because her mood was always as muddy and foul as a pig pen.

As the Kennesons' chatter turned to a woman's suffrage meeting to be held in their parlor the next week, I banished all thoughts of home.

"You must come with Nellie," Mindy said. "You do support the cause, don't you?"

"Oh yes!" I did believe—fervently believe—that women should have the right to vote—and the right to draw pictures of anything they desired—and to marry whomever they chose—and to control the purse strings so that shop girls paid proper attention. I welcomed the opportunity to meet others who supported these ideas. Nellie made arrangements for us to attend. I was going to love it here after all.

A few days later, I was so tired I could barely drag myself from bed. I attributed it to being in the family way, but Nellie thought it more than that, had argued that I should call in a doctor even though she didn't trust them. But whatever was wrong passed, and I was glad I hadn't wasted money we didn't have. Jack still hadn't returned. I was both broke and bored.

Finally I realized I could stand there looking out the window at the cable cars below, feeling sorry for myself, or I could remedy my situation. I secured my hair in the latest Gibson girl style (copied from Miss Mindy Kenneson, though her hair leaned toward light honey while mine was more caramel) and positioned a large rose-colored hat on top of my head. I tripped down the stairs to the kitchen, where Nellie was stirring jelly in a six-quart stock pot. The heated air was thick with the scent of sugar syrup, purple grapes and melted wax.

I tilted my chin up with purpose. "I'm going to the newspaper office."

Wooden spoon in hand, Nellie sweated profusely over the stove. "Which one—the *Examiner,* the *Chronicle* or the *Call*? Surely you're not planning to walk down to Market Street in your condition."

"Walking's good for a woman when she's expecting. You told me so yourself."

Nellie wiped her brow with a kitchen towel. "But you've been so sick the last few days. You're still a little peaked. Take the cable car."

"I'm feeling better, and I can't go on living here on credit. I'm going to place an ad offering to give art lessons. I might not earn much, but I can at least pay for the food I consume."

Nellie pushed a wilted strand of hair back into a net and dabbed at her face again with the towel. "Let's sit somewhere cooler."

I followed her into the parlor.

"May I see something you've drawn?"

I hesitated. Since coming to the city, I had shown no one my work. Everyone here seemed so sophisticated. What if she scoffed? Oh not openly, she was too polite for that. But I would know if she found my art wanting.

"Please—I'd really like to see what's inside that sketchbook you work on every day."

Reluctantly, I trudged upstairs to retrieve it. When I returned, I presented it, anxiously scouring her face for any reaction. She lingered over a pelican and another of Jack's profile. What was she thinking?

At last she closed the book and beamed. "I have a more suitable idea than an advertisement. Take off that hat and help me put up this jelly. Then I'll send for a carriage."

MY EYES FLITTED FROM ONE LUXURY to the next, awed by the display of sybaritic wealth in the Spanish colonial-style house. Later Nellie labeled all the unfamiliar furnishings for me. A large oriental rug. Dentil-molding around fourteen-foot high ceilings. Peach satin-stripe covered sofas with graceful out-curving feet. "American Empire chairs—Duncan Phyfe," Nellie whispered. What did she mean? I had never heard of this Phyfe fellow. My eyes finally rested on a well-executed painting framed in ornate gold. It was an art style I'd never seen before, impressionist, I later learned. All the while I was absorbing my surroundings, I remained acutely aware of Alexandra Underwood's expressions as she studied my sketches. The furrowed forehead as she studied an egret. The lift of her well-formed brow as she examined Jack's face. I felt as if I were baring my soul to a stranger, a woman who carried herself with the supreme confidence of one born to wealth. She was not beautiful, the planes of her face too sharp, too rigid, yet I suspected few men would be able to resist her commanding presence.

I rose and walked closer to the painting so I wouldn't have to watch this potential patron any longer. The painting's subject was a young woman, perhaps my age, in a white dress. She lay in the grass, her legs bent and slightly apart, which I ascertained even though her limbs were hidden by the folds of cloth. The painting created the impression of innocence, yet the bent legs suggested a careless sexuality, one the young woman was unaware she possessed. The girl was granted the freedom to enjoy a summer sky sheltered by a leafy canopy without worrying if her legs were modestly arranged. As an artist myself, I realized another artist, no doubt male, stood over her as she posed for that painting, probably for many weeks—and then exposed her to public view. My father would be scandalized. I bit my lower lip to still the twitch in my jaw as I heard the rasp of another page of my sketchbook turning. Though I was listening acutely, no other sound escaped until finally—after what seemed like hours—there came the soft slap of the book closing.

I returned to my chair. Alexandra Underwood set my sketchbook down, the white lace cuffs of her plum silk gown brushing against the coffee table. *Say something,* I pleaded mentally.

"You seldom draw portraits, Rosella." Her voice, rich and dark, carried an aura of burgundy and purple. A royal voice. Used to getting what she wanted. "Just this one man." One eyebrow raised. "A very handsome man."

Oh, no, no, no. This woman didn't like my work, didn't like it at all. Why had I let Nellie talk me into coming here? This was beyond humiliating.

"My husband." I forced the words out without making eye contact, my arms pressed so tightly against my sides that the stays of my pregnancy corset felt as if they were cutting into my skin. I risked a glance up. Mrs. Underwood's cheeks were dimpling.

"Your love for him shows. Such a handsome fellow."

The tension left my arms. She liked my work.

Mrs. Underwood poured more tea from a sterling baroque pot into porcelain cups with a pastel floral design. All the cups matched, unlike Nellie's. "Can you manage equally good portraits of my children?"

A flitter of uncertainty tickled my throat. I had far less experience with faces than with landscapes, flowers, and animals, though I had sketched my brothers and my mother long ago.

Nellie folded her hands across the low-hanging monobosom of her blue gown. "I'm sure she could. That's why I brought her to you, Alexandra."

What could I do but agree? Nellie had been good enough to arrange this meeting, and besides, I couldn't afford to be choosy. I'd taken an instant liking for the little boy who reminded me of my brother Timmy. But I'd taken an equally intense dislike for the little girl, a light-haired child of about nine, who already carried herself with that entitled air children of privilege sometimes acquired.

"And art lessons for Lydia," Mrs. Underwood said. "It's important for girls her age to develop appreciation for art and music. Contrary to popular opinion, we haven't abandoned the finer things in life in the West, Rosella, but they can be more difficult to come by."

I tried to show sympathy, though I suspected the kind of money the Underwoods had caused every heart's desire to magically appear. Their ten-bedroom house stood out with its clay-tiled roof and the verdant lawn sided by evergreens. Here, in Russian Hill, there was at least a touch of the greenery I missed so much.

Among the benefits of employment by the Underwoods, the estate would present an amazing variety of sketching subjects. A splendid garden, orange trees, a cat ready to give birth to kittens.

"Yes, art can bring so much enjoyment," I said. "It certainly has to me." I thought of the destroyed sketches. Art could bring grief, too. And resentment.

"It's settled then. I'll send the carriage tomorrow morning at nine."

On the way back, Nellie smiled wistfully. Her voice rose in volume so to project over the clatter of Mrs. Underwood's horses. "That could have been me. Our husbands were business partners. Mine caught pneumonia and died. Hers lived and became wealthy."

"What business were they in?" Following Nellie's example, I covered my nose and mouth with a handkerchief to avoid breathing in the dust kicked up by the horses.

"Brick kilns. All the buildings you see downtown—our house, lots of these houses—they were built with our bricks. The streets— paved with our bricks."

Wasn't it odd, though, that the Underwoods had chosen stucco for their own home?

"Ro, you don't have to take my advice, but if I were you, I'd keep my little income a secret from your husband. Squirrel it away with your unmentionables and you'll always have that little notion of independence, money that is yours and yours alone. Once your husband knows about it, he controls it."

Hardly fair, but it was the law. Nor did it seem fair that Nellie had to take in boarders and sell needlework. She should have inherited her husband's business. Life was so much harder for women than men. Our carriage passed by fleets of working women in their drab dresses walking home, most with hands coarsened by hard labor. They were the maids, factory workers, store clerks, and teachers. A woman had to be prepared to take care of herself in this world. A memory surfaced of my father's hands tugging on the overalls and boots he wore to tend the cattle, an ordinary act of love I had taken for granted. I swallowed and shook my head, dismissing these thoughts lest I become sentimental. I still found it hard to forgive the way he scorned artwork as useless. It wasn't useless if it brought pleasure and joy. And it wasn't useless if it paid the bills. Then, as if he were sitting beside me in the carriage, I heard my father's admonition: *You wouldn't have to worry about paying the bills if you'd married someone steady like Gunner Beck.*

THREE ROUGH SKETCHES OF LYDIA lay on the coffee table. One straight on with Lydia's haughty chin tilted up; the next a profile, a pose that again emphasized the chin; and the third, purely my invention, because the royal princess Lydia never held her head in that sweet, humble pose. Yet I intuited the child appeared this way to her mother.

Sure enough, Alexandra chose the third sketch. "You have captured my Lydia so beautifully. Work it into a larger piece to match the one you did of Will."

"Yes, ma'am." I scooped up the preliminary drawings and sought out Lydia to continue her art lessons. We went outside to sketch the chrysanthemums sprawling out of urns on either side of an arch leading into the gardens. I had to admit Lydia was capturing a fair representation of the shaggy blooms. She paid attention when I suggested she hold the pencil at a different angle.

A large pink ribbon gathered the girl's straw-colored hair at the nape of her neck. A few short tendrils curled over her ears. "Mother says these lessons are a good place to start. Next year I'll move on to oils. Mother says a lady is expected to have certain accomplishments if she wants to make a good marriage."

"I'm sure she's right." What qualified as a good marriage? Not in the sense Mrs. Underwood meant, but *good* meaning happy. Jack had finally come home and seemed pleasantly surprised by my rounding abdomen. Flush with cash he'd won at poker, he advanced Nellie three months rent and paid our other bills as well. Slyly, Nellie returned the money I'd given her for rent. I followed her advice and kept it in a hatbox on top of the chiffarobe.

In a romantic mood, Jack whisked me away to a deserted stretch of coastline to sketch the gulls and seals. I shivered, with equal parts fear and delight, remembering how, despite the chilly October air, he made love to me on a blanket laid across the rocks—such a terribly uncivilized thing to do. The blood had thundered through my head, nagging, *What if someone sees us?* My thoughts had nearly drowned out the surf and stolen my pleasure. Nearly, not quite.

Another morning, he drove a carriage to Cliff House so I could see the mansion jutting out above the ocean. I sketched the rocks, the crenellations, the waves breaking on the beach. He took me shopping for new gowns, one of which I was wearing today. *Jealous? Of Mindy Kenneson? You will never need to be jealous of that prissy little thing again, he told me. I'm shocked that her father allows her to work in his art gallery. It's unseemly for a well-off woman to work.* Nellie, I knew then, had been right about keeping some secrets. Jack needn't know I was earning money with my portraits and art lessons. I defended Mindy and her desire to help her father, but Jack silenced me with a kiss. He laughed and we made love. And I laughed and we made love. Laugh and love, love and laugh—our life had been perfect for two weeks, and then he took off again, this time to Tucson.

So here I was, back to teaching Lydia. Not because I needed the money now, but it gave me something constructive to do with my days. I had several other students, two recommended by the fellow on the third floor, Val Martin. He often stopped to talk in the parlor, tossing Tootsie Rolls onto the coffee table and filling my head with amazing facts or discoveries. He could rattle off the average salary of a factory worker ($489 a month) and segue straight into a recitation of Marx Brothers' jokes or Will Rogers' quotations or an analysis of how Harry Houdini performed his great escapes. Listening to him was an education. Many evenings he played his cello for Nellie and me, sorrowful yet soothing pieces, while I sketched flowers and birds from memory and Nellie crocheted. I began to feel a sense of being at home. A home without Jack, I realized sadly.

A sudden kick against my ribs riveted me to the present moment. I held one hand against my belly and couldn't suppress a giggle. Lydia Underwood looked up, a question in her eyes, but I wasn't about to explain. Already her mother had dictated that this would be the last lesson until after my delivery lest the girl question the rounding abdomen my clothing barely disguised. I directed Lydia's attention to a problem with her drawing, holding my own sketch up for her to see. "Make the front bloom larger, the back smaller."

Lydia's chin went up. "But they're almost exactly the same size."

"True, but you're trying to create perspective. See how narrow I've made the edge of the urn as it curves away? It's the same size all the way around in reality, but your eye wouldn't see it that way. Perspective."

It all came down to that, didn't it? When Jack was here, he dominated the canvas of my existence. When he was gone, though, he didn't shrink away like the edge of the urn. Instead the focus of my existence was missing. His absence was like removing the chrysanthemums from the sketch. All that was left, an empty urn. But I was learning to fill my life with other people, other activities. Nellie taught me to embroider garments for the baby. I even invented my own pattern for the front of an infant gown, a whimsical frog catching a ladybug with its long tongue. Embroidery was like sketching with thread. The design wouldn't be all that appropriate for a girl, but I was certain I was carrying a boy.

Lydia thrust her revised drawing in front of me. "Is this better?"

"Much. Now we'll try sketching the same thing from a different spot." I led Lydia to a low concrete bench. "Really look at the urn and flowers and see what's changed. From a different perspective, everything changes."

Working as an artist had changed my own perspective. An income of my own nurtured not only confidence, but also my independent spirit.

DOZENS OF FASHIONABLY DRESSED WOMEN crowded the Kennesons' parlor, decorated with furnishings every bit as lovely as the Underwoods' but understated rather than flamboyant. A carousel of conversations spiked with laughter swirled around the room and down the hallways. The palpable energy barely contained by those pale green walls electrified me. The only events I'd ever attended that aroused anything close to the same excitement in a crowd were tent revivals my father held each summer. These women assured me that they would continue the campaign until they won the vote. Eight years earlier, the referendum had failed, a crushing defeat, especially here in San Francisco. It was distressing to know women in Wyoming, Utah, Colorado, and Idaho had already secured their rights.

"We will succeed this time," Alexandra Underwood declared

with a queen's assurance, her arm resting on a handsome man's sleeve and looking up at him with approval bordering on adoration. "George is organizing all his friends, aren't you, darling?"

"We men will march with you on the capital one of these days." The only male in the room, he clasped his hand over Alexandra's.

I had seen a man's portrait in the Underwood's home and this fellow seemed a decade younger and far more handsome, and unless I was mistaken, they were more than mere acquaintances. "Is that her husband?" I whispered.

Nellie shook her head, eyebrows raised. "Later," she whispered back.

With Nellie's encouragement, I became a member of the National American Woman Suffrage Association that night. "Don't you see, Ro, it's important not only that women get the vote, but also better legal protections in divorce cases," Nellie said.

"And equal pay for work and the right to control any income we earn," Mindy Kenneson chimed in, her voice as flouncy as her dress. "Why should a husband get to control his wife's income? Mama took me to hear Aunt Susan speak, and I intend to follow in her footsteps. I shall never marry."

That was a bold assertion. "Aunt Susan?"

"Miss Anthony," Mindy clarified. "She's been in practically every town in California encouraging women to fight for the rights stated in the constitution. Aunt Susan says those rights were granted to 'we the people,' not only men, but all people. San Francisco had a lot to do with why we were defeated in '96, but as Aunt Susan says, 'Failure is impossible.' It's up to us, her lieutenants, to make sure we win this time."

Lieutenants—I liked the sound of that. Mindy, I was learning, was far more than the pretty face (well, semi-pretty—there was that odd concave shape to consider) in the society pages I had first taken her for. Mindy had drawn her own friends into NAWSA and they were passing out brochures of their own design all over the city. She introduced me to two young women close to my age. When they made plans for a shopping expedition that was to include distribution of brochures, they included me. Even though I lacked their wealth, I was thrilled to make connections in my new city. It didn't cost anything to window shop or campaign for equal rights.

"We need to promote family planning too," Alexandra said. "Women should have control over their own bodies."

I couldn't have agreed more. We women needed control over all aspects of our lives. Wasn't that why I'd left the farm to begin with? But I knew little to nothing about controlling births. Well, I knew some. On the farm my father gelded horses and castrated bulls. No humans would willingly tolerate that.

"It's just as important that we support improvement of the human race," Alexandra said.

"Too many immigrants having hordes of children," George said. "We need to start breeding humans more like we do animals. Increase the best and brightest and stop propagating undesirable traits."

"We must eliminate weakness," Alexandra said.

"Yes," George added, "those with mental and physical defects, and those who carry socially transmitted disease."

Eliminate? How? I didn't want to appear ignorant, so I waited until we were in the carriage ride home to ask Nellie. Thunder rumbled in the distant hills and we pulled a blanket across our laps as light sprinkles fell on the brick pavement outside.

She wrinkled her nose at my question. "They're talking about the eugenics movement. Sterilization of immigrants like our dear Valentine. Can you imagine? They think most immigrants aren't as bright and hard working as English stock. Idiocy, if you ask me. All of us except the Indians came from somewhere else, didn't we?"

I couldn't imagine anyone objecting to Val Martin.

"Alexandra didn't get caught up with all this eugenics nonsense until she started this fling with George." Nellie explained that Alexandra had an understanding with her husband. They remained married and shared a residence, but each led separate lives. "Alexandra calls this a modern marriage. I'll grant you it allows her a degree of independence many of us envy. No man fussing over where she is and what she is doing, no money worries, and dalliances with whomever she likes. If she wasn't so rich, she would lose her social standing. Lucky for her, the Underwoods give to every charitable cause, so everyone overlooks her flings. But I do wonder if she ever misses having emotional attachment."

Yes, love mattered. So did independence and autonomy—the goals these vibrant women preached about tonight. Was it possible to have both—love and self-determination? I was so young. I still had great hope.

Angie

IS IT POSSIBLE TO HAVE BOTH LOVE AND SELF-DETERMINATION?
At fifty, I still can't answer that question. Any marriage means compromise, so your course isn't steered by your needs alone. There were probably a thousand and one things I would have preferred to spend money on last year than Dewey's dream truck, but I gave in. Hard to deny the man you love his dream. If he does lose his job, we'd have been much better off paying down our mortgage. I will not say *I told you so*. He makes sacrifices for our relationship, too. There are probably a thousand and one ways he'd rather spend his time, but nonetheless, he accompanies me and my students on summer field trips and keeps the boys in line.

I'm intrigued by Ro, but can't figure out from Mom's drawing of my family tree exactly how I'm related to her. Her name doesn't appear on my birth mother's side, where the Wellingtons and Springers are traced back to the days of the American Revolution. Rosella must be on my father's side, but the family tree is incomplete, with the most recent generations missing. When I asked Mom about it, her explanation only added to the mystery. Said she was still working on that part of the story, but it is only logical that she would have started with the most recent generations and worked backward. I feel sure she is hiding something. Is my birth father a criminal? A terrible man?

I can't read any further in the scrapbook tonight. Too tired. I turn out the light and rub Dewey's back. He's not quite asleep, but almost.

Now that the light is out, I can't quiet my thoughts. That Alexandra Underwood—was she happy bucking all the norms of her day? I don't think I could behave like she did, having affairs openly, even today—not that I want to. It'd be pretty nice to have no money worries though. Like Ro, we have trouble paying the bills, but not because one of us is absent or lazy or gambling or not working.

Is there a gene for working hard and hardly working? Since my DNA test results came back, the company quizzes me on everything from smelling asparagus pee to liking cilantro. My DNA yielded nothing interesting or alarming in the health portion. I expected the one quarter German ancestry, but the half English-Irish ancestry surprised me, as did the quarter Italian heritage. I thought the latter would be more. Don't see a thing in the reports helpful to Trish and Bella—unless knowing they may have a preference for chocolate over vanilla ice cream is useful. Seems like something you'd want to figure out on your own. The hard way—by eating lots of ice cream.

I turn over on my stomach and wiggle down so my feet hang over the end of the bed. Paint fumes—that's what's keeping me awake. I told Dewey we're gonna have to do something to air out Bella's room better. Leave the windows open all night or something. They are moving in soon and we can't leave them open once the baby's here. Dewey acts like we have all the time in the world. Sometimes he drives me crazy.

I feel as if I have just drifted off when the phone rings. Barely coherent, Mom finally makes me understand the reason for the call: Poppy has wandered off.

Dewey and I throw on clothes, hurl ourselves into his truck, and speed through town toward the farm. Every light in Mom's house is on, a beacon in the moonless, starless night. The sky, black felt. Once parked, Dewey and I hurry toward the house, our feet crunching against the hard frost coating the grass. The front door opens, Mom's thin silhouette backlit. It is freezing cold and she is shivering.

I close the door behind us. "Where have you already looked?"

"Everywhere in the house and garage. I yelled for him outside, but I was afraid to wander out there in the dark, afraid I'd fall."

"The last thing we need is for you to break something," I say. "You stay here and we'll search. You might put some coffee on for when we get back."

Dewey digs through the messy conglomeration of junk in his

truck. I've accused him before of keeping everything but the kitchen sink in there, so it's no wonder he comes up with exactly what we need: a couple of lanterns and chemically activated heat packs to slip into our gloves.

With the help of the lanterns, Dewey spots footprints in the frost leading toward the tree line. We head out there, calling for Poppy. Under the trees his path is harder to follow. We split up to cover more territory. My face stings in the frigid air. After almost an hour of searching, Dewey calls out. "Over here, Ange. His footsteps circle around and head out toward the back of the barn."

There is a rear entrance we used to let the cows in and out. We haven't kept cattle for years.

The heavy wooden door creaks as Dewey pulls it open. "Hambone, you in here?"

I finally catch up to him. The air inside is musty from moldering hay. "Poppy? It's me, Angie. Where are you?"

There is no answer as Dewey and I stomp around, shining the lantern into corners. I grab Dewey's arm. "I think I heard something." We stand still, listening. And there it is again—a high-pitched, drawn out meeeooooow.

I run toward a wheelbarrow leaning up against the wall. Dewey maneuvers it out of the way and there is Poppy, huddled barefoot, shivering in thin pajamas, no coat. One of the barn cats—an old tabby—is dragging itself against Poppy's arm. It meows loudly as if to ask what took us so long.

I crouch down. "Poppy, what are you doing out here? We have been worried sick."

Through chattering teeth, he gets out, "Sss-Sun-ddance."

We haven't had horses for decades—we sold Sundance when MacKenzie graduated from high school.

"What about Sundance?" I ask.

"F-f--feed."

"You came to feed the horses."

Poppy nods.

Dewey picks Poppy up as if he is a sack of potatoes, slings him over his shoulder, and carries him to the truck. He pulls a pair of extra hunting socks onto Poppy's feet and takes his own gloves off and tugs them onto Poppy's hands. He wraps an old blanket around him with a few hot packs for extra warmth. By this time, Mom has joined us.

"I'm taking him to the hospital to get him checked out. You all follow me in the car."

"I'll drive," I tell Mom. I know she hasn't driven at night for many years.

With impressive efficiency, the hospital staff soon has Poppy recovering with heated blankets and intravenous solutions. They want to keep him overnight. Mom says she is staying with him. Her head drops into her lap. "What are we going to do? I just can't manage him anymore."

"We'll figure something out," I tell her.

It is four in the morning before Dewey and I get home. I don't bother going to bed. In two hours I have to get up for work anyway.

YAWNING, I SEND MARLA TO THE LIBRARY with a copy of a childish book on dinosaurs her mother would approve of and strict instructions not to read Chapter Five on Evolution in our textbook. By the time her backpack hits the table, she'll be deep into the study of evolution. Not the text—I suspect she's already read it at home, intellectually curious gal that she is. No, she'll have that copy of Darwin's *On the Origin of Species* off the shelf again—the librarian is my spy and has ratted Marla out, much to my delight. Her mother would be horrified to know she is harboring a budding scientist in her home, a rebel, an anarchist who dares to read Darwin. Furthermore, when Dewey and I have walked around Veteran's Memorial Park on Saturday afternoons, I have seen Marla hanging around the particular patch of land assigned to her. She sits on a stadium cushion, which she moves around to various positions, and takes notes after consulting field guides. I can't see which ones from a distance, but I can't wait to read her science journal.

Once Marla leaves for the library, I ask each student to jot down the five most interesting ideas they discover while reading Chapter Five in the text or other resource materials on evolution. I motion to books scattered across a tabletop. Chairs scrape and chatter ensues as everyone chooses a book, and it sounds a bit chaotic until they settle down to read. Then, blessed silence for a while.

Something has to be done about Poppy. I hate to think of a nursing home, not only having to confine him away from family, but also the expense. How could we ever afford it—unless we sign up for Medicaid but then won't we lose the farm after Mom passes away?

I'm too worn out to dwell on it today and a room full of teenagers waits on further directions. "Tomorrow you will meet with your group to compare and discuss your five points. "Fifteen minutes total, three for each person," I suggest. "Then the team leaders will type your group's top five points into a SharePoint doc. At the end of class tomorrow we'll talk about your findings and I'll answer any questions you have."

Somehow I make it through the day—which isn't over when the dismissal bell rings. I have to attend an AFT meeting as Rebecca's vice president. Normally that might be yawn, yawn, yawn, but not in the inferno bubbling near the surface of any room where more than one teacher gathers these days. Still, not many show up for the meeting. No surprise. Usually I was one of the no-shows. Those who come express concern about the funding behind our health insurance program. It isn't stable. Instead of buttressing the system, rumor has it the legislature plans to cut benefits.

After the meeting, I comb my hair as I wait for Rebecca in the restroom. I hear a whimper—so muted I decide it might be my imagination. Finally, Rebecca emerges from a stall, her face pale and pinched.

"You okay?" I ask.

She nods, but I don't think either of us is convinced.

When I get home, with a groan I hurl my book bag onto a chair and hurl myself into the cushiony recliner beside it. Dewey takes in my utterly wretched face, my raccoon-rimmed eyes and glowering mouth; he nods as if he has anticipated my exhaustion. He, in contrast, wears a superior little smile as if he hasn't lost a wink of sleep—or most likely his job. Heaven help me, I am not in the mood to see a happy face. I want to unload, I want to share my gloom, but the cushions begin to absorb my tension, and I detect the aroma of tomato sauce and yeasty crust. "Do I smell pizza?"

"You do. I knew you wouldn't feel like cooking, but that's not all." His expression grows even more smug.

Curious, even though I hate to move out of my chair, I let him lead me by the hand into the kitchen where he holds forth a canvas shopping bag as if presenting, at the very least, frankincense and myrrh.

"Inside this bag are door alarms. After we eat, you're going to sack out in front of the TV or soak in a hot bath or whatever floats your little boat, and I'm going over to your folks' house and install the alarms. From now on, your mom will know if Hambone tries to make another jailbreak in the middle of the night."

"My hero." I plant a big old smoocher on his cheek.

After pizza and iced tea, I feel revived enough to delve into my book bag for a set of worksheets that need checking.

Dewey snatches the papers from my hands.

I try to hang onto them. "Hey—what do you think you're doing?"

"You need to relax tonight. No more work."

"Since when did you get promoted to be my boss?"

"Since I bought door alarms so you could get a good night's sleep." He has a point and he won't let go of the papers, so I let him stuff them in my bag. "When I get back from your mom's tonight, you better already be asleep."

On his way out the door, his arms are loaded with tools and shopping bags. I land a hearty pinch on his butt.

He yelps and delivers a threat over his shoulder. "Payback will come when you least expect it."

A SUBSTITUTE IS STANDING IN FRONT OF REBECCA'S DOOR on Monday morning. She never, ever misses school. I text her: *What's up?*

Seconds later, I see three wiggly dots, indicating she is typing. An incoming message pings: *Had blood in urine again over weekend. Bad back pain too. Doc insists on more tests. Carry on AFT without me tonight. Organize troops. Show strength to tight-wad legislators.*

Rebecca has had too many pee problems lately, dismissing her pain as nerves over the rising tension with the legislature. I warned her it could be more serious. Should have pressed her harder to see a doctor. Not that she would have listened.

I text back: *Will handle AFT. Don't give it another thought. Listen to doc. Get well.*

My stomach twists in knots. Something's really wrong with her. I just know it. I wrack my brain thinking of what I can do to help.

I have just enough time before class starts to call Dewey so he can take a pan of lasagna out to thaw and run it over to Rebecca's house later this afternoon. Her kids and husband will still have to eat.

"Leave it to me," Dewey says. "I'll fix a salad and get some good bread to take over, too."

"You're a gem."

During my lunch break, I text Rebecca: *Any news?* No response. I figure she's wearing one of those attractive tie-on gowns in some halfway sterile room submitting her body to a humiliating assault on her dignity.

After work, my heart races as I stand in front of my colleagues. My throat is so constricted I wonder if I'll be able to speak, if my voice will quiver, but I can't let Rebecca down. Especially not now when the stakes are so high. The whole state is in an uproar because the legislature once again is failing to properly fund our health care or offer a significant raise. I take a deep breath and imagine that these adults are simply more students. I explain where Rebecca is and let them know they are stuck with me for now, their vice president.

"Don't be silly, Angie, we're happy you are here, and rest assured, we've got your back." That was Eve Carstairs, our English department chair, one of the stalwarts of the school. The staff joked she has been teaching since Melvil Dewey invented the decimal classification for books. Students, however, swear she was the Eve formed from Adam's rib. With iron-gray hair and an iron-stiff spine, she is not to be trifled with. If Eve Carstairs has my back, I am in good shape. The meeting continues with little resolution to our problems, but at least my voice doesn't shake.

In the morning I check my messages. Still no word from Rebecca. I call and reach her husband Chad. "It's bladder cancer," he says.

My heart leaps into my throat. For a moment I can't talk. "Oh, Chad, I'm so sorry. What do the doctors say?"

He explains she'll have surgery and then some crazy procedure where they fill her bladder up with an infusion of tuberculosis-like germs. He says the doctor is upbeat about her prognosis and Rebecca is in good spirits.

"What can I do to help?" I ask.

"Nothing else. Thanks for the casserole. The kids enjoyed it."

"The least we could do."

Rebecca's mom is coming to help with the kids. Chad promises to keep me posted with regular updates. I tell him I will organize a meal team, where all her friends and colleagues can sign up to send food over to them.

After work I pick up a bouquet of daisies and button mums at the grocery store and take them to Rebecca. As soon as I enter the room, the smell gobsmacks me. I hyperventilate and feel dizzy. I force myself to take deep breaths and calm down. It's not the usual hospital smells that have plunged me down the rabbit hole. I can take the disinfectants and bodily fluids. It's the vase of Stargazer lilies sitting on Rebecca's overbed table that slay me with their lovely speckled strawberry and white blooms and heady scent. The smell that I will always associate with Daddy's funeral. Observing Rebecca accelerates my panic. Her spiky hair is squashed flat against the white pillow. Her essential perkiness is flatlined, too. I smile and say the expected platitudes and pass along AFT news, but I turn tail and exit as soon as I can without seeming rude. I can't let her see how distressed I am by the sight of her in that bed, how worried I am for her and Chad and their kids. The surgery is slated for the next day, with the germ infusion to follow soon after.

That night I research bladder cancer on the Internet. If all goes well, the surgery is relatively non-invasive and she should recover quickly. The germ treatment, called Bacillus Calmette-Guerin, appears standard; it activates the body's immune system to fight any cancer cells remaining after surgery. The prognosis is good, thank God. She will be all right. She has to be.

IT IS THE FIRST DAY OF MY CHRISTMAS BREAK, so I am in a great mood as I drop a poinsettia by Rebecca's house. She is home and doing well, though she will not be back at school any time soon, she tells me over a cup of hot chocolate.

"Chad wants me to take the next semester off. Which means AFT will be your baby for the rest of the year. Is that okay?"

"Definitely. What are friends for?"

"I'm still going to come to some meetings once I get better, but I don't want the stress of being in charge."

"Got you covered. You concentrate on getting well." I promise to bring over a batch of Christmas cookies for her kids later in the week. I can't help but wonder what happens to her health insurance if she takes the semester off, but she explains she's covered by Chad's. Lucky for her.

On the drive home, I catch a red light by the Robinson Grand Theater. It has been more than restored; it is grander than it ever was in my childhood. A beautiful, Broadway-worthy building. The marquee advertises a production of "The Nutcracker." It's been many long years since I've seen a ballet. I can imagine the lovely dancers floating across the stage. Clara and the Land of the Sweets. The Sugar Plum Fairy. And my favorite, Mother Ginger with the horde of children scurrying from beneath her skirt. Dewey would opt for a root canal over going to the ballet, but I could see if Trish would like a night out. The light changes and I drive on. The uncertain state of our finances dispels my daydream. This is not the year for indulgences. Maybe next year things will be better.

At home, I set a pair of ruby-red poinsettias on either side of the fireplace hearth, a ritual I've carried out ever since we moved into this house. I hang red felt stockings along the mantel. It's beginning to look like Christmas!

Later I drag our artificial tree out of the garage and pull boxes of decorations from the attic. While the Carpenters Christmas album plays in the background, I shake out the tree's limbs. The musty odors make me sneeze. Twice. The old thing looks rather wretched and raggedy. "Once the ornaments are hung, it will look fine," I say aloud even though no one is around to hear. I begin unwrapping treasures from folds of tissue paper. A photo of Trish pasted on a tree-shaped piece of green felt, an ornament she'd made in kindergarten. I slide its twist of pipe cleaner over a limb. Next is a carved wooden moose Mom and Poppy had brought back from Alaska, and then gifts from Trish, a miniature lawnmower for Dewey and a tiny garden spade lying in front of tulips for me. The most delicate and time-consuming to unwrap are the old-world glass bulbs passed down from grandparents. My heart overflows with memories.

One look at Dewey as he comes through the front door tells me something's wrong. "Bad day?" I ask.

He angles straight for the refrigerator without stopping to remove his wool sport coat. I hear the familiar pop as a beer can is opened. He returns to the family room and drops into the couch cushions like a stone. As seconds pass, my heartbeat escalates.

When he finally answers, he avoids looking at me. "Worse than bad."

I sink down beside him and place my hand on his knee. I notice I've ironed parallel creases down one leg of his khakis. I feel I have failed him by adding one more imperfection to his day, though I doubt he even noticed the dual creases.

He slugs down almost half the contents of the can and then lowers it to rest on his right knee. "I laid off the last of my crew." He laughs mirthlessly. "I have now joined the ranks of the unemployed."

"Oh, Dew, I'm sorry." We knew this was coming, but the timing just before Christmas lands like a gut punch.

He finishes off the beer and muffles a burp. The way he is fidgeting alarms me.

"Look, I shouldn't have kept this from you, but two weeks ago, I called Ted and asked if he could get us the loan. He hemmed and hawed, didn't say yes, didn't say no. I didn't see what harm it could do."

I clench my teeth. He wouldn't—because I'd kept things from him as well, so how mad could I get? But I am mad. Spitting mad.

"What did Ted say?"

"He'd get back to me and he didn't, so I called your sister today to see if she could twist his arm a little."

I get up and fetch him another beer and grab one for myself too. Damn it, I told him it wasn't a good idea and he has gone and done it anyway. I sit down beside him again and take a sip of beer to calm myself. Even without Ted's and my hidden history, without their suspected marital problems, I wouldn't willingly ask my sister for anything. Ever. Especially money.

"I'm surprised she took your call. She lets mine go to voicemail. What did she say?"

Dewey scrunches up his mouth. "That she can't help us." He sets the beer I brought down on the coffee table, untouched. "Mac didn't exactly say so, but I get the impression she and Ted are having trouble."

"I told you that might be the case when we got her Christmas card last week." My sister has always done family photo cards with a two- or three-page typed letter of all their accomplishments. This year's card—generic variety you can buy at the drugstore. No letter.

I push down my anger. It is only getting in the way of the important decisions we have to make. I've been thinking about our options for a while now, and only one seems feasible. "Maybe we should sell the house and move in with Mom and Poppy. Just for a while until you get another job or we figure out something better."

He bends his torso forward, hands clasped between his knees. His thumbs worry against each other, picking at the cuticles. "There's a job I could have tomorrow if I wanted it."

"It's not a good position?"

"Actually, it's a great position. One of my old college friends owns a commercial construction firm. He wants to groom me to take over financial management when the current fellow retires."

"Sounds like a great opportunity, so what's the catch?"

"The firm's in D.C."

I deposit my beer beside his on the coffee table. One more sip and I might vomit.

"Oh no, Dew. Visiting Washington once or twice for the museums and history is fine, but the whole idea living there totally creeps me out. I just don't think I could deal with the traffic, the high rises, all that asphalt and concrete." Would he really consider leaving Trish and Bella just when they needed us most? We wouldn't be here to help Mom with Poppy either.

"I don't want to live there any more than you do." Dewey sighs. "Guess we could move out to the farm, temporarily. It would get the mortgage off our backs. How would your mom feel about it?"

"You kidding? She gets a whiff of this and she'll be over here packing up the moving truck."

"We wouldn't be total freeloaders. I could help take care of Poppy and fix things up around the farm."

I lean over to kiss his cheek. "You're the best fixer-upper ever, Dew. Mom definitely could use our help."

One person down; a few more to persuade.

Dewey read my mind. "What about Trish and the baby?"

They were supposed to move in with us right after Christmas. Four generations under one old farmhouse roof—what could possibly go wrong? I call Mom first, and she is ecstatic.

"I've been so afraid I'd have to put Ham in a nursing home," she says. "It's getting really hard for me to manage him on my own."

When I phone Trish that evening, she says she's okay with the change in plans.

"Have you talked to your aunt lately?" I ask. Dewey's not always that astute at reading people, so if he noticed something amiss, MacKenzie must be a mess.

Trish hasn't talked to Mac, but she promises to check her on-line sources.

"I've already checked Facebook and everything on Mac's page looks normal," I say.

"There's a lot of other places to look. Give me a few secs." She disconnects.

Fifteen minutes later, Trish calls me back.

"Mom, you aren't going to believe this."

"What?"

"No, you gotta see for yourself. I sent you a link. I'll wait."

I boot my laptop and click on the link. I shriek, "Oh my God!"

Trish snickers. "If you're calling on God for help, I hope you warn Him to close his eyes."

My screech attracts Dewey's attention. I scoop up my laptop and shut myself and the offending device in the bedroom.

"Trish, this can't be Mac. It must be Photoshopped."

"I don't think so. Didn't she tell you she was playing a lot of tennis?"

She did, and she bragged about being buff. I had no idea she meant *in the buff.* Yet the evidence is right there on the screen. Mac and her tennis partner, naked as Adam and Eve in the garden, with-out a fig leaf anywhere in sight.

"I'm going to call her."

"And say what, Mom?"

"I'll ask what in the hell she thinks she's doing.

"You should sleep on it."

I may never sleep again after seeing my sister on her—I slam the laptop screen down. Try to blank the photo from my mind—reformat my hard drive. No, no, no.

"I can't deal with this, Trish."

"She can get the photo taken down. It's called revenge porn—happens to people all the time."

"Not to anyone I know." What a hypocrite my sister's been! All her holier-than-thou, my-choices-have-been-better-than-yours attitude, just one big load of manure.

We agree I should take time to consider what I am going to say.

"But it has to be soon. She has to get that horrible photo taken down. Allison and James will have a heart attack if they see it." No mother wants her children to think of her—let alone see her—in such a compromising position.

The baby is crying in the background and Trish has to go.

Staring at my closed laptop, I debate whether or not to tell Dewey. Finally, I open the bedroom door.

He pauses the TV show he's been watching. "You gonna tell me what that was all about?"

"Can't." I inch toward him, the laptop pressed against my waist.

He shrugs and picks up the remote.

I sit beside him, open the laptop, and turn the screen so it faces him. He glances over and his eyes pop right out of his head.

"Holy shee-it!"

Exactly.

I LEAVE NUMEROUS VOICEMAILS on MacKenzie's cell, but she doesn't return my calls, even when I tell her it's an emergency. Finally, I admit I've seen the photo and she should contact a professional about getting it wiped out of cyberspace. That is, unless she wants her children or mother or social circle to accidentally stumble onto it.

Still she doesn't return my call. I have done all I can.

It's not as if I don't have other business to occupy my time. Before an ad can even be placed in the newspaper, the real estate agent sells our home to a guy who drives water trucks out to fracking sites. As an environmentalist who loves our state's beauty, I hate the whole idea of hydraulic fracturing and what it is doing to our land and water—but I can appreciate the jobs it brings for some families. The week after Christmas whizzes by, a flurry of taking down the tree far earlier than usual, packing boxes, loading trucks, seemingly endless trips back and forth to the farm. We move Trish and the baby into MacKenzie's old room first. The next day we move ourselves. Leaving the house we'd lived in for two decades proves more emotionally wrenching than I'd anticipated. We'd celebrated Christmas mornings and birthdays in the living room, satisfied our hunger in the kitchen—and other hungers in the bedroom—spilled snacks on nearly all the family room furniture, collected gobs of knickknacks and memories. Many of our belongings get stacked in the barn until we have a place of our own again. I get through the transition by staying busy. I'm scared it will hit me once I have a moment to sit down for a second and think.

By that time, school is starting up again and we all adjust to new routines. I have to get up earlier in the morning because I no longer have a garage to park my car in. That means scraping ice from the windshield, not to mention a longer drive to work.

Dewey spends his days fixing up the farmhouse. He replaces ancient electrical wiring. Spreads sheets of insulation in the attic. Weather-strips windows and doors. He takes Poppy with him to the grocery store, doctor's appointments, the barber shop. Plays "Go Fish" with him so Mom can visit the beauty parlor—a real treat, she says. If Poppy sets off the door alarm in the middle of the night, Dewey intercepts him. Poppy plays Dean Martin CDs constantly—and if it drives me crazy in the evening hours, I can only imagine the effect it is having on Dewey, trapped in the house all day. He drinks beer, more and more, starting earlier and continuing late into the night. I don't complain. I worry. He needs a paying job but there aren't many out there.

Many mornings I go to work half asleep because at Bella's first miniscule wail, I wake and can't get back to sleep, an instinctual response to a crying infant I can't repress. A few weeks pass, cold and dreary, and I wonder as I always do this time of year if I will ever see a blue sky again and if I will ever go outside again without my eyes watering from freezing gusts of wind. The ride to work offers a respite, a few blessed minutes of silence, alone in my own space, no moon hitting my eye with a big pizza pie, no infant wails, no dirty diaper odors. I love my family. I love them better when there are not so many of us crammed into one small space. I love them best when I've had a good night's sleep.

I am not the only one with sleep deficit. Kev, a first period student who is never a bundle of energy, drags through the door so slowly on Monday, I wonder if he could be stoned—but how likely is that at this hour of the day? I think he's wearing the same flannel shirt he had on Friday and the day before that. The odors coming off him would embarrass a homeless person. His curly brown hair is unwashed, uncombed, his eyes riddled with red lines—a road map spelling trouble. I make a mental note to find a moment to talk privately with him.

The tables along one wall are covered with flats of Black-Seeded Simpson lettuce. Every kind of experiment imaginable will be performed on my saved seeds before the year is out. In the past my students sowed seeds in sand and clay. We sowed them on sponges. Students manipulated the pH of the soil with everything from tomato juice and soda pop to powdered limestone and laundry detergent. We played with the temperature and the light—both natural and artificial. We are growing lettuce hydroponically.

They design their own experiments, and it looks as if one group this morning is hooking up a battery to electrically charge the soil. I move over to quiz Marla about the experimental design, as she is the one taking notes and directing activity. In theory, electrically pulsed soil could affect bacterial action, which could affect plant growth. A cool idea, and it seems to interest everyone in the group. Except Kev. He hangs back, uninvolved. Eventually, he retreats to a desk and lays his head down. It's not allowed, but I let it slide. Five minutes before the end of class while students are writing results of the day's work in their science journals, I call him out into the hallway.

"What's going on, Kev?"

His eyes flick away. "Nothing."

"I know something's wrong."

"Nothing, just tired."

"I'm not buying that. You can talk to me about whatever's going on, or one of the counselors."

"Nothing to talk about." He shuffles his weight from one foot to the other.

"Not talking isn't an option. The choice is in listeners: me or a counselor."

In the silence, I can almost see his brain twisting and wrestling, a push and pull between the desire to unburden himself and the desire to hold in whatever is wrong. He is only fifteen. Whatever it is, he shouldn't carry the load alone.

"I haven't gotten much sleep lately. That's all."

"Hmmm. Why is that?"

He shrugs. "My dad hasn't been very happy."

"Oh?"

"Lost his job."

Naturally Dewey flashes through my mind, but I'm aware our situation is unique. My mother's home had empty rooms and she welcomed the help. Dewey feels needed. Is needed. We are lucky, although it doesn't feel lucky to lose your home when you are fifty years old. And the stress is getting to him, hence the increased beer consumption. Still, it could be worse. Much worse.

"That's tough. How's your dad handling it?"

Wild rage ignites in Kev's eyes, overriding tears I sense just below the surface. "He ain't, he ain't handling it. Now you happy? Glad you asked?"

"Yes, I'm glad I asked. I'm worried about you."

I understand his reluctance to talk. We are taught to hide our dirty laundry. I don't know if it's like that everywhere, but that's how it is around here. We cope. We make do with what we have. We don't whine when the last glass company leaves the state or the coal mine shuts down after stripping the hillside of every living thing. We don't cry when the last mom-and-pop store downtown shutters its windows, or when even Dynamo Deals closes its doors. Instead we let the frackers come in and drill wells beside the grade schools and on the edges of our farms because they promise jobs. We take our college degree in business and wait tables or flip burgers if we have to. We go back to college or a vo-tech school and learn to empty bedpans or take X-rays because people are always going to be sick. Especially if they worked in the mines or drank polluted well water near the fracking sites.

We suck it up. Until we can't suck it up anymore.

The bell to dismiss class rings. From my classroom come the murmur of voices, the creak of desks releasing bodies, the scuffle of book bags scooped up and slung to shoulders, and slap of shoes against the wooden floor.

Kev needs more help than I can deliver between classes. "Look, I'm going to walk you down to Mr. Bryant's office. He might know of ways the community can help."

The look Kev shoots me plainly says I am denser than granite. "Help? Dad's beyond help. It's heroin."

Kev stalks off, every step, every swing of his arms, shedding sparks of anger. Stone-still, I watch, heartsick, my attempts to help a complete fumble, my words, inadequate to deal with such pain.

But at the end of the hallway, Kev turns into the counselor's office, and I am relieved. I hope Mr. Bryant has the right tools and a strong dose of magic in his bag of counselor tricks. Drug problems in our state have risen to the crisis level. Opioids and fentanyl I knew about from news coverage. But this is the first I've heard of heroin abuse here locally. I hope it's the last.

Down the hallway I see Rebecca's substitute teacher for the second semester. I call to check on my pal and she has a surprise: her brother owns a carwash and needs another worker immediately. I text Dewey about the opportunity: *Not a great job, part time, but could help until something better turns up. You could start today.*

He texts back: *I didn't work my ass off to get an MBA so I could wash cars.*

Yeah, well, I didn't work my ass off to get a masters in science education just so I could move back in with my parents either, but we all have to make the best of a bad situation.

After work, I have to call an emergency meeting of AFT. I phone Dewey to let him know.

"It's about the forbidden S word," I say, pausing for effect. "Not the first one that popped into your mind."

He considers this a second. "Strike," he guesses.

"Strike. I'm supposed to sound out our members and report to the higher-ups."

"I don't like it." Worry hovers in his voice. "You could lose your job. Get arrested. Get hurt. Strikes can be violent."

"Progress rarely comes without struggle."

"Our family is struggling enough right now, Ange."

"You think I don't know that?" I close the door to my room, before someone overhears the rising tension. "But what we're facing is nothing compared to what Rebecca and Chad have to deal with. Look, the legislature isn't going to throw fistfuls of cash at education and healthcare unless we push them, either through negotiation—or through a walkout."

"You can't do this."

My teeth clench, and there is a banging in my chest, an angry beast demanding to be uncaged. I never have taken well to the word *can't*. Who is this? Surely not my laid-back Dewey speaking!

"I don't see as I have much choice."

"Sure you do. Resign. You didn't want to be president anyway."

"I promised Rebecca I'd do this for her. I can't quit."

"Yes, you can. Listen, I didn't want to say anything until I'm further along in the interview process, but I applied for a job with the FBI fingerprint division, their business administration. Your name in the paper as an AFT president might ruin my chances. It's illegal for public employees to strike."

I suppose the FBI gig is why he turned down the carwash job. But why is his potential job more important than my career?

"I love you, Dew, and I hope you get this job, I really do, but AFT is about the job I already have. It's about better wages for me, and don't forget it affects Trish too. I'm trying to get our health insurance to cover more stuff like Bella's hearing aids."

"Someone else can lead AFT."

"I promised."

"You want to move to D.C.—is that it? Because that's what's gonna happen if I don't get this FBI gig."

"You say that like there aren't other choices, other jobs you could get."

"Companies aren't chomping at the bit to hire a fifty-four-year-old man."

"Something will turn up. I can't believe there aren't other jobs out there for an MBA."

"Believe what you want, but if the FBI falls through, I'm taking the job in D.C."

How quickly a man's hand can turn into a fist—a my-way-or-the-highway demand! This is the last thing I ever expected from Dewey. "Don't I have a say in that?"

"No."

I don't know who he thinks he's talking to, but it isn't me. I signed onto a partnership, not dictatorship.

"I'm not moving and I won't resign." As I disconnect, my hands are shaking.

When I get home, Dewey isn't sitting in front of the television with Poppy. He's not in the kitchen with Mom.

"Seen Dewey?" I ask Mom.

She says he went out right after I phoned. "Going to see a friend. Said not to hold up dinner for him."

My stomach lurches as I open our bedroom door. I discover Dewey's note on the bed. It is written on a notepad designed for grocery lists: *I'm going to stay with a friend for a few days while we both think about our situation.*

Does he mean my participation in strike talks? My standing up to him? Or the overall situation of living with Mom and Poppy? I sink onto his side of the bed, holding the note. I can't believe he's left me. How long is "a few days"?

I check the closet and drawers. Not much missing. A clean shirt, socks, and underwear. We have always maintained separate checking accounts, so I'm not worried about his draining a joint account.

I brush my hand over his pillow. It's not the first argument we've had in twenty-nine years of marriage, but he's never left before. Then again, we've always lived under our own roof. He hasn't even told me which friend he went to stay with, although I can guess. Probably Phil, an old high school friend who is a thrice-divorced alcoholic. I clench my teeth. I refuse to call him to ask. And I won't give in.

I put on a cheery smile to face Mom and Trish. "Dewey says he's staying with a friend for a few days."

"Okay," Mom says. She doesn't say anything more about his absence, but her worry hangs in the silence like a high-pitched buzz.

After dinner, I go in the bathroom to brush my teeth. His toothbrush is missing from the cup. Its absence punches a hole in my chest.

Dewey and I met on an outing to Arden Party Rock with friends at the start of my senior year in college. Arden was a popular spot for drinking and shooting the rapids between two rock formations called Devil's Den and Hell's Gate. Over the years, more than one person had imbibed too much and drowned in the strong currents. In early September the water was far too icy to tempt me and I wasn't a strong enough swimmer to feel comfortable plunging over the small waterfalls, so I spent the afternoon lounging on the dark sandy beach watching those brave—and foolhardy—souls who cascaded down the river. Dewey was one. He had arrived with a different bunch of kids. As my group's designated driver, I had sucked down only one beer early in the afternoon. When it came time to leave, I discovered my VW had a flat tire. Arnold Schwarzenegger must have tightened the lug nuts, because try as I might, I couldn't loosen them. More than one expletive passed through my lips and attracted Dewey's attention. Before I knew it, he had fixed my flat and secured a date for the following weekend. Over plates of spaghetti, we discovered we both liked hiking, camping, gardening, and pasta. A foster child, he had no real family of his own, and he readily adopted mine. We have been together ever since. Until now.

His side of the bed is empty, but not as empty as I feel without him. I go through the motions. I get up for work, come home, help Mom with dinner, play with Bella, go to bed. I can't sleep. I feel as if I am stumbling around in two left shoes.

The next evening I break down and call Dewey.

"Yeah?" He doesn't sound overjoyed to hear from me.

"I wondered when you were planning to come home."

"Not sure. Do you want me to?"

"Of course. I miss you."

"But not enough to turn down a starring role on the evening news."

"What was I supposed to do? Refuse to talk to the reporters? They were there covering the meeting."

"If you were one of hundreds in a crowd of other teachers, it wouldn't matter to the FBI or any other employer. But when you insist on standing out in front of cameras, pounding a gavel on a podium, you're kind of hard to miss. You come across as an agitator. Another teacher could take the lead in the strike. It doesn't have to be you. Doesn't have to be your face on the TV for everyone to see. I need this FBI gig, Angie. I can't go eleven months without work again. I just can't."

"I hear you. I understand."

"I wonder if you do."

He disconnects.

Great. That's what I get for trying.

~~~

THREE DAYS LATER, I PULL OUT of the school parking lot. Everything happens in slow motion. I hear the crunch of metal. I feel the impact, a jarring of the bones. The airbag slams into my face and my eyes sting. My left ankle twists. A few seconds pass before I comprehend that a truck has tee-boned my little car. Coach Jones pulls me out through the passenger side while Mr. Esposito calls paramedics. They must have been on parking lot patrol.

"No ambulance—that's not necessary. I'll be fine." I say this even though I can't stand without support. Mr. Esposito cleans my face with his handkerchief. When he finishes, the white cloth is blood stained.

He appears pale and beads of sweat dot his upper lip. I don't know what to make of this. With his years of experience, he's seen plenty of football injuries, broken up fights in the halls. Do I look that bad?

"Best to get yourself checked out," he insists.

A crowd of students and teachers lurk around the smashed vehicles. The truck's driver is telling anyone who'll listen that he didn't see me. He is uninjured but the truck's front end sustained damage. "It's a good thing I wasn't going fast," he tells Coach Jones.

"Maybe not, but you ran that stop sign," Coach says.

"I stopped, and I wasn't speeding in the school zone, I swear I wasn't."

"Any faster and that door would have been on top of her, buddy," Coach says.

With sirens and flashing lights, paramedics arrive. While they secure my ankle in one of those thick support booties, Dewey's truck skids in behind them.

Our eyes lock as he walks toward me where I am sitting in the back of the paramedics' van. He hasn't shaved. His clothes look rumpled, grubby, and he smells like a funky dishcloth.

"How is she?" he asks the fellow pasting one of those little butterfly bandages on my chin.

"You the husband?" the paramedic asks.

Dewey nods.

"She refuses to go to the hospital. Her ankle is sprained, nothing broken as far as we can tell."

His partner adds, "She'll be sore. Could have a concussion. Watch for headaches, nausea, vomiting, or numbness. Don't let her fall asleep for a while and get her to the emergency room right away if her condition deteriorates in any way."

"You got it," Dewey says.

The paramedic looks at him suspiciously. "You been drinking?"

Dewey turns his head away. "No, sir."

Even in my disoriented state, I can smell his lie.

The paramedic accepts Dewey's answer, and I let him help me hobble into his truck. My car will have to be towed away. Mr. E. says not to worry; he'll take care of it.

The adrenaline is wearing off and I realize I am bone-weary.

On the way to the farm, we don't discuss where he's been or if he's leaving again. We have always found it easy to talk about our preferred brand of coffee, the best streams for trout fishing, what week to plant potatoes—the trivia of everyday life. Yet broaching our deepest feelings requires a language we never learned. We become as mute as Bella might have been without hearing aids.

Mom and Trish make a ridiculous fuss over me. Poppy admires my ankle boot and asks if I want to dance. I decline. Dewey accepts the offer and swings Poppy around the room in a crazy two-step.

Dewey's toothbrush is back in the cup on the bathroom sink, but when I get a call from one of the higher-ups in the AFT, he scowls and slams into the bedroom.

Rosella

After the meeting at the Kennesons', I was more determined than ever to be part of the struggle. We women had to force the legislature to accord us equality. They would never give in unless pushed relentlessly. Jack came home the morning after the meeting. He'd turned out to have a bossy streak, a desire to dominate, a trait I found quite commonplace in men. Fear that he'd forbid me to attend future meetings kept me from confiding in him—even though persuading men to vote in favor of women's right to vote was the only way we would ever gain that privilege. First, I wanted to ferret out his feelings on the issue. I wasn't sure how to broach the subject. While I brooded over this, he proposed a change which would have an immediate (and completely unwelcome) impact on our lives.

"I suppose," he said over Nellie's biscuits and beef stew, "we'd better look for larger accommodations before the new Joyner makes his appearance. We can rent a house while we build our own."

"Oh." I almost swallowed a carrot chunk whole. Only a few months ago those words would have thrilled me. Now they caused pain. What if Jack was away when the baby arrived? I would have given anything to have my mother beside me. If I couldn't have my mother, Nellie was the next best thing. Without her, how would I know whether the baby just needed a hot toddy for croup or whether it needed to see a doctor?

Nellie set down her fork. "I was planning to fix up another room for the baby."

Jack scoffed. "What room? They're all occupied."

"My sitting room. It's on the other side of your bedroom, and when I want to crochet or embroider, I can use the parlor down-stairs. I usually do anyway."

"Oh, Nellie, we couldn't impose on your privacy." Inside, I was praying Nellie would insist. The boarding house was far from the grand hacienda Jack dreamed of building, but I didn't want to go through a birthing without the woman who'd become so much more than landlady. She was a dear friend, a confidante. The sister I never had.

"What do I need with privacy? It'll be such fun to have a baby in the house. I thought I'd paint the room yellow. What do you think? Make some dotted Swiss curtains. And I have an old chest of draw-ers in the attic we could drag down and paint."

"Sounds perfect. What do you say, Jack? We could stay here un-til our own home is built."

He shrugged. "Suit yourself. At least you'll have company when I'm away."

Yes, at least there was that.

Two days later he trained to El Paso.

May 1920

After the planning meeting for my reception, Nellie drove us past the house where Solina had spent the first years of her life and Nellie's second boarding house so Solina could see them. She had only the vaguest memories of living in San Francisco, understand-able since she had been such a wee one then. Everything about the city seemed enormous to her. The buildings, the ocean, the num-ber of people. Watching her expressions reminded me of how I felt when I first arrived here as a fifteen year old, how strange it all was.

Nellie still wore her hair in a slightly disheveled updo, but now it was shot through with gray. Her gait had changed as well, sug-gesting sore knees, or perhaps hip trouble.

Solina was impressed by Nellie's new Model T. "You must be rich," she said. Nellie explained she wasn't wealthy, that the auto had cost less than $300, but to Solina, the sum seemed enormous. We rarely had extra cash on hand. Val's patients often gifted us with half of a butchered pig or a chicken or whatever else they could spare. He never turned anyone away if they couldn't pay cash, especially during the war years and the recession that followed. As a doctor, Val had been exempt from serving in the Great War, and Timmy had been exempt as a coal miner. Not all were so fortunate. A construction worker, my brother Josiah was never quite the same after he returned. Shell shock, Val called it. A common ailment of returning soldiers. We were all doing what we could to help Josiah's family as he was often unable to work. Even so, we weren't poor. We were managing.

"Your Papa says we may have enough saved up to buy a car later this year," I said.

We parked in front of the hotel again. The reception was still on, though Mindy's smile had been somewhat strained. She had gone to considerable expense and effort to arrange this exhibit for me. I prayed the newspaper's lies wouldn't harm her gallery's reputation by association with me. The big event would take place two nights from now. Enough time to correct the original story—if anyone would print the truth.

We exited the car into a pleasant evening, no rain this time of year and no need of a coat. I loved the western states in late spring, especially California. I continued with my life story, filling in a few more pieces for my daughter.

"So Nellie, you aren't really my aunt?" Solina asked.

I hurried to answer. "Not in the blood sense, but she's been like an older sister to me ever since she took us in, and like an aunt to you ever since . . ."

Solina completed my sentence. ". . . ever since I was born."

Nellie raised an eyebrow to see if I intended to elaborate, but I wasn't ready to talk about my daughter's birth.

Solina smiled. "And Aunt Nellie introduced you to the Kennesons and Underwoods. She has played such an important role in your life. More than most blood sisters, I would guess."

"She has indeed." When Nellie came into a room, it was as if a lamp went on and the world became a little brighter, a little happier.

"You are the family I chose for myself, I couldn't love you any more than I already do." Nellie headed toward the hotel, swaying side to side, duck-like. Her increased weight had intensified what had been a barely noticeable tendency when she was younger.

The three of us entered the hotel lobby, waiting until we'd greeted the doorman before resuming our conversation.

Solina wrinkled her nose as she bounced with youthful enthusiasm toward the grand staircase. "Mama, I liked your friend Miss Mindy, but that Lydia Underwood seems stuck up. I didn't much care for her. She wasn't kind at all toward Mindy's helpers and barely had two words for me."

Never let it be said that my daughter was a poor judge of character. Miss Lydia had grown up to be every bit as witchy as her mother. Alexandra had aged since I had last seen her, crow's feet near her eyes, creases at the corners of her mouth, yet she had put on none of the weight that girded Nellie's middle. She and her daughter had their hair bobbed fashionably short. Alexandra's style secured bangs to one side of her face with a stretchy headband. A red silk flower was attached on the left. In slight contrast, a fringe of bangs hovered just above Lydia's large blue eyes. They both looked low-class, if you asked me.

Nellie spared me the necessity of a response. "Lydia was born a child of privilege and sometimes forgets the virtue of kindness toward others is cherished above all others." Nellie ventured to take her leave. "I'll expect you for dinner, then."

We hugged and she returned to her auto.

As we climbed the stairs, Solina looked thoughtful, puzzled. "What happened to the baby, Mama?"

I sighed. That poor little creature. "Two weeks after Jack left town, I delivered a baby girl, far too soon for her to survive."

Solina reached for my hand. "My sister. How sad."

Yes, I had been heartbroken. And where was Jack? In El Paso or Seattle or Timbuktu. What did particulars matter? He wasn't at my bedside when I nearly bled to death.

"I'm so glad you had Aunt Nellie, that you got to stay on with her."

It had fallen upon Nellie to comfort me, a pattern that repeated itself often in my life. "Sometimes nature knows best," she said, refusing to let me see the baby, insisting it would only upset me. I could read in the creases around Nellie's eyes that something was terribly wrong with my little girl. She gave the tiny body to Val Martin to bury while I was still packed in ice to stop the bleeding.

Years later Val confessed the child had horrible deformities, the details of which he refused to disclose, thinking to spare me further distress. I'm not sure it was a kindness, since my imagination leapt from one nightmarish vision to another. The reason for the deformities was something I couldn't bring myself to explain to Solina. Not yet.

I had stood in front of auditoriums full of women and lectured on delicate health issues. But this talk was so much harder. So personal. So degrading.

No matter how many times I told myself I had nothing to be ashamed of, nonetheless I was.

My reticence to tell my daughter the truth, ugly as it was, illustrated the problem. If no one spoke frankly, if we kept seeing disease as sin, as shame, nothing would change.

"It's time to tell you Jack's story, what I know of it." Some was supposition from receipts I'd found. "I've pieced together fragments of his life from what he told me and what I learned later from your papa and Lourdes."

Solina frowned. "Who's Lourdes?"

Courage, Ro, I told myself. "I'll tell you all about it once we are in our rooms."

Jack

LOURDES STOMPED HER FOOT. "I bet you would buy it for *her,* your Ro-*zell*-uh. I bet *she* doesn't have to beg for necessaries."

Jack would hardly call a hat with a real stuffed hummingbird nesting on top of gaudy silk flowers a necessity. More of an abomination. The hat was inordinately expensive, but he supposed he was going to have to buy it. Ever since he'd gotten married, Lourdes had been difficult. She was always demanding money and had conveniently forgotten he first met her in a saloon across the border in Juarez. She had vindictive brothers who already looked at him as if they were sighting a snake through a rifle. Not that their dislike surprised him. Women had always loved him, and men begrudged him for it. Been that way all his life. But her brothers were crazy if they thought she was pure. She was hardly a virgin when they'd met three years ago, even if she was only thirteen then. In fact, he'd gotten a sore and rash soon after they first became intimate. She'd scrunched up her face and shrugged. "Bed bugs, big deal."

She was probably right. His skin cleared up, but there were still times he worried about that rash. One evening over cards, his boss, Mr. Whiting, told a story that gave Jack some assurance he knew the cure even if he had contracted an unspeakable infection: "Being with a virgin is a sure-fire remedy for anything untoward you catch in a whorehouse, if you get my drift, Jack."

Leroy Whiting had never steered him wrong, so soon after their talk, Jack had married Rosella, as pure a girl as ever was.

Jack chucked Lourdes under the chin. "I would prefer you didn't cover up your beautiful tresses, that's all." Especially with a dead bird.

She arched her back, raised both hands to her thick tresses, and fanned them away from her neck. "You like my hair?"

"I've told you so a thousand times." He liked her dusky skin, too, the way it contrasted with the white she always wore. This dress was one of the new straight silhouettes with dozens of little tucks across her full breasts. Another one of the "necessaries" she insisted he buy for her.

Her smile fell away. "I still want this hat."

Jack knew when he'd lost an argument. He told the vendor he'd be back to buy it the next day, even though it cost enough to feed a family of four for a week.

Then she had the nerve to demand five dollars for more necessities, unspecified.

"Sorry, I can't spare any more, Lourdes, not on top of the hat."

Soon, he would finish engineering this spur of the railroad and he could steer clear of El Paso for a while. Let Lourdes find someone new to warm her bed and feather her head.

They strolled arm in arm down the street, the October air so stifling at midday it felt to Jack as if he were inhaling cotton. Unseasonably hot, especially compared to San Francisco. He had never liked El Paso. North Franklin Peak was visible in the West. No matter where he stood in the city, he could see the mountain, a reminder of Rosella waiting for him, the baby due in February. To think, he would be a father. It made him smile. His kid would have an easier life than he had growing up. He would make sure of that. He couldn't wait to ride the tracks home. San Francisco was never this hot. Never this complicated.

THE COWBOY AND BANKER TOOK A QUICK PEEK at their cards and folded. Jack palmed his two replacement cards up, fanned them just enough to glimpse the additional queen, and snapped them closed. Aces over queens—a winning hand if ever there was one. About time his luck turned. Jack leaned back in his chair and eyed the pile of coins in the center of the table. Enough to make up for everything he'd lost so far this evening. And then some. Enough to pay for Lourdes's dead bird hat. He shoved the last of his silver into the pot and called. He threw back a shot of whiskey and signaled for another. The rancher—went by the name of Parsons, just Parsons, no first name—was the only one left now. Cocky bastard was obviously going to see it through to the end.

Jack laid his cards down and reached for the pot. Parsons crushed his hand. Once Parsons eased up, Jack jerked his hand away. Under the table, he massaged the bones. What a freak! Jack wouldn't be surprised if his hand bruised. There weren't many men who could best Jack, but Parsons was a regular Paul Bunyan. One by one, Parsons laid down his cards. Son of a gun. Jack couldn't believe it. Four kings. What were the odds these two hands could occur in the same deal? A million to one, he guessed. If there was a God, He had it in for Jack. Maybe this was punishment for Lourdes, for adultery. He pondered the possibility for a moment, and then decided *Nah*. It was all a matter of luck, and he must have used up every lick of his when he persuaded Rosella to marry him.

They'd met when he visited his aunt in West Virginia. He first noticed her in church, an angel singing in the choir. Then, to his surprise, later in the week she came to his aunt's home to help pick and can green beans. He remembered how she looked that day. A fine-featured face and brownish hair that gleamed almost golden in the sunlight. When she entered a room, she filled every corner as if no one else existed. And she did it not because she was chatty, not because she put herself forward, but because she glowed with loving kindness, with a feisty goodness he was hard-put to define. Even so, it was her curiosity about the world, her way of observing details he overlooked—like a crumbling autumn leaf that resembled lace or a witch-shaped cloud—that stoked him until he had no choice but to marry her. Unlike Lourdes, it was the only way to get her into bed.

Lourdes, too, dominated a room when she slipped along with cat-like steps. If she and Rosella were in the same room, he wondered what would happen, whether Lourdes's feline ways would get the best of Rosella's feisty goodness. The two were nearly the same age. But what a difference—Lourdes, already granite-eyed and womanly, while Rosella was sheltered, barely formed.

He thought it would be fun to shape the woman Rosella would become, but to his surprise, she was shaping him. For the first time in his life, he knew fear. Used to be, he would have faced the Devil down. He scaled cliffs, braved the desert, shot rattlers. Now, he worried every time he rode the rails, wondered if this would be the time some faceless, nameless brakeman would forget to set his flag to warn of a stopped train ahead. Or a dispatcher in a far-off city would make a miscalculation and two trains would meet head-on round the bend. Or any of a dozen other human or equipment malfunctions might occur and boom—Jack's train would smash its way into railroad history. With single-track roads, collisions were bound to happen. More often than the public knew. But railroad men like Jack knew. And it was clear to him his luck wasn't what it used to be.

The worst fear was that Rosella would find out about Lourdes or one of the other women who kept him company. He was afraid his wife would leave him. He was afraid she'd die in childbirth. Fear, he thought, ruined luck. Fear made you fold when you should hang in there.

He threw back another shot while Parsons raked over the coins, the silver pieces clinking merrily as if they mocked Jack. He shoved away from the table and staggered through the door into the street. The moon was nearly full, and North Franklin Peak towered above the city to the West. Now he had to explain to Lourdes why he couldn't buy her the hat. Worse yet, how was he going to explain lost wages to a pregnant wife? A voice called out, and he turned, his eyes trying to adjust to the dark. He couldn't make out who it was. By the time Jack saw the face, it was too late.

Lourdes's brother Hernando crashed a fist into Jack's jaw. "So you don't got any money?"

Another brother—Jack couldn't remember his name—pinned Jack's arms behind his back while Hernando searched Jack's pockets.

"Hey, Hernando, what the hell?"

"You stick it to one of my women, you pay, you got it?"

One of his women? "Wait just a doggone minute—Lourdes said—aren't you her brother?"

Hernando laughed. To the beefy fellow restraining Jack's hands, he said, "He thinks I'm her brother." He laughed again. "Her brother, yeah, sure, we're all brothers, all us Mexicans look alike."

Two more hits: one to the gut, one to the side of the head. "You think I'd let my sister sell herself to a gringo—is that what you think?"

The next blow plowed Jack's chin skyward and that was it. All he could remember.

When he came to, he smelled vomit. His own. And something else—hay, manure, musk? A swaying sensation and sound of metal scraping told him he was in an empty freight car. One used to transport animals, he surmised. He lay still a few more moments, and then crawled to the half-opened door. Slightly to the east towered North Franklin Peak. He was headed out of El Paso, thank God. He hated that city. He would telegraph the copper refinery to go ahead with the spur as planned. Local yokels could finalize details like exact elevations as they built the track. Jack's plans provided a good start. He would have left in a few days anyway.

At the next station he cleaned up as best he could in the restroom. He assessed the damage in the mirror. One eye badly swollen. Jaw beginning to purple. No money. He couldn't go home, not like this. The solution was to lay up in Tucson for a few weeks. He knew a woman there who might take him in. This was the last time. He was giving up loose women and poker for good. Soon as he scraped up a respectable sum of money, he would head on home.

NOVEMBER 1904

A THICK MIST HUNG in the air, not quite rain, the sort of evening when chill seeped into your bones, yet Jack lingered outside the boarding house, reluctant to face his wife. He knew from Mr. Whiting she had called the railroad office in El Paso and was told they didn't know where he was. For days now, he'd chewed around several fabrications and was still unsure of their relative merits. The trouble with a lie is you never knew which detail was going to trip you up. What exactly had the office manager said to her? Had anyone seen him in Tucson who might have reported his whereabouts to her? Unlikely. And she was sure to have called the hotel he usually stayed at, so she may expect an explanation of where he stayed these past two weeks. At least he'd made back some of what he'd lost at the poker table.

He shivered—not only from the damp cold—and entered the boarding house as quietly as possible. He would rather not encounter Nellie Priester if he could help it. Censure too often showed plainly when she directed her gaze on him. He expected she'd heard gossip concerning his less savory activities, but as far as he could tell, she hadn't repeated it to Rosella. That old woman ran her mouth all day long, her and her uppity friends.

He hung his wet coat and hat on the rack near the entrance and mounted the creaky staircase. When he reached the second floor, Nellie's bedroom door cracked open long enough for her to scowl and shake her head, before she ducked back inside.

Throwing open the door to their sitting room, he declared in a hearty voice, "There's my girl!"

Rosella set her needlework aside and clumsily rose from the chair, leaning backward slightly to balance the weight of her abdomen, expecting again, against Nellie's advice, the old busybody.

"Where on earth have you been?" she demanded. "I've been worried sick about you."

Thankfully, she spoke in a heated whisper so her voice wouldn't carry through the bedroom wall to the old biddy's ears.

Jack tried to stroke Rosella's cheek with the back of his fingers, but she jerked away. "Honey, you know I have to work."

"If you think you can waltz in here and 'honey' me a few times and make everything okay, you have another think coming. I telephoned the railroad office in El Paso and they said you'd left over a week ago."

Jack paced across the room in bear-like strides that Nellie could surely hear. "What a mix-up! Somebody's going to get a royal chewing out for this mistake, I can promise you that. I was out working on a site. They knew how to reach me. Wait until I get hold of that fool in the office."

The doubt on her face as she sank back into her chair made him flush with guilt. He wasn't sure she'd forgiven him for not being by her side when she lost that first baby. Jack had to come through for his wife this time.

Rosella's arms were crossed, never a good sign. "You don't know what I've been through. I imagined all sorts of terrible things. That you were kidnapped by Indians or shot by bandits or robbed and beaten by thieves and left in an alley to die. There's no reason you couldn't have telephoned or sent word. You have obligations now."

"It's not easy to get to a phone out at a work site."

She shot him a warning look: *Not good enough.*

"I'll do better from now on. I'll find a way." He crossed the room and knelt beside her. One side of her face was lit by the glow of the lamp; the other, shadowed. He placed a hand on the sleeve of her dress, a silent entreaty. "I'm here now. I'll stay until the baby's born—and I'll ask to stay in the area for a while after."

He leaned closer, intending to kiss her if she was amenable. At first he sensed a stone in her heart, but eventually she softened.

One knee still on the floor, he straightened his back leg to move closer. "Rosella," he whispered into her hair. Her name sounded like a poem. Or a prayer. He did love her, he did. He cradled her head between his hands and traced fingers around the backs of her ears.

With half-gasp, half-giggle, she moved his hand to her belly. "Feel that? The baby's kicking." She smiled, teasing. "I think he's jealous of sharing attention with you."

"He?"

"I think it's a boy."

The kicking spree was quite vigorous. "What's that little rascal doing in there?" Jack asked. "Square dancing?"

"I think he forgot to take off his spurs."

Jack relaxed. Everything was going to be okay. She would forgive him. She had to. With each little flutter kick, he felt more fused to her than ever.

TRUE TO HIS WORD, Jack asked Mr. Whiting to stay in San Francisco for a while after the baby was born. Not only that, the boss gave him a raise and more responsibility.

Benjamin Roosevelt Joyner was wrinkled and red, and if you asked Jack, rather ugly, but when he discreetly asked Nellie about the baby's condition, she pronounced Benjamin perfect.

"All babies arrive a little disgruntled. Give him a week, you'll see."

Nellie was right. Benjamin's skin became smooth and white as a hard-boiled egg—bald as an egg, too, Jack thought. The baby's face lost that squeezed look it had on the day of his arrival. Jack's only complaint was that the child woke up in the middle of the night expecting to be fed. Rosella only laughed at him when he commented on the oddness of the hour.

"You really are ignorant about babies, aren't you?" she said. "Didn't you have any brothers or sisters?"

Jack's face hardened. "No."

He didn't have family except for his aunt. None he wanted to think about, anyway. His mother was mean-spirited, a first-class nag. His father, a coal miner, up and walked away one night from the supper table in Ashley, Pennsylvania. Never said he was going, never said he wasn't coming back. Left Jack's mother with six kids to raise. Jack had already been working two years at the Huber Coal Breaker, where they busted up anthracite into smaller transportable chunks. But with his father gone, the family needed a bigger paycheck than Huber provided. So at thirteen, Jack descended into the belly of the earth, down into the Baltimore Number 14. From the beginning, he hated the stale quality of air underground, the narrowness of the shafts. Then one day when he was fifteen, an explosion rocked their house. He knew immediately it was the mine and took off running, along with everyone else in Ashley. He got to the entrance in time to watch his friend Frank stagger out, his head blood-encrusted, face scratched and sooty.

"Jack, it's something terrible inside. A great rush of air blew out my light. Right after that I heard someone calling out further on the gangway that the lower split was caving. I hitched the mules and tried to get them along, but they wouldn't move. Not for nothing. Not in the dark, so I went on myself up the gangway. Behind me I heard the roof chipping and cracking. Other men were running, too, but all the lights were out and I couldn't see a thing. There's men in there, Jack. My dad, my dad's in there."

Jack stood ready with the other volunteers to go after survivors, though that dark tomb was the last place on earth he wanted to enter. But he would. The men in there would have done it for him. He watched while they drilled into the caved-in areas. He felt lucky when they chose five others to go in. They carried three out, their faces charred, unrecognizable. For weeks the memory of their groans roused him from sleep.

The mine explosions had caused the boards on one side of the Joyners' house to tumble loose. Jack and the next two oldest boys spent the following week doing their best to fortify, to rebuild.

The morning after they finished the repairs, his mother stirred up a pot of oatmeal, complaining about there never being enough money. Jack, who'd gotten maybe two hours sleep undisturbed by the ghosts of those entombed men, dropped his head against his folded arms on the kitchen table.

"You boys is just like your father. Lazy. You should be out looking for another job. Heard they was hiring over at Sugar Notch."

Jack's heart hardened like a lump of anthracite. The next day, like his father before him, he hopped a train and never looked back. He didn't want to know if his brothers went down into the Sugar Notch mines. Didn't want to know if they were charred or crushed or were buried alive. They were fools if they descended into that hell.

The strangest piece of luck befell him when Collis P. Huntington himself, the railroad magnate, was on Jack's getaway train. Huntington saw he was hungry and bought him a meal. Took a shine to him, one of the few men who ever did. Introduced him to Mr. Whiting, who taught him everything there was to know about trains and tracks. Never having to climb down into the black bowels of the earth again was motivation enough for Jack to learn fast and work hard.

The only relative he allowed himself to care about was Aunt Elizabeth. He had spent several summers with her in Clarksburg, West Virginia. Every time he smelled cinnamon he remembered the oatmeal cookies she baked. Oatmeal was for cookies. Not the sticky old mush his mother served. Breakfast at Aunt Elizabeth's was eggs, bacon, toast, and milk. A happy soul, her laugh pealed out like the church bells at noon, deep and sonorous. He had Elizabeth to thank for showing him a life outside the mines was possible. It had led to this new version of himself: husband and father.

During those first weeks after the baby was born a glow surrounded Rosella. For the first time, Jack understood why the Madonna always was painted with a golden aura. Motherhood was—or should be—a sacred thing. Jack couldn't remember his own mother showing any joy when his brothers and sisters arrived. Instead, a general weariness hung over her: another mouth to feed, another bottom to clean, another nose to wipe. Occasionally, she raged against them all, as if they were to blame for their own births, as if they were holding her back from the life she would have claimed if not for them.

Watching Rosella exposed Jack to something new. He loved to see his wife cuddling and fussing over the baby as she sat on the loveseat by the window, her hair glinting with golden highlights in the sun. He would become the good husband she deserved. This home, this family, *his* family, was the happiness and respectability he'd been searching for ever since he left Pennsylvania.

One morning when the baby was a month old, Rosella laid the baby on the dresser to change his diaper. "Oh, nasty—look at this."

Jack clasped both hands on her shoulders and leaned his head to one side to see. Benjamin's beautiful egg-white skin was peppered with a rash. They trooped downstairs to consult the expert. Nellie knew quite a bit about childhood ills. Sadly, she had lost her own two children to influenza.

"Baking soda mixed with a little water."

Rosella made soda pastes and applied them every few hours. Ben wailed. Unable to comfort him, Rosella cried. Jack didn't know what else to do, so he paced.

By the next morning when they diapered Ben, the red spots had grown into ugly sores and spread beyond the diapered area. Nellie frowned. "Doesn't really look like diaper rash."

Jack blanched when he saw the blistered skin. It reminded him of the sores that had peppered his own thighs, the sores Lourdes had dismissed as bed bug bites. Was Leroy Whiting wrong about virgins? Was this another sign his luck had run out?

Nellie suggested trying honey.

Rosella brightened. "Yes, I remember my mother using it for many things. Coughs as well as cuts." She smoothed the amber stickiness over the sores and placed two layers of clean white cloth over the mess to spare the baby's embroidered infant gowns.

Still the sores persisted. Jack was disgusted by all the herbs and concoctions. "Let's call in a doctor."

Nellie sniffed. "Quickest way I know of to lose six dollars and maybe your life, too. I don't know what your doctors were like back East, Mr. Joyner, but I'd sooner throw myself under a cable car's wheels than trust the likes of the quacks we have out here. If Val hadn't gone off to Johns Hopkins for training, I'd ask him. He's almost a doctor now and the only one I'd trust. Let's try tea leaves."

Miraculously the spots began to fade. Rosella and Nellie were ecstatic, congratulating themselves for thinking of tea leaves.

Jack? He was just relieved his luck hadn't run out.

HE TOOK THE STACK OF CLEAN BABY CLOTHES from his wife and set them on top of the dressing table. "Let's ride out to the Bay this morning. Walk along the beach. Just the two of us, Rosella. You can take your sketchbook."

"Sounds lovely, but the baby will wake up soon and need feeding."

Rosella retrieved the clothes and tucked them one by one into the chest of drawers. Diapers in the second drawer, gowns in the third, crocheted caps and sweaters and odds and ends in the bottom. His wife reserved the top drawer for special keepsakes. A baptismal gown. A silver-plated rattle. A stuffed bunny from Rosella's brother Timmy. It was a toy her mother had made for him when he was a baby. Rosella had cried when she opened the package. Jack had been at a loss to understand her tears, at a loss to comfort what he couldn't understand.

Nellie had tsk-tsked and clasped Rosella in her arms and rocked her, patting her back as if the mother of his child was a baby herself. "When a woman has a baby, 'tis only natural-like she wants her own mother nearby. Course Ro misses her mum, course she does. You can see that, can't you Mr. Joyner?"

No, he couldn't. He didn't want his mother nearby. Nor his father. And Rosella had been so ready to leave home, to run away with him, he couldn't understand her desire to go back now. She had taken to nagging him about getting train tickets to West Virginia, the three of them going for a visit. He couldn't go taking time off work on a whim like that, and he sure as hell wasn't going to let her and the baby go across the country by themselves.

He couldn't understand the changes in Rosella either. Before the baby, she would have jumped at the chance to walk the beach with him, jumped at the chance to sketch. Now she turned him down for a shopping expedition for new gowns. She had no interest in going to the Grand Opera House or Delmonico's for oysters and champagne, or to soak in the salt waters of the Sutro Baths, even though they could now indulge in a few of the luxuries afforded to the best people of the city. Every waking moment was about the baby. Feeding the baby. Burping the baby. Wiping the baby's bottom. Keeping the baby in clean clothes. She wouldn't hear of having a wet nurse. In what little spare time she squeezed out of the day, she sketched the baby from every angle, awake or asleep. Jack loved the baby, too, but he couldn't help feeling Rosella was shutting him out of her life, the way she cocooned herself and the baby into a shawl to feed him, the way she pushed Jack's hands away.

"Too soon. I can't risk having a second child so soon."

Too soon. Always too soon. Yet the baby was four months old. Jack suspected that old busybody Nellie was responsible for Rosella's reluctance. Before the baby, his wife had been eager enough for his hands. The old crone probably was, no doubt, filling Rosella full of tales about the wife's duty to control her husband's appetites. Jack had thought Rosella smarter than that, thought her different from other married women.

When the baby was five months old, Jack's boss told him it was time to get back out on the road, designing spurs for the many business concerns sprouting up across the West. Whiting said Jack's talents were wasted behind a desk. Jack thought he might as well go back on the road. He wasn't needed at home. The morning Jack was to leave, he leaned over to kiss Benjamin. The baby grabbed Jack's mustache and gave it a good yank. He must have thought it was quite funny because his round little face lit up with a huge smile, a smile that seemed to have extra shine because his chin dripped with drool. All the while Benjamin warbled animal noises. He was trying to tell Jack something, but what? Jack wished he knew. He kissed Rosella goodbye, picked up his suitcase, and would have headed out the door that instant, but he passed by Rosella's sketchbook. She was occupied, her back to him, while she changed Benjamin's diaper. Jack set down the suitcase and fanned through the sketches until he came to one that captured the earnestness of that drooly smile. He slipped it out of the sketchbook and tucked it into his suitcase. He left without looking back.

On the road, it was all too easy to resume his former habits. The gambling. The women. He was no damn good at celibacy. Hell, he was just no damn good, and he'd be the first to admit it. But these women—they didn't mean anything, they didn't mean he didn't love his family. At the oddest moments—as he was unlacing a woman's corset, as he was eating eggs the next morning—he would think of Rosella, remember her sitting by the window, the light shining in her hair, her mouth pursed in concentration as she tried to capture the expression on Benjamin's face with her pencils. He hardened himself against such softness. The worst moments came when he would remember the baby's intense efforts to talk to him. What was it Benjamin wanted so to convey with the gurgles and wild waving of his fat little fists? Only when Jack was alone and stinking drunk would he take out the sketch of the baby he'd spirited away. That little piece of paper always blew a hole in him as wide as a ton of dynamite packed into the side of a mountain.

Yet the next night, drunk and lonely again, he'd find himself sending a half-smile toward the prettiest woman in the saloon. One night he was back in El Paso and it was Lourdes.

"Where's your pimp?" he asked.

After that, she behaved like a bitch, but he bought her a drink anyway, and then another.

She pushed her chair away from the table. "I'm sick of this place."

He looked around the room, took in the dim lanterns, the line of smelly cowhands bellied up to the bar, the sticky floor. Thought of the barren land outside the city, far as the eye could see, thought of the midday heat, the way the sun could give you lizard-skin in only a few days time.

"Never been my favorite place either. Now, San Francisco is something to behold. Never too hot, never too cold. It's a city with class. There's an opera and the restaurants treat you like a king."

She tilted her head back and slung the shot glass at her lips. She arched one shoulder like a cat. "I don't believe you."

Jack felt his blood warming, the effect of whiskey and Lourdes's sensuality. "Believe me or not. There's this one hotel that has a courtyard surrounded by dozens of arched windows and lined with palms. The hotel restaurant serves you champagne and oysters on white linen table cloths. If that's not treating you like a king, I don't know what is."

"What's the name of this restaurant, King Jack?"

"The Palace."

"You will take me there."

He realized too late she'd manipulated him into a corner. "Sure, someday we'll go."

"Not someday. Now."

Drat. Why had he shot off his big mouth? He should have known better. Lourdes harbored illusions that it was possible for her to scale social barriers. As if a pretty dress or a hat with a stuffed bird would make her something more than a saloon girl. "That's not such a good idea, Lourdes. You are so beautiful I fear someone will steal you away from me."

She pushed away from the table. "Either you take me or I'm leaving you." When he hesitated, she added, "For good."

"Sure, okay. When I finish this job, we'll take off for San Francisco, you and me."

Her wanting to visit the coast wasn't a great idea, but it wasn't that bad, either. On the first floor of popular establishments like the Palace, husbands dined with their wives. On the second floor, hoteliers accommodated more intimate arrangements. There, in private dining rooms, Jack could offer a woman like Lourdes a taste of the life of the rich. She could eat the same oysters, drink the same champagne, sit at the same elegantly arrayed tables as the elite set. She just couldn't do it in their company.

Jack made a bet on a half-breed he'd met when he was overseeing the laying of track on a new southern spur. Best man Jack had ever seen on a horse. Jack didn't know anything about the two horses being raced, but he knew the half-breed. If he was riding the brown stallion, it was a sure thing. He put all the money he could muster on the half-breed and won a considerable sum and a godforsaken piece of desert. He hated the land around El Paso, and he promptly deeded the plot to Hernando. Jack didn't quite think of it as payment for taking Lourdes. More like an insurance policy that Hernando wouldn't feel obligated to bust Jack's head next time he rode into town. He nodded at Jack with eyes black and hard as obsidian, and then strode off and it was done.

Clouds formed as Jack and Lourdes boarded the train to leave El Paso. The brakes hissed and the familiar clack of the wheels began. It was Lourdes's first train ride and she couldn't stop smiling. The sky appeared to be boiling with dark clouds as they passed Thunderbird Mountain. Jack could barely make out the red clay formation that gave the mountain its name.

A streak of lightning split the sky, so close it seemed as if it stretched from the mountain right to the passenger car they were sitting in. Unfazed, Lourdes babbled about how she couldn't believe she was actually going to San Francisco, she was actually going to drink champagne.

Jack hardly heard her. It almost never rained in El Paso, but he was remembering an Indian legend about the mountain. That half-breed had shared the story over a poker game. Said a big bird lived in the mountain. When it flapped its wings it thundered, and lightning flashed from its beak. Only happened when the Great Spirit was really displeased. When you'd really pissed him off.

Total nonsense. Still, Jack felt uneasy until he rode past the storm. Had he really just bought a woman?

JACK LEANED BACK in his chair and lit the cigar Mr. Whiting offered him. Smoke hung thick inside the club, covering everything with a slight haze.

Thick white eyebrows that angled toward his nose dominated Mr. Whiting's face, especially when he waggled them, which he did now. "That li'l Mexican girl I saw you with last night's a looker, Jack."

Jack frowned. Whiting lost all discretion when drunk. In a city this large, you'd think you could keep a secret. What were the odds he'd run into his boss only a month after Lourdes's arrival? Jack took his last card. "Raise you two dollars."

Pullen and Scholtz made their final bets.

Whiting downed a shot of whiskey. "She looks like she has expensive tastes."

"You gonna play?"

Whiting's forehead wrinkled, and his eyebrows connected over his nose. "Yeah, sure, what'sa hurry?"

The old man lost the hand, and Jack swept up his winnings. Pullen and Scholtz called it a night. It was after 2 a.m. Jack should head home, too.

As he pushed back his chair, Whiting laid a hand bristling with white hairs on Jack's forearm. His speech was slurred. "Jus' 'tween you an' me, someone could make a lotta money. A lotta money. Southern Pacific's gonna gain control of Pacific Electric. You wait'n see, if it don't."

Jack's brain whipped into focus. His boss often met with the movers and the shakers, sometimes with Henry Huntington himself. Henry was the nephew of Collis, the man who'd turned Jack over to Whiting to begin with. Collis had died a few years back and Henry inherited a fortune. Whiting must have overheard some big plans.

The old man staggered as he tried to stand up. By morning, Jack figured Whiting wouldn't even remember he'd let that tidbit slip.

He slapped Whiting's back lightly and kept an arm around his shoulder. "Let's get you home, Sir, while we both can still walk."

They both laughed as if that were the funniest thing in the world.

In the morning, Jack took all his winnings, all the cash he could scrabble together and took out a small loan. He bought stock in Pacific Electric. A few months later, he sold it and the windfall left him a wealthy man. He consulted with several men about various banks in the city and was leaning toward Wells Fargo, but as he was strolling past North Beach, a handsome fellow had a group gathered around him, telling anyone who'd listen about his bank, the Bank of Little Italy—and he would do business with anyone, not just the wealthy. Even better, his bank would pay interest. Jack liked the sound of that, and stashed his coins with A. P. Giannini.

Immediately Jack set to work on plans for a substantial home to be built on Russian Hill. He would give Rosella and Ben the home they deserved. The home he deserved. When he finally held the architect's finished blueprints in his hands, he imagined his mother visiting him, her awestruck face, a coal miner's wife who'd never left her home county, never had two spare nickels to rub together. She couldn't accuse him of being lazy or no-account once he and his family lived in the fine house of his dreams.

Rosella

I OPENED A WINDOW that looked down onto the busy street, letting in not only air, but a cacophony of noise. Streetcars, horns, talk—everyone rushing about. I needed a breath of air after admitting to what I knew of Jack's sordid past.

"He bought a woman? That's disgusting, Mama." Solina's nose wrinkled.

"Yes, and she wasn't much more than a child when he first met her, younger than you. Thirteen and an orphan."

"You sound as if you feel sorry for her, a filthy whore."

"What choice did that little girl have? There but for the grace of God go you and I, never forget that, Solina." She had no idea how true my platitude was, how that poor girl's fate could have been her own. Part of me would always despise Lourdes, but my better angel would always cry for her, a little girl whose life was far from easy. I wondered what had become of her and her child.

"Still, Jack must have loved you both very much, Mama, to build you a fine house, even though he wasn't perfect."

"Far from perfect."

"Did you forgive him?"

"I tried."

My daughter's sour expression spoke volumes but she didn't let that stop her from voicing her opinions. "You can be rather hard on people."

Buying a teenage girl was a rather serious mistake. "What? If you mean because I stopped you from bobbing your hair—"

"Forget it."

Gladly. Girls her age could be so difficult. Ro supposed she deserved it after the fits she'd given her father. "Tidy yourself up now, so we aren't late for dinner at Nellie's. After we eat, I'll tell you what happened to Ben."

Nellie had been by my side through all of it. She would back up my story, and then Solina would understand. Let her write the whole truth in that diary of hers. The truth wasn't pretty, but it wasn't what the newspaper said either.

Forgive. Some things were unforgivable.

1905

UNAWARE OF MY PRESENCE—and what's more, totally naked— Ben laughed hysterically and careened off the wool rug and onto the oak floor, his feet spanking the planks as he flung raisin after raisin into the air. They rained down behind him, creating hazards Nellie tried her best to dodge. She'd already crushed two with her black-buttoned boots.

One skittered off the hem of her dark rose gown. "Stop that, you little scamp." She bent over to grab Ben, but he twisted away, giggling breathlessly. It was good to see him healthy and energetic for a change.

Head cocked to one side, I stood with arms akimbo. "So, this is what you mean by 'He's no trouble'?"

Nellie straightened up. "My goodness, you gave me quite a start. I didn't expect you back this early."

"Mrs. Underwood wanted to take Lydia and her cousin shopping this afternoon, so we cut our lesson short."

"Mama, mama, up." Ben ran toward me, arms stretching upwards, a supplication for me to pick him up.

"Not until you pick up those raisins. Go on, now. Be a good boy."

Ben looked sorrowful, as though his nearly two-year-old heart would break, but when he saw I was not going to acquiesce, he began to retrieve the raisins.

I smiled, shaking my head. "And why, may I ask, was he eating raisins in his birthday suit?"

Nellie adjusted her gown, which had gone somewhat off-kilter during the chase. "Our boy was a tad rambunctious this morning. I thought I could get him dressed more easily if he had something to nibble on, something to keep his hands occupied."

A *tad* rambunctious, indeed. But he felt poorly so often I welcomed any display of boyish energy.

I had missed a couple of monthlies and hoped Ben might soon have a brother or sister. Ever since Jack had made some money in the market, he seemed obsessed with building a mansion.

He tried to explain. "Don't you see? We'll have the stability of that investment, security for our family, something to pass down to Ben when he grows up."

I wanted a home, too, someday, but I didn't feel the same urgency that propelled Jack into a flurry of meetings with builders and real estate men. If that's where he really was. Some meetings lasted rather late into the night. During his absences, I sat in the parlor where Nellie plied her needle and Val read his medical books or played his cello. He was a doctor now, but continued to study and often used Nellie's kitchen to distill unusual concoctions he believed might effect cures of one illness or another.

This afternoon, I had an appointment to have Ben's photograph taken by a photographer Val recommended. An indulgence, since I'd sketched my son over and over and photographed him incessantly with the new Brownie camera.

Ben deposited the raisins in my outstretched hand. I discarded them and picked him up. "Time to get dressed, Mister Benjamin."

I pulled a white Buster Brown tunic over his head and tied a black silk scarf around the neck, smoothing down the wide collar. Short knickers, white socks, and black strap shoes finished his outfit.

Nellie adjusted the bow. "Handsome as a little prince, he is."

Before we left, I grabbed Teddy's bear. While not a favorite with Ben, it was something familiar he could hold if he suddenly took shy.

We caught the next cable car as it passed by the house and headed for the business district. It was a mild March day warmed by a golden sun. I was glad to see the early morning fog had lifted. As we got underway, Ben studied the passing cable cars, trains, carriages, and automobiles. Anything with wheels or engines fascinated him.

The photographer's studio was on the fourth floor of a brick building in the heart of the business district. A rather barren room, with two staging areas. First, Mr. Brown played a game of hide and seek with Ben. I couldn't imagine how the man expected to get the boy to sit still after all that squealing—on both their parts.

Ben began coughing, putting an end to the chase.

"Is the boy ill?" Mr. Brown asked.

"No, he's perfectly fine," I said.

Nellie's lips pressed together but she said nothing to contradict me.

"Well, then," Mr. Brown put his hands on his hips in a woman-ish way, "Ben, are you ready to play another game?"

"Yeah."

The photographer's face was gravely serious, examining Ben as if to determine his worthiness. "The hardest game of all?"

Ben nodded, his face mirroring Mr. Brown's gravity.

"You have to sit very, very still on this bench and not move a muscle. The bear can sit beside you and it has to sit very still too. Neither of you can even blink or the biggest, baddest monster in the world will get you. Can you sit that still?"

Ben's eyes widened and he nodded.

A skeptic, I would believe it when I saw it.

But Ben and the bear sat still. Neither blinked when the photographer flashed his blinding light. And no big monster got Ben or the bear.

Not then.

FIVE DAYS AFTER BEN SAT for that photograph, he suffered a severe setback.

I dipped another cloth in cool water, wrung it out, and held it against his head. The amber light cast by the gas lamp beside the child's crib revealed his fevered skin and the sweat-soaked hair souring against his scalp. He twitched in his sleep.

Nellie, a wrapper loosely tied on over her nightclothes, ducked her head in the door. "Any better?"

I shook my head. "Thought you went to bed a long time ago."

"Can't sleep for worrying about our boy." She padded closer in her stocking feet, stopping just behind me, one hand coming to rest on my shoulder.

I was grateful to have someone to share my worry, but it should have been Jack. He should have been home hours ago. Just because San Francisco was known as the City That Never Sleeps didn't mean he had to work so hard personally to maintain its reputation. I'd told him this morning Ben was sick. He should be here.

"The rash is worse," I said.

"Might be measles. Mother love is the best cure of all."

Nellie was usually right, but what if this once she was wrong? "I wish Jack was here."

Nellie patted my shoulder. "Any idea where he was off to this evening? I could send someone out to fetch him."

Who knew where Jack was? Delmonico's. The Alcazar Theater. Marchand's. The Majestic. Before Ben's birth I had frequently gone out with him, much less so now. This evening Jack had the nerve to ask if I wanted to accompany him. As if I could leave Ben when he was sick.

A short while later, I heard the front door open and, with relief, thought surely it was Jack. It was not. I overheard Nellie rushing to greet Val, imploring him to attend to Ben, and then I heard the rapid fire tapping of his hard-soled shoes on the steps.

I moved aside to let Val examine my fevered child. "Thank goodness you are here. I am beside myself with worry."

Val cautiously examined Ben's blistered skin, frowning intently at the soles of my boy's feet. The exam lasted less than a minute. When Val looked up, the alarm in his eyes terrified me.

"I'm going to ask Dr. Kasbarian to take a look at him."

That Val would consult with the doctor who shared his practice told me he considered Ben's situation grave. I knew Val and Dr. Kasbarian frequently disagreed over treatments, even though the older doctor had been one of Val's early mentors and teachers.

A short while later, I crept down the stairs to freshen up the bowl of water I was using to cool Ben. I was careful to step on the outside of the wooden stairs as the center tended to creak, and I didn't want to wake Nellie if she'd finally fallen asleep.

As I reached the landing, I heard hushed voices. I recognized Val's voice.

"Dr. Kasbarian should be here soon. I want to consult on proper dosages for a child so young. I've sent a messenger for Jack, Nellie. The boy's case is serious. I saw Mr. Joyner earlier this evening at The Palace with that young woman he keeps company with. I told the messenger to check there first."

I anchored one palm against the flowered wallpaper, holding my breath. The bowl tipped and water sloshed onto my skirt.

Nellie's voice floated up the stairwell. "Thank you, Val. The child's burning up."

"Yes, his father should be here, just in case."

In case—? Surely Val didn't think—no, I would not allow myself to entertain such dreadful thoughts.

The front door made a sucking sound as it opened and closed. The stairs creaked as Nellie's heavy tread landed on them. A few more steps and she would reach the landing.

"I'm just on my way down for a cup of tea," I called softly, "and to fetch more cool water for Ben."

"Oh, you gave me a scare."

"Sorry. I was trying to be quiet so I wouldn't wake anyone."

Nellie turned and descended the stairs again. "Let me make the tea. Can't sleep anyway."

THE FIRST VAGUE HINT OF DAWN seeped through Ben's bedroom window, not like the sunny mornings I knew in West Virginia, but the pearl gray of a fog-obscured sky. I stood on the opposite side of the room, watching my husband with Ben. Would I ever look at him again without hearing Val's words: *that young woman he keeps company with*? I could never forgive Jack for consorting with his mistress while Ben suffered through convulsions. It should have been the boy's father, not Nellie and Val, who brought me ice to pack around my son to lower the fever.

Voices, muffled but carrying the distinct heat of anger, carried up the stairwell. I could make out bits and pieces. *She needs . . .* and a voice answering, *You can't . . . against the law.*

I was the "she" they were talking about, but what was against the law?

Finally, Nellie showed Dr. Kasbarian upstairs. She waited in the hall while Kasbarian examined my child. In late middle age, the doctor sported a full white beard and a belly that would make him a fine Santa Claus. Was his age a good thing—would experience provide more insight into Ben's illness than Val's more recent training? It was impossible to know, and Ben's life hung in the balance. *Dear God*, I prayed, *have mercy.*

Dr. Kasbarian pulled the damp sheet from Ben and began the examination. I pressed in on the other side of Jack to watch, though the room was so tiny that four adults seemed to displace all the air inside. Jack put his arm around me. I shuddered and shifted away from him. His arm had, no doubt, been around *that young woman* a short time ago. I banished Val's words from my mind. Ben was all that mattered. The doctor handled the child's foot with a damp cloth, frowning at the blisters on the soles. I could see from the look he exchanged with Val that they both felt the blisters were a dreadful sign. The doctor's eyes cut to Jack with—what? Distaste? Anger? I didn't know how to interpret his look.

"Mrs. Joyner, I'd like to be alone with the boy and his father for a few minutes. Dr. Martin will stay."

"But—" I protested.

"Please." He took my elbow and practically pushed me through the door, then reverting to gentlemanly behavior, held it open with a slight bow. He pulled it shut behind them, excluding Nellie and me from their conversation.

I waited, pacing nervously, certain now that Ben's illness must be something terrible. Jack's strangled cry pierced the wall and sliced my heart. Nellie gripped my shoulders.

I threw open the door and clutched the frame for fear I would collapse. "What's wrong with my baby?"

The doctor glanced at me, and then turned back toward my husband even though his remarks seemed meant for me. "It's serious. Possibly a tropical fever of some sort, a pox. Your husband tells me he travels near the border frequently. Perhaps he was exposed to an equatorial ague, which didn't affect him, but he might have brought the illness back with him. The child could have grown ill because his defenses are still undeveloped."

My knees were crumpling beneath me. I gripped the doorframe tighter. How I disliked this man, this bearer of devastating news, his dismissal of me as though I was of no consequence.

Nellie took charge. "What can you do?"

"I recommend continuing the treatments begun by Dr. Martin, the Cascara amarga, Echinacea, iris, and phytolacca. I have found the Cascara works sometimes by itself, but because of the involvement of his glands and throat, I recommend the additional medicines as a precaution. For conditions of the skin, I use this ointment. Rub it all over the boy." He handed a jar to Nellie. "Even with these treatments, you should know the situation is grave."

I bent at the waist and wailed. Jack nudged the doctor aside and wrapped his arms around me. "I'm sorry, I'm so, so sorry, darling."

Grief squeezed everything else but Ben from the world.

"The rest of the medicine," Nellie said. "Let's have it. How much and how often?" She took careful note of the doctor's directions as he mixed solutions.

He handed her a cobalt blue bottle. "In addition to the other treatments, half a dram of the potassium iodide to three ounces of water, a teaspoon three times a day for a week. As a precaution, I'm going to recommend that the parents take a double dose of the iodide for two weeks. These illnesses can sometimes travel through a family."

"What about me?" Nellie asked.

The doctor looked sharply at her. "Have you handled the boy since the rash broke out?"

"No. His mother has insisted on taking care of him herself."

The doctor handed Nellie two more vials and packed up his bag. "No need then. I have another patient to see this morning, but I'll be back in a few hours to see how he's doing."

He took me aside and gave me some tablets and a medicinal douche. I'd never heard of the latter but immediately suspected this had something to do with intimate relations with my husband. I blushed as the doctor explained how to use it, grateful no one else could overhear such personal instructions. I was seething—I knew there was more they weren't telling me.

I sat at Ben's side, bathing his forehead with cool cloths, maintaining my vigil all day, backing away only when Val visited to examine Ben. I sat by the crib into the next night. Jack stayed with me, fetching ice and fresh water, bringing soup I couldn't eat, preparing the medicinal doses. Sometime near dawn of the third day I nodded off. When I awoke, Ben's hand was cold and Jack's face heavy with the weight of the world's sorrows.

MAY 1920

FOR PRIVACY, WE WERE CLUSTERED in Nellie's sitting room rather than the communal parlor in the boarding house. I couldn't help noticing this sitting room was considerably larger than the one in her old home, the home that had burned down, but she had painted the walls the same shade of lemon, and suddenly I felt the present collapse and I was sitting once again in Ben's nursery, watching over him as he slept, watching him as he woke and called, "Up, Mama, Up." I closed my eyes and in my mind my arms reached for him. My fingers almost touched him . . . almost . . .

Solina's sobs brought me back to the present. Her head lay on Nellie's shoulder. I should be the one comforting her, but I was depleted of all energy by this journey into the past. *Forgive.* Now Solina would understand some sins were past forgiveness, even when unintentional. After Ben's death, Jack and Nellie put the child's things in storage or gave them away. I never knew what happened to most of them. I was too distraught, and what little thought I was capable of was fogged by the medications I was taking. Jack stayed in Ben's little room when he was home. He knew better than to come near me again.

Solina's handkerchief, already quite sodden, rose once more to her dark lashes. "All this time I didn't know I had another brother, Mama. You should have told me."

"I have tried to put those days with all their anguish behind me."

A frown creased Nellie's face. "Anguish indeed. That poor baby suffered every day of his life." Perhaps she noticed the distress her observation caused me, for she changed the subject. "Tell me more about your brothers, Solina."

My daughter made a face. "They are as different as night and day. Michael makes a complete pest of himself all the time and Thomas is so shy he barely speaks."

"I dare say they will grow out of these phases before long." I feared for Thomas. His parents had been badly injured in an accident when their horse panicked and their wagon had tumbled down a steep hill, overturning on top of them. Neither survived their injuries, despite Val's best efforts to save them. Thomas was thrown clear and suffered only a few scratches. Physically. Emotionally, he was traumatized. He had no other family, so we took him into ours. He was polite and well behaved but distant. All I knew to offer him was a consistent routine so he might feel secure again.

"Maybe Thomas will grow up, but Michael will forever be a nuisance," Solina declared.

I shook my head. "You can see why I left the boys home with Val. I would have lost my mind locked in a small train compartment with all the squabbling."

Screeching brakes and clanging bells drifted in from the street outside. There was always some sort of commotion going on here in the city. I missed the relative quiet of our small town. I wouldn't want to live here again, even though I missed Nellie.

Solina's eyes seemed to focus inward as if something had just occurred to her. Her head bobbed off Nellie's shoulder. "What's a medicinal douche?"

I swallowed and opened my mouth to respond, but Nellie came to my rescue. She explained its purpose, but we both knew there was still so much Solina didn't grasp. I hadn't understood the cause of Ben's death myself right away. I had been barely older than my daughter and not even doctors understood much about such diseases back then. I was treated with a mercury compound, Val later told me. Today, he said, doctors used an arsenic compound that was more effective and less toxic. All I knew was the pills and douche made me horribly ill.

Nellie took over. "Solina, I could hear Jack pacing the length of his room—he was staying in Ben's old room— over and over he paced on the floor above the kitchen. I could tell he kept stopping by the window, so I went over to the parlor and drew aside the curtain. A woman lingered outside, and I knew at once it was Jack's mistress. Surely she knew the meaning of the black wreath on the front door. I remember thinking if she had any decency, she would have left.

"Your papa decided if Jack Joyner wasn't going to do anything about her lurking about, he would. He ran down from the third floor so fast I swear his shoes sounded like a machine gun—at least what I imagine one would sound like. I've never actually heard one.

"Anyway, I heard the front door slam and next thing I knew, our Val had seized the hussy by her arms and was shaking her. I watched him yelling and thought he accused her of having no shame, but I couldn't really make out his words. But then he must have turned his face toward the house because I could hear what he said next plain as day. 'They lost their son. For the love of God, go away and leave them in peace,' he said that just as plain as day. She pulled away from him, and Val let her go. Later he confessed he apologized to her for his lapse of manners. He hadn't realized he was hurting her."

That was Val. Always chivalrous, but I sincerely doubted Nellie could hear Val speaking outside the house. She did like to embellish her stories. I chimed in, "Lourdes told him she had the right to be wherever she wished. Some nerve."

"Outrageous," Nellie agreed. "I was still watching from the parlor window. As soon as I saw the way her arms clasped over her belly, I realized she was swollen with child. I knew it would crush Ro if she learned this, so I would not be the one to tell her. In the months after Ben had died, she hadn't noticed anything. She got out of bed, ate very little of what was put in front of her, and went back to bed. Nothing could cheer her up. Losing two that close together is enough to knock any woman down," Nellie said.

Actually it was three. With Val's help, I had aborted the child I was carrying in my womb when Ben died. Val had been certain that even if the mercury treatment cured me, it would harm my unborn child irreparably. I vowed I would never give birth again unless I was pronounced cured. Fortunately, the time came when I carried no trace of disease.

I didn't care for this picture of myself as poor, pitiful victim. That was not who I wanted to be to my daughter and I didn't want her writing that in her diary. I hurried the story along. "After Ben's death, I vowed I would do all in my power to prevent any other baby from suffering as Ben had."

Solina's head swiveled in confusion from one of us to the other. "Why would another baby—"

"Jack had syphilis, a serious disease he got because he wasn't faithful in our marriage. He passed the disease along to me, and it killed our babies."

"How horrible!" Solina drew back in the loveseat, one hand pressed to her mouth, her eyes wide and round.

Nellie nodded. "Dr. Kasbarian kept the truth from your mother about her illness and Ben's death. It was cowardly, but he was following the law."

"The Comstock laws were dead wrong. In fairness to Lourdes," I added, "you should know Jack wronged her too. She told your Papa that Jack knew her first, before he met me, and had promised her they would marry one day." One of many lies he'd told her, no doubt.

"How did you find out about the disease, Mama?"

"Overheard your papa chastising Jack."

"I was there," Nellie said. "Val is such a gentleman, he hesitated to speak in plain language in front of me but I pushed him. Told them I wasn't afraid to hear the word *syphilis* spoken aloud. Told Val and Jack if people were more open and honest, there'd be less disease around."

"Amen," I said. "Maybe, Solina, you can understand why I feel the need to march for women's rights."

"I never said—" Solina protested.

"Admit it. You were angry when I left you and your papa behind to go to the capital. You were ashamed when I got arrested."

Solina screwed up her face. "Was I supposed to be proud of having a jailbird for a mother?"

"Yes indeed," Nellie said. "I'm proud of your mother. It took great courage to stand up against such powerful men. She stands up—"

"We," I corrected her.

Nellie acknowledged the correction. "We stand up against ignorance that harms men as well as women. I suppose the *Examiner* called your mother a baby killer because she has spoken out in favor of family planning, the right for women to control our own bodies."

Yes, my stand on family planning was likely how the reporter derived that particular inflammatory statement. Who from those family planning gatherings fed information to the reporter? A traitor lurked in our midst.

Nellie continued, "I'm sure she's told you how we marched on the state Republican convention meeting in Oakland demanding the right to vote."

"She told me those men called you fifty thousand mice. Very rude of them. It's fine that women in California can vote for some things, but they can't vote for president yet."

"True," Nellie said. "We are still treated like second-class citizens."

I clasped Solina's hand. "That's why I became one of the Silent Sentinels, why I marched on Washington three years ago, so when you are old enough, you and every other woman in this country will have that right. We're almost there. Nearly every state has ratified now."

Solina squeezed my hand briefly. "I know. Papa told me. He told me how thankful he was that you only spent one night in jail."

"I would have stuck it out with my fellow Sentinels, but you took ill."

"Papa only said that so you'd pay the fine and come home, but he told me the truth: he feared your tuberculosis would return if you were ill treated. He says those women were beaten and tortured and you wouldn't have survived. Papa fibbed to save your life."

Even though I'd always suspected this manipulation, it still infuriated me. "It should have been my choice. My decision."

Nellie's chin lifted. "Your lungs *are* weak, Ro. Val did the right thing. Frankly, I'm surprised he let you make the journey out here."

Fiddlesticks. I was stronger than my family and Nellie believed. Why must there always be *Papa this, Papa that*? I supposed I should be glad Val was so close to Solina, but it stung when she gave more credence to his words than mine. Male superiority was so ingrained in our culture, how would we ever overcome it? Even Nellie—how could she agree that Val had a right to lie to me?

"So, back to that man, Jack," Solina said. "What happened when you found out?"

I sighed. "I overheard everything your papa and Jack said. I made Nellie explain what syphilis was. I had no idea such a disease existed. I realize now Jack never intended to hurt me or Ben. He honestly thought marrying a virgin would cure him of his disease."

Nellie shook her head. "Such foolishness."

"For a long time, I hated him." If I could have pulled myself out of the dark hole I'd fallen into, if I hadn't needed Nellie's consoling so badly, if the medicine hadn't made me so ill, I would have fled back to West Virginia immediately. After Ben's death, nothing could ever have been set right between us, but even I have to give Jack credit for trying.

Jack

No matter whom else Jack tried to blame, he knew who was at fault. Even God tried to warn him. He remembered how it had thundered when he left El Paso with Lourdes, how lightning split the sky.

Making it up to Rosella was the only way he knew how to live with his guilt. He put on his coat and straightened his tie. Streetside, he handed a nickel to the trolley conductor and rode to the business district. It had been months since he had carried that white casket to the grave. All this time gloom hung over Nellie's house. Rosella refused to leave the house. He didn't think the pills the doctor had prescribed were making her so ill that she couldn't leave her bed, just an excuse. In any case, they weren't affecting him so severely. It was time for her to get out and rejoin the world.

On Market Street, Jack disembarked in front of the Emporium. The domed glass ceiling gave the department store an almost religious air. Jack circulated through the various departments, amassing purchases. He bought gowns—dark rose, emerald, deep blue. When he presented them to his wife, she smiled weakly, thanked him, explained she would only be wearing black for at least a year, and turned her face away.

Another day he brought home an assortment of imported teas and chocolates. Another, six bouquets of assorted flowers.

Rosella needed a change of scenery. Once she moved out of this boarding house and into her own home, one without memories, he hoped she would rebound. The pallets of bricks dwindled each day and the façade of their new home neared completion. Only a couple of arches to go. She would eventually forgive him, wouldn't she? He never intended Mrs. Priester's to be a permanent residence. It had gone on far too long already. A man of Jack's wealth should have a home of his own. He showed Rosella drawings of the large parlor, the kitchen, the modern bathroom with the latest plumbing fixtures, wallpaper patterns selected by Nellie. Rosella slumped listlessly, staring out the window while he waxed enthusiastically about foundations and furnaces, bricks and shingles, windows and walls. At the mention of a garden, she perked up slightly but quickly fell into disinterest again, her face pale and pinched.

Nellie tried to point out the positives of the new house. "You'll be near the Underwoods on Russian Hill. Won't that be fine?"

Rosella smiled wanly. Jack thought she seemed fearful of leaving Nellie. He could find no trace of the adventuresome girl he'd married.

He bought two bicycles, thinking a ride in the fresh air would do her good. Nellie begged her to give it a try, but Rosella just looked angry, even at Nellie.

Jack's boss wasn't going to let him keep spending most of his time in San Francisco forever. Every day new industries cropped up in the West, and each wanted a spur connecting their site to the main rail lines. Jack was the company's best at engineering the spurs, a fact Leroy Whiting reminded him of daily, raising those bushy white brows. "Women lose children all the time. She has to move on, Jack."

Jack agreed. They both needed to move on—but how? Especially since she blamed him. Rightfully so, he acknowledged, but he hadn't meant to hurt anyone, least of all his wife and son.

Ignoring the masses of ladies flocking to the Bargain Basement of the Emporium, the next week Jack mounted the grand staircase, and with rising spirits, he ordered a set of crystal goblets. Soon the interior of their home would be complete. He'd walked on the red oak floors for the first time that very morning. Planning the furnishings would give Rosella something fresh to focus on. She would need to set her own table. He nearly purchased china, but decided he would bring her back to choose the plate pattern herself. They would start over.

Another day, in an attempt to cheer her up, he insisted they visit the Underwood home to see their furnishings, for decorating ideas. He had never been to their home and had been angry and shamed when he learned that his wife had been taking money from the Underwoods. As a lady's hobby, painting was fine, but anything more was unseemly. Still, he was willing to try anything that brought back the zest for life Rosella once possessed. Prior to their visit, Nellie would suggest to Mrs. Underwood that Rosella paint something for the family again, perhaps her portrait.

Not bothering to hide her lack of enthusiasm, Rosella agreed to go.

The elegance of the Underwoods' home was evident from the meticulously manicured gardens to the stunning Spanish colonial façade. All the furnishings were top quality, exactly what Jack had in mind for his own home. Everything about the Underwoods was what he'd been led to expect.

Everything but the electric elegance of Alexandra Underwood herself. She shimmered sensually in a way his wife had not since Ben's death. No, that wasn't true. Since his birth.

When his mustache brushed Alexandra's smooth hand in a brief kiss, the vibrations he felt flowing from her left him stunned.

OVER THE NEXT MONTH, JACK FOUND EXCUSES to return to the Underwoods, at first with Nellie and Rosella, later on his own. Nevertheless, he didn't quit trying to revive his wife. He brought home chocolates, flowers, a book on portrait painting. Still, Rosella refused to paint Alexandra's portrait.

On another visit to the Emporium, he passed a menagerie of animals—cats, exotic birds, dogs. He told the saleslady he was looking for anything that would encourage his wife to take an interest in the world. She held up a puppy with black and white fur and funny mashed face. "This little fellow is just what she needs, a Boston Terrier, America's dog," she said. "A puppy is just the thing to pull your wife back into the world. Give her something to take care of."

A puppy might be just the thing.

When the goblets were delivered, he unpacked one and twirled it about, admiring its sparkle. Rosella walked to the window and held the glass to the light.

"Why, this is Fostoria glass," she said. "It's made in West Virginia, you know. Moundsville." She looked happy, lost in fond memories.

Jack had forgotten about all the glass factories near Aunt Elizabeth's. He'd worked on spurs for the railway to several of them. He felt encouraged by her interest. "Our home will be finished soon. You'll need to order furnishings—maybe you can find more things made in West Virginia and it will remind you of growing up there."

She set the glass on the nearest table and sank back down onto the loveseat. "You do it."

"Nonsense," he said, sitting beside her. "I wouldn't have any idea how to properly furnish a home."

"Whatever you choose will be fine."

He rose from the loveseat and called for Nellie. She carried in a wide canvas bag and handed it to him. She was beaming, nodding and deepening that double chin, her eyes teary.

Jack played his last card.

He took the puppy from the bag and set him on Rosella's lap.

"His name's Prince and he's come to live with us."

Rosella stroked the short fur with a smile that lit up her eyes for the first time since Ben died. The smile collapsed. Her hands covered her face and she sobbed. "Take him away. A dog is no replacement for a child."

Of course not. Nothing was.

Rosella

I LET THE PUPPY CRY, HOPING NELLIE would come in and care for it, but either she was asleep or didn't like dogs. Half an hour of mournful whining grinded on my nerves and finally severed the last one. Didn't the dog know it was the middle of the night?

I slid out of bed, lit a candle, and padded barefoot across the floor to the puppy's box. Jack had a lot of nerve buying a puppy and taking off like that. Whoosh! Off to Oregon or Utah or somewhere. He'd told me his destination when he bid me goodbye, but I couldn't remember. I hadn't listened well enough and felt a pinch of regret. He was trying. Even through my fog of grief and anger and ill effects from the mercury treatment, I could acknowledge that.

The box smelled of urine and poo. "Prince. What kind of name is that for a smelly puppy?"

I pulled on a wrapper and slid into slippers before wadding up the newspapers that lined the bottom of the box. I carried the mess and the puppy in one hand and the candle in the other, making my way down the back staircase and into the kitchen. I disposed of the mess in the trash barrel just outside the back door. When I set the puppy down in the kitchen, he went right to the water bowl and slurped. He sniffed an empty bowl beside the water and licked the ceramic surface for any traces of leftover food. Jack must have left the bowls out for the puppy. The puppy sniffed the bowl again.

"Let me see what I can find." Rummaging through the ice box and cabinets, I rounded up bread scraps and leftover chicken. I minced them with a chef's knife.

While the animal ate, I lit a small lantern. When he finished eating, I carried him outside behind the house. A sickle-shaped moon hung low in the sky and the air smelled as if it were going to rain. I closed my eyes, longing for childhood nights when I'd chased fireflies in the creeping dusk and for the innocence of that child who lay in the field wondering how far away the moon was, how many stars peopled the heavens and was each one the shining soul of some person who had passed on—was one my mother? I looked up at the sky, the same sky, now and wondered if my babies were bright sparkles in that velvety darkness. I longed for them. I longed for Timmy, for green hills and pastures. I longed for Jack to come home, the Jack who had swept me away, not the one who'd betrayed me with another woman.

The puppy sniffed all around the foundation of the house before he finally tinkled in the dirt. Afterward he started sniffing again.

I picked him up. "Enough of that."

Back upstairs, I laid fresh newspaper in the box and set the puppy inside. I went back to bed, but the puppy mewled and scratched at the cardboard. I listened with annoyance for what seemed like a long while, but time had a way of feeling eternal in the middle of the night, as eternal as the moon and stars. I had no idea how much time really passed. Finally I pulled the puppy from the box and laid him on the bed beside me. He snuggled into my armpit and promptly fell asleep. Fantastic. How was I supposed to sleep with a rat-sized pup under my arm? If I rolled over I'd smother him. The little beast would force me to lie awake all night. Eyes squeezed shut, unable to block the furry burden from my mind, I lay there and thought up hateful names for him. Nuisance. Pest. Monster. Maybe the store would take him back. I would talk to a clerk in the morning. In the morning, I would—I would…

Something poked my cheek. I rolled over. Something wet sandpapered my ear. I squinted through eyelids still heavy with sleep. It was very early, perhaps six judging by the gentle fingers of yellow light creeping through the window. A damp spot bloomed on the sheet where the puppy had peed. "Ewww—nasty, you little cuss! Look what you've done now." Stripping the sheet from the bed, I flung it to the floor in disgust and settled back on the pillow. Immediately whiskers tickled my cheek. I pushed the pup away. "Stop being such a disagreeable pest."

The puppy climbed on my chest again, rear end raised, and he lunged toward my chin.

I put him down on the floor, fighting off tendrils of guilt. The little critter was probably lonely, finding himself in a strange place, surrounded by strange people, none of his own kind around. I knew how that felt. Although I'd polished my speech patterns and customs to match those of San Franciscan society, I was still an outsider and always would feel that way on the inside. I'd hoped children of my own would make me feel as if I belonged here. And for a while, Ben did, he nearly did. But Ben was gone. Jack was gone, and even when he wasn't, most of the time I wished him gone. His vile disease had killed my babies and the medication I was prescribed made me so violently ill I thought I might follow them to the grave. Yet I refused to complain. What was my suffering compared to Ben's?

That woman was expecting—the thought kept returning to me. Her hair, dark as midnight, swung thick and lush about her shoulders, I had seen that much from my window. I hated her—completely and totally—but what if her baby was born deformed? What if it suffered like Ben had? Did I hate her enough to let that happen? Had anyone told her about the syphilis—or had she been kept in ignorance like me?

I clamped my eyes closed and willed my breathing to slow into a normal sleep pattern, but my thoughts were too troubling, and the persistent thumps and grrrs from the floor became alarming. I cracked my eyes. Drat! The puppy was chewing the corner of Nellie's Persian rug.

I bolted from bed, blankets trailing to the floor behind me. "Can't you stay out of trouble for one minute?"

Since there was to be no peace, I dressed. I poured water into a basin and washed my face. Before I could begin the rest of my toilette, the puppy deposited a sticky brown clump on the carpet.

"Now look what you've done!" I cleaned up the mess as best I could and finished dressing while the puppy sniffed the perimeter of the sitting room. Dark fur clung to the bodice of my nightdress and several tufts already dotted the rug. For such a small creature, he managed to shed an awful lot. I pulled on an old black skirt and a dark shirtwaist I hadn't worn for ages. No sense in letting the puppy ruin good clothes on the way to the Emporium. The little monster was going back. I would demand a refund.

The puppy pulled one of my stockings from the wicker laundry basket and scurried with it under the loveseat. I knelt on all fours and tried to retrieve the sock, but the puppy tugged and backed further under the loveseat, shaking his head ferociously. I laughed out loud. "You actually think you can win this war, don't you?"

Nellie knocked and peeped in. "How did our little guest fare the night?"

"Monstrous. I hardly got any sleep at all. Look at the wee devil." I tried again to pull Jack's sock away, but the puppy clamped sharp little teeth even more firmly into the sock.

"You're a determined little cuss. Give it up." As the puppy fought with all his might, Nellie and I both laughed. Then for no reason I could fathom, he suddenly lost interest in the sock and smiled at me, tilting his head from side to side as if to say, "Aren't I cute?"

And hang it all, he was.

All young creatures were cute. And precious.

I had to make sure that woman, that horrible creature, Lourdes Garcia—I shuddered even thinking her name—I had to make sure she knew about the medicine that would save her baby. The hell with her, but that baby didn't deserve to suffer or die the way my Ben did. I didn't think Jack was man enough to tell her, so I would assume responsibility. But how would I find her? I had no idea where she lived, if she had family here, or who her employer might be. No doubt Jack knew all this, but I couldn't bear the humiliation of asking him.

I checked the street directory. No Garcias listed. But an advertisement in the directory gave me an idea. I would hire an attorney to track her down and deliver a letter discreetly. No one else ever needed to know the contents of that letter, and I could rest easier, knowing I had discharged my duty to that child. I took out a piece of stationery, but when I took up my pen, my hand trembled. I took a deep breath, thought of the blisters on Ben's feet, his dear, fevered face. I bit my lip and proceeded to compose a brief, pointed letter. I put on my finest hat and set out for Drown, Leicester, & Drown, Attorneys and Counselors at Law, the first suitable firm I found in the directory. If they couldn't handle the job, I'd move on to the next.

1905

SLOWLY, I FOUND A MEASURE OF PEACE AGAIN, especially when Nellie would fix up a picnic basket with ham sandwiches and apples, and Val would drive a wagon north of the city into the redwood forests. Mindy, who had recently lost her mother, often came along if she wasn't helping her father in the gallery. The four of us took long walks together, silent, each alone with his or her thoughts, listening to the ancient trees sing their hymns. Their towering trunks formed a cathedral that touched the sky. In the half-light filtering down through limbs that had spanned the ages, I glimpsed the edges of something eternal, and was absorbed into the essence of something greater than myself. If Ben's spirit was anywhere on this earth, I believed it must linger here like a fragrance in the refreshing air or float along a sunbeam, sacred and warm against my skin.

Then an extraordinary injustice occurred in Los Angeles that ignited my interest in suffrage all over again. The Central Library fired the head librarian of five years, Mary Jones, simply because she wasn't a man. A graduate of a library school, Mary Jones, by all reports, was pleasant and professional. And the man chosen to replace her, by all reports, was a drinker and philanderer, with no library training whatsoever.

Mindy came to tea at Nellie's, all aflutter with excitement. Aunt Susan—Susan B. Anthony herself—was coming to California to protest the firing. "We have to go and march in support of Mary Jones." Mindy's pitch careened upward, surely in a range to match the reach of the great soprano Lillian Nordica, whose recording Val had treated us to one evening. "Say you all will come, please, please, oh, say you will!"

How could anyone refuse such an impassioned plea? Val, always a supporter of women's rights, agreed to accompany us on the train. Jack was off in Arizona or somewhere—I made no attempt to keep abreast of his travels. We were married in name only.

It was a short ride down the coast, but our plans were rather hazy other than doing whatever we could to support the fired librarian.

Despite Mindy's prior acquaintance with Miss Anthony, we were not fortunate enough to meet with her personally on our visit to

Los Angeles. Nonetheless, we found ourselves surrounded by like-minded women, who were appalled by the city's harsh dismissal of Mary Jones. At first I wasn't sure how much credence to give to the scandalous tales about her replacement, this Charles Lummis character, but the reports added up. The marchers' tongues were wagging about his wild parties and dozens of adulterous affairs, the newspapers reported that he swore like a sailor and he had at least one illegitimate child. We did have the privilege of meeting Miss Jones and offering our allegiance to her cause. Little good it did. The city attorney declared she could be fired at will.

Nellie disagreed with the terminology. "At their merest whim, they should have said." She had heard rumors Miss Jones had turned away unseemly advances from a member of the library board and that was the real reason she was fired.

When we returned to San Francisco, we learned a telegram had arrived in our absence. Nellie delivered the envelope into my hands.

I turned it over and turned it over once more, transfixed, terrified. I took it with me to the sofa and settled onto its cushions, resting the envelope on my lap. I breathed in and out slowly, touched a strand of hair next to my cheek to see if it had come loose from the hair pins. It hadn't.

Having followed me into the parlor, Nellie angled toward me on the sofa. "Aren't you going to open it?"

As long as I didn't open it, I didn't have to know. Was I an aunt again? Or suddenly richer? Or bereaved?

"Shall I open it for you?" she asked.

"I can manage, thank you." I sighed, sure the telegram bore news I didn't care to learn. When I felt I couldn't put it off any longer, I slowly slid my finger under the yellow flap and withdrew the telegram. As the words sank in, I shuddered and a small cry escaped through the fingers I had instinctively pressed to my lips. The paper fluttered from my hands.

"He's dead!" I cried.

Nellie retrieved the missive and scanned it quickly. Tears shimmered in her eyes. "Oh, you poor dear girl. You must be devastated."

Appalled. Stunned. Horrified. I wouldn't have wished such a horrible death on anyone! I shuddered again, hoping, praying, that Jack had died from smoke inhalation rather than burning when the

Grand Star Hotel went up in flames.

I felt remorse that I hadn't been able to offer Jack the forgiveness he'd tried to win with all his gifts. Especially the puppy. I should have written to let him know how much I enjoyed having the little terrier around.

As sunlight slanted through the parlor windows, I remembered how, three years earlier, the sun shone behind Jack as he walked into my father's church that first morning, how he appeared like a savior, the answer to prayer. How he saved me from marriage to Gunner Beck.

But I couldn't help but remember this, too: the disease he brought into our home had killed my babies. When would I be able to stop blaming him for that? Maybe now that he was dead I could bury my bitterness along with his ashes.

I broke into sobs and bent at the waist until my forehead touched my knees, while dear Nellie held me and muttered comforting words.

Sometime later, I pulled myself upright and made an effort to tidy my face with a handkerchief.

"I know what you're going through." Nellie patted my back. "I didn't know how I would ever hold myself together after my husband died. At the time, I didn't know if I would ever stop crying over losing him."

Unlike Nellie, I wasn't even sure what I was crying for. Jack. Ben. Myself—the betrayed wife. All of us who might have occupied the house that Jack built.

As Nellie fixed me a cup of tea, I was thinking not of Jack, exactly, but of my father. Of this parable from the book of Matthew that he told about a fool who built a house upon the sand and the rain came down, the streams rose, and the winds blew and beat against that house, and it fell with a great crash. And I could hear my father speaking as clearly as if he were in the room: *Only a fool would marry a railroad man. Might as well build your house upon the sand.*

MAY 1920

DUSKY LIGHT FILTERED through the sitting room window, dulling the color of the walls until they appeared less yellow than beige. "My goodness, look at the time," I said. "It's nearly dark outside. We had best return to our rooms, Solina."

Nellie and I stood, but Solina, persistent creature that she was, remained seated. "Mama, I don't understand. If Jack died, why is that reporter calling you a bigamist?"

Nellie took the girl's hand and pulled her to her feet. "That story can wait for another day, dear girl."

"Later tonight, Mama?"

I pursed my lips. "I think we've dwelled on the past enough for one day."

"Tomorrow then?" she asked hopefully.

"Tomorrow morning I should oversee the uncrating of the collection," I said, "but I'll come back here in time for the meeting, Nellie."

Nellie had arranged for a gathering of women at her home. I had brought information on the latest contraceptive methods from back east, materials I had picked up after the march on Washington. Now, I was wondering if it was such a good idea to distribute the flyers on pessaries here. Dissemination of such information was still technically illegal, and the newspaper had already drawn unwelcome attention to me.

We three descended the stairs, chatting as we went along, still in no hurry. A sharp knock sounded on the front door of the boarding house. Nellie swept past us to answer it.

I stopped on the staircase, instinctively holding my arm out to block Solina from descending any further.

Three policemen stood outside. The stocky one in front pushed his way past Nellie. "We're here for Rosella Martin."

My heart caught in my throat. Could they really charge me with bigamy like the headline suggested? The kitchen—I could slip out the back door. I grabbed Solina's hand and tugged her down the last two steps and toward the rear of the house.

"Who?" Nellie said.

"None of your dissembling, now," he said. "We know she's here."

"There she goes." Over my shoulder I saw the tallest officer pointing. I picked up my skirts and began to run. He charged through the parlor, overturning a small table in the rush to apprehend me.

One of Nellie's permanent boarders, an elderly gentleman who had been reading, stood up, his book and eyeglasses abandoned on a needlepoint-covered chair. "There's no call to behave like animals," he chastised the officers. "This is our home."

I was vaguely aware of Solina pulling away from me, heard her shoes clattering up the staircase, while Nellie berated the police. "What right do you have to charge in here like this? Ro hasn't done anything wrong."

Just as I reached the kitchen door, the tall officer seized my arm roughly. "Rosella Martin, you are under arrest for intent to distribute lewd and lascivious materials."

Blood boiled in my ears. "Define *lewd*. Define *lascivious*." When there was silence, I continued. "You obviously don't know the meaning of those words.

The stocky one held up a handful of pamphlets. "We found these in her hotel room."

They had searched through my travel case. "I'll define *lewd* for you. *Lewd* is your grubby fingers slithering through my undergarments to find those educational materials. My husband will be furious!"

The tallest officer's bushy mustache quivered as his face contorted with hatred. He yanked me toward the front door. Not to be outdone by his colleague, he added, "We have it on good authority that she planned to distribute that trash tomorrow."

"Women have a right to—" Nellie interjected.

"You'd best shut up or we'll arrest you, too, for aiding and abetting a criminal," the tall one said.

Nellie presented her arms. "I *demand* you arrest me too."

I interceded. "No, Nellie, you mustn't. Take care of Solina for me. Please." In my mind I could still hear those footsteps running away from me. I had embarrassed my child again. Maybe Nellie could smooth things over.

To the officers, I said, "There's nothing criminal about a woman taking charge of her own health and well-being." My voice sounded far too shrill and strident, rather than the firm, decisive one I hoped to project. It only served to make me angrier. "*Lewd* is what goes on in the upstairs of the Palace and other fine establishments in this town. Why don't you harass the married men taking their mistresses to private rooms?"

Nellie's gentleman boarder stepped forward. "Shame on you, shame on all of you. You've no call to burst in here and treat these ladies this way."

The third officer hung back as if he was indeed ashamed of their mission. Probably married and practiced contraception in his home. He would be the one I appealed to for decent treatment, if I could get him alone.

"I'm calling Val's father right now," Nellie said. To the policemen's backs, she shouted, "Mr. Martin works at the Mint and he knows people. You're going to be sorry for this. Really sorry. Wait and see if you're not."

The stocky fellow snorted.

"Very attractive," I said, as he hustled me down the street. "I grew up in farm country and heard hogs make that very noise."

How had they known to search my hotel room? Or that I would be at the boarding house? The traitor had to be someone who knew about tomorrow's meeting. It wasn't as if it were advertised. Only Nellie's close friends had been invited. Or was someone shadowing my movements?

Since there was no way my arrest would stay a secret anyway, I would use it to stir up anger against those who would repress our right to understand and control our own bodies.

With effort, I twisted my head back toward the boarding house. "Make sure my arrest gets in the newspapers, Nellie. Call Mindy and Alexandra. Organize the women—we must show strength!"

The arrest made headlines the next day even though I spent only a few hours in jail. I had barely been shoved behind bars, when Mindy Kenneson showed up in a lovely mint green gown and exquisitely styled hair that looked as if she had been ready to go out on the town for the evening. She berated the police quite forcefully, a sight to behold in all her outrage—and she'd dragged a reporter along to make sure my release was known to the public. A photograph was taken of the two of us leaving the jail. The meeting on birth control, however, would be postponed, Mindy said, until after the pottery exhibition.

"Are you sure you want to go ahead with the show after all this bad publicity?" I asked. "Perhaps we should cancel it."

She linked her arm through mine, her face lit by the happiest of smiles. "I won't hear of it. We can't let them win. Besides, everyone in town knows your name now. The gallery will have the grandest turnout ever."

I couldn't share her optimism, but she certainly knew the gallery business better than I.

Angie

"**WE ARE AT A CRITICAL JUNCTURE,**" I say, gaining assurance as my voice stays steady, strong, while surveying the teachers and reporters in the meeting room. I feel myself getting comfortable with this leadership role. I only wish Dewey could understand how important fighting for public education has become to me. How it is changing the way I see myself. A leader, not just of children but of adults. Someone who could make a difference in the world outside the classroom.

I lean into the podium. "As you know, some southern counties have staged rolling walkouts the last couple of weeks, but our AFT leadership thinks we should keep negotiating."

The room erupts with so many protesting voices I can't keep track of who says what, but it's impossible to miss the gist: the raise the legislature passed isn't enough.

"Two percent sucks," a middle school math teacher says. "We've been four years without a raise. Two percent won't even cover the increase in our health insurance premiums. It actually amounts to a pay cut."

Eve Carstairs stands, seeming to tower over us with far more than the actual five feet of her height. "He's right. We're forty-eighth in the nation in teacher pay. That's pathetic. The state can do better. It must."

Someone calls out, "Yeah, no wonder the state can't find enough teachers. Everyone's leaving for states that pay more."

It's the math teacher again, Rick, I think his name is. "They have to fix our healthcare. Having to wear a Fitbit and reach a certain number of steps or pay a penalty is ridiculous."

Since I'm still wearing the ankle bootie, I have to agree. I'm sure I'm not the only teacher who would have trouble meeting the proposed requirements.

"That's only one of the impossible changes they have proposed," Mrs. Carstairs says. "Under the new schedule, my premiums would skyrocket."

"So will everyone who has a family covered by our insurance if anyone else in the household works," Rick says. "My fear is no one is paying attention to all these changes. We have to do something."

Calls of "Strike!" come from every corner.

I try to restore calm. "The proposed raise isn't enough, but the governor says he is trying to find more money. AFT wants to continue to negotiate with him."

Mrs. Carstairs has not given up the floor. "Empty promises. Jim Justice is a billionaire coal baron—what does he know about living on a public employee's paycheck? If Governor Justice signs that bill into law, we need to walk out."

Dewey's job loss, Bella's hearing, Poppy's dementia, Rebecca's bladder problems—all these thoughts tumble through my brain. I have to take a stand. Judging by the temperature in this room, it probably doesn't matter what I do anyway. The walkout is coming. Especially if Mrs. Carstairs favors it.

Time for a vote. "Let's see a show of hands of those in favor of walking out if the governor and legislature don't come up with better numbers?"

As hands shoot up, I raise my own. Four fence-sitters raise their hands, perhaps reluctantly, when they see I support a walkout.

Ron Wilson from the technical school suggests we wait until Rebecca Knight returns to vote. "I don't think you represent the thinking of our union, no offense, Mrs. Fisher."

"None taken," I say, though I am offended, "but Mrs. Knight has every confidence in my assuming this role until she returns next fall. Our union leaders have tried negotiating and haven't gotten results. A walkout is the next logical step."

Wilson shouts, "What kind of role models are we for students if we break the law?"

"Role models who stand up for education," says Mrs. Carstairs, "for our students."

You tell him, Mrs. Carstairs. I feel myself leaping into the spirit of this protest.

Wilson won't give up. "I saw on Facebook that we aren't going to get paid if we strike. I can't get along without my paycheck."

"None of us could, but that's not true," I say. "All the school superintendents have decided to close schools if there's a strike and not dock our pay. We'll probably make up the missed days at the end of the year. That's straight from the source, not a silly rumor on social media."

Wilson isn't buying it.

"Our country and our state have a long history of public protest and strikes," says a young man I recognize as a Liberty High social studies teacher, "from the Boston Tea Party to the coal wars in Matewan."

Mrs. Carstairs adds, "Civil disobedience as practiced by Thoreau."

It's the social studies teacher's turn again. "This is a teachable moment, a chance for students to see history being made, my friends."

"Well, let's make some history then." I bang the gavel and the meeting is over, but the hard work is just beginning. I talk briefly with the reporters present and then shoot off emails to other AFT and WVEA chapters to see where their members stand and to let them know what's going on in Harrison County. Clusters of teachers hang around talking about the next steps: making posters and organizing carloads to drive to Charleston. I suggest a poster-making party at my home after dinner for anyone interested. Mrs. Carstairs volunteers to bring supplies.

I call home to let the family know we'll have guests.

Dewey answers. "That's just great, Angie. Like it isn't crowded enough here."

"It'll only be for a little while."

"I'm going to remind you once again how much this family is counting on your income. I heard the state may not pay you for days missed."

"That's not true."

He's planted a seed of doubt in my mind again, so I call Mr. Esposito to scope him out on the strike. He has already discussed the possibility of a walkout with the county superintendent and reaffirms that we won't be docked pay for our absence.

In 1990, our pay had been docked, but no one else depended on my salary for food. I picketed outside the school during the strike. We succeeded in boosting teacher pay from forty-ninth in the nation to thirty-first. We won better services for students and better training for teachers to impact the quality of education across the state. We want no less this time.

When I get home, Dewey isn't there. Mom says he left in a huff after seeing me on the evening news. That sick feeling in my stomach returns and I wonder if our marriage will survive the strike. Am I doing the right thing?

Trish, though, is beaming as if I'd been selected for a mission to the moon. "You're famous, Mom."

Have to admit, I am sort of proud. I made it through the meeting and reporters' questions without my knees knocking at all.

Trish plants a kiss on my cheek. "You did good."

"You bet she did," Mom says. "She comes from a long line of strong women."

"True." I turn to my daughter. "Did you know a famous suffragist is in our family tree? She helped California women get the right to vote—ten years before the nineteenth amendment gave all women that right."

Trish pops a chocolate chip cookie in her mouth, chewing and talking simultaneously. "Change starts with one person willing to stand up—that's you, Mom."

"Change may start with one person, but strength comes from numbers. From what I'm hearing, all fifty-five counties will walk out if the governor signs that bill tomorrow as he's expected to."

"*55 Strong* would make a great hashtag," Trish says.

"Tell me again what a hashtag is," Mom asks.

I don't get hashtags either. Facebook I understand. Twitter, not so much, but I guess I'm going to learn if I want us to succeed. There have been a lot of protest movements in the last decade. Occupy Wall Street. Black Lives Matter. Me Too. They have had mixed success, but I think we are different. Those movements had broad, rather vague goals and their members were scattered all over the country. We West Virginia teachers know exactly what we want and we are all centered in one place. We are going to succeed in ways the others have not. I can feel it. I call a local shop that prints tee-shirts and order four dozen with an outline of West Virginia on the front, the word *UNITED* in all caps and the hashtag *#55Strong*. I think I can sell at least that many at cost to local teachers. The shop owner's wife is a cafeteria worker, who will also benefit if our walkout is successful. He agrees to rush the order through immediately and promises they will be ready in the morning even if he has to work all night.

"I'll meet you in the school parking lot in the morning," he says.

That evening, five teachers from my school, armed with magic markers and poster board, arrive at our house. We commandeer the kitchen table while Mom and Poppy watch sit-coms in the living room. Dewey comes home, sullen-faced with an open beer in hand. He slouches beside Poppy, pretending to watch a sitcom, but his disapproval seeps across the room. After a while, he pops the top on another beer and disappears into the bedroom to stream an episode of *The Rookie* on his laptop.

While the TV blares in rooms to every side of us, we teachers create signs: "The Power of the People is Stronger Than the People in Power," "Students, Because You're Mine, I Walk the Line" with a photo of Johnny Cash, "Fix PEIA and 5% Raise."

On commercial break, Mom comes over to inspect our work. "What's PEIA?" she asks.

"PEIA is the Public Employees Insurance Agency," Mrs. Carstairs says. "They administer our health plan."

I am proud of my sign, block letters filled in with green magic marker: "They tried to bury us. They didn't know we are seeds." The slogan isn't entirely original. Other protest groups have used it, but the metaphor speaks to me and I can't resist co-opting it. I staple an empty packet of lettuce seeds to the poster board.

We finalize plans to meet in the morning in the school parking lot to make the two-hour drive to Charleston. Our local teachers will go down in rotating shifts, some one day and others the next for however long the strike lasts. Around ten, my little gang of sign-making protesters breaks up, driving off into the dark night—though it's dark any time after six this time of year.

Mom and Poppy have dozed off in their favorite reclining chairs, so I tune into a news channel and catch my brother-in-law, Senator Ted McNeil, making a pitch for charter schools. "Public schools are broken," he intones. "It's time to give parents and students another choice."

"And drain what little funding public schools have!" I shout at the jerk, even though he can't hear me.

"He's an ass, always has been," Trish says. "No wonder Auntie Mac is looking elsewhere."

I glance at Mom and Poppy. Luckily, they are still snoozing. "Careful, there, Trish. Besides, that picture must have been Photoshopped."

I still have to pack, and head for our bedroom. Propped up on the bed with his laptop, Dewey ignores me, earbuds tuned into some show. Fine, if that's the way he wants to play it. From the coffin-sized closet Dewey and I share, I lay out jeans to wear on the ride down, with a blue polo shirt sporting the school logo. Later, I can change into a hashtag tee-shirt if they are really ready first thing in the morning, as promised.

He takes the earbuds out long enough to issue another warning: "It's either the FBI job or I leave, Angie. With or without you."

My throat constricts until I think I'll choke. He's never said he'd go without me before. It's the television interview. I knew he wouldn't like it.

"Dew, what I'm doing isn't wrong. I can't think the FBI would withhold a job just because your wife is involved in the strike. Every teacher in the state is involved."

"It's illegal for public employees to strike. You are going to break a law and—"

"An unjust law," I interject.

"The FBI is law enforcement. They frown on breaking the law."

I can feel my face turn red. "They can't be that stupid."

I close the bedroom door behind me and lean against it with my eyes closed. The damn FBI better give him that job because I sure don't want to live in D. C. Would he really go without me?

I return to the living room, ready to kiss Mom and Poppy goodnight when to everyone's surprise, my sister flings open the front door—dramatically, because that's how she does everything.

"It's over," Mac announces in a voice so loud pictures rattle against the walls. She slams the door behind her and wheels in an over-sized suitcase, a medium-sized suitcase, a garment hanging bag, and overnight bag. "I've left Ted."

Mom blinks until she is fully awake, motors the recliner down, and hitches herself up. Her bones crackle and pop like wood snapping and resettling in a campfire. "Oh, honey, it can't be that bad."

That's Mom, the eternal optimist, the original Miss Sunshine. Me? I'm thinking, *What took so long?*

MacKenzie starts crying. In Trish's bedroom the baby starts crying.

If I don't get some sleep before I have to drive to Charleston, I'm going to cry too. If I think for one minute about living in D.C., I'm going to cry. If I think about Dewey's threat, I'm going to cry. So I'm not going to think. I'm not going to cry.

Mom folds MacKenzie into her arms and makes little hushy noises. In the bedroom Trish is making the same sounds to quiet Bella.

"Have you tried counseling?" Mom wants to know.

MacKenzie boohoos even louder. "It's beyond that."

"Why don't you tell us what happened," I suggest, leading them to the couch while I take a chair.

It takes a long time to tell the story, but the crux is an old, old tale we've all heard many times before: he's been having an affair with a younger woman named Natalie for some time—years, it seems, maybe since she was jailbait—and now she's pregnant. He plans to marry her—has even ripped the wedding and engagement rings off MacKenzie's hand. Says he is giving them to the Child Bride since MacKenzie won't need them anymore.

Mom's mouth falls open. "I never heard tell of any man being so . . . so disrespectful, so insensitive."

"So cheap, so despicable." I wonder if Ted found out about the tennis partner. Ripping the rings off her finger sounds extreme, even for Ted.

"How can I possibly tell the kids?" MacKenzie asks. "Natalie's two years younger than our daughter, for Pete's sake."

For Pete's sake—whoever the hell Pete was—MacKenzie's so-called "kids" are somewhere around thirty. They will handle the bad news. Unless they happen upon The Photo. That would freak them out, for sure.

"You've raised James and Allison right," Mom says, "and they have full lives of their own now. They'll be fine. Let's focus on helping you through this."

Mom's and my eyes travel to MacKenzie's suitcases and we are thinking the same thing: *Where is she going to sleep?* Trish and the baby are in MacKenzie's old room. Dewey and I are in my old bedroom. This farm house, whose empty rooms echoed for decades, is suddenly busier than the freaking Holiday Inn.

Finally Mom offers the best she can for the night. The sofa that makes into a bed.

MacKenzie's eyes flick to the door of her room and it dawns on her that it is occupied. She would have known this if she had bothered to stay in touch. Irritation creases her face and she shakes her head as if to say, *What else could go wrong?*

She stayed in a hotel the last time she visited, and that makes me suspicious. "MacKenzie, how are you set financially?"

My sister collapses in sobs. "Ted canceled my credit cards and wiped out our bank account. I don't know what I'm going to do."

"The snake!" I sit down beside her and pull her head onto my shoulder. I bet he's seen The Photo.

"You'll stay here with us," Mom says. "That's what family is for."

"That's right," I say.

"It'll be fun having the whole family under one roof again," Mom adds. "When's the last time that happened?"

I vow I won't say one negative word about the situation, but we are already tripping over each other here, what with bouncy seats and diaper pails, differing opinions over television shows, and Deano Martino's pizza pie songs blaring in the background. The only place I can grade papers in peace is in the bedroom—and that's only if Dewey hasn't come in there to stream his own shows. My sister will be one more source of tension in a too-crowded space, but it doesn't matter. We will make this work.

I hug Mac tighter. "Yeah, it'll be fun—like the old days. If it snows, we'll drag the old saucers out of the barn and slide down the hill behind the house. Remember when we used to do that?"

My sister smiles half-heartedly and nods. "What about money?"

"We'll make do," Mom says.

Dewey, who has wandered in to watch this spectacle, mostly in silence until now, speaks up. "First thing tomorrow we'll get you the best lawyer in the state."

Tomorrow—I will be on my way to Charleston. My eyes meet Dewey's and knowledge flashes between us: I won't be able to go with them. I am torn. I want to be with my sister. Should be with my sister, yet no way am I letting down my fellow teachers.

I explain my dilemma to MacKenzie, but instead of disappointment, a small flame glimmers in her eyes. "The lawyer can wait until another day. I want to help you with social media and publicity."

"No one is better at campaigns than you, Mac. I'm so sorry for what you're going through with Ted, but I know you'll help me figure out tweets and hashtags." An added bonus: helping me with social media will keep her mind off her troubles while she gets her life sorted out.

She smiles for the first time tonight.

After I make sure MacKenzie is settled in with fresh sheets, a blanket, and pillow, I head into the bedroom and find Dewey on his cell making arrangements to pick up a friend's RV and park it near the garage. When he hangs up, he takes a long slug of beer. "He'll let us rent it with an option to buy. He's been wanting to get rid of it anyway. I can run electric out to it, and it could be ready for Trish and the baby right away. Give them a place of their own, sort of. It might take me a few more days, but I think I can run a sewer line from it to the house's septic system. It'll be nice and cozy for them."

I'm not sure where things stand between us, but clearly he is still part of this family, still fixing whatever is broken. "Thanks. That should be perfect until we figure out where everyone's gonna end up."

Where will everyone end up? Not in D. C. Never. Yet our lives all seem to be at loose ends—jobs, marriages, illness, strikes. I wish I could see the whole tapestry, how all the threads would weave together into our future. One consolation: if there's strength in numbers, this family ought to be getting pretty darn strong.

Just then, Dewey upends the beer can and, finding it empty, crushes it in his fist.

I flinch. The sound hangs in the air like an electrical charge.

Twenty minutes later, my husband is snoring. Though I am only inches away, the gulf between us feels enormous, an empty space I don't know how to fill. We haven't touched each other since I first brought up the strike. I can't bring myself to reach out first.

After another half an hour, I get up and tiptoe through the living room, thinking a glass of milk might help me sleep. In the dark Mac calls out that she can't sleep either. She turns on the light by the sofa. "These springs and mattress are shot. I think it's the same old sofa Mom had when we were growing up."

"Right you are. New plaid upholstery, same weary bones." I tug on her arm. "Mac, why didn't you return my phone calls?"

"Didn't want to talk about it."

I get it. She's ashamed—and it might be the first time in her life she has reason to be. "Did Ted find out?"

"Oh, please, he went ballistic. Called me a whore, a liability. He's dying to be governor." Mac presses a tissue to her nose, sniffling. "It's not fair."

No, it isn't. Mac has always played the part of the good wife. The good citizen. The super mom. The one time she allows herself to be a mere mortal, she is publicly flayed.

"He's cheated for years, and I've looked the other way. Tried to focus on his good qualities. He's a born leader. A good provider. A good father."

That's Mac. Still trying to be the good wife. "A crappy husband."

"Yeah." She sniffles some more. "Not always."

"What are you going to do about The Photo?"

"Took your advice and hired a professional to wipe it off the face of the earth."

Good. Her kids will never see it. "Are you still seeing the . . ." I am not sure what to call him. "The tennis partner?"

Her arms pull tight across her abdomen. "I broke it off. He kept pushing me to have plastic surgery."

"What? You look fantastic." We both hear echoes of the words the whole world thinks but doesn't say aloud about women like us: *for a woman your age.* Geez, if this man thinks my sister isn't perfect, heaven only knows what he'd think of me.

"I don't feel fantastic. I feel old. He's a plastic surgeon. First he pressed me to get rid of my stretch marks, and then he suggested I reshape my butt and tits. It got so I didn't want to take my clothes off in front of him anymore."

I shake her arm. "Don't you dare let that loser reduce you to nothing more than the shape of your body. You are so much more than that."

Her smile is so weak it barely moves her cheeks.

"Mac, you are Chair of the Hospital Fundraising Foundation, Woman's Club President, and most important of all—" I pause, laying on the full-fledged Drama Queen—"you are my sister."

That produces a barely audible chuckle. Her lips part, close again, and then she whispers, "Ted told me about the ring . . . and you."

Damn. I swallow the lump in my throat. "I'm sorry. He only told you because he wanted to hurt you. Couples going through divorce pull out every weapon they can find."

"Wish you'd told me—way back then."

"How could I? You were happy. You would have hated me for ruining it for you. *I* would have hated me for ruining it for you."

She weighs this in silence, and finally admits, "Yeah, I would have."

She pulls my scrapbook from the shelf under the coffee table. She's had enough dissection of Ted for one night. "What's this?"

I explain Mom's gift. We share memories stirred by childhood photos: Easter egg hunts, snowmen with carrot noses and rock eyes, and carefully wrapped presents under Christmas trees. We giggle over Halloween costumes. I feel something shift between us.

When Mac sees the photo of Val Martin, she swears I have his nose.

"Horrors! Really?" I turn and swivel on one knee to check out my schnoz in the mirror hanging behind the sofa. Sure enough, Val could be the source of my gigantic proboscis. If only I could return the gift.

Mom schleps out of her bedroom, wrapped in a fuzzy pink robe I'd given her. "I thought I heard voices and I couldn't sleep anyway. Is it okay if I join you, or is this a private party?"

"Definitely okay." I don't know how I'm going to drive to Charleston in the morning, but a second wind has caught my sails tonight.

I scoot over and invite Mom to sit between us. She wants to know how far along I am in Rosella's story. I show her where I left off and she smiles. "Oh, you're coming up on the best part of the story. Would you read it aloud?"

When she smiles, I would do anything for her. Drive her to the moon and back.

And so I begin.

Rosella

MINDY KENNESON PASSED ME A ROUGH SKETCH of her ideas for window displays supporting the National American Woman Suffrage Association. "We can get all the local stores to put these up to show their support."

Nellie leans over my shoulder to see the sketch. "The more, the better. There's strength in numbers. We have to push harder for voting rights, especially here in the city."

I passed the sketch along to one of Alexandra's friends. About ten of us were gathered in at the Underwoods' just down the street from my new home, the house that Jack built.

We were waiting for the other NAWSA members to arrive. When chatter turned to fashion, my thoughts wandered. What color to wear wasn't an issue for me, since I had worn only mourning dress since Jack's death three months earlier. I was beginning to appreciate the practicality of dark skirts that hid dirt—but not dog fur.

I had moved into my new house without Jack. It was so unfair that he never got to live in it after he'd put so much energy into the planning. Yet if there was one lesson I had learned in my eighteen and a half years it was this: no one could predict what the future held. Jack had been right about my needing a change of scenery. Facing the empty nursery every day rubbed my face in Ben's absence.

Even so, I still enjoyed a morning cup of tea with Nellie twice a week.

Finally everyone arrived. Alexandra paraded her children, Lydia and Will, through the parlor to greet us, and then she shooed them and the nanny outside for a walk. After tea and cookies, Alexandra called the meeting to order, but instead of talking up suffrage, Alexandra started in on eugenics again. My teeth clenched. I could feel my face flushing as she repeated the now-familiar litany: how the Italians and Chinese were taking over the town and breeding like rabbits, how socially transmitted diseases were spread by these degenerates in the lower social classes, how carriers should be involuntarily sterilized. How only the Underwoods and their kind deserved to have children.

Mindy knew how I felt about eugenics, and I was grateful when she interrupted. "Could we please stick to women's rights? This is supposed to be a meeting on women's rights."

Alexandra's smile was so laced with condescension I longed to slap her. "The meeting is in my home, so I will talk about whatever I please."

"Not all of us support eugenics," Mindy said. "It's a different issue."

"But surely you can see society can't go on this way, letting inferior—"

I had heard enough and cut her off. "I disagree strongly, Alexandra. There's not a finer man in San Francisco than—" I remembered Val Martin's Italian heritage was supposed to be secret—"an immigrant who boarded with us once," I finished lamely.

Nellie jumped in. "Diseases have nothing to do with social class. Rich and poor alike can get sick."

Bless Nellie for realizing how I would feel about being classified as one undeserving of children!

Alexandra's smile narrowed into a grimace. "Anyone who doesn't appreciate my conversation is certainly free to leave at any time."

Nellie stood and pulled on her gloves. "Fine."

Mindy and I followed her out the door. I hated the disagreement for Nellie's sake, and said so as we marched up the street to my house. "This is an unfortunate estrangement. Alexandra is your oldest friend."

Nellie's chin tilted upward. "Oldest, not dearest. She wasn't supportive when my husband died. You must have noticed she never visited, just sent her card. Besides, I won't stand for anyone putting down our Val."

I heard what she didn't say—and I appreciated it: She wouldn't stand for anyone putting me down either, even if said person didn't know I was included in the category of degenerates who had experienced socially transmitted disease.

"I never did like her," Mindy admitted. "She and that little girl of hers are snooty."

True, but I held my tongue. I invited them in for tea and further gossip. Five other ladies who'd been at Alexandra's soon came knocking at my door. They, too, wanted to make plans for the next speakers promoting rights for women.

We had barely begun, when a frantic rapping sent me scurrying to the door once again. It was another lady from Alexandra's, Audine Hall. Her sobs alarmed me, but I had no time to ask what was wrong, for she announced it immediately.

"We just got the news. Aunt Susan is dead!"

Much commotion and distress followed. Susan B. Anthony was well known by most of the ladies; many had met her personally on one of her frequent visits to California. I had not been so fortunate.

"Whatever will we do without her?" Nellie moaned.

Agreement traveled through the room until Mindy interrupted.

"What we shall do is carry on. We are her lieutenants. Failure is impossible!"

I stood and raised my cup of tea and led a toast to the Mother of the Movement. "Failure is impossible!"

APRIL 18, 1906

I EXTINGUISHED THE CANDLE BEFORE OPENING the back door and setting the dog down. "Hurry up, Little Cuss, do your business." The name I'd given the dog still tickled me every time it rolled off my tongue, even though I'd come to adore the little devil. Only a hint of light softened the sky, but I was in a hurry because I had plans for the day.

After tea with Nellie, I had an art lesson scheduled at a school that served the children of factory workers. I charged no fee. I simply wanted to be around the children, to give them appreciation of the natural world. I took simple objects—pinecone, shells, a beetle in a jar—and taught them to draw. Seeing the wonder in their eyes was all the reward required. Besides, I wasn't in bad shape financially. Jack had paid for the house as it was being built. Not much was left in the bank when he died, but the Kennesons had recommended me to several of their friends, so I made enough money painting portraits to cover my expenses.

The sweet blossoms of my lemon tree scented the morning air. With shears, I clipped a branch, careful not to snag a finger on the thorns. The limb offered so many shapes and textures for the children to study and draw: shiny leaves, white blossoms, silky stamens, spiky thorns.

Little Cuss sniffed about the new shrubbery and perennials I had planted around the foundation. A Rose of Sharon and hollyhocks because my mother had grown them. Sasanqua camellias, a gift from my new neighbors, the Grays. A pair of plum trees. The large lot allowed a bit of greenery in my life again. Jack had come to understand my need for it. One of his good points. He had many, but I refused to romanticize him just because he'd died young. Memories of that woman haunting the street in front of Nellie's still hung fresh in my mind, her abundant hair flouncing as she walked, that sun-darkened skin.

Lost in these musings, I had ignored Little Cuss, who was shoveling furiously with both front paws at the loose soil around the plum tree.

"Cussy-Poo, stop that." I lunged for him, but he edged away, ears drawn back, tail curled under. He yapped, which wasn't unusual in itself, but he held his whole body stiff, as if bracing against an unseen threat. At least no threat I could see. No cats. No thunderstorm approaching. What was the crazy dog's problem this time? He had one problem or another every morning, a constant source of amusement and aggravation.

"Hush—you'll wake the neighbors." It was only 5 a.m. and not my choice to be up quite so early, but the lunatic dog refused to sleep in. Ever.

I reached for him again and he let me pick him up, the bark transforming into a pitiful whine. Suddenly he let out such a shrill yelp, I nearly dropped him. He clawed my wrapper, scrambling closer to my face. He was shaking all over, every little nerve a-jitter. "What's wrong, baby-poo?"

I cradled him against my chest and rocked him a bit, my face buried against the soft fur. When I drew back a little, I eyed his dirt-caked paws with dismay, and was doubly dismayed to discover how much filth he'd transferred to my wrapper. "You little rat! This means a good brushing before we go to Nellie's. That'll teach you to dig up my plants."

Nellie would keep the dog while I visited the elementary school, though on occasion I kept the puppy with me because the children loved petting him. I sniggered, remembering the teacher's shocked expression when she first heard the dog's name. Well-practiced by then in explaining the dog's name to neighbors and my maid, I smoothed things over: "Little Cuss is short for Little Cousin. I named him after my favorite little cousin." The relief on people's faces amused me. Only Nellie knew the truth—and she agreed the name fit the dog perfectly.

I had one hand on the back door when a great roar—not quite like any thunder I'd ever heard—began in the distance and swelled like the approach of a train, only much, much louder. Abruptly the ground shifted up and down in waves, shooting sideways at the same time. I was thrown to the ground, screaming as I fell, barely able to hang onto to my terrified dog; he was shivering, digging his claws into my chest. Terror surged through my body. I was going to die and Little Cuss was going to die with me. I couldn't even protect a dog. The earth bucked like an unbroken horse, cracking the bones of houses, rocking the street beds. Animals and humans screeched in horror. Neighbors' houses looked like a row of stiff-legged clog-gers, bobbing up and down. Maybe this was the end of the earth, the apocalypse predicted in the Bible.

Just as quickly as the shaking had started, it was over. Stagger-ing to my feet, I plunged inside the house with Little Cuss. My heart in my throat, I felt a surge of energy through every pore, propelling me forward.

No sooner had I entered than a second wave, stronger than the first, hit. I grabbed anything relatively stable in my path for balance. A wall, a door frame, a chair. But nothing seemed an iota more stable than my own buckling legs. In shock, I absorbed these strange facts: the kitchen table was dancing a jig; one of the ladderback chairs had toppled over; my new china rattled in the cupboard; a goblet on the huntboard skittered to the edge and shattered on the tile floor; the chandelier above the dining room table swayed, its crystals tinkling nervously; the framed oval photo of Ben tumbled from its easel and the easel itself collapsed; a potted philodendron in the living room window crashed to the floor spraying dirt across the red oak planks and onto the imported rugs Jack had ordered.

Without quite knowing how, I made my way from the rear to the front of the house and found myself standing in the street in my nightclothes and wrapper. So were my neighbors, the Grays, staring, slack-jawed, at the brick pavers which were hurling their way up or shoving their way down or twisting sideways. A jagged line four to six inches deep divided the street in half. With a whip-like crack, the concrete cornice on the house across the street tumbled loose, barely missing Mrs. Gray. It shattered into pieces on their lawn. Suddenly the earth was still again, and after all the commotion, an unearthly quiet stole over the city.

Mr. and Mrs. Gray ventured out to the center of the street, staying a foot back from where bricks lay in chaotic upheaval. I approached the other side of the jagged line, also keeping a fair distance. What if the earth opened wider along that seam and we all got sucked in, crushed by heaving rock?

I tucked Little Cuss tightly into the crook of my arm, stroking his ears in a futile attempt to stop his trembling. I spoke in hushed tones. "Have you ever felt one like this before?"

Mr. Gray cleared his throat, oblivious to the fact he was dressed only in a sleep shirt with white legs thin as an egret's poking out beneath. He looked every bit of his sixty years as he hung onto his wife's arm—to give support or for support?

He swallowed visibly. "Never. Nothing even close. This is the worst earthquake we've ever had."

I had thought as much, but hearing someone put it into words gave credence to my opinion. A label. A category of occurrence. An earthquake. Jack had told me about the one in '98, but hearing stories about quakes and feeling the center of gravity disappear—the very center that had anchored me, my world, and everything in it every second since my birth—were two immeasurably different things.

Alexandra Underwood stood out in the yard with her children. As usual, she pointedly ignored me, as she had ever since I had criticized the eugenics movement and stalked out of her house.

"This earthquake," Mr. Gray proclaimed loudly enough to be

sure Alexandra could hear, "is God's punishment for the immorality of some people in this city."

Ridiculous! Everyone knew earthquakes happened because of pressure that built up underground, naturally occurring events that had nothing to do with the Underwoods' modern marriage.

I stared at my home, overtaken by a sudden lethargy, an inability to function. The house rested, as Jack had told me, on pilings driven deep into the clay, designed to sway with the ground's movement. The circular drive bordered by cedars was intact, despite the damage to the front street. The Italianate façade, the arched brick supports for the front porch, the square windows, the clay-tile roof with its slight pitch—all appeared to have withstood the violent shaking. Jack had wisely insisted on a strong foundation. The clay of these outlying neighborhoods, he said, would withstand quakes better than the sandy soils in the southern parts of the city. Jack had befriended the city's fire chief, Mr. Sullivan, and thus knew a litany of facts about the city's disaster plans, but I couldn't shake the fog from my mind long enough to recall details.

Feeling light-headed and headachy as my initial fear subsided, I surveyed the street. A column supporting the portico of one house had toppled, leaving the left portion of the roof listing precariously. I noticed no other damage. A miracle. Mrs. Gray went back inside, while other neighbors wandered up and down the street, assessing damage, making sure everyone was accounted for. One man called out for everyone to shut off their gas mains. I still couldn't command my body to move, though I knew I should.

I looked down the hill toward the city. Small clouds of black rose in isolated spots. Fires. To be expected after a quake, Jack had warned me. I supposed candles or gas lamps or cook stoves tipped over. Those things would happen, Jack said, and the fire departments were ready to respond.

Well, I was a strong woman of sturdy stock who'd survived the death of a mother, my son, and a husband; suffered a stillborn and a terminated pregnancy; and now I'd survived an earthquake. Others, I realized, would not have been so lucky. I strode toward my front door.

Mrs. Gray emerged from her house, this time fully clothed. She wrapped a blanket around her husband, whose face reddened now that he became aware of the indelicacy of his appearance. "Phone lines are down," she said. "George, you'll have to drive downtown to find out if Austin is all right."

The earth shuddered again and my heart leapt into my throat.

"This happens," Mrs. Gray told me. "The aftershocks. They are likely to go on all day. George, we must find Austin."

Austin, the Gray's grown son, worked in the business district where buildings stood tall, crowded, and, according to Jack, many were built on fill dirt. A disaster waiting to happen. A new surge of energy shot through me. Nellie. Was she all right? How self-centered not to have thought of her already. Yet I had no doubt Val would look after her—unless something dire had happened to him as well. Nellie's home angled down a hill, sandwiched between two others in a long line of buildings. Did they still stand? And my new maid—the young Polish girl. I didn't even know where she lived to check on her. I sent up a quick prayer for all the citizens of the city.

While Mr. Gray dressed, I obtained permission from Mrs. Gray to let me ride in the rumble seat of their new Lambert.

I rushed inside and threw on a dark skirt, white blouse, and a light jacket with sensible shoes. I tucked the dog into the afghan-lined wicker basket he slept in and covered him with another of Nellie's baby afghans. For once, he didn't shake it off. I thought to fill a Mason jar with water in case Little Cuss got thirsty and tucked that and some hard-boiled eggs into the side of the basket as well. I had no idea how long we would be gone.

Mrs. Gray knocked on the door and advised me to fill the bathtub with water. "A precaution in case aftershocks rupture the water mains." The older woman adjusted the pins that anchored her hat. "You never know what's going to happen after one of these things. The shaking is likely to go on for days."

It was 6:45 by the time we secured our homes and set out for downtown. Mr. Gray wove cautiously through the hordes of people thronged in the streets. We passed a few cars and carriages, but most people traveled by foot. Trolleys weren't running, the reason obvious as the Lambert negotiated its way around mangled cables sprawled across the street.

As we left the outlying neighborhoods, I was shocked by the devastation. A whole row of homes thrown off their foundations, some leaning on the next, another two completely collapsed. Firemen gathered around the rubble, frantically hauling it away, board by board.

Mr. Gray leaned out and asked a civilian what was happening.

The man paused from clearing away rubble long enough to wipe his face with a bandana. "Family trapped in there." He pointed to the splintered remains of a wooden structure.

"Don't stop," Mrs. Gray implored her husband.

His face hardened. "I must."

"What about Austin?"

"If he's buried under rubble like these people, I'm sure everyone around is pitching in to dig him out."

I sympathized with the anguished concern for her son, but feared for those trapped here as well. I was relieved when Mr. Gray got out of the car, tossed his jacket back inside and made his way to the front of the line of rescue workers. Despite his age, he and another man lifted a board and carried it aside. And then another. And another. I got out for a closer look. Surely there was something I could do to assist. Shouts erupted as a child's hand came into view—and even from a distance I could see it was moving.

On the stoop of a house across the street, a young woman about my age lifted her apron until it covered her mouth as if to hold in a cry too horrible to unleash. Her own child, a boy in short pants, twined his hands into the folds of her skirt. Assuming the woman lived there, I approached and asked her to fetch water and some blankets.

The suggestion dispelled the woman's shock and she let go of the apron. "Yes, I should have thought of it. Come and help me." Gently she pushed the little boy's shoulders. "Off to the linen closet, Joseph, quick now, and fetch some blankets." She introduced herself as Margaret O'Halloran and led me by the hand into the kitchen, motioning toward a large pitcher sitting by the sink. I set the wicker basket with the dog down. This young mother and I would never have exchanged more than greetings under other circumstances. Her perceived lower social class would have barred a friendly exchange. Extraordinary, how the earthquake had leveled more than buildings.

I filled the pitcher while Margaret clanged through a drawer, coming up with a dipper. "That wee girl, Essie, the one they found, she's my Joseph's age. I pray God she'll be all right, but how will she be, what with the rest of her family still buried over there?"

Margaret sank the dipper into the pitcher. "For the men." She filled a separate tin cup for the child, who surely would be pulled free any moment. "I hope Essie makes it. I lost one of mine, my Charlotte, two years ago. Was the scarlet fever took her. Don't seem right when such a wee one goes."

No, it didn't seem right. A mother's grief transcended social barriers too.

Joseph thumped down the stairs with a pile of blankets, worn but colorful. I crossed the street just as the little girl was pulled loose.

Margaret held out a quilt to receive the child. The girl didn't look quite human. More like a plaster-casting, so thickly coated were her face, hair, clothing—even her eyelids—encrusted with dust. "Essie, baby, it's going to be all right," Margaret soothed.

I felt it would be, even if Essie was the only survivor. Margaret carried the girl onto her porch where she paused to wipe Essie's face with the edge of a blanket. Someone would care for the child. We would all pull together to help each other.

More cries arose from the rescue workers as they found the father. Not so lucky. Under him, the wife. He'd tried to shield her with his arms, his body, but she was dead, too—but no—there came shouts for water. I rushed forward with the pitcher, brushed the crumbled plaster from the mother's lips, and held a dipper of cool water to them. Her eyelids fluttered. Her lips parted and she made sounds—unintelligible, but good to hear nonetheless.

"Easy," I said. "Don't try to talk. Your little girl is safe." I directed the men to carry the woman to Margaret's home.

By the time I washed and treated the woman's cuts and abrasions and thought to look outside, the Grays had disappeared in their Lambert, venturing further into the city to find their son, I supposed. On foot, I set out for Nellie's with Little Cuss and my basket, moving through dazed citizens clogging the streets. Nine blocks later, after a lengthy detour because of a carriage accident and dead horse in the street, I reached Sacramento Street. Thank the Lord, Nellie's home looked intact. I knocked. One of Nellie's itinerant boarders, an elderly gentleman, ashen-faced and clearly in shock, answered. Disintegrated plaster peppered what little hair he had.

I looked over his shoulders to scan the foyer and the entrances to the dining room and parlor and saw Nellie lying stationary on the sofa. "Oh no, no, no," I sobbed, a hand pressed to my lips.

The boarder hurried to reassure me. "No, she's not—she'll be fine. She just took a fall and needs to rest."

I calmed myself.

He thought then to introduce himself as Mr. Longfield. "Dr. Martin rushed in to the hospital. He'll find himself in high demand today."

I lifted Little Cuss from the basket and poured him a little water in the lid of the Mason jar. He slurped it noisily and I refilled the lid twice. The dog was still shaky on his legs. We all were.

The boarder's hands trembled as he spoke. "The couple next door lost their baby—a cabinet fell on the little fellow. I helped the father move the furniture but . . . too late." His eyes flicked to Nellie. "Since you've come to look after her, I'm going out to see what I can do. Fires are cropping up everywhere. I expect the firemen need every pair of available hands."

When the door clicked shut and I knew Mr. Longfield had departed, I let my eyes close. I breathed deeply and felt strangely calm. For a few moments, I stroked through the dog's thick fur. Another child dead. *The Lord giveth and the Lord taketh away.* He'd taken away so much.

Since Ben's death I had felt nothing but anger at a God that would allow my child to die and to take my other babies before they even had a chance to draw breath. But the earthquake had shaken all the anger out of me. All these people—Ben, my husband—they were gifts, not possessions. Even the dog. A gift. A life that could be snatched away at any moment. My own life was a precious gift too. I vowed to put the rest of it to good use. How? I didn't know, but had to trust that God would show me the path.

Right now my paramount duty was caring for Nellie as long as she needed me. I propped a small blue trapunto-quilted pillow under her head, and covered her from feet to waist with a crocheted afghan in shades of blue. Kneeling by her side, I prayed silently, some words vaguely recalled and the rest of my own making: *Lord, shelter this woman under your wings. She is my friend, true and honest. I am pleading with you to make her well and keep her walking along the path of life. Amen.*

Her neck was sprinkled with crumbs of plaster. I brushed off what I could without disturbing her. I climbed the stairs to fetch fresh clothing for her to put on when she woke. When I returned, I set the clean dress and petticoat on a chair and went to the kitchen for water to wash her face and hands. I turned on the tap, and with dismay found not even a drip. The water mains here must have broken. I remembered the clay pots Nellie kept in the yard to gather rainwater for her plants. Those small cisterns would be a godsend. I slipped outside, dipped water into a pan, and took it inside.

Gently I washed Nellie's face with a clean cloth. Her eyelids fluttered.

"What—?" Her voice dropped off and her eyes closed. Then her palms pushed against the sofa as if to raise up.

"Shhh, don't try to sit yet. It was an earthquake."

Nellie swallowed visibly, tongue flicking across parched lips. I retrieved the mason jar and raised her head enough to allow her to sip a little. I settled her back on the pillow.

"Oh, that feels better," she said. ". . . so dry." Her eyelids closed for a moment and I thought she was going back to sleep, but when she opened her eyes again, she seemed fully alert. "I remember now, I was near the top of the stairway, coming down to start breakfast for Val and Mr. Longfield when the shaking started. I lost my footing and took a tumble."

I cringed. It was a tall staircase. Val and Mr. Longfield must have carried her down from the landing. No bleeding that I could see, and she didn't appear to have broken bones, but she would certainly be badly bruised and sore and perhaps have lumps and sprains.

"How are you feeling now?"

"Stiff. Achy." She stirred as if to sit up again.

"Are you sure you're ready to get up?" I asked.

"I can't lie here all day, now can I?"

I smiled. "Yes, actually, you could if you wanted to—and you should if you aren't feeling well. But if you insist on getting up, let me help."

I started to steady her as she rose, but another aftershock sent us both onto the sofa. We squeezed each other's hands until it passed.

Together we inspected her body, which—other than two goose

eggs on her left leg, a gash on her forehead, and a probable sprained wrist from trying to break her fall—seemed intact. I cleaned the gash with a dab of whiskey, and then helped her put on fresh clothing. As she was hungry, I gave her some hard boiled eggs from the ice-box and a slice of bread with butter and jam. We decided to forgo tea since neither of us was sure the gas lines were safe.

"Better not risk a fire," she agreed, nibbling on an egg.

"Several buildings are burning in the city. Mr. Longfield went to assist the firemen." I told her about the child and mother I'd seen pulled from the rubble—and the father that didn't make it, and about the neighbor's child crushed by furniture.

"It's bad out there," I said.

Nellie looked thoughtful while she washed down her bread with water. "You must go out and help others," she said.

I shook my head. "I promised I would stay with you."

"Nonsense. I'll be fine now. I'd go too, but as wobbly as I am, I might be more hindrance than help. Please go. Lives may depend on it. Take food, water, blankets—and take that whiskey with you. Whatever you think people will need."

I let her talk me into it. As Mr. Longfield had pointed out, the city would need every pair of available hands.

In the root cellar, I located one of Ben's favorite toys, a large wagon Nellie had been using to move her canned goods around. I wheeled it into the house and filled it with afghans, bed linens, quarts of apple juice from the cellar, two loaves of bread and a jar of jam, the whiskey, and a few carrots from the larder. I didn't want to take too much—Nellie would need nourishment herself. I left Little Cuss with Nellie and made her promise not to try to take him outside. Poor thing was still shivering. "I'll be back before dark," I promised.

CINDERS DRIFTED DOWN FROM THE SKY like fat black snowflakes. I brushed one off my cheek, steadying myself as the ground trembled again. I passed by a woman in a rocking chair in the middle of the street. Another family sat on a four-poster bed with their cat as if it were the most normal thing in the world to be lounging in the road. I skirted rivulets from a broken water main and moved toward the corner to intercept the mass of people streaming out of the Market district. Refugees carried large trunks filled with their belongings, all they had left in the world. I lifted the first jar of apple juice from the wagon and offered a drink and a slice of bread to an old man shouldering a packing crate in one hand and a caged parrot in the other.

He set his load down. "Thank you kindly, ma'am."

Soon a line formed. I continued to hand out food and drink to an assortment of people fleeing the fires: a woman carrying her new spring hat in a band-box, while her servants carried her trunks behind her; several painted ladies; and an Italian vegetable peddler with his entire family—dozens of them. Every one of them appeared extremely overweight until I realized they wore all their clothes in layers. Easier than trying to carry them. Newlyweds, quite cheerful, stopped next, the husband exclaiming that this was a honeymoon never to be forgotten. I felt more connected to these people, more a part of the city, than I had at any time since moving here.

Two couples still dressed in opera attire asked for a drink. The men wore tuxedos, but incongruously the stout one's feet were clad in bedroom slippers. One of the women was wrapped in gold lamé; the other, in a pearl-encrusted cape. They seemed in good spirits, chatting about Caruso and how there'd never be another *Carmen* like the one they'd seen the night before. "Not in our opera house anyway," the pearl-encrusted lady said. "Did you know it's on fire?" she asked.

"No." I looked anxiously at the smoke-filled sky. A great boom reverberated somewhere at a distance from us, south of town. What was happening now?

"Yes, indeed, and City Hall collapsed as if it were made from playing cards," the one in gold said.

"The walls were stuffed with newspaper," a tall fellow added. "Saw it with my own eyes. Newspaper! Heads will fall over that, I can tell you."

Two horses clopped by, hauling a wagon loaded with a grand piano, and a man banged on the keyboard and sang, "It'll be a hot time in the old town tonight." The opera refugees laughed. One shouted, "That's the spirit!"

"Rosella," Mindy Kenneson called out from a mule-drawn wagon. Her father held the reins. "Nellie told us you'd headed this way. We came over to check on you. Whole city's on fire! Come on."

The pearl-caped woman waved. "Ta-ta!"

Mr. Kenneson helped me up into the seat. Once I was settled, he put Ben's toy wagon and what was left of its contents in the back. A strong aftershock rattled my nerves all over again as the wagon jittered and the mules brayed their fear. Mr. Kenneson did his best to steady the poor beasts. Bricks tumbled from a house across the street. Supports on a porch collapsed. And then, the ground stilled again—temporarily. I tried to steel my nerves against the shocks I knew to come.

"Where'd you get the rig?" I asked. I had never seen Mindy's father so disheveled. He always dressed impeccably. Even his mustache looked unkempt, unwaxed, as was his custom.

Mr. Kenneson snapped the reins. "Volunteered as an emergency policeman, and we're commandeering every available transport."

"What are the booms I keep hearing?"

"Gas mains exploding. They say they have shut down the gas supply to the city, but the lines keep exploding. Dozens of burn victims, heard some died."

I shuddered. Burn victims. Like Jack. I shuddered again—and began to cough. The air, so thick with smoke, made breathing difficult. I held a handkerchief over the lower part of my face.

"We're going to pick up bedding from buildings nearest the fires and take them to the hospital they're setting up at the Mechanics' Pavilion. Mindy insists on coming with me."

"I want to help, too."

"I'd feel better if you young ladies stayed somewhere safe, but if you insist."

Safe? An illusion. There was no safety—anywhere. "I appreciate your concern, but I can make beds up as well as anyone. I can clean a wound. I want to be useful."

Seeing he couldn't win the argument, Mr. Kenneson turned the rig around and drove it to within a block of burning buildings on Powell Street. We filled the wagon with mattresses and linens. I noticed a cistern behind the building and filled several containers Mr. Kenneson had brought along with water. We dropped off our load at the makeshift hospital.

"Thank God you brought water," a nurse said.

Next they sent us out to procure groceries. At the first store we happened upon, angry customers clustered outside. I approached a woman with a bandana wrapped around her head to keep off the cinders. "What's going on here?"

"Fifty cents he charged for this bread—it's robbery, that's what it is!" Others around her shouted agreement. Two soldiers, bayonets drawn, barked orders and parted the crowd to enter the store.

Less than a minute later they emerged, one soldier holding the grocer by the scruff of the neck, the other poking the fellow's ribs with the bayonet. The mob fought their way into the store and plundered the shelves.

Tight-lipped, Mr. Kenneson tried to steer us toward the wagon. "Let's try another store. We don't want to get in the middle of those folks."

The soldiers pushed the grocer down the alley beside the store. I stepped tentatively, toward them, drawn yet repelled by the tense drama. "But what are they—"

Two shots resounded. Instinctively Mindy and I jumped backward. The grocer bucked against the brick wall of his store. As blood seeped through his apron front, I could feel my own blood draining from my head. I staggered, woozy, as he slid to the ground. Mr. Kenneson gripped one of my elbows. He had his arm around Mindy's waist and almost carried her to the wagon.

This couldn't be happening. Not in the United States of America. "They can't do that," I whispered.

Mindy's father helped us into the wagon. "The mayor issued a proclamation this morning. No price gouging. No looters. Violators will be shot." The wagon moved on. "Shall I take you girls home now?"

Mindy's chin came up. "No."

I felt lost in a nightmare and would have liked nothing more than to crawl into bed and pull the covers over my head. It was so tempting, but I would never forgive myself if my courage failed when my neighbors needed me most. I shifted my shoulders back and adjusted the gathers of my skirt. "Let's find another grocery."

We delivered two wagonloads of supplies to the hospital before Mr. Kenneson received word that the fire had marched through the Emporium and was headed toward the Mint.

He whipped the wagon around toward Market Street. "I have

to go. We have to save the Mint."

At the corner of Market and Powell, soldiers stopped them. One recognized Mr. Kenneson and let him through the barricade on foot.

Reins now in hand, Mindy shouted, "Papa, be careful, please."

He tipped his hat and bowed slightly. "You girls do the same."

We entered the hospital and went to work.

SOMEONE KEPT CALLING MY NAME. An unwelcome intrusion. *Go away,* I wanted to say. But then I'd have to wake up, something I was trying to avoid. A catnap—that's all I wanted. I'd been on my feet since the first tremors. I'd helped move over three hundred patients and supplies out of the Mechanics Pavilion when it caught fire. I made beds, washed the dead, cleansed wounds, secured and prepared food for the injured and the medical staff. I deserved a nap.

"Ro."

All right. All right. My eyelids raised halfway and I jerked my neck upright, kneading it with my fingers. It ached abominably.

Val had squatted down beside me. Soot begrimed his face and his clothes reeked of smoke. "Sorry to disturb you."

I pushed a loose hank of hair back from my cheek. I must look a sight. To sleep, I had found the only unoccupied space, a tiny corner of the hospital floor, where I had slouched against the wall. "What time is it?"

"Near eleven."

I tried to focus, to pull sense from his words. "Eleven when?"

"Eleven o'clock Thursday night. The earthquake was yesterday morning."

"What news?"

"Nothing good. A broken water main flooded Valencia Street and three whole stories of the hotel sank into the old marsh. Everyone drowned. Hundreds of people."

"Dear God!"

"I wouldn't have disturbed you, but fire is creeping up Russian Hill. I want to take you and Mindy home so you can rescue some belongings. Mr. Kenneson has already fetched his wife, Nellie and Little Cuss. I promised him I would bring you and Mindy."

Home. Yes. The house that Jack built.

Slowly I rose and brushed off my skirt. "The Mint—did they save it?"

His teeth shone white against the grime of his face. "They did. Every building surrounding it is gone. Everywhere you turn in the city, it's utter devastation, but the men watered the Mint down from the inside and saved her. She stands."

"Your father—he is all right?"

"He is. He took charge of the men who saved the Mint. You can't imagine how important She'll be to rebuilding the city."

I would stay. Long enough to help my neighbors and nurse the injured. Long enough to get started with the rebuilding. Afterward, I thought I would go back to West Virginia. I missed those gentle rolling hills. I'd heard the postal service would accept letters at all the refugee camps the next day. My family would be so worried. I would get word to Timmy somehow, even if I had to write my message with ashes on a remnant of my petticoat.

The night sky glowed an eerie orange, the air clotted thick with smoke that stung my throat. We rode in an Oldsmobile, a vehicle Val had commandeered. I made a mental list of the things I wanted to take. The framed photo of Ben, my sketchbooks, the afghan Nellie gave me as a wedding gift, a change of clothing, water, food, my favorite teacup—one Nellie had given me. The cash box Jack insisted we keep in the chiffarobe for emergencies like earthquakes. Another boom shook the ground. Dynamite. Soldiers were blowing up houses and buildings, whole blocks of them, trying to create a firewall. They'd been blowing things up since yesterday afternoon. One boom after another.

"The dynamite doesn't seem to be doing much good," I said.

Val turned left to avoid soldiers blocking the road ahead. "It isn't. I tried to tell General Funston's aide they shouldn't be using black gunpowder. The sparks are only setting more fires."

"What did he say?"

Val lowered his pitch and mustered an uncharacteristic sternness. "He said, 'Sir, what exactly are your qualifications to contradict the army's dynamite expert?' And I said no particular qualifications were required, other than common sense and sobriety. Why, the fellow they have directing the dynamite operation is so inebriated he can barely stand up."

Nothing could surprise me anymore. Val turned right at the next intersection and ran into another blockade. "I'll talk to them."

He argued with the young soldiers and flashed his medical pass. No luck.

He returned. "Come on then. We'll have to walk in."

On foot we worked our way around the blockades. Mr. Gray stood in his front yard. His wife, he said, was inside collecting her treasures. "I'll warn you if the soldiers come this way or if I hear talk of dynamiting."

I thanked him. "Austin? You found him?"

"Safe and sound, though the bank where he worked is gone."

I smiled. "That's good news about Austin indeed." I walked slowly across the road to my home, absorbing the details: the arched brick supports for the front porch, the square windows, the clay-tile roof. Jack had built a fine house and selected beautiful furnishings for it. Now they would all disappear. It seemed nothing in life was permanent. Nothing stayed the same.

Quickly I gathered my precious keepsakes and belongings and tied them up inside a sheet, hobo-style. Val raided the pantry for food, piled it in a deep drawer he pulled out of a chiffarobe. He looped a belt through the slot in the front of the drawer. From torn linens he fashioned a harness. We joined the Grays and other neighbors drifting up the street. It was an exodus, just like in the Bible. Val hauled the food up the hill, and I trudged behind. Halfway up, it dawned on me that Val didn't have a change of clothes.

He tugged on the harness, which had shifted to one side. "Afraid they burned up while I was putting out the fire at the Mint. My cello, too."

Mr. Gray overheard. "Son, I can't replace your cello, but run back down the hill. My bedroom's on the second floor, first room on the right. You're about my size. Take anything you want."

The Kennesons, Nellie, and Little Cuss waved to us from the top of the hill. The Grays and I joined them to wait for Val. He returned in fresh clothing with spare clothes wrapped in a sheet. The pants revealed two inches of Val's socks and the jacket revealed wrists, but so what? I could alter them for him—if I could find a needle and thread.

By now orange and golden flames licked the walls of the house beside the Grays'. The heat warmed my face and sweat rose on my brow, yet we seemed to have reached a tacit agreement. We would stay and watch our homes burn.

"I almost forgot." Val dug in the pocket of his jacket—Mr. Gray's jacket—and took out a handful of Tootsie Rolls.

I burst out laughing. "Where did you find those?"

"I can tell you," Mrs. Gray said. "The dish on my dining room table."

After Val distributed the chocolate, he pulled a bottle from his other pocket. "That's not all I found."

Mr. Gray slapped Val's back. "Good man!" He took a swig.

Mrs. Gray coughed. "These ashes are mighty irritating to the throat. I believe I'll have a sip for medicinal purposes. No sense asking for a cold."

My father and brothers drank moonshine, but I had never tasted hard liquor. If ever there was a time for new experiences, a time to stick together, this was it. I asked for the bottle and took a small sip and choked. Everyone laughed. I had to cover my mouth to keep from spewing it out. What awful stuff! And then I was laughing with them, and it seemed so strange and yet so right to laugh while fire approached first the Grays' home and then my own. Nellie's and the Kennesons' were already gone.

As fire engulfed the walls, the roofs, and furnishings with its terrible roar, we watched in silence. We breathed in the smoke. We shed no tears.

Val was the first to speak. "We'll be safe at the Presidio." He referred to Fort Mason, about ten blocks away.

Safe. There was that word again. As if safety was something we could control. With our few belongings, we survivors moved on.

JUNE 27, 1906

VAL MARTIN HEAVED THE DOOR UPRIGHT and I steadied it while he guided the hinges into place and secured them with pins.

I stood back to admire the handiwork and laughed, hands on my hips. "I'll feel like a queen, having a door instead of a tent flap to call my own."

I figured I was more useful than most queens, doing my best to be a helpful resource to everyone in the Golden Gate tent city. If my ailing neighbor needed a cup of tea, I scoured the countryside for herbs and brewed a pot. I knew how to find wild chicory to make a substitute coffee. Every day I cooked massive amounts of food for the displaced citizenry. When I saw the children weren't learning to read, I found primers and taught them. They learned their letters by writing with sticks in the dirt until I could obtain better supplies. Eventually, I organized makeshift classrooms for the children. I took Little Cuss on visits to the hospital where he cheered patients by tilting his head from side to side and wagging his tail. He had gotten quite plump from successful begging.

A girl had come to San Francisco, but a woman emerged from the earthquake. All the energy suppressed by grieving had accumulated and was pouring out in every direction at once.

Thousands had evacuated to other cities, but Val, Nellie and I chose to stay. Right after the quake, the Bank of Little Italy gave out loans to refugees when none of the other banks could open their vaults—they were too hot. I wondered what Alexandra Underwood thought of Italians after hearing about that.

The time I spent in the shack was the happiest I'd been since Ben died. I felt connected to everyone, a vitally important piece of the community. In the tent city, rich and poor, immigrant and blue-blood, mingled. There I discovered neither money nor position had anything to do with character. Despite the losses people endured, few whined or cried or bemoaned their fate. I felt shamed by their strength and vowed never to allow myself to sink into self-pity again.

I had been pounding nails into walls since early in the morning, both in my own new shanty and a neighbor's. Around noon, I took a break. To my surprise, a letter awaited me, a missive from Timmy that set me yearning to return home to the hills where I'd grown up.

JUNE 1906

Dear Ro,

You will hardly know Father when you come home. Sometimes I hardly recognize him myself and I have witnessed his decline. One side of his face droops and it takes near to forever for him to spit out a word. Not that he was ever much a one for words cepting behind a pulpit, but now even less so. His energy is jest gone. I fear Martha abuses him with near constant fussing. Time hasn't softened her atall.

We are very proud of the way you're helping those children in the tent camps. Seeing those sweet smiles every day must be very rewarding. Thank you for sending the newspaper photographs. Now that much of the rebuilding is done, perhaps you can find your way back to us.

I have been walking out with Ava Wallace after church on Sundays.

Josiah and Pauline took an anniversary trip to Chicago. The gowns, the traffic, and the entertainment up there are all she can talk about. I think she'd move to the city if Josie would agree.

We do hope you'll come for a visit soon. Better yet—move back. Family doesn't hold you to San Francisco any longer, and we miss you terribly.

Much love,
Timmy (Still your favorite brother)

LITTLE TIMMY WAS TOO YOUNG TO WALK OUT with a girl, and I couldn't wait to tell him so. How I missed him! I put the letter aside. If only I could go home for a visit. But I had to wait for the insurance money for the house. With that check in hand, I could go east as an independent woman. A woman who could take care of her own needs, beholden to no one.

Soon after the quake, Nellie had moved into a room in a boarding house while waiting on her insurance payout, and Val's father had arranged a loan for him. He would have a real home soon, one whose foundation was already being laid. The tent city was shrinking, day by day, and soon it would be quite lonely. It would be time to head back east.

After lunch, I grabbed a hammer and went to find Val where I'd left him shoveling a trench behind a row of shanties. "Let's get your roof on over that tarpaper."

He leaned on his shovel. "Tomorrow."

"Don't be silly. There's hours of daylight left. Those shingles might disappear by morning."

"True, but it's not like I paid for them. Finders, keepers; losers, weepers. If someone else takes them, I'll scrounge for more."

I was practically skipping, already making my way down the row of tents to his shanty. He was two steps behind when I stopped. A plaintive bleating came from within one of the tents. My heart leapt— a baby! The bleat became a wail. I stood still, unable to move on.

One minute passed. My hand touched the tent flap, but still I didn't open it. "Hello? Do you need help?"

No answer.

"Anything we can do?" Val called out.

Though it violated unspoken rules of courtesy to enter a tent un-invited, I lifted the flap, peeked inside, and a strangled cry escaped before I could stifle it. Just beyond the opening a young woman lay sprawled in a puddle of blood, her baby squalling, beating its spindly arms and legs between the mother's thighs, umbilical cord still attached. I dropped the hammer and rushed inside, Val right behind me. I raised and stroked the baby's head and made shushy noises of comfort, letting it suckle on a finger, while Val dropped to his knees, trying to find the mother's pulse.

I watched, anxious, but he shook his head and gently closed the mother's eyes. She looked so young, still in her early teens, long, damp strands of dark hair plastered against a sweet heart-shaped face. Had she given birth alone? Had no one heard her cries? Val flew into doctor mode and sent me for water and whiskey and clean towels. Moments later I returned. He rinsed his pocket knife in whis-key and cut the cord. I cleaned the baby girl's body and swaddled her in a towel.

Val strode from tent to tent, inquiring if anyone knew the young woman. No one did. One man claimed he had heard moaning but thought it was just another case of digestive problems. They plagued everyone in camp from time to time.

I took the baby back to my lean-to. Val followed and I handed the child to him. I cut the tip from a glove and filled the finger with sugar water. The baby hushed immediately.

"Where'd you learn to do that?" Val asked.

"On the farm where I grew up. When we had an orphaned cow or kitten, we made a sugar tit like this. It will only do until I can find a wet nurse or a goat. This child will need nourishment."

"I'll put up notices to find her family. There must be a father, grandparents, someone who will want this wee one."

I cradled the tiny body tighter against my breasts, smoothing the dark hair away from her forehead. "No one nearby knew the mother."

"Ro." My ears heard the warning in his voice, but my heart ignored it. "We have to keep looking. She must have family here."

"Some family. No one helped her birth the baby." I tried to beat down the hope from my voice.

Val closed his eyes. "Ro, you can't just take someone else's child."

"I know." But maybe I could. Maybe I had found her for a reason. Maybe she was meant to be mine. *Finders, keepers.*

Every day I cared for her. I scrounged for milk, clothes, nappies. I cuddled, bathed, kissed.

Every day Val reminded me this was temporary, that the baby had family somewhere. He put up flyers and inquired of everyone he could find in the tent city. No one came for the baby. We buried the mother and pounded a wooden cross at the head of her grave.

We took the baby to visit with Nellie, who agreed she was exceptionally beautiful. "That head of dark fuzzy hair—just adorable!"

I beamed as if Nellie were praising my own accomplishment. Nellie suggested the baby and I move into her rented room. It would be crowded but safer. Val thought we should stay near the birth mother's tent in case a relative came for the baby. Another two weeks passed.

Things might have continued as they were, but a telegram arrived from Timmy that forced my hand: *Father's condition worse. If you don't come soon, it will be too late. If money needed, will wire immediately.*

When I showed Val the message, he insisted I should leave the baby with Nellie.

I cuddled my little one closer and didn't answer. How could I part with that tiny rosebud mouth, the sweet grasp of precious fingers, even for a day? I had failed to keep Ben safe. I would not fail this baby.

In the pre-dawn hours the next morning, I knocked on Val's shanty door and I invited him to walk with us out to the Bay.

As rays of light filled the sky, I extended my arms outward, a sacred offering of the baby to the sun. "Her name is Solina. It means sunlight."

I was meant to be this baby's mother. I could feel maternal light shining within, warming my every pore.

MAY 1920

SOLINA'S MOUTH FELL WIDE OPEN. "That baby was me? You just found me—that's what you're saying?"

I pressed my lips together. At the conclusion of this installment of my tale, recited at length in our hotel room's tiny sitting area, I didn't expect gratitude exactly—well, maybe I did—but I didn't expect—well, I don't know what I expected. I had never quite been able to picture this moment, to anticipate her reaction, and that was one reason I had not shared her origins with her until now. The main reason was that I wasn't sure what I had done was quite legal. I was terrified someone would emerge from the shadows and try to take her from me.

"Didn't you try to find my father? My grandparents?"

"Yes, but without a name to work from, there was little chance of success." In truth, I hadn't tried very hard.

Her lips quivered. "What about Michael? Did you just find him too?"

"It's not as if I go around searching for stray children under bushes. I gave birth to Michael soon after we moved to West Virginia. You were old enough you should remember my pregnancy."

Her face crumpled. "He's yours. You love him more; you let him get by with everything."

I rose from my seat and knelt beside her, cradling her beautiful, tear-streaked face in my hands. "Don't be ridiculous, you silly goose. With you, it was love at first sight. I would have died if someone had stepped forward and claimed you. You must know I love all my children just the same. And you, Solina, are one of the greatest blessings in my life."

She threw her arms around me, weeping quietly. I stroked her back and ignored the tears running down my own face. I didn't know how to make her understand how much I loved her. I was grateful to be alone in our hotel room as Solina learned about her origins rather than at home with the rest of the family or in Nellie's boarding house. This revelation needed to occur privately. The moment was too fraught with emotion to be shared with anyone else, not even Nellie or Val. It was fitting, too, that it happened in the city of Solina's birth.

"What would have happened to me if you hadn't . . ." Mumbled against my shoulder, her question floundered and dropped off altogether.

I intuited she was wondering what one did with a foundling. Did you take it to the police, the fireman, the city council, a minister? I had refused to consider the proper procedure, because whatever authority took her, the end result would likely have been some horrible institutional setting.

"Solina, as God is my witness, I would never have let them take you to an orphanage. You have no idea how terrible the conditions in those places can be. Some children suffer horribly; many are malnourished or abused. Most are barely educated. They certainly don't have pretty dresses and hair ribbons. Some end up like that woman—Jack's mistress." I squeezed her tighter. "That was never, ever going to happen to *my* baby, and you were *my* baby from the first moment I picked you up and your tiny hand gripped my finger, and you will always be my baby, no matter how old you get."

She leaned away from me, wiped away her tears. "I guess I'm lucky then."

I nodded, with no small measure of relief. "We both are. I was desperate for a baby to love and you were in desperate need of a mother."

Angie

I FINISH READING ALOUD RO'S DECLARATION of how she loved all her children the same, and close the scrapbook. We sit in silence, MacKenzie on one side of Mom, me on the other. We are alone, the three of us, holding hands at two in the morning.

So this is why Mom pushed me so hard to read about my ancestors, her special way of telling me one more time that she loves both of us, MacKenzie and me. I've known this in my heart all along. I am so glad MacKenzie is here, that she heard the story. Mom may have constructed some scenes straight from Solina's diary, but her loving heart beats beneath the words, infusing them with her warmth.

MacKenzie sighs. "That's the most beautiful story I ever heard. Rosella's so much like you, Mom. She was meant to be a mother. She was Angie's great great grandmother, is that right? And she became a famous potter?"

"Yes," Mom agrees. "MacKenzie, you have an important woman in your family tree, too. A great great aunt on my mother's side, Susan Dew Hoff. She became the first West Virginia woman licensed to be a physician. Happened right here in Harrison County, over in West Milford. They wouldn't let her go to school to study medicine, so she studied with her father, who was a doctor, and she passed the exam back in 1889. I've been working on the scrapbook with your special family story. It will be your birthday gift this year."

Leave it to my mother to understand that MacKenzie doesn't need the surprise on her birthday; she needs to be wrapped in our love right now.

I want to do something to boost Mac's spirits, too. I put the scrapbook away and set up my laptop on the kitchen table. "Mac, come over here and teach me what a hashtag is."

"Me, too," Mom says.

Mac's enthusiasm glows in her eyes. "Do you have twitter accounts?"

Mom and I both shake our heads. Mac sets up accounts for both of us and explains how tweeting and retweeting works.

After a while, Mom says she's going to bed. "Twitter is for the birds."

"Seriously. I don't get why anyone wants to limit the number of words they can use."

"You two are so out of it," Mac says.

I can see she is going to be my official tweeter of AFT strike news. After she posts tweets supporting the strike, I check out the teachers' Facebook page. I am not the only one who can't sleep tonight. Before I know it, morning creeps near. Time for a shower and lots of coffee.

Get ready, Charleston! Big doings ahead.

Rosella

I PROMISED TO SHOW SOLINA her birth mother's grave after the exhibition was over.

The exhibition—I glanced at my watch and had a moment of panic. There was so much work to be done before the big event. We had best get on with it. "Right now we need to get ourselves over to Mindy's gallery and uncrate the pottery, so pretty yourself up, quickly now."

Pushing aside my tea, I hurried to wash my face and choose fresh clothing. I finished long before Solina, who dawdled as teenage girls will, certain that all eyes will be focused on them and them alone, when in truth, others are rarely all that interested in us, being more interested in themselves. We are self-centered creatures, even the best of us. When others praise me for Solina's adoption, I am quick to point out I received at least as much benefit as she.

As we boarded a streetcar, Solina whispered darkly, "I hope no one recognizes you from the newspaper stories."

"Not likely, my dear." News photos never were very clear, merely blurred ink dabs. It set me to wondering again who might have told the reporter about our scheduled event on family planning. Such a shame that those policemen had confiscated my brochures. They represented a significant personal financial investment. I didn't suppose there was the slightest hope of recovering them. Who had set the police on me? I suspected a single culprit lurked behind both stories, the one claiming I was a bigamist and the other on my arrest for intent to disseminate lewd materials. I supposed I was becoming quite famous, though not in the way I'd hoped.

At the gallery, the story of my arrest wagged every tongue.

Four copies of the *Examiner* were on hand for all to see, much to Solina's dismay—as if the poor girl hadn't had enough to cope with this morning.

I took her hand and squeezed, our eyes meeting with what I hoped was mutual understanding. "Everything will be okay."

"I know." Doubt lingered in her words.

I mouthed *I love you* to her before turning to greet Alexandra Underwood.

I can't say I was pleased by the gossiping tongues any more than Solina. Especially as I was certain I detected a smirk on Alexandra's smile. Both Alexandra and her daughter wore the shorter dress lengths, black and beaded. I noticed Solina studying their fashions and bobbed hair with obvious admiration. I sighed. She reminded me of myself at that age. I supposed she would be eager to copy the new look, no matter what I said about frivolous pursuits. I might as well save my breath.

Although we had our differences, Alexandra and I, she had collected a considerable amount of my work and had loaned it to Mindy for the exhibition. For that, I was grateful. I still didn't understand why she bought my pottery. Was it to support Mindy's gallery—since Mindy earned commission on all the pieces sold? Or did she take some secret satisfaction from owning the work made by the wife of the man she'd had an affair with? After Jack had disappeared, Nellie let it slip that Alexandra's open marriage had been open to the husbands of her friends, including mine. I shouldn't have been surprised. Jack was a pretty thing, and Alexandra collected pretty things. I wondered if he had transmitted his disease to her—and if so, if she still supported sterilization of people who contracted social diseases.

I thanked Mindy again for persuading the police to release me.

"It wouldn't do for the guest of honor to miss her own show." Mindy's smile dimpled her cheeks. Such a shame that the caved-in features resulted in a vessel that missed being as beautiful outside as I found her inside to be. Was that why no young man had claimed my excellent friend as his wife? Or had it truly been Mindy's decision to eschew marriage? I remembered that long-ago proclamation she'd made that she would never relinquish her freedom to a husband.

We proceeded to unpack my pottery—Solina, Nellie, and me—

unwrapping piece after piece from folds of newspaper, afterward wiping each down with a soft, damp cloth. We left the arrangement of the pieces up to Mindy and Alexandra, as they had already created small placards identifying each piece and distinguishing the work done in California from that done in West Virginia.

"You made all of these?" Wonderment resonated in Solina's voice.

I was pleased for the distraction from the emotional revelations of the past few days. I was feeling overwhelmed myself. It was the first time I'd seen so much of my work gathered in one place. Even I could see it was an impressive array of pottery, the glazes of crushed raspberry, soft olive, butternut, and matte blue predominating. Shapes varied from tall vases with outward sloping sides to squat pots with narrow-lipped openings. What distinguished my work from other artists' was the slip trail: designs of leaves, flowers, or trees created with slightly raised lines of clay squeezed through a narrow tube, a technique I learned under the direction of the renowned Frederick Hurten Rhead at Arequipa, north of the Bay area. My early pieces were made there from clay dug by boys Arequipa hired. At first, I simply did the decorating, like the other girls, but eventually I was allowed to shape pots. I created my later pieces in my own shed in West Virginia. I loved the texture of wet clay on my hands, the way it smoothed and soothed as it rotated on the wheel, the way it whispered my mother's name, reminding me of those first vessels we'd made together. These new pots were my creations from beginning to end. Most were similar in shape to those made at Arequipa, but recently I had begun sculpting the clay into shapes: a flowering dogwood branch, a hen, a spray of roses. Even plates and cups. Fanciful pieces attracted attention; the practical earned my bread and butter. Tableware sets disappeared from shopkeepers' shelves as fast as I could make them.

"I wish Papa were here to see this," Solina said.

"Yes, that is a shame," I agreed. "If it weren't for him, I never would have learned to make pottery. It was he who arranged for my recuperation at Arequipa."

"Tell me the story of how he proposed again," Solina begged. "It's so romantic!"

This was a story I knew she had already written in her diary—not because I'd read it but because she told me so. I ignored the lift of Nellie's right eyebrow, the narrowing of her eyes, the downward tilt of her chin.

JULY 1906

THE STRAW BASKET FELT UNSUBSTANTIAL beneath my feet. I clung to Val's arm, half afraid I would float away into the pale yellow light of the morning. The balloon lurched a bit as it rose. I gasped, giggled, and looked up to meet Val's brown eyes smiling down. Odd, how his narrow face became so beautiful when he smiled. Quite possibly more beautiful than any other man I'd ever known. Even Jack. It came from a different source, something inside, rather than an agreeable aggregate of facial features. A couple in a carriage on the outskirts of the city looked up and pointed when they heard the whoosh of the burner. I laughed and waved from the basket of the hot air balloon. I didn't know what possessed Val to arrange this adventure, but I was glad he had. What would my family think if they could see me now? Soon I would be seeing them again.

The balloon rose higher and higher until the city receded below and left me with a stomach-dropping feeling of unreality. This is what the world looks like to birds, I thought with amazement. Houses resembled children's blocks; people, Ben's toy soldiers. How he would have loved this! I suddenly felt Ben's presence, as if his spirit shared in the joy of my journey.

For the first time in ages, I reached in my canvas bag and took out the sketchbook. I drew the world below. I flipped to another blank page and sketched clouds above. I could feel Val watching as I outlined sailboats in the harbor.

His breath touched my neck and I felt little shivers of happiness as he leaned near to see the details. "It's good to see you drawing again."

I closed the sketchpad and flung out my arms. "I feel as if I am flying. A bird catching the air in my wings." I closed my eyes. The world was so beautiful, I couldn't possibly hold all its splendors inside, couldn't possibly cherish each moment before it slid away and became the past.

Val cleared his throat. The man he hired to take up the balloon turned away. "There's something I want to ask you. We've known each other for some time now, and—I mean, I hope I am not pre-suming—well, I am presuming, but I hope you'll forgive me. You are a fascinating woman, one with great courage and fortitude—"

I opened my eyes and looked at him curiously. What was he go-ing on about? His thin face narrowed even more when he became this intense. He wore the same expression when he started in on the efficacy of some newly discovered herbal cure or the possibilities of cross-continent flight opened up by the Wright Brothers or the need to have federal inspection of meat, food, and drugs. His many enthusiasms tickled me. It suddenly occurred to me that perhaps he had arranged this outing—perhaps he was going to overlook the many things that made me an unsuitable match. The humiliation I'd suffered by Jack's attention to other women. Being a widow. The long depression after Ben's death. My lack of family position. Maybe Val could overlook all these flaws. We did get along famously well. Was it possible he felt the same tingles in my presence I felt in his?

MAY 1920

"AND THEN HE ASKED ME THE QUESTION EVERY WOMAN IN LOVE wants to hear," I said, distracted from my tale as across the room Mindy placed a pink matte vase with iris blooms on top of a white box. Two similar boxes, each slightly taller, stood ready to accept additional pieces for display.

"Oh, Mama, that's the most romantic story ever!" Solina's dark eyes sparkled.

"Yes, wasn't it?" Her response filled me with delight, though I should have turned my talents toward fiction writing, instead of visual arts, for fiction it was. The truth was constructed of consid-erably more dirt and less air, but I wanted my daughter to hold on to some illusions a while longer.

Val had taken me on a balloon ride that morning, that much was true. As soon as we rose above the trees, he reached inside a large picnic basket and took out an assortment of Petri dishes, which he uncovered one by one. He exposed the contents of each container to air in the upper atmosphere because he entertained the notion that differences in air and gravity in the sky could affect mold growth on food and other substances. Grass. Soil. Snot. Those containers were bad enough, but I confess I covered my nose with my hankie when he uncovered the dish containing a sample of Little Cuss's poo. He had prepared slides of these same substances yesterday. When he returned to earth, he would prepare a separate set of slides of the substances after exposure to the upper atmosphere to examine under a microscope.

If he was so keen on diagnosing something, he should diagnose the nature of the disorder that sent him careening from one enthusiasm to another willy-nilly.

Satisfied the containers had been exposed long enough, he re-covered them.

Val turned away and fished around in the picnic hamper for apples, tucked inside, probably bumping up against the unsavory contents of the containers. He gave me an apple and began to munch on one himself. A chunk of apple stuck in his throat and he coughed, and then chattered on. "Settlers mostly planted them for the purpose of making hard cider rather than to eat. When people happen onto one that produces tasty fruit, they graft new trees from the original. The first ones originated in Eastern Europe near the Caucasus Mountains. These—" he waved his apple in the air—"are a variety known as American Beauties."

I stared out at the clouds. "You must really like apples to have learned so much about them."

He reached into the basket again, and with a broad smile, an-nounced, "Champagne! I understand it's traditional to sip it on these flights."

The balloon master agreed. "Yes, sir, it is."

Val poured the bubbly into two glasses and proffered one to me. "Here's to you, Ro, and to the success of my experiments."

Heavens, yes, let us drink to snot and poo.

I COULD HARDLY CONFESS THE TRUE VERSION to my daughter. A touch of foreboding washed over me. In spinning my story, I had cast myself and Val in too grand a light. I wanted her to love us, to admire us, and yes, to see that even if life knocked you down one day, the next it could bring you joy. But was I filling the girl's head with too many romantic notions?

"Could we go up in a balloon while we're here?" Solina asked.

Heaven forbid. "Oh, I doubt we'll have time."

Nellie smiled angelically, her hands clasped over her midsection. "I am sure we'll make time, my dear. Who knows when you'll have another opportunity."

Nellie winked at me, taking devilish delight in my predicament. She knew I had grown quite airsick on that balloon ride. I had purged the contents of my stomach, including the champagne, all over the basket's floor. So much for romance. So much for the friend who knew all my secrets. She also knew the real story about the proposal.

I had been sure he would propose on the balloon ride—but for whatever reason, he didn't. Could have been his excitement over his experiments. Could have been my airsickness. Could have been the man was shy and bumbling around women. Or, most likely, as my life with him later bore out, Val Martin was a remarkably asexual man. Anyway, afterwards, we went to dinner at a fine restaurant and I decided if there was to be advancement in our relationship beyond the platonic, it would be up to me. I had planned to pop the question as soon as we were seated, but first there was the ordering and then the waiter hovered about and couples at nearby tables seemed to be listening to every word we said. I cut my amberjack into small pieces and pushed them around on my plate, unable to swallow more than a few morsels. As luck would have it, on a platform in a nearby corner of the restaurant, a pianist fingered his way across a Baby Grand and a stunningly beautiful songstress warbled along with him. The song was "I Love You Truly." I took an unseemly large gulp of wine and set down my glass. It really was now or never.

"Well, Val, in two days Solina and I will be off to West Virginia on the Southern Pacific. If you are coming with me, we had best get married tomorrow."

And so we were. For the second time that day, we opened a bottle of champagne. This time I savored every drop.

I had heretofore regarded that "Love You Truly" song as rather mushy and overwrought. From that night on, whenever I heard its melodic refrain—"Life with its sorrow, life with its tear/Fades into dreams when I feel you are near"—my lips trembled. It is truly the greatest love song ever written.

Solina need never know I was the one who did the proposing. A mother has to have some secrets.

While I had been musing over the less than romantic beginning to my marriage, Nellie finished the fictional tale for Solina. "Your mother and Val married right away, and you and your papa both accompanied her back to West Virginia. I was so lonely without your mother and couldn't wait for your return. I have always thought of you, Solina, as my niece. I am so glad you have come to visit. You must make your mother bring you back more often."

My daughter enthusiastically agreed. I was lost in my memories. After we married, I had gone home at last. I had arrived in time to tell my father goodbye and for him to make his peace with me. Everyone assumed Solina was our own child, mine and Val's, and we saw no reason to tell anyone any different. After the funeral, Jack's Aunt Elizabeth declared Solina looked exactly like me when I was a baby, though I knew there wasn't a shred of truth in that. Solina was far, far more beautiful than I had ever been, and goodness knows she didn't resemble Val in the least beyond the dark eyes. In fact, Nellie was the only other one who ever knew the truth about Solina's birth. She was the keeper of all my secrets.

The thought caused me to turn and look at her with fresh—and newly suspicious—eyes. Could Nellie have let my secrets spill to a reporter? She would never betray me deliberately, but the old dear could be a bit of a gossip.

I watched Mindy Kenneson and Alexandra Underwood debate the placement of a green amphora and a blue vase with oranges. High or low. This side forward or that one. Alexandra was pushy, prone to getting her way, even though this was Mindy's gallery. I crossed the room and turned the vase with oranges to show off what I considered the best side. After all, it was my work—even though Alexandra owned the vase. The set of her lips dismissed my opinion as inconsequential. As soon as she thought I wasn't looking, she rotated the vase back.

"Well, then, I'll see you tomorrow for the opening," I said to Mindy and collected Solina and Nellie.

I glanced over my shoulder one last time. Of all the people I knew in this city, Alexandra was the one I clashed with most frequently. She had been so angry when I led the revolt against eugenics. Had she somehow learned my secrets and fed them to a newspaper?

~~~

1907-1911

AFTER MY FATHER'S FUNERAL, we returned to San Francisco to live in Val's newly built home. My insurance check for the destroyed house Jack had built finally came, so, added to his income, we had an adequate nest egg to live on.

Sadly, I learned from Timmy that my father had left the farmhouse we'd been raised in to Martha. Each of my brothers would inherit some acreage. I wondered if they would keep it or sell it. Our neighbor Gunner Beck was courting Martha, and it was only a matter of time until the family home belonged to him. Timmy reckoned Gunner was finally going to get a piece of our land, and a piece of Martha's temper, as well.

Nellie, Mindy, and I resumed the push for women's rights, with Val's support. Attorney Clara Shortridge Foltz spearheaded our campaign in the Bay area. To my delight, the legislature agreed to put the issue on the ballot, so we redoubled our efforts to contact every male we could find and appeal to them as mothers, grandmothers, wives, teachers, and nurses. We distributed millions of flyers and "Votes for Women" buttons. We held a massive rally in October, enlivened by fireworks and a band playing. I insisted on attending, even though I had developed a rather serious cold.

On October 10, 1911, my friends and fellow suffragists gathered in our parlor awaiting election results. I truly lacked the energy to leave the house, so my friends came to me instead. We had been pushing for our rights together for so long, they wouldn't hear of leaving me out of what we hoped would be a grand celebration.

But early in the evening, Val brought us the terrible news: the measure was failing in San Francisco again, and it had barely passed in Los Angeles. We were devastated.

"All our work for naught," Nellie said.

Mindy reminded us of Aunt Susan's slogan: Failure is Impossible! "She fought her whole life and never gave up. Neither shall we."

Eventually, I knew we would pick up our broken hearts and carry on, but it was difficult to think of that now. I pressed a handkerchief to my lips to catch a cough. Weariness dragged at my soul. Our gathering adjourned and I trudged to bed. Val brought me a cup of hot broth. Nellie took Solina and Little Cuss home with her so I could rest.

News the next day heartened me. The rural counties were voting in favor of the measure. It took several days for all the ballots to be counted, but in the end, California women won the right to vote. The headlines declared that San Francisco was the largest city in the world where women could vote. My friends gathered in our parlor again to celebrate and our spirits were lifted by the victory, though Mindy reminded us the fight wasn't over until women everywhere in the United States shared our rights.

"It isn't over until we can vote for President," I said.

Mindy and I planned to take a train to Washington, D.C., to protest, but by the time November came, my coughing had increased, persistent, sometimes violent, wearing me down more than I cared to admit. When Solina napped, so did I. A long journey anywhere was out of the question.

One afternoon Val came home early after visiting patients. He found me asleep on the bed, Little Cuss snuggled against me, a sketchbook and pencils abandoned at my side. Solina was napping in her own room.

The most recent sketch was one of Solina sleeping, thumb in mouth, looking like the angel she was. He moved the drawings and pencil from the bed where I was resting. "You have filled so many sketchbooks with drawings of that child, I might just get jealous." I knew he was teasing because he adored her as much as I did.

I started to laugh but it quickly descended into a coughing jag. Afterward I kept my handkerchief crimped in my hand to hide the blood.

"Not feeling any better?"

I shook my head, not trusting myself to talk yet for fear of coughing again.

"Are you using the tincture of cannabis?"

I took a sip of water from the glass by the bedside table. "Yes, thank you, it eases the sore throat."

"And the oranges I brought you—two a day?"

I nodded.

"And carrots?"

I wrinkled my nose. "My skin is turning orange as a pumpkin."

"More like pale as a ghost. What did you think of the yoghurt this morning?"

"Didn't much care for it, a bit sour, but thank you for the trouble you went to in procuring it for me."

"No trouble, since I've decided to take it daily myself. Yoghurt has many fine medicinal qualities. Dr. Grigorov from Bulgaria has convinced me of its efficacy in treating many disorders."

I smiled weakly. Val was always on the hunt for the newest, the latest, the best health remedies. "Perhaps I'll try it again, maybe with honey or mashed fruit."

"Good, good." He frowned. "There are tears in your eyes. Is something wrong? Something I've said?"

"You never are anything but kind, Val." I dabbed my eyes with a clean corner of the handkerchief. "I'm worried Solina will catch my cold."

"I fear it is more than a cold."

"No, it's just—"

"You've been coughing for months, and I've seen the bloody handkerchiefs you've been trying to hide. It could be tuberculosis. I'm seeing cases everywhere I turn, more women than men. Breathing in all those ashes after the fire has caused an increase in the number of cases, I think."

"It's just a cold. Once the weather warms, I'm sure it will clear up." Solina was nearly four—she deserved a healthy mother to look after her. I refused to be sick.

"Colds go away after a few weeks, Ro."

I could hold in my grief no longer. I bawled. I couldn't fail another child. I just couldn't.

Val sat on the bed beside me. "It would be best if you spent a few months resting."

I shook my head but that exertion only started me coughing again.

"Real rest without a child, a dog, and a husband to care for—my prescription for you, Ro. You need to concentrate on taking care of you, so you get well. Nellie is coming over in the morning to look after Solina. I have found just the place for you to rest. I went to visit the facility, and I was most impressed."

I dug my fingers in his arm. "No, I can rest here, please."

He kissed my forehead. "I know you don't want to risk infecting Solina. Besides, you're going to love this place, I promise. If you don't, you don't have to stay."

I agreed to a visit, only to make him happy. He had gone to so much trouble. But I had no intention of staying there, let alone loving it.

I was wrong. I liked Arequipa immediately. The way the buildings nestled into the lush green hillside, as though they were natural as the trees and shrubbery. The openness of the graceful structures. Even the air was scented by new-cut wood and smoky leaves.

Dr. Philip Brown, the handsome friend of Val's who conceived this place, led us on a tour of the facilities. His eyes lit with enthusiasm as he showed off the open design of the dormitory. At times, clefts appeared in his cheeks balancing the deeper one in his chin. The dorm's sleeping porch was walled in for three-and-a-half feet at the bottom, with the next four feet to the roof left open. A breeze ruffled the doctor's thick white hair even though they stood indoors. I could see why Val liked this place.

Next Dr. Brown led us to the pottery studio, which Val had kept secret from me. "For the first month, patients rest most of the day, but for the rest of their six-month stay at Arequipa they can work here if they wish."

"Arequipa is a lovely name," I said. "What does it mean?"

"It's a Peruvian word that translates roughly to 'Place of Peace' or 'Place of Rest.'" Dr. Brown motioned to the walls, which boasted banks of windows. In between were shelves of pots ready to be decorated. "The women work for a few hours a day, whatever they feel up to. This isn't a charity. Patients can feel comfortable knowing they earn their keep. But the biggest benefit is the pleasure derived from creating something with their hands. Your husband tells me you are an excellent artist, Mrs. Martin."

Blushing, I examined the potter's wheel and the lathe. "Not excellent, but I do enjoy it."

"She's being modest, Dr. Brown," Val said.

"Our facility is founded on the philosophy of the Arts and Craft movement. We believe contact with beauty is healing, good for the body and the soul. We strive to make the surroundings beautiful—" the doctor motioned to the tree-covered hills—"and provide women with the opportunity to create something lovely with their hands. They will leave Arequipa with good health and with a skill enabling them to get decent jobs."

Val nodded. "It's a fine plan. Lying in bed for months on end is debilitating, not only to the body, but to the spirit."

"Exactly," Dr. Brown said. "The experience at other institutions has been that patients recover more quickly if they have something useful to do. Make baskets. Carve wood. Weave cloth. Different hospitals are trying different approaches, but the result seems to be the same. Improved health."

I remembered my own months in bed after Ben's death. The doctor's words rang true.

Val left off his fiddling with the mechanisms of the wheel and lathe. "When I heard about the artistic elements of Dr. Brown's treatment, I immediately thought of you, Ro."

Dr. Brown inclined his white head toward me. "Your husband showed me some of your sketches, Mrs. Martin, the sunflowers and hydrangeas and the hen. I think you can work these designs into a different medium. Pottery. In time, you could assist with the design of our first molds. I've hired the renowned art director Frederick Rhead to oversee that aspect of the work. He was educated at the Wedgwood Institute and Stoke-on-Trent in England."

What an opportunity to learn from a trained artist! If I had to leave my family behind for a few weeks, there could be no better place than Arequipa to rest and recover.

"But Solina—"

Val hushed me. "Nellie and I will see to it that she is cared for in every way."

I knew it was true, but my heart was sore at the thought of separation.

The doctor herded us outside along a narrow path to view the benches backed against Satsuki azaleas where patients could sit and paint pottery under the shade of various hardwoods. "Many women would jump at the chance to be tutored by Mr. Rhead," the doctor said. "I've turned several of the finest ladies of San Francisco down when they asked if they could visit Arequipa to study with him. I think perhaps you know one of the families. Alexandra and Lydia Underwood."

I was hooked.

LITTLE CUSS RAN AHEAD OF VAL AND SOLINA, gobbling like a piglet. Laughing, I stood and picked him up and let him lick and sniff at my cheeks and neck. I nuzzled my nose into his black and white fur and laughed. "I missed you, too, Sweetheart."

"What about me?" Solina demanded as she caught up to us.

I scooped her up into a bear hug and kissed both her cheeks. "You most of all, my darling girl."

I was grateful for a morning when it wasn't raining so we could sit outside on a stone bench, my heart aching as I watched Solina's little legs swinging in the air beneath the seat. She was still so small. Val settled on the other side of her, holding Little Cuss. My husband was hatless today, perhaps a nod to the spring afternoon, though he wore the usual dark suit.

My colleagues or sisters-in-illness—whatever you wanted to call them—scurried toward us to make over Solina and pet the dog. Pamela offered my daughter a cookie and Little Cuss a bread scrap she'd wrapped in a clean cloth at lunch time expressly for this purpose. Not to be outdone, Jane gave Solina a bouquet of wildflowers and let the dog lick a bacon morsel from her hand.

"Enough," I protested in a sunny voice. "You're spoiling both of them. Besides, Little Cuss is much too chubby as it is. Dr. Brown says if we aren't careful we'll kill the poor little creature with kindness." I had saved a few bits of cheese for him myself. For Solina, I had sculpted a teensy dog from clay. It wasn't a very good effort, but Solina seemed to like it. It was hard not to overdo the treats when I only saw my babies once a week. I struggled against the instinct to make up for all the days we were apart.

We all walked over to the pottery. The art director, Frederick Rhead, held one of my vases in his hands, running his fingers over the daffodil blossoms and spiky leaves I'd carved into the clay. Rhead was a wild-haired fellow with curls that sprang out in all directions from his scalp.

Rhead set the bowl down and teased me. "You're sure you just learned to do this? You didn't sneak into the Weller pottery factory over in Ohio when you were little?"

I laughed. "Never did." I introduced Val.

"Mrs. Martin tells me you're a doctor."

The men exchanged pleasantries before Rhead turned the talk back to his passion: pottery.

"Your wife has a gift, Mr. Martin. She is the best student by far at Arequipa. I shall be loath to lose her in another month." The art director nodded once, setting his tight curls in motion. He turned on his heel and left.

Embarrassed yet pleased by Rhead's flattery, I led Val to another shelf of pottery. "This week Mr. Rhead is going to let me apply all the slip trail decoration for the other ladies' vases." I held up a bowl Rhead had designed himself as an example. "See the raised lines? They are applied with a squeeze bag—like cake decorating! Oh, he's a master, Val. I'm so lucky to have this opportunity to learn from him."

Other patients restricted themselves to painting designs Rhead created because they didn't like the mucky feel of wet clay on their hands, but I reveled in it. I liked to see a piece through from beginning to end. Shaping the damp clay on the potter's wheel which I spun by means of a foot treadle. Shaving the base and sides of the piece to define the curves. Decorating with carving or slip trail. Spraying on glaze. Only men fired the pieces, but Mr. Rhead had invited me into the kiln room to view the process. Soon, he said, he would teach me to do sgraffito, which involved scratching through one contrasting layer of slip with a darning needle to reveal the layer beneath. So much to learn—and so little time remaining in my stay! I couldn't believe I'd been at Arequipa for nearly six months. My health had improved immeasurably during the past five months, and though I relished learning everything Mr. Rhead had to teach me, I couldn't wait to return home to my little family.

We walked the dog along the narrow path that ran between the rhododendrons, Solina skipping ahead. We returned to the same stone bench we'd occupied before. I knelt to inspect two bright yellow slugs among the damp, decaying leaves. Their bodies curled near each other without touching, one a c-shape, the other a backwards c inserted into the curve of the other. "Look, Solina, aren't they pretty?"

"Banana slugs," Val said. "They're courting."

He could still surprise me with the odd things he knew—the courtship habits of slugs, indeed! How long would the slugs remain like that, their lives linked to each other, encircling each other without touching? Not nearly as long as Val and I had.

After Val and Solina left, Pamela clucked her tongue. "Honey, that man looks at you as if you were the sun that gives rise to his days. And your daughter is adorable with all that beautiful dark hair and sweet smile. No wonder you have worked so hard at getting well."

Hmmm. What they didn't know is that Val looked at everything in the world with effervescent enthusiasm. Even banana slugs. I was happy to be included as one of his many interests. I believe we were both content with the family life we had forged together.

WHEN CERTAIN NO ONE WAS PRESENT, I pulled off a chunk of the Tootsie Roll Val smuggled in for me. I savored the sweet chewy chocolate, slowly rolling it around my mouth with my tongue. The remaining candy I slipped into my locker and tucked it between my unmentionables. It was against the rules to bring food to patients from the outside. Arequipa had many rules. Patients must be prompt to meals. No food could be in the wards. Shoes must have rubber heels. Only eight items of clothing per patient could be laundered by the staff a week. Fancy articles like dresses or shirts had to be fumigated and sent to town for laundering. If your temperature rose to 99.5 or above, you were confined to bed. (Fortunately, mine had remained normal after the first month.) And the rule I hated most: standing by with my chart at 10 a.m. for the doctor's visit. I would rather be in the pottery at work long before that. But rules were rules, and you kept them or hid your violations well. I was now allowed to work five hours a day, a great improvement over the solitary hour I'd been allowed in the beginning. I dawdled on the way to brush my teeth this morning, so I could finish the candy, rationalizing that is was such a small pleasure. It was a shame to have to wash the luscious taste away with the nasty flavor of salt and baking soda.

After I'd readied myself for the day and seen the doctor, I headed for the pottery with Pamela and Jane. I greeted Agnes, Frederick Rhead's wife, and slipped a smock over my white lingerie dress.

Agnes handed Pamela a container of glaze and turned her attention to me. "Are you painting the fruited vase today, then?"

"Yes, ma'am."

"The vase would have been quite pretty with a simple glaze, you know."

"Yes, ma'am, but the oranges and greens will pop against that deep blue background. They will draw the eye and give the piece a beautiful balance, don't you think?" Besides, I'd already added the slip trail. It would be a shame not to use the contrasting colors.

"My husband has taught you well." Agnes turned her attention toward Jane's bowl, much to my relief. I got along much better with Mr. Rhead than his wife, though I couldn't have said why. When Agnes spoke to me there always seemed to be an undercurrent of disapproval.

Carefully, I painted the oranges. The raised brown lines of slip trail formed a boundary that confined the paint so it didn't bleed into the background—much the way the walls of a well held water in place. Or the way a trench filled with water. I painted until lunchtime, chatting amiably with the other women. Then there was the required hour-long nap at 1:30. Wasted time. No, I reminded myself. This was nothing like the months I'd taken to bed after Ben's death. Getting well wasn't wasting my life. This place of peace and rest was saving it.

I loved Arequipa.

I couldn't wait to leave.

VAL'S LIPS CURLED WITH AMUSEMENT as he stole glances at my filling page after page of my sketchbook. I'd get a few curves of a landscape drawn, perhaps the horizon and a few hills, maybe the angles of a few trees and something new would catch my eye. I'd flip the page and start again. I felt as if I were seeing the world again after being shut away for years rather than six months. The windshield of his Ford did little to prevent my hat or my paper from flapping about. These automobiles were drafty affairs.

He grimaced as we hit yet another rut. "I hope all this air doesn't cause you to relapse."

"Don't be such a worrywart. I'm never going to be sick again. I've made up my mind—pull over! Right now, Val. Would you look at those Shooting Stars?"

Practically before he could stop the car, I opened the door and was tripping through a field of lavender and gentian blue flowers with strongly recurved petals, gold eyes with a thin wavy red edge, and a dark, exposed base that held short stamens. For half an hour while Solina happily picked posies, I sketched. Single blooms. Small groupings. Whole fields.

I closed my sketchbook and Solina presented me with the bouquet she'd gathered. "Oh, sweetie, aren't they the most beautiful things you ever saw?"

Joy lit up my daughter's face and I pulled her down into my lap and nuzzled my cheek against her curls. I held her at arm's length. "I take that back—your smile is the most beautiful thing I've ever seen."

Solina giggled and then wiggled free to chase after a tiger swallowtail butterfly that flitted by.

When we arrived home, I found Nellie in the kitchen, a full meal prepared for us. "Your favorites," she said. "Chicken pot pie with peas and carrots and my best gravy, along with baked apples and ice cream for dessert. "I'll be over every day to help with chores and cooking until you are settled back in and feeling stronger."

"It smells heavenly—you'll spoil me." I already felt stronger, perfectly capable of fixing our meals, but I had no intention of shooing her away. No one was a better cook than Nellie.

Soon we settled back into our routines, the only difference being Nellie insisted on coming to our house to share tea and gossip in the afternoons. When the letter arrived, she was there ensconced in a well-cushioned Queen Anne chair across from the sofa where I sat. Nellie preferred sitting in the Queen Anne because the arms supported her when it was time to stand again. She blamed her difficulty in rising on her age, but it was every bit as much the fault of the weight she had put on in the years since the earthquake. I feared for her health.

"This is a surprise," I said, opening the envelope that arrived in the post. I extracted a thick bundle—five handwritten pages. "I haven't heard from Jack's aunt for years, and now it appears she's practically written a book to me." I scanned the first paragraph and was ready to lay it aside. It didn't seem to hold important news, and I feared reading the whole thing and leaving Nellie sitting there twiddling her thumbs would be inexcusably rude.

"Read it aloud," Nellie suggested. "I do enjoy a good letter. Always full of news to share."

Nellie collected gossipy tidbits the way young girls collected hair ribbons or Val collected new ideas for good health. Well, I wasn't going to deny her the opportunity to hear the latest from back East. So sitting in my parlor, while Solina napped and Nellie drank tea, I began:

APRIL 10, 1912

My dear Rosella,

I am sure you are wondering why I have written to you after such a long time. I will soon make the circumstances clear, but first let me say it was such a pleasure meeting your new husband and baby. Though it seems like just yesterday you returned home to bury your father, your little girl must be nearly five already. Time surely flies as you get older. Please know that I wish the three of you nothing but happiness.

I have kept abreast of your life through your brother Timmy. Naturally, I have an interest in your well being. Since you were a tiny girl yourself, I have known you through the church where your father preached, and moreover, I have thought of you as a daughter ever since you married my nephew Jack. After your brother informed our congregation of your illness, we all prayed for you each Sunday. Your brother assures me that God has answered our prayers and you are feeling stronger now.

My health, alas, has lapsed even as yours has rebounded, but this is as it should be. You are young, and I am a silly old lady and have nothing to look forward to now except arranging for proper disposal of my worldly goods. No pity, please! I have not known the happiness of having children of my own, but I have experienced good fortune and known the love of a good man. Yet these blessings came at a cost. I will lay open my great sin to you, Rosella, because you deserve to understand my family history. After all, you have been a part of it. You will remember my husband Israel. My sister Joy was in love with Israel from the time she was a young girl, and even though I knew how deeply she cared for him, I contrived to turn him away from her. If ever a person was misnamed, it was Joy, for never was there a more joyless person. Even as a child, she was a complainer, but I have never shaken the guilt for the exaggerations—no, I shall be honest and admit the tales I told Israel about my sister bordered on lies. In any case, he turned from her to me. After I married him, Joy ran off with a coal miner. I don't know if she ever loved him but she couldn't tolerate seeing me and Israel together, so she took the first opportunity to elope. One day her miner up and deserted her, leaving Joy to raise four sons and two daughters alone. Israel and I offered assistance, but she refused and held a grudge against me until her death. I cannot blame her.

Neither can I blame Jack for abandoning Joy and his younger siblings. Like many a young man, Jack yearned for a better life than that of a coal miner, and Israel and I were somewhat to blame for those notions. Joy allowed him to stay with us in summers to help with our garden and one of his younger brothers took over his job in the mines for those months. It took the feeding and clothing of one child off my sister's hands, and I always sent him home with extras for his brothers. But living with us showed Jack a different sort of life than the one my poor sister could offer her brood. She blamed me for Jack's running off and refused to let any of the other boys visit us. I wouldn't know Jack's brothers if they knocked on my door. In truth, she was to blame for Jack's leaving, too. He had confided in me concerning her nagging and meanness to the boys.

I hoped my small role as a matchmaker between you and Jack in some measure atoned for the hardships of his early years. I know your father frowned on the match, and perhaps

he had good reasons, but I hoped the love of a fine girl raised
in my own church would stand my nephew in good stead.
As I face the end of my days, one of my deepest regrets has
been that my nephew preceded me in death, a horrible death
at that, and he passed on without my revealing my role in his
family's poor circumstances.

Now, to the point of this letter. You can imagine my
surprise—a complete shock, really—when Alistair Partnow—
you will remember him, he owned the feed and grain store—
returned two months ago from a trip to Seattle, swearing
as God was his witness, that he had seen my nephew Jack
Joyner—

My voice failed me for a moment, but then I managed to gasp
out the end of Elizabeth's sentence.

and he was very much . . . alive.

The pages slipped from my hands. I fell back against the sofa,
the blood draining from my head.

Nellie hoisted her bulk from her seat with far greater speed than
typical and was at my side, thrusting decorative pillows beside me
and arranging my head against them.

"You just lie down here, Ro. This is bizarre, quite bizarre indeed.
Shall I fetch water? Smelling salts?"

When I shook my head weakly against the pillows and managed
to breathe in again, she suggested sending for Val.

"For heaven's sake, no." I started to sit up, but with a gentle hand
on my chest, she encouraged me to remain supine.

"I won't send for him. I only thought—well, I don't know what
I was thinking. What shall we do?"

That *we* was why I loved her. Nellie stayed by my side through
every trial. The stillbirth. Ben's death. My illness. Jack's affairs and
his death—if indeed he was dead. She had engineered my accep-
tance in the finest parlors in San Francisco—Nellie was a true friend.

I recovered my wits enough to turn attention to the letter. "Surely
this man was mistaken."

"Mistaken identity, that must be it." Nellie retrieved the fallen pages and offered them to me. "Perhaps the letter goes on to explain that very thing."

I pushed the pages back into her hands. "You read the rest to me, please." My chest felt so tight; my breath, so strained. I prayed the consumption wasn't returning.

Nellie rustled through the sheets until she found the place I'd left off.

You can imagine my surprise—a complete shock, really—when Alistair Partnow—you will remember him, he owned the feed and grain store—returned two months ago from a trip to Seattle, swearing as God was his witness, that he had seen my nephew Jack Joyner and he was very much alive.

I had no idea what to make of this. Was it an old gentleman's mistaken eyesight? Or was Jack alive?

To make a long story short, I hired a Pinkerton to discover the truth. My dear, I wouldn't even share this news if you were still convalescing, but your brother assures me this is not the case. I haven't divulged the Pinkerton's findings to another living soul, except my solicitor, because this news rightfully belongs to you first, as Jack's wife. My nephew is truly alive and well in Seattle. He sent the Pinkerton packing, claiming he was Arnold Hyde now and that's the way he wanted it to stay. The Pinkerton has delivered a letter to Jack revealing my betrayal of his mother. Mea culpa.

I have no idea why my nephew deserted you as he apparently has done, why he has chosen to assume the alias of Arnold Hyde, who died in the hotel fire. Maybe Jack was more of his father's son than I believed him to be—the apple not falling far from the tree and all that. If so, I am ashamed for my role in encouraging his courtship of you.

My dear girl, I cannot imagine how shocking, how alarming, this news must be to you and pray it doesn't cause a relapse. I considered leaving you in ignorance, but I concluded how much worse if you found out some other way. I imagine you have many questions you would like my nephew to answer, but whether or not you choose to confront him is up to you.

In any case, you may have need of a solicitor regarding your compromised position as the wife of Dr. Martin. I hope you will forgive me for bearing such distressing news.

> With all fondness,
> Your Aunt Elizabeth

As each word passed through Nellie's lips, my head ached worse—and still worse. Jack, alive. It seemed I had two husbands. As the depths of Jack's duplicity sank in, my nails clenched tighter and tighter into my flesh. I held up my hands and examined the half moons my nails had cut into my palms, laughing bitterly.

"Do you think it's illegal to kill someone who is already dead?"

As soon as I entered Father martin's office at the Mint, he stood and pulled out a chair, every bit as solicitous and well-mannered as his son. Although we had shared Sunday meals together twice a month as a family, this was the first time I had occasion to visit him at the Mint. The first occasion I found myself in his presence unaccompanied by his son and our child. The strangeness of those circumstances by themselves would have made me uncomfortable. My mission made me even more nervous—except I had no idea whom else I could trust. He inquired about the health of his son and granddaughter. I reciprocated and then it seemed my tongue was lodged permanently in my throat. I could see by the senior Mr. Martin's raised eyebrows, that he, too, wondered what I was doing in his office.

I cleared my throat. "I was hoping you could recommend a competent lawyer to handle a small but important matter for me."

His eyebrows raised even further, and I am sure he was wondering why I had come to him rather than my husband, but I hadn't found the courage to tell Val about Aunt Elizabeth's letter. In typical elder-statesman style, Val's father leaned forward and offered to handle my problem himself or at least to take the problem to a lawyer for me. "Dealings with lawyers are best handled by men."

How tiresome! Men assumed they were better at everything occurring outside of a kitchen or nursery. "Very kind of you, but no,

I must do this myself."

He drew back, all business now, clearly offended by my dismissal of his offer. The first two men the senior Mr. Martin suggested were of "good" families. Too visible for what I had in mind. I needed a working lawyer, not one of those rich men who needed something to fill in their daylight hours—if nothing more important came along.

"Someone of more modest means would suit my purposes better," I said.

Mr. Martin twiddled one end of his waxed mustache. "William Nelson, then. People take little notice of him, but he's handled several matters for me. He's a single fellow, sharp and hard-working."

"Let me call and make an appointment for you," he said. "Since we have worked together before, I am sure he will expedite matters for you."

I waited nervously while he exchanged a few pleasantries with the lawyer and arranged for me to meet with him later that day. At the end of the call, I stood, unwilling to take up any more of his time—and fearful of questions he might ask.

"Thank you, Father Martin. I appreciate your help and your discretion."

He brushed off my thanks. "Such a small bit of assistance isn't worthy of mention. What is family for? I am always at your service, Rosella."

Later that afternoon I walked down the hand-cut stone path along the side of Mr. Nelson's modest home where a shingle marked his law office. Through the window, I saw the lawyer peering at a newspaper through wire-rimmed glasses. He wore a neat but inexpensive suit. The books lining his office shelves were arranged just unevenly enough I could tell he actually referred to them. I would have been embarrassed if he caught me looking in his window, so I took a few more steps to his office door and knocked.

I accepted his invitation to sit down and began immediately before my courage faltered. "Mr. Nelson, I have come to you about a matter that requires the utmost, complete discretion."

"That goes without saying, Mrs. Martin. My profession is bound by a code of ethics and discretion is always paramount in our conduct."

I doubted many lawyers practiced that code to the degree which

I required. There could be no gossip repeated to a wife or drinking friend, which would be repeated at church or to a bartender. I wanted to know all my options.

"I need to understand certain laws, Mr. Nelson." How dare I go on? What would he think of me? It didn't matter. "I need to thoroughly understand laws regarding matrimony."

I coughed discreetly into a handkerchief. Nerves, I hoped, not the consumption returning. I looked out the window to avoid the lawyer's eyes, which I felt penetrated to my very soul. "Bigamy, to be specific. And laws regarding divorce. I would like to know about these"—I searched for a word and couldn't think of one—"things. And I need to know quickly."

I dared to look at him and discovered Mr. Nelson hadn't so much as blinked. "Mrs. Martin, I will need further details."

I coughed again. "These are not matters I wish to divulge in detail."

"I understand. Yet the more I know, the more I will be able to assist you. Laws vary somewhat from state to state, you understand. Perhaps you can start with that. Name the state whose laws you wish me to explain."

What state should I name? West Virginia where Jack and I had married? California where a tombstone marked Jack Joyner's grave? Or Washington state where he was living now under another name? Could I trust this man? I studied William Nelson again. The unwavering gaze. If he felt disapproval or shock, nothing in his face betrayed it.

I leaned forward in my chair, my gloved hands resting on the edge of Mr. Nelson's worn desk. "Six years ago I received a telegram informing me my husband died in a hotel fire and the only remains I received were ashes. I erected his tombstone in the Oakland cemetery, not far from where we lived."

"Ahhh, with your permission, I'm going to interrupt and tell you about laws in California that might govern your situation. I don't need to know if they actually govern it. Let's deal in hypotheticals." He searched along his bookshelf, pulled out a fat volume, and searched the index. "According to the California Penal Code, the state exempts from its laws regarding bigamy any person by reason of any former marriage whose husband or wife by such marriage has been absent for five successive years without being known to such person within that time to be living."

I let myself lean back into the padded leather chair. Thanks be to God!

"The key," Mr. Nelson continued, "is that the husband or wife must remarry believing the spouse is dead. Then he or she would not be guilty of bigamy."

I closed my eyes and held the handkerchief to my mouth but no cough came. "And if a wife has remarried and the first husband is found to be alive after six years, would she—should she—would it be necessary to seek divorce?"

"No, since the first husband has deserted and not provided sustenance during that time, divorce would not be necessary."

The relief that swept over me was palpable, releasing the tension in every muscle. I needn't bother Val with Elizabeth's letter at all. Jack might as well be dead as far as we were concerned.

Still somewhat dazed by all that had transpired over the past day, I wandered down the street and stopped to buy carrots and onions at the market. I selected those vegetables and idled on toward the bin of green beans. Their color had faded slightly, past their prime and likely stringy. I gathered my purchases and prepared to leave when I noticed a tall, dark-haired man looking in the window of the store across the street. Jack! I felt my blood seize up. The silence of the world was deafening, its axis, the crowds, the streetcars and horses—all stilled.

When the man turned, I saw at once it wasn't Jack at all, just a tall fellow with dark hair, one of thousands, millions. With relief, I laughed at myself. My imagination had run amuck.

I hurried home, more carefree than I'd felt in ages, eager to embrace my husband. I fixed his favorite chicken pot pie for dinner, a dish that could rest in the oven. Solina would be napping when Val got home and I planned to take advantage of the opportunity. Finally, there he was, with his gaunt face, that mountain slope of a nose, and legs as long and lean and gawky as an egret's. We looked at each other for a long second, and I was remembering everything I loved about him. His smile, his enthusiasm, his sense of honor. The way he'd worked tirelessly in the makeshift hospital for the people of San Francisco yet still managed to see me to safety. The way he'd doctored Ben and found Arequipa for me. The way he encouraged my art. The passion he put into playing the cello. His quirky experiments and unending efforts to help his patients. His standing by me in sickness and health, for better or worse—even before we'd taken any vows.

I raised up onto my toes and kissed him slowly, passionately on the mouth.

"That was nice." He drew back and held me at arm's length. "Now, what's this I hear about Jack's being alive?"

There went my plans to seduce my husband. Dear Nellie never could keep a secret.

1912

RUMBLING AND A WHISTLE ANNOUNCED the approaching train. I continued to have misgivings even as our departure neared. Were we doing the right thing by moving to West Virginia? It meant leaving Nellie behind, and Little Cuss, who would remain with her. She had often taken care of him and loved the little terrier as much as I did, had begged me to leave her something to love. I would miss them both terribly but I would be closer to my brothers and their families—and oh, how I missed the hills I'd once called home!

The catalyst for this change was a surprising letter from a solicitor informing me that Aunt Elizabeth had passed away and left her home to me. I couldn't help but wonder why me—and not Jack—but her will explained since she felt her matchmaking had resulted in the sad state of affairs that left me alone in San Francisco, the least she could do was make it possible for me to return to my family and community. I could read between the lines. She blamed herself for Jack's abdication of his marital responsibilities. It was not her fault, but guilt is a hard taskmaster. The rest of her estate, a considerable sum of money, she divided among Jack's three still living brothers and sisters.

I could have sold Elizabeth's home and remained in California, but the relationship between Val and Dr. Kasbarian had long been strained, Val being excessively progressive for the older man's taste. I had noticed, too, that Val's quirkier experiments embarrassed his father and had caused a certain stiffness in their interactions. So when Val learned Harrison County had need of another doctor, he eagerly agreed to begin his own practice there. Aunt Elizabeth's carriage house would be ideal for conversion into a doctor's office.

The train whistle crowed again, much closer now, I thought—although sounds could carry unusual distances in the rain. Despite the inclement weather, the shed master was out directing his crew to shunt cars from one track to another. But as the rain pelted down harder, he withdrew into the roundhouse. Finally the engine came into view, the cattle pusher and cab out in front, a long procession of box cars, Pullmans, dining cars, gondolas, and hoppers coupled behind. The brakes squealed and steam hissed as the train slowed near the platform.

A redcap disembarked first, carrying luggage. Behind him, two more redcaps shouldered a trunk between them. Passengers swarmed off the train and into the station house.

I felt as if I'd swallowed a lump of sand. In minutes, I would bid Nellie goodbye. Who knew when we would see each other again? Val, Solina, and I would board the train and head off to a new and different life.

I would still be able to make pottery. I had a letter from Mr. Rhead and learned that the clay near the Ohio River made excellent pottery. Several factories were producing beautiful wares: Roseville, Weller, McCoy. Val promised me I would have my own small studio so I could perfect the techniques I'd learned at Arequipa.

It was time to board. I went through the motions of hugs for Nellie and Little Cuss and my father-in-law, who'd come to see us off, but I felt as if my movements occurred underwater, the sounds muted, distorted, my limbs moving unnaturally.

I raised my umbrella and stepped outside to board, clutching Solina close at my side so she wouldn't get wet. Raindrops beat like a drum on my umbrella and splashed off the ground onto the dark skirt I'd chosen for travel. We hurried to stay as dry as possible. Once inside and seated, I glanced out the window long enough to see Nellie standing in the rain, one hand over her mouth, and I knew she was crying. I looked away, wanting to cry too. I didn't dare or I'd gather my daughter and husband and run back into the station house, back to the city I'd called home since I was fifteen. Back to the city where I'd buried my son and a husband whose grave was empty.

I hugged Solina to my side and held onto Val's hand. They were my life now.

I COULDN'T TAKE MY EYES OFF the well-remembered redbuds and dogwoods that painted the West Virginia countryside pink and white as the train rolled over the mountains from Kentucky to West Virginia. Yellow-green leaves were bursting forth on trees. These things, once too familiar to notice, I absorbed with newfound appreciation. What a relief, when we finally disembarked in Clarksburg. Timmy (everyone called him Tim now but he would always be Timmy to me) and his wife were there to welcome us and carry us to our new home, a dozen or so blocks from the station. We made plans to gather the family under one roof in a few days' time.

It had been years since I'd seen Aunt Elizabeth's house, but it was every bit as impressive as I'd remembered. My eyes leapt from the white exterior with its gingerbread trim and wraparound porch to the lilacs leaning over, heavy with wet buds, to the chickens scratching the dirt in the side yard. Aunt Elizabeth's solicitor had continued to pay a gardener and housekeeper to make sure the home remained in good condition. It was fully furnished with her family's good pieces, ready for us to make it our own.

"Storybook perfect," Val said, as he stood before the house for the first time. "This is what home should look like, the perfect place to raise a family. I think I'll hang a swing on that big oak tree in the side yard—how would you like that, Solina?"

"Yes, Papa, please! Tomorrow." She skipped over to the tree and ran around it and around it until she became dizzy and collapsed on the ground. I could hardly scold her. The long train journey had been hard on a six year old—all that energy confined to a small compartment. I'd done my best to entertain her with stories about the cousins she was going to meet.

I laughed. "You might have to wait for that swing until we unpack our belongings."

Oh, I knew Val was romanticizing the place—after all I'd grown up here and knew the folks were pretty much the same as those in San Francisco, the good and the bad mixed up in each one. People were people. Yet, as soon as we stepped off that train to start our lives here, I could feel the mask peel away, feel my true self shining through. I no longer needed fancy gowns as armor and disguise. I belonged here. I wasn't the same Rosella Krause who had left home or even the Rosella Joyner who'd shaped herself into a lady. As Rosella Martin, I could be myself—and Val wouldn't have me any other way.

I shared his hopes that our lives here would be good. We had a decent sum of money put aside to build a pottery shed and fix up Val's office. And our property, very close to downtown Clarksburg, was situated ideally for a doctor's practice.

I wandered from room to room, remembering the times I'd spent here, nursing Elizabeth through an illness, helping her can the bounty of her garden. The last room I entered was Elizabeth's sitting room, and it was as though time had stopped. On the wall hung a sketch of her cat, the paper yellowed and curling around the edges, my childish signature embellishing the bottom right corner. I couldn't believe she'd kept it all these years.

In the morning, I watched the sunrise from our bedroom window and then made breakfast in our new kitchen from fresh eggs Solina and I gathered from our own chickens. What fun for her! I made toast from bread Timmy's wife had brought over the night before. I spent the rest of the day unpacking, necessities first, but I couldn't resist sneaking in one special box that would make this house feel as if it belonged to me. Carefully, I stripped away one piece of wadded newspaper after another and at last I held it in my hands. A vase I'd made at Arequipa, my own design with maple leaves and seed pods. Our farm had a pair of maples that turned glorious gold and orange and burgundy in fall. My mother would help us rake the leaves into a pile and then Timmy and I would fling ourselves on top, relishing the crisp textures that crumbled beneath the pressure of our bodies. We inhaled their smoky fragrance while our mother untangled broken fragments from our hair. The vase would always remind me of those joyous childhood days when my mother watched over us with such love. Reverently I placed the piece on a credenza in the dining room.

The home now felt like my own.

MAY 1920

Of all my pieces, the maple leaf vase generated the most interest because people mistook the seed pods for angel wings.

"You should just go along with them and agree they are wings," Mindy said. "There would be a bidding war for it."

I would never sell the only piece I still owned from my days at Arequipa, yet it could be that the ladies who saw an angel's presence in the vase weren't entirely wrong. During its creation, I yearned for my mother's comforting touch, a longing I've felt all my life whenever I was ill. I had wanted so badly to heal and go home to my family, perhaps my mother's spirit had hovered over the sanitarium and blown in a kiss to make me better. Perhaps her love had grazed my brush.

A steady flow of guests filtered through Mindy's gallery. Many of the newer pieces I'd made already had "SOLD" tags beside them. I had shipped them to Mindy well in advance of the show. Alexandra had exorbitant price tags by several of the pieces she owned, because, I overheard her tell a guest, she didn't really want to sell them since they had been made by her dear friend. Fiddlesticks! If even one sold at those prices, it would drive the value of all my pottery up, which she well knew.

For over an hour, Solina wandered through the gallery with Nellie. I had told her no champagne—she was far too young—but I noticed Nellie let her have several sips when she thought I wasn't paying attention. At last there was a gap in people demanding my attention, and Solina and Mindy approached.

Mindy held out her arms as though she was ready to embrace the world, her honeysuckle perfume dispersing with the graceful movement. "The turnout is better than I could have hoped for."

"Mama, I've heard many of those ladies talking about the newspaper articles. Why don't you tell them what that scoundrel did to you?"

I could, I suppose, give a speech, but many would not believe my version anyway. People liked to gossip, to think the worst of others, especially a woman who talked openly about family planning. "I won't give them the satisfaction of thinking their opinion matters. Let them have their fun."

Solina crossed her arms and pouted. "It's not fun when I hear them say such dreadful things. It's embarrassing."

Mindy laid a well-manicured hand on Solina's shoulder, again sending such an overpowering dose of perfume my way that I held a handkerchief to my nose to suppress a sneeze. "Honey, always look for the blessings the good Lord has chosen to provide. Those articles, dreadful as they may be, brought all these people into the gallery. Why, we've never had a show open to such a large crowd. We were on the verge of bankruptcy. Your mother's show is going to save us. Not only have we sold a lot of her pieces for record prices, other artists' works have sold tonight as well. Hallelujah!"

Mindy's approval of the news articles stunned me. We had been such good friends—how could she receive joy from scandal that was causing my daughter such pain? Mindy drew my daughter to the other side of the room to introduce her to a young man near her age, surely a welcome distraction from the ugly gossip. As I watched them, Mindy's words echoed through my mind. This was the first inkling I had that her gallery was failing. I had assumed it was as successful under her as it had been under her father. Until this moment, I thought perhaps the reporter had come across someone who knew Jack and had seen him in Seattle. Or that Alexandra had been communicating with him—he had been a beneficiary of her modern marriage. If Mindy had known of Jack's shenanigans, I might have suspected her of planting the stories to draw a crowd, but I had never told a soul except for Val and Nellie. Certainly Val had told no one. That left only one possibility.

I marched across the room. "Nellie, could I have a word?" I drew her into a small storage room where the crates and boxes were kept. "I keep wondering how that reporter knew Jack was still alive. I know you wouldn't have told the reporter, but did you let it slip to someone else?"

Nellie's face crumbled and she wept. "I've been so afraid you would find out, and I love you so much, I never would have done anything to hurt you, you know that."

I hugged her. "Yes, I know you love me, and I love you too, but did you let it slip to someone?"

She hid her face in her hands, a handkerchief pressed to her eyes. Between sobs, she gasped out her confession. "Mindy and I were talking one day over tea, you know how it is, and it just popped out, how terrible he'd treated you. But Mindy adores you. She would never have told your story to a reporter."

Oh, yes, she would. Mindy valued our friendship, but that was nothing compared to the love she had for her father. She wanted to preserve his legacy, his gallery. And she was one of the few people who knew about the family planning meeting and who also knew where I was staying.

All this time, I'd been thinking evil thoughts about Alexandra, that she had known Jack was alive and tried to wound me by publishing my secrets. I thought my enemy had spread the ugly rumors; instead, it was my friends.

I couldn't stand to see Nellie cry. "Dry your eyes. Everything's going to be okay."

When we returned to the gallery floor, Mindy was conversing with a reporter. "Rosella isn't a bigamist—far from it. Her first husband deserted her. His grave is in the Oakland Cemetery—empty grave, I should say. Wouldn't that make an excellent photo to accompany your story?"

During our women's vote campaign, I had witnessed Mindy's knack for marketing. Hosting the Equality Tea at the Emporium and stenciling 'Votes for Women' slogans on napkins in ice cream parlors—those had been her ideas. Time had only sharpened her skills. I had underestimated her cleverness, her cunning. From the beginning, she had the gallery's publicity campaign all mapped out to the last detail, a plan to keep the story on the front pages until my show closed. Nothing like scandal to sell newspapers. Or pottery, apparently. All sunny smiles, she turned and caught sight of me.

"Here she comes now," Mindy said. "She'll tell you herself."

The reporter and I shook hands, and I affirmed that Jack had faked his death. Across the room, Solina traced her finger absently over the slip trail that ran down the face of a blue pot, her shoulders slumped.

I was going to forgive Mindy, I knew that. I had her to thank for the impressive turnout, but also for my daughter's glum appearance on what should have been a fun trip to the city of her birth.

I would forgive Mindy, but I intended to make her squirm and grovel first.

CLARKSBURG, WEST VIRGINIA, AUGUST 17, 1920

SOLINA SCREECHED AND SWIPED HER ARM to fling off a corn earworm, an unwelcome gift deposited by Michael. She stomped her feet a dozen times, screaming, "I'll get you back, you miserable little pest."

Michael hooted with laughter and the chase was on, between two long rows of corn until they disappeared around the corner of the house. Another three weeks until school started. It couldn't come soon enough. Those two were going to drive me crazy. I still couldn't get used to seeing my daughter's cropped hair. For all her insistence that she didn't care for Lydia Underwood, she had persuaded Nellie to lop off the long curls of her childhood. Her hair would never lay straight, so she adopted a finger-wave style that made her look quite the young lady, even if she didn't always act it.

I cupped a hand at my brow to shade my eyes from the blinding rays of late afternoon sun. Sweat patches were plainly visible around my armpits. A cool bath would be in order before dinner, if I could make time for one.

Thomas, bless his heart, continued to harvest green beans from the little patch he'd planted himself in early summer. He picked carefully, methodically, joylessly, dropping each bean into a small basket. Not that I wanted more squabbling, but I longed for the day when he would join Solina and Michael in childish pursuits. I hoped the little fellow would eventually move past the sorrow of losing his parents —though I certainly knew how difficult it was to lose those you loved. Grief took hold of people in different ways. It left at its own speed, not because someone else told you it was time to move on. All I could do was offer a safe space where Thomas could grieve and grow, a space where he felt loved and cared for, a place where he belonged.

Michael and Solina came tearing around the other side of the house, making enough racket to raise the dead.

I pulled another brown-tasseled ear from a stalk and tucked it into my basket, not bothering to turn around. "Don't you come trampling through the garden, you hooligans! Solina, what boy is going to want to look at you if you don't settle down a little? You're too old for this nonsense."

"I didn't start—" she broke off. "Mama, someone's here."

A stranger, I heard it in her voice.

Looping my arm through the basket handle, I turned.

I knew at once—yet didn't know at all—the tall figure that stood still, hat in hand, watching the house, watching the children, watching me. For years I had expected, had dreaded, that this day would come. Across a crowded city street or stepping around a tall building, my breath would catch and I would imagine I'd caught a glimpse of him. It never was. I'd shake my head to dispel the eerie sensation and go about my business. This time, his flesh occupied space too solidly to be easily dismissed. This was no ghost, no optical illusion.

For some moments, we both stood still, silent. Even Michael was quiet for once.

As he approached, Jack swept one arm wide as if to embrace the scene or some memory, and the fragrance of apple-scented tobacco drifted toward me. The sound of my name in his mouth was dangerous, as it always had been, his cheeks dimpling, the gold specks in his eyes glimmering, threatening to upend my hard-won sensibility once again. The love, the hurt, the grief—they all flashed over me, inundating me in a rush of memory. As quickly as these came, they dispelled, hardening into anger I thought I'd let go of long ago.

"Jack. Or should I call you Arnold. What do you want?"

He winced slightly, before calling up that lopsided smile that had once won my heart. "I came to see my aunt's house, to see you."

I felt so cold toward him, this man I had once burned for. "So you've seen us both." Implying, quite clearly, I thought, he should go back to wherever he'd come from.

He moved closer, clutching his hat. "I was hoping we might talk."

"Nothing to talk about."

"I think there is. I still have feelings—"

"Stop right there."

"Fear made me fold when I should have hung in there."

How like him to treat marriage like a bad hand of cards. When I didn't respond, he changed tactics.

"Elizabeth was my aunt. I have fond memories of this place." His eyes swept over the swing, the fresh paint, the garden. "You've kept it up real nice."

"I take care of what's mine." So that was it. He was after the house. "Solina, please go in the house and fetch the letter from my attorney. It's tucked into the side of the coat rack." For once, she did as I asked without argument, and Michael went with her. I had kept the documents handy ever since moving into Elizabeth's house, certain Jack would one day appear just as suddenly as he'd disappeared.

His eyes darkened as if a cloud had wiped out every trace of green and gold.

"She was my aunt."

"She left the house to me, not you. She had her reasons."

"She was old. Her faculties weren't that sharp anymore."

The screen door banged and Solina returned with the documents from the attorney. I proffered them to Jack. He opened the envelope and began to read. I didn't wait for him to finish. He could peruse the rest at his leisure.

"I made certain before I moved back here that her will is absolutely incontestable. Since your aunt knew you were still alive but couldn't be bothered to visit her on her dying bed, she asked her lawyer to specify you could never inherit a dime from her. I think you had better leave."

The screen door banged shut behind us again. Michael tramped down the steps toting the breechloader. He stopped beside me. The shotgun, thank goodness, was angled toward the ground, not at Jack's gut.

"My mama asked you to leave."

I had never heard my eight year old sound so stern. Obviously Solina had regaled Michael with every detail of her San Francisco visit. She was as incapable of keeping secrets as Nellie.

"Whoa, son, take it easy. Is that thing loaded?"

"Yep."

Jack looked at me. "I don't suppose he knows how to use it."

"Quite a few squirrels and birds and one deer would tell you different," I said.

He shifted his weight from one foot to the other. "I never meant to hurt you, Rosella, never meant you any harm."

Solina stepped forward, her voice seething with fury. "But you did hurt her. I hate you for what you did to her!"

Michael raised the shotgun. "I hate you, too."

Alarmed, I pushed the barrel back toward the ground. There

would be no murder on my front lawn. And if there was, I would be the one to do it.

The carriage house door opened and our contentious tableau paused. Out limped Thaddeus Haynes, followed by Val, his step boisterous, as usual.

"Thanks, Doc. That ointment's fixed me right up."

"Glad to hear it, Thaddeus. You stop by again any time you need more."

"'Preciate it mightily." Thaddeus slogged down the street, elbows bent, bow-legged, in his jeans and plaid flannel shirt, Val watching until the old man moved out of sight.

"I heard you'd married Val Martin," Jack said. "Have to say, your first husband was a far better looking chap."

"My first husband lies in a grave in the Oakland cemetery."

He tried to smile, but the attempt wobbled and disappeared. His eyes roamed over our house with what I interpreted as longing, whether for the past, prompted by his memories of Aunt Elizabeth, or a longing for a future he could never have, a safe and warm family life inside this solid white house.

"Okay, then. I just wanted to check on you, see how things were."

"A little late for that," Solina said.

He looked as if he might leave, but hesitated, his weight shifting back toward us. "Look, my finances are a bit underwater right now. I would appreciate it if you could see your way to loaning me—"

I squinted, my lips curled in, and I swear I was close to taking that shotgun from Michael and pointing it at Jack's gut myself.

My expression served answer enough, and Jack turned and strode up the street, disappearing in the same direction as Thaddeus Haynes. At last I allowed myself a deep breath.

Val made his way across the lawn to us. "Who was that?"

"No one important. We sent him on his way."

I knew the children would eventually relay every little detail of the encounter anyway. "Michael, put that shotgun back where you found it now—make sure it's not loaded." The gun was darn near as long as Michael was tall. He was too young to learn to use it, but Val insisted all boys in West Virginia learned to hunt at his age, child-rearing advice he'd gleaned from his patients. I disagreed, but I had learned to pick my battles. I couldn't win every time.

"Why was the shotgun out? It's not a toy," he hollered to Michael's back.

"He wasn't playing with it, but we will have a talk about using it safely again." I put my arm around Solina and she leaned into my embrace. "My children did me proud today."

My children—where was Thomas? My stomach contracted and I spun around, my eyes searching for some sign of him. Where had I last seen him? I dashed to the garden and found his basket abandoned by the bean patch. "Thomas!" I shouted. Where had he been during the commotion? "Solina, help me find your brother."

We searched the house, the yard, and then Val knocked on neighbors' doors. No one had seen him. Where would he have gone?

At last Michael thought to look under their bunk bed. "Mom, I found him, but he won't come out. Want me to pull him out?"

I charged up the stairs, ordering Michael not to forcibly remove his brother. Solina and Val began to follow me up the stairs, but I motioned them away. I wanted to see Thomas alone. When I got to the boys' room, I thanked Michael for finding Thomas. "You've been such a big help to me today already, I hate to ask you for anything else, but could you go shuck that corn? I have a hankering for one of those sweet ears tonight, and you're the best corn shucker around."

Michael thundered down the staircase at top speed. Just this once I didn't scold him for risking a fall.

"Ask Solina to put a kettle of water on to boil," I called after him.

Gathering my skirt out of the way, I sat down on the pine floor, shifting my legs to one side. Since I still couldn't see Thomas, I lay flat on my back and twisted my head until my cheek rested on the floor. There he was, a little mouse nestled into the corner. My view was still limited and awkward, so I scooted sideways until I lay beside him. The bottom bunk practically touched my nose and breasts.

"What are you doing?" His voice, so small, so surprised, so dear.

"I thought it might get lonely under here with only the dust bunnies to keep you company." I wasn't making up the dust bunnies. I felt a sneeze coming on and pinched my nose to prevent an eruption.

"Oh."

"It feels nice and snug under here, doesn't it? Safe."

"Yeah."

I waited, hoping he would open up to me. Seconds ticked by.

I still felt like sneezing, my back was starting to ache, and I could hear the screen door slam, which meant Michael had finished the shucking. I feared I would have to hurry Thomas along so I could fix supper, but then—

"Did that man leave?"

"He did." I didn't have to ask who he meant.

"Was he here to take me away?"

I jerked my head from the floor and banged my nose on a slat. "Sch—" I broke off. It wouldn't do to curse, even with my Grand-mother Krause's *Scheisse,* but by golly that hurt. "Absolutely not. Why did you think he or anyone would take you away?"

He didn't answer. What terrible fears sent him into this corner?

"Where did you think he'd take you to?" I asked.

"An orphanage."

"Thomas Henderson Helmick, no one is ever taking you away from this family. Ever. Put that right out of your head."

"But what if someone does come?"

I searched for the right words, the best words, to make this child feel secure and safe in an unsafe world. "When that man came to our house this afternoon and your brother and sister thought he might hurt me, they both stood by my side, ready to do battle to protect me. When we thought you were lost today, every one of us searched high and low because you are important to us. That's what it means to be part of this family. We'll always stand up for you."

"But I don't know who I am anymore."

"What do you mean? You are part of this family, that's who you are."

"I'm a Helmick. The rest of you are Martins."

"Oh." I rolled my head carefully to look him in the eye. I was ready to utter sensitive words of wisdom, I swear I was. Instead I sneezed and my snot blew all over the poor boy's face. I was horrified.

Thomas laughed. He laughed and he laughed. Out loud. A glorious, uninhibited, spontaneous belly shaker. One of the most wonderful sounds I'd ever heard. In the ten months he'd lived with us, I had never heard him laugh. It infected me like a virus and I laughed with him.

"Do you think we could get out from under here now to finish this discussion?"

After we rolled out, I washed his face off and we pounded the dust from our clothes. I sneezed again, but this time my hands were free to catch it in my handkerchief. We laughed all over again. I caught him up in my arms and whirled around and around.

"Thomas Henderson Helmick, I love you dearly." I set him back down and swatted his backside playfully. "Now, hustle on out to the garden and fetch your beans inside. We have a supper to prepare."

A good while later, after we said grace and passed around platters of vegetables, I suggested Thomas might like to change his last name to Martin. I thought it would make him happy. Instead, he looked worried.

I was quick to take it back. "It was only a suggestion. You don't have to."

"If I change my name, it might make me forget my mom and dad."

Val hurried to reassure him. "We put their photograph in your bedroom so you will always remember them. We won't let that happen."

I knew it wasn't true and so did Thomas—and I understood why losing the memories scared him. Already he was forgetting the sparkle of their eyes, the vigor of their walk, the dynamics of their faces in motion. Eventually he would only remember faces frozen in a photograph. When I thought of Ben, my mother, my father, the memories contained less and less life with each passing year. Only in my dreams did I see them again as joyful or sad, stern or loving, their faces and bodies animated by all the hopes, dreams, and activity that made them human. Forgetting was sad, but also a blessing. Forgetting helped us move past grief.

I set down my fork. "Thomas and I had a chat. He says he isn't sure who he is anymore. That's why I thought he might want to change his last name."

"You dolt." Michael shoved Thomas's shoulder. "You're my brother, that's who you are."

Leave it to Michael to combine insult with exactly the right assurance Thomas needed.

"Ignore Michael," Solina said. "He's just a pest. You're *my* brother, the one who isn't a pest."

Michael stuck his tongue out at her.

"Solina and Michael, table manners, please," I said. "You're supposed to be setting a good example for your little brother."

"No one will ever put me in an orphanage?" Thomas asked.

Michael laughed hysterically. "Thomas, if they've kept Solina out of an orphanage all these years, as much trouble as she causes, believe me, your place in this family is safe."

He looked from Michael to Solina, addressing her alone, shaking his head. "But you're a Martin. Why would they put you in an orphanage?"

"I'm adopted too." She sounded almost proud of her status.

Thomas's eyes widened but he said nothing. He hadn't known and we hadn't ever thought to mention it.

We resumed eating the bounty of our garden.

As Solina carried plates to the sink, affecting a snooty, nasal tone, she suggested hyphenating Thomas's last name. "He could be Mr. Thomas Helmick-Martin."

"You read too many of those stuffy British novels," Michael said.

Val declared her solution pure genius. "Thomas can keep his old identity and yet forge ahead with a new identity as part of this family."

"What's hyphenating mean?" Thomas asked.

After Solina explained, Thomas nodded his approval.

I thought the discussion was over, but while Solina and I washed and dried dishes, it took an unexpected twist.

"He doesn't realize how lucky he is," my daughter said. "At least he knows his parents' real names."

Moisture crept to the corners of my eyes. I lowered the plate I had been washing into the sink, fearing I would drop it. "I'm sorry, I'm so sorry."

"Sometimes I wonder who I really am, you know? Who were they, my parents?"

I wanted to tell her she was my dearly beloved daughter, but she already knew that.

She surprised me again by smiling. "Don't look so sad and worried, Mama. I'll be all right. I'm a Martin. And I love you and Papa extra special bunches because you gave my birth mother a name. Jane Martin. You didn't have to do that, but I'm glad you did."

We had visited the cemetery in Oakland and she had seen how

we'd placed her mother's gravestone right beside Ben's. Val and I hadn't known what else to call Solina's mother. We had done the best we could to give her an identity and decent burial.

"I will be eternally grateful to your mother. If not for her, I wouldn't have a beautiful, intelligent, kind daughter." Jane had lost her life, and I had gained a daughter. It wasn't fair, but life rarely was.

The next morning we woke up to a headline declaring women had finally won the right to vote. Tennessee was the thirty-sixth state to ratify the nineteenth amendment, fourteen months after Congress had passed it.

I had to smile when Solina informed Thomas that his adoptive mother had marched on Congress to help make it happen. For once, she actually sounded proud of me.

Angie

AT FOUR IN THE MORNING, I creep into the bathroom to get showered and dressed. Dewey pretends to be asleep. I gather my purse and the keys to Mom's ancient Olds from the dresser. My car is still in the body shop, and I don't want to take Dewey's truck in case he needs it for a job interview or a family emergency. I glance at him, weighted with sorrow over what we've lost. My mouth shapes a soundless goodbye, and I turn to leave. His voice stops me.

"I checked the air in the tires of your Mom's car. You're good to go."

"Thanks." I cross the room and stand beside the bed, grateful he's broken the silence.

"You and Mac be careful today."

"We'll try." I lean down and kiss his forehead. It appears we will carry on with daily routines and hope the injuries heal on their own.

Outside, the pre-dawn sky glows midnight blue, enough light to spot Mom's daffodils pushing slim green tips through the soil. I am grateful for even this hint of spring because I detest the barren nature of these winter months. I long for green, for growth. Mac scrapes ice off the windshield of Mom's Olds and drives us to the school parking lot to meet my colleagues. The tee-shirt company fellow is already there, passing out shirts with "55 Strong" emblazoned on the front. I give him a check and hand over the carton with the remainder of the shirts to Becca's husband Chad.

"She feels well enough to picket in front of the school for a while today," he says. She will sell shirts to whoever wants one and get the word out to AFT members that they are available.

That settled, our crew of four—plus Mac—are set to make the

two-hour drive to Charleston in Emily Harris's compact car. The front seat is roomy; the back seat has plenty of legroom if you are eight years old. One of the youngest teachers in our school, Seth is quite a bit older than eight, and at six foot two, his knees will be folded into his chest the whole ride. Mrs. Carstairs has the front seat, due to her bad knees, and I share the back seat with my sister and Seth. My ankle bootie makes it awkward to get situated inside. We're nervous and excited. It's the first protest at the capital for all but Mrs. Carstairs, who had driven down in 1990.

I press my face near the car's window and watch the pale light of dawn spread across the sky. Silhouetted treetops are black lace against peach silk. Gradually the sky turns rose, blending to gold. Finally the hills become visible. I have a sudden urge to sing, "Oh those West Virginia hills, how majestic and how grand." The others join in.

Afterward, Mrs. Carstairs leads off with John Denver's "Country Roads."

"I know that's an iconic West Virginia song," Emily says, "but the only place in the state it could apply to is Harper's Ferry."

Mrs. Carstairs says, "I still love it."

Finally traffic becomes thick and I know we have reached the outskirts of Charleston.

Fifty years old—and I've only been to the capital one time. That was in junior high when I won the Golden Horseshoe award for knowing a lot about West Virginia history. I can't remember a darn thing about that trip except the capitol building sits on a bank above the Kanawha River and the dome is gold. Is it *ever* gold! The whole shebang is covered in twenty-three-and-one-half karat gold leaf, one of those dubiously useful facts I learned for the Golden Horseshoe exam.

We park the car and head toward the crowd noise, with Mrs. Carstairs, Mac and me bringing up the rear. The ankle boot makes jogging along at Seth- and Emily-speed impossible. My sister makes sure I don't fall. As we near the big dome, we hear "We're not going to take it!" The crowd is ginormous—a scientific term, meaning, who the heck knows how big—maybe 5,000, maybe 10,000 teachers out there already.

It is about forty-eight degrees, maybe fifty, I judge; nevertheless,

I keep on my gloves. My hands and feet are always cold these days, while the rest of my body bakes. My internal thermostat is broken.

We encounter a sea of red at the capitol lawn and join a red wave flowing across the grounds. Everywhere there are signs. I have to laugh when I spot a young teacher standing on one of the huge decorative posts in front of the building. I bet she teaches biology, like me, because she is holding a sign about seeds, too. I am proud of us, proud to be part of this moment. Our numbers are growing, and so is our strength and vocal power. Those weaselly legislators have to take notice now.

My sister takes a photo of my crew of four with a teacher decked out in an Uncle Sam outfit. He says the costume is symbolic of justice and unity and our fight for our country's children, for their education. I wander through the crowd, and am suddenly confronted by another symbol of justice. A statue of Lincoln towers over us.

I seize Mac's hand, staring up at the craggy face. "I feel crushed by the weight of history here," I say.

Her brow crinkles as if she is amused. "Well, it is impressive."

Guess if you live in Charleston you take all the grandeur for granted.

We cheer along with another teacher who mounts the capitol steps to lead us in chants. Almost every car driving by honks support.

Mac and I chat with a woman in a knitted cap who is passing out cups of coffee. "I recognize you," she says to my sister. "You're in the newspaper all the time. I just live up the street from here."

My sister accepts a cup of coffee, beaming at the recognition. "I'm here today with my sister." She nods at me. "She's a teacher."

When the woman nods, the funny knitted braids dangling from the sides of her cap nod with her. "My mother was a teacher, so I know how hard your job is."

The heat from the coffee warms my hands. I have to blow on it before I take a sip. It's really hot. "Thanks for coming out here this morning, and you aren't lying about how hard it is."

Another lady offers a donut, but Mac and I decline. I can't afford to gain more weight. Mrs. Carstairs and Emily accept a donut. Seth scarfs down two and then burns his mouth by gulping the coffee.

"Serves you right," I tell him.

A couple of police officers stop their cruiser and get out. I grab my sister's arm, adrenaline flowing. If they arrest us, Dewey will never forgive me. I am ready to run. But then they smile and drop off a few more boxes of pastries to the ladies distributing food. I relax. Police officers and state workers aren't allowed to strike with us or they will lose their jobs, but they will benefit from better insurance if our efforts succeed.

"Look at those kids." Mac points at a pair of grade-schoolers carrying their own signs: *This is my Homework!* and *We Stand with Our Teachers!* "Aren't they cute?"

"This is like a civics field trip for them," Seth says. "Look over there." He motions toward United Mine Workers wearing their union jackets.

A teamster shakes my hand; in his other hand he carries a sign declaring solidarity with us.

"These union workers know strikes like penguins know ice and whales know water," Seth says.

Not everyone approves. A passenger in one passing car rolls down the window and screeches, "If you cared about the children, you'd be in the classroom."

"Wrong!" Mrs. Carstairs yells, not caring that the passenger can't hear her. "We care that teachers are leaving the state because they can't live on their paychecks or afford their medical insurance."

She's right. More than seven hundred teaching positions sit vacant and over a third of the state's math teachers are uncertified. We care that every child receives quality instruction from qualified teachers in well-funded public schools. I am doing this for Bella and every other child deserving of a chance at a good life.

Near lunch time, more locals show up with kettles of hot soup, bags of pepperoni rolls, and boxes of pizza. I was good in the morning, turning down those donuts, but I'm starved and I never can resist pepperoni rolls and pizza. I take a little of each. The afternoon drags on endlessly. I keep pushing up my jacket sleeve to check my watch.

Mac nudges my arm. "That isn't going to make time go by any faster."

"I know." The excitement is wearing off. "I worry we aren't accomplishing much."

"We're in it for the long haul," Seth reminds us. "The longer we're out, the more pressure it puts on the legislature to act."

Mrs. Carstairs stamps her feet to stay warm. "You can bet parents will pressure them. It's a major inconvenience when those kiddies are their responsibility all day instead of ours."

I am exhausted by the time I reach home around eight that night. Dewey isn't there. Around eleven he stumbles in, so drunk his friend Phil had to drive him home.

THE NEXT MORNING MY CREW pickets in front of our school and Mac delivers coffee and hot chocolate to us throughout the day. Other squads of protesters take our place at the capitol. My crew makes the Charleston run two more times over the week-long strike in Emily's car. Mac stays home to meet with a top-notch lawyer. She promises to tweet out strike news periodically. Dewey says very little to me, but the air in our bedroom vibrates with the tension of everything we aren't saying to each other.

On my next trip to the big city, my cell rings. The governor's staff says he's willing to meet with us. I am chosen to attend along with several others. I can hardly breathe as I climb the steps from the Rotunda. I enter a room that smells of furniture polish and power. Here I am, seated around a conference table with the governor and his staff. Me. A genuine Mover and Shaker.

Heart racing, I listen as other AFT leaders lay out our issues. One of the governor's staff members begins to tread quietly across the carpet, and when I sense he's preparing to end the meeting, I panic. We haven't pushed hard enough on healthcare.

I stand, my fingers resting on the conference table so they won't tremble. I can do this. "Governor, every family has its own reasons to need strong health insurance. I want to share mine. My daughter is a public employee and recently my granddaughter Bella was born with impaired hearing. She will need expensive hearing aids the rest of her life. Without them, her ability to learn and interact with others would be seriously curtailed. Our insurance doesn't cover medically necessary devices like these. Twenty-two other states do. Over twenty thousand teachers and their families are covered by PEIA. They all face different health issues. Each one is as important as your own family members are to you, as Bella is to me. We are counting on you to fix the problems with our health insurance."

He smiles and responds with vague promises. I leave the meeting uncertain that anything will really change—except me. A sense of power and purpose has flooded through me.

And then, February 27, our AFT and WVEA union leaders say we are heading back to work on March 3 after a "cooling off" day. The deal? The governor promises a five percent raise and freeze on health insurance changes. The House passes the five percent raise. I tune in to Hoppy Kercheval's radio show *Talkline* and hear Senate Majority Leader Mitch Carmichael sneer that he doesn't think the governor's proposal will pass. He has taken the pay raise off the senate's agenda. Seriously?

Facebook posts roil with anger. I roil with anger. We are not going back to work after a "cooling off" day.

The strike becomes a wildcat in defiance of the governor and union leadership. In all fifty-five counties, schools are closed again.

Rebecca calls. "Guess what? Chad and my doctor think it will be okay if I come with you to the capital this time."

"Hallelujah! After all the time you've devoted to AFT, you deserve to be in on the excitement now."

"My moment on the battlefield," she says.

"My doc said I can remove my ankle bootie, so I can drive. You can ride with me." We plan to spend the night.

On the ride downstate, we listen to radio coverage of our strike.

We are inching through Charleston's traffic when Rebecca's voice reverberates through the car. "Hey, Angie, isn't your brother-in-law a senator? Have you tried swaying him to our side?"

Somehow I manage not to wreck. My mother's voice repeats in my inner ear: *A car is a lethal weapon. Keep your mind clear and focused on your driving—lives depend on it.*

"Really?" Mrs. Carstairs regards me through her eyeglasses. "If you have a personal connection, we should use it to our advantage."

"We aren't close."

"Still, more deals get made over lunch than in meeting halls," Seth says.

"A great idea," Rebecca says. "Let's take him to lunch."

"He's soon to be my ex-brother-in-law."

I can feel Mrs. Carstairs frown—*feel* because I am keeping my eyes on the road.

With the wisdom that comes with age, she says, "That complicates matters."

"Sure does," I agree.

"Even so, it's a personal connection," Seth says. "Let's work it, baby!"

"Is his phone number in your cell?" Rebecca wants to know.

"No."

Rebecca pulls out her phone. "Piece of cake to get his office number."

I park. By the time Mrs. Carstairs and I climb out of the car, Rebecca has Ted's office on the phone. She explains that Senator McNeil's sister-in-law is in town and would like to meet him for lunch. Rebecca is laughing and charming Ted's aide. Unbelievably, by the time we reach the capitol grounds, she has Ted on the line. She tries to hand her cell to me.

I push it back at her.

She insists.

Crap. Now what am I supposed to do?

"Hi, Ted."

"Angela, always good to hear from you. My aide said something about wanting to meet me for lunch, but I'm afraid I'm tied up in meetings all day."

Venom oozes beneath the smooth dismissal. On top of everything he's doing to my sister, it boils my blood. Mac said he went ballistic over the photo. That's what I want to provoke. Rage equal to mine. I have the power and I intend to use it.

"Perhaps you'll reconsider, Ted. I know about The Photo." I feel lightheaded and wonder if it is possible to faint from an amputated conscience. Am I as venal as Ted? He doesn't respond and I wonder if he's hung up, but then I hear footsteps and the click of a door closing.

"I'll have my aide clear my schedule."

"There will be four of us. I hope that's okay."

"Angela, the photo . . . they don't know about . . . you haven't shown . . ."

"No."

"Excellent. Let's keep it that way."

We make arrangements to meet at The Block at 11:30.

Rebecca is ecstatic. "We have a chance to make a difference."

Seth high fives her. "Change starts by flipping one senator at a time over to our side."

I am unable to share their enthusiasm. I have just threatened my brother-in-law, an implied threat, anyway. The words poured out of some dark hole inside me without forethought. I've become as despicable as he is. What does Ted think I could do with knowledge of the photo anyway? I couldn't expose it without hurting my sister.

We merge into the crowd. Today the chants in the rotunda are "Get Out of the Way, Mitch!" The sound seems to climb the white columns and echo off the white marble.

"They can't get any business done up there with all this commotion," Rebecca yells in my ear. "They have to give in soon."

"Hope so." Mitch is the problem right now, and Ted has his ear. We have one shot at persuading the snake to join our side. That pay raise has got to get back on the agenda.

NOT FAR FROM THE GOLDEN DOME, The Block is an attractive restaurant. Brick interior walls, cushy booths and modern wood tables give the place a warm, welcoming feel, the kind of place you'd meet friends for lunch or share a drink on date night. We are here to meet the enemy. When we arrive, I give the hostess my name. She leads us to a private dining room. Good grief—it could hold at least fifty people.

From a table in a discreet corner, Ted hops up and greets us, shaking hands with everyone but me. I merit a hug. Ugh—he smells musky like a small furry animal.

"I reserved the private dining room so we'd have a quiet space to talk," he says.

I suspect my smile resembles Wile E. Coyote's. "How thoughtful. I hope meeting with us hasn't upset your day too much."

"Not at all. Got me out of boring meetings. I should be thanking you."

"You can thank us by making sure we get that raise and decent health insurance rates," Mrs. Carstairs says.

"And keeping charter schools out of West Virginia," I add. "We can't afford to drain our limited resources."

Ted smiles and nods. "Let's save the business part of lunch for later. I want to get to know you all better first."

When a waiter appears, Ted tells us to order whatever we want; he's picking up the tab. "These are important people," he tells the waiter. "They are the teachers of our children."

I order the most expensive item I can find: a salad with field greens, prawns, goat cheese, cinnamon toasted pecans, roasted beets, and dates with a fig balsamic glaze. Actually nothing is overly expensive, darn it. I hate to waste a chance to get even with this man who cleaned out my sister's bank account and canceled her credit cards.

Once the orders are in, Ted continues to play an unctuous politician, asking pertinent questions around the table: what subjects everyone teaches, how long they've been working, what their spouses do for a living. They are all behaving oh so politely! I say very little. Every time I think of his ripping that ring from my sister's finger I want to stick a knife between his eyes.

After we eat, Ted listens to my colleagues make their best pitch. He swears he hears their concerns.

He stands, signaling the end of our lunch. "I can't promise anything, but I'll try."

"It's all we can ask." Seth engages in another handshake and seems quite charmed by my brother-in-law.

Ted suggests the others go back to the Capitol while he and I catch up on family news. "I'll bring her over later."

Like hell he will. I'll catch a cab or walk.

We sit back down. I hold my arms stiffly in my lap, anchoring them. There are only dirty butter knives on the table, but I'm not taking any chances.

"How's Mac?"

"She's fabulous. Looks much better without you."

"Let's talk about the photo."

"What about it?"

"What do you plan to do with it?"

I shrug. I hope the horrible photo has been erased from every dark corner of the Internet.

"If it fell into the wrong hands, became public, people would get hurt . . ."

"Come off it. You're not worried about 'people.' You don't want to hurt your career."

"You always did cut right to the chase, Angela. What exactly do you want?"

"What do you mean?"

"If it's the raise and all that stuff, you know it's not up to me. The whole senate has to vote. Be reasonable. Natalie was really young when that photo was taken. She didn't realize how it could be used against her . . . against me when we get married."

Natalie—the girl Mac refers to as the future Child Bride! What photo is he talking about?

"Is it money—is that what you want?"

My brain seizes on the reference to money—Lord knows we need it, what with Dewey out of work, all the family squeezed up against each other, bumping elbows and knees. How much money is Ted talking about? I could do this for my family. We could afford a good memory care facility for Poppy, if it comes to that. Bella could get cochlear implants if she needs them down the road. Dewey and I could buy a house again and take a real vacation, one that didn't involve a tent and beans heated over a campfire.

"How much are we talking about?" he prods.

My mouth feels as dry as snakeskin. All I have to do is pick a number. A thousand. Ten thousand. Fifty thousand.

"Don't you have a number in mind?" he asks.

I shove away from the table and stand. "All I want is for my sister to be treated fairly. After raising your children and putting up with you all these years, she deserves a decent settlement."

"I'll take care of it."

Geez—what had Natalie done in that photo? Not that I really want to know.

"And give my sister back that stupid ring so she can hock it or throw it in the Kanawha River or flush it down the commode where it belongs."

The snake smiles. "You liked that ring, admit it."

"That ring sucks, almost as much as you do."

I stride out of the private dining room and leave the restaurant. The air outside is brisk and refreshing.

BY THE TIME WE RETURN TO CLARKSBURG around six the following night, I am weary yet exuberant. We are making progress in talks with individual senators. Some of the meetings were arranged by Ted.

As I turn down our road, I know immediately something is wrong. Every light in the farmhouse is on. My exuberance collapses.

Mom meets me at the door. "It's Hambone. He wandered off again while Mac and I were at the beauty parlor."

Which means Dewey was supposed to be watching him. How could a senile man in his eighties outfox him?

"When did you realize Poppy was gone?"

"Around two."

"Why didn't you call me?"

"Nothing you could do all the way down there in Charleston."

"I would've come back sooner." My sharp tone has only served to upset Mom. "Sorry, I'm just worried. Who's looking for him?"

"Dewey, Mac, the minister, and a couple of neighbors." She texts the others that I am on the hunt also. "Whoever finds him will notify the others by text. Dewey called the police to put out a Silver Alert."

Poppy's had four hours on his own. He could have walked a long way. It's so cold. I hope he wore a coat this time. The others are searching the area near the farm, assuming he walked aimlessly. What if he had a goal, something from the past, motivating him? Last time it was feeding the horse.

I drive back toward town, making stops at the graveyard where Poppy's family is buried, the closest convenience store where he used to stop on the way home from the restaurant, the house where his sister used to live. Finally I check the building where his first restaurant used to be. A police car sits in front of the boarded-up establishment. Poppy is in the back seat.

I pull in behind them and hop out. I start to introduce myself, but stop when I recognize the officer as a former student. "Johnny?"

"Mrs. Fisher, you remembered me." He sounds surprised. As if I could forget the rascal who painted one of his lettuce plants turquoise and tried to convince me it happened because of a gemstone he had embedded in the soil.

"That's my Poppy in your car. He wandered off."

Moments before I arrived, Johnny had figured out Hamilton was the man in the Silver Alert. "He can't tell me his name, but he remembers this restaurant was his."

"How'd he get here? It's miles from our place."

"Hitched a ride, he says. Doesn't know who with."

I'm just thankful we've found Poppy and he's safe. Johnny gets Mom on his phone and passes it to me. I let her know Poppy had on shoes and a warm coat and gloves this time.

I ask Johnny if he's seen any turquoise lettuce lately. He grins and helps Poppy into my car.

When we get back to the farm, all the lights are still on. Mom is passing out cups of coffee and sandwiches to the search party. Finally the house empties out. As soon as the bedroom door closes behind Dewey and me, I unload.

"How'd you let this happen? Were you drunk? Playing video games? What?"

His lips part as if he is going to answer, but instead grabs his pillow and a blanket and stretches out on the floor, his back turned to me.

"We should talk about this, Dewey."

He pulls one leg closer to his chest.

In the morning, his badass truck slings gravel before I am out of bed. Over breakfast, my mother tells me Dewey spent all afternoon combing the woods, searching the barn, the neighbors' property, every place he could think of.

"I've tried to give you and Dewey space, to stay out of your marriage, but Angie, this time you are wrong. Last night even a blind person could have seen you were wound up and ready to unleash on him. Dewey felt terrible Poppy escaped, Angie, but it wasn't his fault."

My mother has rarely been this angry with me. Not since I was grown. I don't get it. "Whose fault was it then?"

"No one's. You jumped to the wrong conclusion. Poppy was napping when the phone rang. It was the FBI about that job Dewey wants. He couldn't very well hang up on them. While he was looking up information on references they needed, Poppy slipped out. "

I have stepped in it this time. My hand trembles as I phone my husband. My mother slips away to her bedroom so I can have a moment of privacy, something that's been sorely missing from our lives.

"Dew, don't hang up. I'm sorry. So, so sorry. I was wrong. I know how much stress you've been under and now I've added to it and

I'm just so sorry. Please, please come home."

"I don't want to come home."

"What can I do to make this right—please forgive me. I don't want to lose you."

"I don't want to come home," he repeats.

My chest hurts so bad I think it might burst. What else can I say or do? A slideshow flashes through my mind. The day we met at Arden. Our honeymoon hiking part of the Appalachian Trail—the tender flesh of the trout we pan-fried, my blistered heels, his ripped jeans when he stumbled over a root, making love in that stuffy tent that smelled of mildew and hormones by week's end. The way his eyes lit up when he held Trish for the first time. The joy of our first grandchild. After all these years, are we at an end?

"Home's a little crowded these days," he says. "We can't really talk there." He pauses. "Or do anything else without everyone else listening in. How about we snuggle up in a cheap hotel room the rest of the morning instead?"

He doesn't have to ask twice.

The manager pushes an electronic key across the front desk and informs me that Mr. Fisher has already arrived. I locate room 215 and fumble with the key card until I get it turned the right way. With curtains drawn, the room is dark. One small light on the desk is on. Just enough light to make out the bed, where Dewey is propped up with pillows, his upper torso exposed above the top sheet. A deep pink rose rests on my pillow. The romantic gesture, so unlike Dewey, amazes me. He even remembered my favorite color. I pick up the blossom and touch it to my nose, an instinct I can't resist, even though it won't share the heady fragrance of the Abraham Darby bush I had to leave behind when we sold our house. The memory of that sensual fragrance travels through my body.

"I'm sorry I've been such an ass lately," he says.

"You've been under a lot of stress."

"We've both been under a lot of stress."

I toss the rose aside and kiss my husband. He pulls my sweater over my head and unhooks my bra. I can't even remember the last time I didn't undress myself when we made love, even before the clash concerning the strike.

In a very ordinary bed in a very ordinary hotel, we make extraordinary love, provoked by how close we came to losing each other. Losing what really matters.

Afterward, I stroke my fingers down the cleft created by his spine. It's now or never. Time to have a serious talk. "I know it's tough being out of work."

"It is, but I shouldn't take it out on you. It's just . . . a business manager is who I am, not a car wash attendant."

I don't want to ruin our reconciliation, but the moment to speak my mind may never come again. I think of my ancestor Rosella and Susan B. Anthony, how they stood up for women. It's time for me to stand up, too. I have to slough off the skin of inferiority that's held me back. I am not the child who caused the accident. I am better than my grandmother's ethnic slur. I am becoming a Mover and a Shaker.

"What upset me more than anything else was your trying to tell me what I could and couldn't do. It was your acting as if your work was more important than mine. I want to be your partner, Dew, not a servant who has to walk two steps behind you or an employee who has to say yes to the boss."

He strokes my hair, chin touching my nose, so he won't have to meet my eyes. "I'm sorry if I made you feel that way."

"I did."

"I'll try to do better."

He still can't look at me, but it's enough that he's apologized. He's a good man, not perfect, but good, and I believe our marriage will survive, maybe even thrive, because of what we've been through. And I'm strong enough to accept major change, if it comes to that. "I'll go to D.C. with you if that's what you want."

"I don't *want* to anymore than you do."

"I know."

"I have a good feeling about the FBI position, but if it doesn't come through . . ."

"We should go where there's work for you. I can get a job teaching most anywhere."

"We can always come back to visit, only a four-hour drive, more or less." He lays his knuckles against my cheek, and noticing my impossible-to-miss anguish at the thought, adds, "Maybe we won't have to. Let's wait and see what happens."

"If we have to move, Trish and Bella could come with us." It would still leave Mom alone with Poppy.

"You can't control everyone's lives, Ange."

I know, but I want to.

ON MARCH 7 THE DAFFODILS start to open their golden, cream, and rose-eyed blooms. Mom has a lovely array of both traditional and unusual bulbs. The blooms are a fitting way to mark the day we head back to our beloved classrooms.

I arrive at school forty minutes before first period, the way I always do. To my surprise, Kev is leaning against the wall beside my door. Alert. Hair brushed. Fresh clothing.

"Morning, Kev. What's up?" I unlock my door. The air in my room smells slightly stale after almost two weeks of being unoccupied.

"Welcome back, Mrs. Fisher. Me and my friends picketed in front of the school one day. It was kinda cool, being part of the strike." He follows me inside and deposits his backpack on his desk. "You teachers really showed those guys in Charleston. You got what you wanted out of them."

Not exactly, though that's the way the media is playing it. We got some of what we wanted. A five percent raise. No health insurance fix yet. The Governor authorized a task force to resolve our insurance issues—I'm not holding my breath.

"Appreciate your support, Kev. It's important to stand up for what's right, and we tried. I wish we could have accomplished our goals without the strike."

"Sometimes you gotta do what you gotta do."

I nod. He hangs around in front of my desk instead of taking his seat—or going back out in the hall to hunt down his friends. What does he really want?

"Have things gotten any better at home, Kev? With your dad?"

He looks out the windows. "I talked to the counselor, like you said, and we decided . . . well, I moved in with my aunt. Just until my dad gets straightened out."

"Sometimes you gotta do what you gotta do."

"I still love him."

"Of course you do. I hope your dad gets the help he needs."

He lifts his chin once, acknowledging my words, and plunges out my door in search of his friends.

I SIT CROSS-LEGGED ON THE FLOOR of Mom's living room, making silly faces at the most beautiful baby in the world. "TGIF," I tell her, even though she has no idea what I mean.

Mom overhears. "I can't believe you're already back to saying that. You were so eager to get back to work."

"Yeah, one week back with those kids and I'm already exhausted."

Bella smiles at me from her bouncy seat. I grab and gently squeeze her little feet. They are encased in tiny soft pink bunny shoes.

"Bay-bee-boo, bay-bee-boo." I cover my face with her blanket. "Where did Nana go?" I snatch the blanket off. "Peek-a-boo!" I cycle through this baby nonsense several times.

Bella flaps her arms and responds with "Baa-baa-baa-baa!" to my delight.

Her hearing aids work well as long as she is sitting with her head turned up. If she turns her head to the side, the aids brush against fabric or someone's shoulder and it causes them to squeal. That feedback annoys her, so we only use the aids when she is awake. It's difficult to find the right balance. Use them too little and she is cut off from the world through one of her senses and she won't learn to vocalize. Too much feedback and she'll learn to hate them.

MacKenzie comes out of her bedroom in a dark rose blazer, charcoal pencil skirt, and stiletto pumps, ready for the big day, a foray to the lawyer's office to finalize her divorce. Every detail of her appearance is perfect—still trying to impress Ted.

I bounce to my feet. "You look absolutely stunning. Eat your heart out, Ted McNeil."

She turns a critical eye on the black slacks I'd worn to work. "Let me grab the lint roller for you."

I'm tempted to snap at her, inform her I don't give a darn what she and Ted think of me and my cheap, lint-laden slacks, but I accept the roller. Mac insists on loaning me a New York designer sweater; the Walmart top I'd worn to work has been washed too many times to pass muster with the Fashion Queen. I fetch my black flats.

Once underway, Mac admits she is petrified. "My lawyer says

Ted has agreed to everything I wanted, but what if he changes his mind again? I don't know what's gotten into him."

"Can't imagine," I lied.

"Think he's having second thoughts about the divorce?"

"You're not having second thoughts, are you?"

"Not at all." Her quavering voice belies her words.

"You're doing the right thing. I bet your kids talked him into treating you right."

Her demeanor brightens at the mention of her children. "That's probably it."

The paper signing goes smoothly, anticlimactic after the bickering. Everyone behaves decently—and I feel better about the indecent role I played in a Charleston restaurant.

On the way home, Mac seems despondent. "Now that I'm not Ted's wife, I'm not sure who I am."

"This is your chance to become anyone you want to be, do anything you want to do in the second half of your life."

"What do I want?"

"You'll figure it out."

As soon as we're home again, I kick off my shoes and change into jeans and a sweatshirt. I drop back onto the floor with Bella.

Mom's front door opens and Dewey charges in and crosses over to stand behind us. "Did I hear my little princess?"

"You did. Bella is doing real good, aren't you, Baby Boo?" I pump her tiny legs again.

"Baa, baa, baa," she babbles.

Everything about Dewey oozes happiness, his stride, his stance, his expression, the light in his eyes. "Guess what? The FBI gig came through."

"Fantastic!" I hop to my feet and kiss Dewey's cheek. I've dodged a bullet. As the initial rush of joy passes, I try to wrap my arms around the changes coming our way.

"Can we look for a house of our own again?"

"Soon."

"Can we afford it?"

"Don't see why not. Good salary, good benefits—and at least the federal government isn't likely to go out of business any time soon."

I pace through the living room. "Do you think Trish and Bella will want to stay in the RV or move in with us? And what about Poppy? Will we need to hire someone to help Mom with his care?"

He takes my arm to halt my pacing. "Angie, Angie. Chill, darlin'. You can't control all of our lives. We're not part of some science experiment."

He's right, yet I long for the certainty of knowing I've made the best decisions for all of us, based on available evidence.

"It will all work out," he says.

Mom pauses in folding a napkin as she sets the table. "That girl's always been a worrier. You can't change that, Dewey."

"Part of my DNA like my big nose." I can tell myself to let go of the big stuff, that it's out of my hands, but I'll always have the urge to shape my family's future. Just like Dewey will always be more of a go-with-the-flow kind of guy. He concentrates on what needs to be fixed right now; I try to analyze all the possibilities the future holds to plot the best way forward. Two different kinds of intelligence, both useful. We make a good team.

A buzzer goes off in the kitchen, signaling the beef burgundy with homemade egg noodles is ready. I open a bottle of champagne and we all gather in the kitchen.

I hold up my glass for a toast. "Two reasons to celebrate. Here's to a fresh start for Mac and a new job for Dewey!"

Chaos and laughter break out as we all talk over each other. Even Bella joins in with "baa, baa baa."

"Three reasons to celebrate," Trish says. "Bella can talk!"

We hear, and life is good.

ON SATURDAY MORNING MAC HELPS DEWEY AND ME hoe and pull weeds that have popped up in Mom's vegetable patch over the winter. We finally get around to transplanting pansies started in the cold frame to pots on Mom's front porch.

Mac firms soil around an apricot pansy with a tiny golden eye. "I always loved Mom's pansies," she says.

"Me, too. Such cheerful little faces!" I lean over and tug out a weed encroaching on the fading hyacinth blooms by the front steps.

Mac has a smudge of dirt on her chin and a smile on her face. "I'd forgotten how good it feels to garden."

After showering, Dewey and MacKenzie babysit. Mom, Trish

and I drive out Rt. 50 until we reach what used to be the Krause family farm. I want to see the land, even though it's a subdivision now. A lone maple shades one yard, and I wonder if it could be the same tree that inspired Rosella's vase. On a vacant lot beyond the homes, metal arms of fracking wells pump natural gas to the surface. A transmission pipeline, inches above ground, traverses the same path used by overhead electrical lines. I can't tell if they are on what once was Krause property or not.

A riot of orange tiger lilies bloom in the ditch alongside the road out of the subdivision. An old apple tree with gnarled limbs remains in one small patch of undeveloped land. Suddenly time bends in on itself, and I catch a glimpse of Rosella Krause traipsing along with her sketchbook dangling from one hand and a box of colored pencils in the other, a basket handle looped over her arm. Her dress gives off a hint of lavender from the sachets her mother tucks into drawers and hangs in closets. Little Timmy lags behind, dragging a stick in the dirt. Ro tells him to hurry up. They are going to pick apples from two long rows of trees, the boughs laden with green and red fruit. Bees buzz and hover over the "drops," attracted by competing scents of ripe fruit, fermentation, and rot. Timmy's job is to pick up the ones that aren't too far gone for cider. Ro's job is to select ones from the tree suitable for applesauce simmered with cinnamon, but soon she is sketching the bees instead. Their mother hollers from the front porch that it's time for dinner.

I shake my head slightly, and the figments of my imagination are gone. So are the orchard and the front porch, long gone. I take a deep breath, surprised at how deeply my mother's research has affected me. I see more clearly how families come in many forms. The ones we are born into. The ones we make for ourselves. What matters are the ties that bind us together, the shared histories, the love, even the arguments.

Next we drive into Clarksburg to find the vacant lot where Aunt Elizabeth's house—and later Ro's house—once stood. It is overgrown with Bahia grass, plantains, nutsedge and nettles. I'm picturing Jack showing up here and little Michael—my great grandfather—charging outside with the shotgun.

So many terrible things happened to Rosella when she was young. With all the illness and deaths, she must have felt as if her life had spun totally outside of her control. And yet in the end she found a measure of contentment. I can understand her so much better than Jack.

"How could Jack leave Rosella after all she'd been through?" I ask Mom.

"Some folks don't handle grief too good, especially being around other people's. Makes them uncomfortable. He couldn't stop her from hurting so he ran off where he wouldn't have to witness that pain anymore."

My mother surprises me with another piece of Ro's story. "You know Jack, for all his faults, was a hero in that fire. He was the first to smell smoke and ran down the hallway of the Grand Star Hotel alerting the other guests. Everyone on the second floor got out safely, including one woman he carried out unconscious and a man he went back for on a second trip. Those on the third floor weren't so lucky. At least three died in the conflagration, including one man Jack had played poker with the night before. A cowboy who drifted from ranch to ranch. That's whose name he took after the fire."

Can't help it—I'm still glad I'm descended from Val Martin instead of Jack Joyner. Even if I am stuck with Val's nose.

OUR WHOLE FAMILY GOES TO WALK ALONG THE RIVER at Veteran's Memorial Park, Bella swaddled in a baby wrap across Trish's chest. The air smells faintly of fish and rotting leaves, the smell of life's endless cycle of death and renewal, the conversion of one form of energy into another. We feed the ducks, an activity which amuses Poppy. His favorite is the one we call "Peg Leg." No one seems to know how it lost its leg, but the loss doesn't hamper its movements. It has adapted. MacKenzie seems to be adapting too.

When the rest of the family walks ahead, she takes something from her jacket's pocket. I watch as she pitches it into the muddy waters of the West Fork River.

"Was that the—"

"The ring," she finishes for me. "I pried the diamond out and donated it to the Alzheimer's Association."

"Good for you."

"I've decided to take classes in nonprofit management," Mac says.

"Heck, Mac, with your experience, you could teach those classes."

"I may make some changes in my life soon, too," I confess. "I'm thinking of running for the state legislature when I retire. I'm already shaping a platform around education and the environment. Both get short shrift around here, if you ask me."

The whole country needs to do a better job tackling these issues, but I have to start somewhere.

Mac approves. "Good for you! Who better than a science teacher to tackle those problems?"

Several of my students are scattered through the park cataloguing the life forms in their assigned corners of the world. Marla, my budding scientist, is one of them. I smile when I see her mother has tagged along. Learning is lifelong; it happens across the generations as we each teach each other to see—really see the web of our world in all its wondrous intricacy. I brush my fingers against little Bella's cheek as she sleeps against Trish's chest, and I amble on down the trail, holding Poppy's hand.

When I think no one is looking, I sneak a pinch on Dewey's backside. Instead of playing our game, he makes a big show of smacking my hand.

"Angie, have you no shame?" He flips his head toward Mom and Trish. "The woman can't keep her hands off me."

I smack his arm. "You rat!"

Mom, Trish, and MacKenzie laugh, and even though Poppy has no idea what's going on, he joins in. I have to laugh, too. "You got me back butt good," I say. "B-u-double t, pun intended."

A couple of teens walk by, cutting their eyes sideways at us. Probably think we're crazy people, what with all the hooting and hollering.

Dewey tears off a bit of stale bread and gives it to Poppy to toss to Peg Leg. They follow the goose on down the path. Trish with her little kangaroo pouch goes with them.

Mom, Mac, and me sink onto a bench shaded by what I think is a Horse Chestnut. I will have to look it up in my tree identification book later.

"So Angela's birth mother's name is Deborah Wellington Springer," Mac says. "What do you know about her?"

Mom chuckles. "Grandmother Adams sure had it all wrong. Angie's mother was hardly a drug addict. She came from a wealthy family in Philadelphia. Her great sin was falling in love with a boy her parents didn't approve of. When she became pregnant, her parents refused to let her marry the father."

A boisterous family group passes our bench, the youngest children bickering in a playful way. I wait until they move on before asking something that's been bothering me.

"Mom, I'm curious. You did so much research, I'm surprised you weren't able to find out who my birth father was."

"Oh, I know who he is."

Mac and I exchange a look. He must be a monster. "Well, who is he?" she asks.

"Actually, you both know him. He's an Italian born to a relatively poor family, and the Wellingtons considered him an unsuitable prospect, so they sent Deborah back to Philadelphia to live with a great aunt until she gave birth."

"For heaven's sake, Mom, out with it—who is my father?"

"Mr. Esposito."

The bag of bread crumbs I've been holding slips from my grasp. No way! I am picturing his salt and pepper slicked back hair, the middle that's thickened over the years I've known him, the khaki pants he wears to work with polo shirts, mostly blue, our school color. I conk my head on the bench arm as I raise back up with the crumbs.

"The principal?" Mac says. "You're kidding, right?"

I massage the bump on my scalp, not sure which hurt I'm trying to ease. Has he always known who I am? Did he never think of reaching out?

"He was only sixteen himself, poor kid, and terribly in love—aren't all young people, though? At that age, we think every clutch and kiss are life and death." Mom chuckles again. I am having trouble finding humor in the moment.

"He has kept an eye on you all these years. He could have retired two years ago, but I think he delayed because he likes knowing what is going on in your life."

Now that Mom mentions it, I realize how often he has stopped by my room and commented on the photo collage on my desk. Dewey. Trish. Bella.

"Wait—which of Rosella's children was Mr. Esposito descended from? I can't keep this family tree stuff straight," Mac says.

"Mr. Esposito is the grandson of Val and Rosella Martin's son Michael, their only natural born child," Mom says. "He gave me Solina's journal and Rosella's maple leaf vase. The journal really helped me flesh out the story."

"Why did you keep Mr. Esposito a secret?" I ask.

Mom sighs. "I didn't know how you'd feel about knowing your boss is your father. It could make things awkward for both of you."

No kidding. How the devil will I keep a straight face the next time I see him?

"Will you tell him you know?" Mom asks.

I don't think so. It's enough to know he's a good man. I have no desire to embarrass him or his family.

His family! I shoot up to standing, flinging my arms out wide. "I know his kids! I have a half sister and brother." They have walked the same streets, gone to the same schools as me. Geez. How weird.

Mom rises to her feet, too. "Quite a bit younger than you, but I'm sure you've seen them at football and basketball games."

"I serve on the library board with Nancy." Not that I go to meetings, but I do send in book recommendations.

We head off to join Dewey, Poppy, Trish, and Bella, who have gotten quite a ways ahead of us.

Mac is very quiet, rather withdrawn. "You have other sisters." She says this without looking at me.

It's taken us so long to find our connection again, there's no way am I going to lose her now.

"No shared history," I scoff. "You're the only one who knows where the wild strawberries grow."

"And you're the only one who knows what I did with that ring."

"You're my forever sister, Mac."

A smile toasts her face. "Always and forever."

IN THE SUMMER OF 2018, Dewey and I plan a family vacation to visit east coast historical towns. Harper's Ferry. Washington, D.C. Boston. And most important, Philadelphia. It figures in my birth family history.

When Dewey and I settle into our Philadelphia hotel room—the cheapest available—I sit on the side of the bed and slip my cell phone out of my purse. Stare at it silently, trying to muster the courage to do what I came here for.

"You want to be alone?" Dewey asks.

I shake my head and pat the bed beside me. He snuggles up and slides an arm around my waist.

"Go ahead, Ange."

"What if she doesn't want to talk to me?"

"Then you will hang up and our lives will go on just fine, the way they always have."

"What if I hate her? After all—"

"Stop with the 'what ifs.' Just do it. Or don't do it. Either way, you'll be okay."

He's right. It's not as if I'm contacting an alien species. Heaps of dirt have been dumped on the people I love this year—job loss, reluctant legislators, Mac's divorce, Poppy's dementia, Rebecca's cancer, Bella's impaired hearing—yet we are still looking out for each other. We do the best we can. In our darkest moments, a fundamental graciousness in the human spirit spurs us on to nurture each other, to heal whatever is broken. I have to believe this woman will be gracious and kind.

Dewey takes a handkerchief from his pocket, drops it in my lap.

"I'm not gonna start crying like some fool," I scoff. "I would rather eat jellied moose nose."

I tap the number I've saved to my cell. Several seconds pass in silence. Have I punched in the wrong number? I know I haven't. I checked it a dozen times. Finally, there's ringing. And ringing. More ringing. She must not be home. Just as I'm ready to give up, a woman answers.

My tongue feels weighted down with sand. Puddles gather in the corners of my eyes. "Mrs. Springer? My name is Angie Fisher. I'm—"

"Oh honey, I know exactly who you are."

I hear a great intake of breath, and then, in a wobbly voice—"For years I've been hoping you would call."

With all my strength, I struggle against the beastly pressure building in my chest. *Suck it up, Angie, suck it up.*

Tears spill in runnels down my face.

I can't suck it up anymore.

EPILOGUE

You can bury seeds and ideas, but you never know for sure if they will germinate. They may stubbornly refuse. Or they may explode into life unexpectedly.

Sequoiadendron giganteum, the largest living thing on Earth, begins life looking very much like a blade of grass, an inch tall, but what potential lies within! General Sherman in Sequoia National Forest is more than half the volume of an Olympic-sized swimming pool, about 52,500 cubic feet. It took 2,000 years to reach that size. Ideas may take a long time to mature, too.

In 2012, scientists regenerated seeds that were thirty-two thousand years old. These seeds of *Silene stenophylla*, a flowering plant native to Siberia, had probably been buried by an Ice Age squirrel. They were entirely encased in ice below the permafrost, surrounded by mammoth, bison, and woolly rhinoceros bones. In this current age of mass extinction, scientists are freezing seeds of thousands of plants in doomsday vaults. Will humans be around to thaw and plant them in a far-off future time? No one knows.

At seventeen, Susan B. Anthony, working closely with Elizabeth Cady Stanton, started a movement to achieve equality for all people. She not only worked tirelessly to improve the lives of women worldwide, she also fought alongside Frederick Douglass in the abolitionist cause. Miss Anthony didn't live to see women achieve the right to vote, but she inspired others to carry on. Fourteen years after her death, the seeds she planted and tended so assiduously bloomed. Her revolution continues as Afghan women push for the right to drive automobiles, American women protest for equal pay and equal rights, and African Americans fight against a biased legal system.

In 2018 and again in 2019, teachers in West Virginia walked

off their jobs and stormed into the dens of power. Their revolution spread across the nation as teachers walked out in Colorado, Oklahoma, California, Arizona, Kentucky, and North Carolina. None of these educators won everything they wanted from their state legislatures, but no one can foresee how widely the forces of activism might spread and take root.

Poppy died more or less peacefully at home in the winter of 2019. We hired full-time help during the last five months of his life when he lost the ability to walk, to feed himself, to talk. On one of his last semi-cognizant days, he gurgled and reached out insistently for something we couldn't see. Without words, his longings remained trapped inside his jumbled neural pathways. Mom played Dean Martin's pizza pie song, and that seemed to quiet his yearning. I hoped in the foggy spaces of his brain he was spinning the Love of his Life around the dance floor one more time.

When spring of 2019 arrived, Kev moved back in with his addicted father and dropped out of school. A short time later he was arrested on charges of breaking and entering. As a juvenile, he got a second chance after time served. His record was expunged. He earned a G.E.D. about the same time he would have graduated anyway and began coursework at Pierpont Community College and Technical School.

In the spring of 2020, Marla Harding graduated as class valedictorian. She won a full scholarship to WVU. Her application essay focused on her plot project in my biology class and expressed her desire to study either environmental science or genetics.

Bella entered preschool in fall of 2020. Her teacher mentioned that Bella talks a lot, maybe too much. What joy that brought to those of us who feared our hearing-impaired child might not learn to talk at all, her thoughts and desires trapped inside, much as Poppy's were. Speak, Bella, speak! Share your beautiful words for all the world to hear, little girl. Nonetheless, we will have a discussion about the need to listen, too.

One thing every parent and every teacher learns: the seed you plant in a child today may never grow into what you hoped for. Or the knowledge and values you plant in a child today may bloom into more than you ever dared imagine. Generations from now, one might become a revolutionary whose passion creates a more just world. Or she might become the scientist who thaws and regenerates seeds long buried, long forgotten.

The End

Acknowledgments

This manuscript languished unfinished for over a decade as I struggled to bring these characters and their stories to life. Any mistakes are my own, but I am grateful to many people for their assistance and support.

Some fine writers took time from their busy lives to help nurture this manuscript. Rhett DeVane, Peggy Kassees, Hannah Mahler, and Susan Womble read and critiqued an early version of Rosella's story. I am also grateful to Peg Holmes, Ursel Homann, Joan Leggitt, Claire Matturro, Phyllis Wilson Moore, Edwina Pendarvis, Diane Schneider, and Pat Spears who served as early readers and provided helpful insights that strengthened the story. And once again, Paula Kiger and her Big Green Pen came through as my editor.

I am so proud of West Virginia's teachers who walked out in 2018 and again in 2019 to try to improve the state's schools. A number of West Virginia teachers provided insights into the 2018 strike. I appreciate the time Erin Bashaw, Stacey Strawderman, and Cindy L. Yazvac took to answer my questions. I am also thankful to Phyllis Wilson Moore, Wendy Oliverio, and Diane Schneider for their assistance in connecting me with these teachers. In addition, the essays in the anthology *55 Strong: Inside the West Virginia Teachers' Strike,* edited by Elizabeth Catte, Emily Hilliard, and Jessica Salfia, broadened my understanding of teachers' frustration with the legislature.

An outstanding science teacher, Jo Farrell, provided me with a wealth of materials on state science standards and how they would impact Angie Fisher in the classroom. I am so grateful for her help in shaping Angie's classroom activities. I also owe a debt to Dr. Weems, my biology instructor at Fairmont State. I have never forgotten his assignment to study the webs of life on a small plot of land.

I attended a lecture on women's health issues at the Knott House in Tallahassee. One speaker was Dr. Jennifer Koslow, an expert on nineteenth century women's health issues. It was through her that I learned mercurial douches were used to cure women of syphilis, often without their knowledge that they were infected. Doctors sometimes withheld information to preserve the marriage and also because the Comstock laws prohibited communication of information of a sexual nature. Both the mercury and later, the arsenic, used as curatives, were toxic. At the same event, Kimberly Berfield, Deputy Secretary of Health for Florida, discussed changes in causes of mortality. In the 1900s tuberculosis, syphilis, and pneumonia were top killers of women. These diseases became a major thread in my novel.

Many books increased my understanding of life during the early 1900s and during the San Francisco earthquake. They include *Three Fearful Days: San Francisco Memoirs of the 1906 earthquake & fire,* compiled and introduced by Malcolm E. Barker; *San Francisco Is Burning: The Untold Story of the 1906 Earthquake and Fire* by Dennis Smith; *Victorian America: Transformations in Everyday Life 1876-1915,* by Thomas J. Schlereth; *The Good Old Days—They Were Terrible* by Otto L. Bettmann; and *Denial of Disaster: The Untold Story and Photographs of the San Francisco Earthquake and Fire of 1906* by Gladys Hansen and Emmet Condon. Ken Joy's film, *The Great San Francisco Earthquake and Fire of 1906* was also useful.

Fired by Ideals: Arequipa Pottery and the Arts and Crafts Movement by Suzanne Baizerman, Lynn Downey, John Toki, and the Oakland Museum of California was invaluable as a resource.

Also I would like to acknowledge Barbara Kingsolver, whose use of transitions between present day and historical times in *Unsheltered* I tried to emulate in this novel.

USE OF HISTORICAL FIGURES AND PLACES

By the time I visited New York State in the summer of 2019, Susan B. Anthony already had a small mention in this story, but after touring her house and museum in Rochester, New York, I enlarged her fictional role. In real life, her role in women's lives, both then and now, could hardly be larger. All of us owe an enormous debt for all she sacrificed for the cause that governed every moment of her adult life: equality for all. The staff at the Susan B. Anthony Museum and House is doing a wonderful job of educating the public about this remarkable woman.

Dr. Philip Brown and Frederick Hurten Rhead were key figures at Arequipa. I used them as fictional creations, but have tried to portray their roles there accurately.

Susan Dew Hoff was also an historical figure, the first West Virginia woman licensed to be a physician.

Hilltop High is an invented school. I feared featuring a real school would lead readers to think my characters represented actual teachers, rather than fictional ones.

DONNA MEREDITH IS THE ASSOCIATE EDITOR of *Southern Literary Review.* Her award-winning novels include *The Glass Madonna, The Color of Lies, Wet Work, Fraccidental Death,* and *Buried Seeds.* The nonfiction title, *Magic in the Mountains: Kelsey Murphy, Robert Bomkamp and the West Virginia Cameo Glass Revolution,* tells the amazing story of a talented couple who revived the ancient art of cameo glass in the twentieth century in West Virginia.

Donna holds degrees from Fairmont State College, West Virginia University, and Nova Southeastern University, and studied creative writing at Florida State University. She taught English, journalism, and TV production in public high schools in West Virginia and Georgia. She lives in Tallahassee, FL, and travels throughout the U.S. in an RV with her husband John and dog Lucca. When home, she likes to garden.

Made in the USA
Columbia, SC
29 July 2020